E. S. Th~~omson~~ ... CWA Endeavour Historical Dagger, a ... Saltire Prize, the Scottis... Award and th... ...Crime Book of the Year Award. She has a PhD in the social history of medicine, and tries to fit as much medical history into her books as possible. She works as a university lecturer by day, and writes by night. Elaine lives in Edinburgh with her two sons.

Surgeons' Hall

E. S. Thomson

CONSTABLE

CONSTABLE

First published in Great Britain in 2019 by Constable

This paperback edition published in 2019 by Constable

A CIP catalogue record for this book
is available from the British Library.

ISBN: 978-1-47212-660-3

Typeset in ITC New Baskerville by SX Composing DTP, Rayleigh, Essex
Printed and bound in Great Britain by Clays Ltd, Elcograf S.p.A.

Papers used by Constable are from well-managed forests
and other responsible sources.

Constable
An imprint of
Constable & Robinson Ltd
Carmelite House
50 Victoria Embankment
London EC4Y 0DZ

An Hachette UK Company
www.hachette.co.uk

www.littlebrown.co.uk

For MMJ

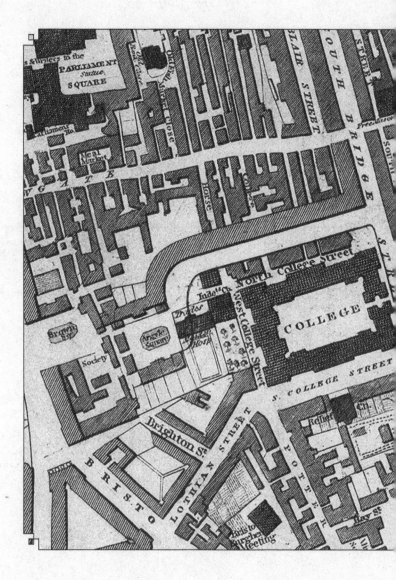

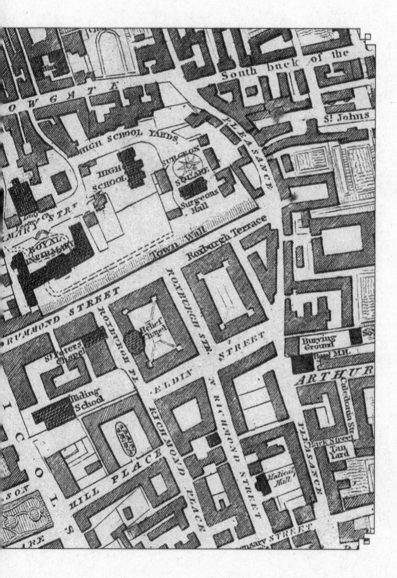

Hands

Not so many years ago it was customary to cut off a felon's right hand and nail it above his head as he swung from the gallows. Why? Because though it is the mind that decides upon murder, it is the hand that commits the act.

The hand of man is the most sophisticated and expressive of all God's creations. He may use it as a tool, as a symbol, as a weapon. The hands can swear, threaten, supplicate, question. We use them to express joy and sorrow. The blind see with them; the deaf speak. And when we wash our hands, do we not purify them? Make them clean? Innocent? What absolution might I achieve by washing mine? None at all.

For the fortune-teller, our lives are mapped out on our palms. Would my wicked deeds be visible there? For the physician, the hand offers signs of poor health: a bluish tinge suggests heart disease, a red hand might be indicative of gout. A cold, moist, flabby hand denotes sickness or emotional disturbance. Fear, perhaps. Or guilt. You see, it is the flesh of the hands that betrays us. What lies beneath – crimson muscle, threaded nerves, silken veins – tells us nothing. Even the bones, the hard, dry, clacking bones of fingers and thumbs are blameless, for one skeleton hand is very much like another. All these elements have their own beauty, their own intricate perfection and divine complexity. But who we are and what we have done is etched upon the flesh. It is in the pale, languid fingers of the leisured lady, or the hard, blistered palms of the labourer. It is in the needle-pricked thumb of the seamstress or the bitten-to-the-quick fingernails of the unhappy schoolboy.

And the hands of a murderer? To know the hands of a murderer you need look no further than mine.

Chapter One

It began innocently enough. A trip to Hyde Park. Will's idea. He had been to the Crystal Palace many times already, though it had taken until the final few weeks of the Exhibition before he'd managed to persuade me.

He held his arms wide as we entered the main transept. 'You see we are now *in*side, Jem? And yet—' He pointed to one of the huge elm trees, dwarfed by the lofty nave of glass and iron that arched high above it. 'And yet to some degree we are still *out*side.' He took my arm, steering me through the crowds. 'Is it not breathtaking? Consider its scope. Its ambition. Its grandeur. Ingenious too! Light but strong. It is modelled on the great glasshouses at Chatsworth, you know.'

'Yes,' I said. 'I think everyone knows.'

'Inspired by the design of the great Amazonian lily pads – gigantic natural structures supported by a network of veins so fine and strong that they can withstand the weight of a small child.'

3

'Mm,' I said. I did not like to admit it, for I had been rather dismissive of Prince Albert's 'greenhouse', but I was impressed. I was not the only one, for there were people everywhere, their faces bright with excitement, the air loud with chatter. As the most skilled draughtsman at Prentice and Hall, his firm of architects and engineers, Will had been seconded to help illustrate the Exhibition catalogue, and had spent a number of happy months drawing images of stoves, ironwork, looms and engines of various kinds. I had already browsed a number of the exhibits whilst sitting at my apothecary table. There were only a few that caught my attention, for most seemed to be a mixture of the grandiose and the absurd.

'A cloak that can be transformed into a boat for the use of country physicians? A mousetrap that can catch an infinite number of mice?' I'd said. 'These things have not been thought through properly. And I have no interest in seeing the world's biggest diamond or a throne carved out of coal.'

'There's nothing that interests you?'

'Only the models of Dr Silas Strangeway.'

Dr Silas Strangeway. Anyone with an interest in anatomy had heard of him. He was known to work in secret, the results of his labours kept in the private anatomy museum of Dr Alexander Crowe, a surgeon and anatomist with the highest reputation, with whom he had worked for over twenty years. Once, when I was an apprentice apothecary at St Saviour's Infirmary, Dr Crowe had brought one of Dr Strangeway's pieces to a meeting of the Pathology Society. It was a replica of the lungs, removed from the chest cavity and opened up to reveal a mass of tubercles clustered within. We had all agreed: it was like staring into a real anatomised lung at a real case of advanced tuberculosis. Somehow Dr Strangeway had even made the cavity glisten, as if it were coated with a layer of mucous. Whether the general public would be similarly impressed by his work I had no idea.

A few yards away a group of young men were gathered about the anatomical display cases. I had seen them going up the stairs ahead of us and had caught snatches of their conversation. Medical students. I wondered where they came from – possibly St George's, which was at the corner of the park, perhaps from St Bride's, which was not far from my physic garden, and was where Silas Strangeway and Dr Crowe were employed. I heard the chink of beer bottles, and saw from the young men's ruddy cheeks and grinning faces that they had been drinking. They loitered in a huddle in front of an exhibit, talking and laughing.

Unwilling to join their ranks, Will and I occupied ourselves with the other wax models, waiting for the students to move off.

'Silas Strangeway is the most gifted artist and anatomist,' I said. 'Though he's known to be something of an eccentric too. Look at this one here – I think you'll like it.'

At first, the model in the crystal and rosewood box appeared to show the face and head of a sleeping man. The right eye was closed, the expression serene, the skin smooth and flawless. And yet as one drew closer the face became something else entirely, for on its left side the skin had been peeled back in layers, flayed open to reveal the secrets beneath. The eye without its lid was a staring orb framed by crimson; the grinning teeth were cemented in bone and laced with blood vessels and nerves made up of the finest waxen thread. It was like beholding the miracle of life and the horror of death at precisely the same moment.

'Taken from life?' said Will, peering into the display case.

'Taken from death,' I replied. 'The heads of a great many corpses will have been dissected to enable something as detailed and astonishing as this to be created.'

'Ingenious,' said Will. 'To show the mechanisms within so clearly and intricately. And you see how the thing is angled, so as to draw the eye from one manifestation of perfection to another?'

'You don't feel faint?' I said, knowing his weakness.

'It's wax,' he replied. 'I should no more faint at the sight of a tallow candle.' He was silent for a moment, then added doubtfully. 'It *is* wax, isn't it?'

Up ahead, with a bellow of laughter the medical students moved on. They were replaced by a man with his wife and children who had entered via the opposite door. Their unfashionable clothes proclaimed them to be from out of town, the sooty bloom on their faces suggesting a recent train journey. They reached the place where the students had been, and the four of them stopped. I saw that they were transfixed by something, though I could not see what it was. And then all at once a commotion broke out. The man collapsed to the ground with a muffled *thump*; his wife began screaming, the children – girls aged some ten or twelve years – joining in with a high-pitched wailing. Will and I bounded over.

'I'm an apothecary, madam,' I said, opening my satchel and groping inside for some *sal volatile*. 'If you would allow me—?'

The woman was babbling something incoherent and

pointing at the exhibits, but there was such a clamour coming from the children that I could not hear what she was saying. I loosened the man's neckerchief and applied my salts to his nostrils. The next moment he dashed the bottle from my fingers and lurched to his feet. He snatched up his hat, and, with a fearful glance over his shoulder, ushered his wife, and still-wailing daughters, out of the gallery. I was about to observe how rude the people from the north of England were – and then I saw for myself what had caused all the fuss.

It was not an exhibit – at least, not in the proper sense of the word for it was not in a box of glass and rosewood. Nor was it made of wax. Instead, what lay before us was of real flesh and blood, the skin a greyish white, the exposed musculature a startling vivid scarlet. It was a hand – a man's hand – and it was lying on its back between a display case of surgical cutlery and a wax model of the human heart. It had been partly anatomised, the skin on the palm slit from fingers to wrist and peeled back to reveal the red glistening stuff beneath. The flaps of flesh were held open with steel pins, stabbed through the skin directly into the table top. The work was neat and precise; skilfully done, given that pinning it in place must surely have been undertaken in haste, for the galleries were busy, and although the medical and scientific instruments exhibits were not the most popular a steady stream of visitors passed through. Most macabre of all, between the tip of the thumb and forefinger was a small square of card, the size of a *carte de visite*. Scrawled upon it in a crude, childish hand, were five ragged words.

It was not the first time I had seen a severed hand. Once, years ago, a workman had been admitted to St Saviour's Infirmary, where I worked as apprentice apothecary. He was brought up on a cart from the warehouses on Gravel Lane, and was carried into the hospital by his friends on a makeshift stretcher – a length of tarpaulin slung between two wooden spars. I could see by their faces, and by the white, waxy skin of the man they carried, that I was about to see something unforgettable.

They told me that the man's name was Henshaw, that he had become caught in the winding gear used to winch materials up from the quayside into the warehouse. His right hand had become trapped, the machinery had turned, and in one sharp vicious movement, it had been partially severed, partially torn off at the wrist. The man who addressed me was white-faced, his gaze appalled beneath the peak of his cap. He nudged his companion, who presented me with a package. I pulled back the bloody folds to find the missing hand, the wrist bones splintered like pale twigs of stripped willow. I remembered the hairs on it, dark and springing; still coated with a fine yellow powder from the sacks of spices the man had been unloading.

By some miracle, the fellow survived. A tourniquet applied by one of his friends had prevented him from bleeding to death, and he managed to avoid septicaemia by being attended to by Dr Bain, the most capable of all the surgeons at St Saviour's. The shock too, which might have killed a lesser man, had been mitigated by the fact that he had been plied with copious quantities of cheap gin as he was brought up from the docks.

I had no idea what happened to him afterwards. With only one hand, and that his left, it was unlikely that his future was a prosperous one. I was more familiar with the fate of his lost appendage. It had been taken away by Dr Graves, St Saviour's most enthusiastic anatomist, who had added it to his private museum, pickling it in spirits of alcohol so that he might show his students how skin, bone and muscle behave when they are torn apart.

∽

I could see straight away that the hand before me had been neither torn nor roughly hacked from a body. Its removal had been a labour of time and precision, the joints of the wrist neatly separated from the larger bones of the lower arm. There was no sawing, slicing or splintering, merely a neat and exact dismemberment.

Behind us, I heard the sound of voices. A group of people had entered the room, their rustic clothing and buzzing accents betraying their provincial origins.

'We must take this away,' I said.

'You cannot walk through London with a severed hand in your bag,' hissed Will. 'Not even you, Jem! Perhaps the police—'

'And while we await them we are to leave this thing here, to terrify visitors?'

'It's probably no more than a prank. Those medical students—'

'Quite possibly.'

And yet there was something about that grisly relic that troubled me. In my work at St Saviour's Infirmary I had seen many a corpse hand; many a severed arm and anatomised body come to that, and I had also known many a student who had horsed around with organs, body parts and cadavers. It was the card that bothered me. The words upon it were scrawled in black ink: a clumsy, inexpertly written note that belied the neatness of the sliced and peeled flesh, as well as the Latin motto it described: *et mortui sua arcana narrabunt*. I slipped the card into my pocket.

I plucked out the pins that held back the skin of the palm, and lifted the hand. It was firm and clammy to the touch, but with no smell of the spirits that were commonly used to preserve anatomical specimens. The wooden surface where it had lain amongst Dr Strangeway's exhibits was not damp, and there was nothing I could feel beneath my fingers that might yield some clue as to the provenance of the thing – no grit or dust or hairs. Opening my satchel, I pulled out a copy of the morning edition of *The Times*. I folded the flaps of skin back over the exposed muscle of the palm and rolled the thing in the paper like a piece of fried fish.

'Where shall we take it?' said Will.

I shrugged. 'To Silas Strangeway, I suppose.'

Precognition for the murder of Mary Anderson,
18th December 1830.

Statement of SILAS STRANGEWAY, anatomist and
anatomical artist, residing at 22 East Newington Street,
Edinburgh. Aged thirty-four years.

19th December 1830

In the spring of this year a pair of beggars appeared at the gates
to the Infirmary. The pavement outside that building has always
attracted those of a curious or hideous physical aspect, and
these particular beggars were sisters known as Thrawn-Leggit
Mary and Clenchie Kate (that is to say, Crooked-Legged Mary
and Club-Footed Kate). The legs of both Anderson women were
painfully bent and knotted with rickets, their spines curved into
a serpentine 'S' by an extreme form of scoliosis. They had recently
removed from the Shore area of the Port of Leith to the medical

quarter of the town, and now lived at the foot of Robertson's Close on the Cowgate, not two hundred yards from the Infirmary. They were remarkable not only for their deformities, but also for the fact that at odds with their twisted bodies they both possessed the most beautiful faces, and, in contrast to their bawdy repartee, were each blessed with a melodious singing voice.

It was widely recognised that the younger of these women, Thrawn-Leggit Mary, bore a close resemblance to my recently deceased sister, the wife of Dr Crowe. Mrs Crowe had been a great beauty, a kind and gentle woman of wit and intelligence beloved by all who knew her. Her death by smallpox was a terrible blow to Dr Crowe, who had married young, and, so it seemed to me, for love.

At almost midday on the morning of the 18th December inst. I was walking towards Surgeons' Square when I saw Kate Anderson ahead of me. There were a number of students gathered outside Dr Crowe's anatomy school. The door was open, and within I could see Dr Cruikshank the anatomy demonstrator. He was talking to Gloag the hunchbacked porter, Mr Franklyn one of our most promising students, and Dr Wragg the curator of the anatomy museum at Surgeons' Hall. Dr Crowe was to instruct the students in dissection that afternoon, a class that usually took place over the course of some three hours. He liked to have everything in order before he began – the bodies brought up, the knives laid out, and all the receptacles and fluids at the ready – and it was Dr Cruikshank, with the help of Mr Franklyn, who saw to it that everything was just so.

It was usual for Dr Crowe to appear as the Tron Kirk on the High Street chimed the hour and not a moment before, and I knew that if he came at his customary time he was sure to meet with Clenchie Kate. Dr Cruikshank knew it too, for I saw him catch sight of the woman through the open door and steal a

*glance at his pocket watch. We all knew what aggrieved Kate,
and why she had come up to Surgeons' Square, for it was the same
reason she came up every day now. Her sister, Thrawn-Leggit
Mary, was pregnant, a condition which, given the extreme
curvature of her spine and the angle of her hips, could lead
only to the grave. The women claimed the child was Dr Crowe's,
and, as her pregnant sister now found it difficult to make the
journey up from the Cowgate, for some weeks it had become a
daily occurrence for Clenchie Kate to appear on her own with
the sole purpose of screaming abuse at Dr Crowe as he entered
the School for his midday class. Dr Crowe's fellow anatomists,
and some of the more robust students, took turns in deflecting
the woman, usually with the aid of a few shillings, for she would
not go away without payment.*

*That morning, Mr Franklyn stepped out. He was hoping to be
appointed demonstrator, and was anxious to show himself to be
worthy of the position.*

*'Go back to your sister, madam,' I heard him say as he tossed her
a few coins. 'Or, better still, bring her to us when her time comes,
and we will do all we can.'*

*Clenchie Kate jabbed her crutch at him, and made the sign of
the evil eye, for Mr Franklyn was known to have visited the sisters
on many occasions. It was said that he had already made an
arrangement with Rabbie McDade, the skeleton maker at High
School Yards, for the stringing up of Mary Anderson's bones.*

*'You will cut her to bits,' she cried. 'You will cut her to bits and
boil her bones. Has she not had enough of men wanting her body
for their own purposes that you must murder her and butcher
her too?'*

*Some of the students laughed at that, as though the idea of
anyone slaking their desires on a body as misshapen and twisted
as Thrawn-Leggit Mary's was most amusing. But there were*

others who looked away, and in their faces I saw that if Dr Crowe had visited the girl then he was not alone.

Kate Anderson saw it too, and her language dissolved into abuse. Two porters appeared from the direction of Surgeons' Hall and dragged her back the way she had come, and we returned to our business. It was reported by Gloag later that day that Clenchie Kate had been seen insensible with drink in the Grassmarket even before the hour was out.

We thought that was an end to it – for that day at least. But there was worse to come. It was late in the afternoon when it happened. I was in attendance because I had made several preparations of the heart – in its entirety, and also in cross section, the aorta and valves, the strings and powerful muscular sides of the organ clearly revealed. I was proud of these creations – undertaken in wax and, if I may say so, an impressive simulacra of that most vital of organs. I was not usually present at Dr Crowe's lectures, but I wanted to see the response of the students to my models. It is well known that Dr Knox, our most famous rival at Surgeons' Square, is dismissive of any teaching aid other than the cadaver itself, and I was keen to prove him mistaken. It was for this reason that I witnessed first-hand the events that took place that afternoon.

It was after half past six. Dr Crowe was concluding his lecture on the circulation of the blood, the last class of the day, when a terrible wailing and moaning came to us from the passage outside. We heard shouting, and a cry of pain – I learned later that the woman had bitten Gloag's hand and thrashed him with her crutch as he tried to drag her back onto the street. There came the sound of cursing, and then the barking of a dog as one of the porters' boys ran to untie the terrier used by Dr Cruikshank to chase the rats from the dissecting room. Before the dog could be brought up, however, the door to the lecture theatre burst open.

Mary Anderson lurched in, her crutches dragging, her gait a

crab-like shuffle. She locked the door behind her and flung the key aside. Mr Allardyce – Dr Crowe's apprentice, and a young man always keen to show his loyalty – leaped to his feet to protest at the intrusion, but Franklyn pulled him back down. I heard him whispering, 'Sit still, Allardyce. This is none of your affair.' The other young gentlemen, clearly in anticipation of a lively ending to the day's work and knowing the deep love and respect Allardyce entertained for Dr Crowe and his late wife, hissed at him to shut up and stay seated.

I could see that Mr Allardyce was aggrieved at this, no doubt because my niece, Miss Crowe, a regular attendee at her father's lectures, was seated in her customary position in the front row and had the best view of what might unfold. I was tempted to go across to her, or to try to halt proceedings myself – and yet I did not. It is an error of judgement I will regret for the rest of my life.

Instead, I sat transfixed. The servitors had lit the lamps hours earlier for it was mid-winter, and in the guttering candlelight Mary Anderson's resemblance to my dear sister was more striking than ever. She had a luminous ethereal loveliness, no matter how bunched and twisted her body, and as I looked at the students' faces I knew they all saw it too. I could not help but take a sketch – a quick ink drawing that caught the lines and angles of the girl's cheeks, the dark, tragic eyes, the fine brows. I had drawn her many times, though never had she looked so distraught, so passionate, as she did that afternoon.

As for Mary, she peered up at us, up at that silent jury of men and her lip curled in a sneer. After that, she paid us no mind at all. She had eyes only for Dr Crowe, who stood motionless before her, a drawing of the heart in red chalk on the blackboard behind him.

'You have killed me,' she cried. Her voice was shrill against the thumping of Gloag's fists against the locked door. 'The babe that you have put inside me is my murderer. And I will take its life as

it takes mine, for there's nothing to be born alive from a body as foul and twisted as this one.' She used the Scots word 'thrawn', 'as thrawn-leggit, an' bough-haunched, as this 'n,' her native tongue giving her words a rough poignancy that was not lost on us.

I thought Dr Crowe might speak, might bluster her remarks away with a wave of his hand, but he did not. Instead, he bowed his head and allowed her words to fall like blows upon his shoulders. 'You have killed me,' she repeated, 'and you have killed our child. Why should you be suffered to live?'

His waistcoat that day was of blood red silk. I had admired it on many occasions, thinking how appropriate a colour it was for a man in his line of work. And so when the woman pulled out the knife and plunged it into his heart we saw nothing but the shock on his face, and the clutching of his fingers about the blade.

True on soul and conscience,

[signed] Silas Strangeway

Chapter Two

⁂

At first we travelled to St Bride's Infirmary. But Dr Crowe had gone, they said, and had taken Dr Strangeway with him. He had opened a new anatomy school. Bigger and better, affiliated with St Bride's Infirmary and St Bride's Workhouse and well supplied with bodies from both. The porter handed me a card, the address, 'Corvus Hall Anatomy School', freshly printed upon it in black and gold. When I saw where we were to go my heart grew cold within me. Somehow, I had always known the place would one day draw me back.

⁂

I should have guessed, or at least had some inkling, for the signs had been there. It had been some two weeks ago. I had gone up to my physic garden on St Saviour's Street to work on the poison beds – I had neglected them of late and the belladonna I had been so proud of was looking particularly sorry for itself. Will had come with me. I remembered him lying on his back in the middle of the camomile lawn, an empty bottle of beer at his side and Hammond's *Principles of Draughtsmanship* over his face. It was warm for mid-September, one of the last hot days of the year, in fact.

'I can hear shouting,' I'd said. 'Can you?'

'No.' His voice was sleepy.

'Hammering too. I'm sure I heard – there it is again! From next door – the house must have been sold. Did you know of it?'

'Did *I* know of it?' He sat up. 'Of course not. Why would I? Didn't you?'

'No.' We were on our feet now, the two of us standing at the gate in the wall, looking over.

The villa beside the physic garden was huge. Set back from the street behind tall black railings and unkempt bushes of laurel, it was a broad Georgian box, flanked by two short, square wings. A colonnaded portico added grandeur to the front, the south-facing windows looking out at the wide sweep of a gravel drive. At the back, in the shadow of the main building, was an ugly low structure of blackened brick, half-hidden in a dark mass of ivy and surrounded by hawthorn and yew.

The name on the gateposts was Sugar-loaf House, and I could remember when the villa had lived up to its name, glinting in the grubby London sunshine as if it had been built from those hard, sweet crystals. That was back when it had been owned by Dr Magorian, the most highly regarded of St Saviour's medical men, back when my father was still alive and St Saviour's Infirmary still standing, and I had loved Eliza, the doctor's only daughter. Since the death of Dr Magorian and his wife, and the disappearance of Eliza, the place had stood empty and silent – the windows boarded up, the paths rank with weeds.

That morning workmen were visible, removing the boards from the first-floor windows. The heavy front door stood open to the afternoon sun.

'Perhaps we should go and introduce ourselves,' I said. 'It would be the neighbourly thing to do, would it not?'

A short, wiry man in a dark woollen jacket and waistcoat stood apart from the others. His tall hat was pushed to the back of his head as he surveyed his men.

'Good morning, sir!' I said as we approached. 'I see the place is waking up again?'

The man looked askance at my face, his gaze lingering in mingled disgust and pity on the scarlet birthmark that covered my eyes and nose.

'Yes, sir,' he said, touching the brim of his hat. 'The place has been sold at last.'

'To whom?'

'My instructions came through the solicitor. I've no idea who the new owner is.'

'May we look around?' I said.

'I'm not sure as you should, sir. It's not like most other places. Not like any place I've ever seen, in fact.' He looked up at the building, his face troubled. 'I heard the previous owner was a doctor, but I can't think what sort of a man he must have been—'

'This is Mr Flockhart, formerly apothecary of St Saviour's Infirmary,' interrupted Will. 'I'm Mr Quartermain.' He shook the fellow's hand. 'From Prentice and Hall—'

'Prentice's, you say?' said the foreman, clearly more impressed with Will's provenance than mine. He shrugged.

'Look around, sir, by all means. But there are things in there that no one should ever want to see.' And he turned from us and hurried away, as if he no longer wished to speak of it.

❧

The house smelled old and stale. The air was damp, with a chill not unlike that found in a mortuary. There was a stillness to it too, as if the building were holding its breath.

'Why have we come?' whispered Will. 'There's only sorrow here. Can't you feel it?'

'Not at all,' I lied. 'It is only bricks and mortar to me.' I grinned, and clapped him on the shoulder. 'Shall we look around?'

For all that I felt strange and sad to be in the place my Eliza had called home, I would not let him see it. Will was my dearest friend, the one man who knew that beneath my gentleman's shirt and britches I concealed the body of a woman. It was a lonely path, one upon which my father had set my feet before I was old enough to ask why, for it was he who had given me my brother's identity almost as soon as the two of us had emerged from the womb – me alive and screaming to be heard, my brother slipping out after me, dead and silent. How else might he get the male heir he wanted if not through deceit, for my mother had died birthing us, and my father's developing madness had prevented him seeking out another wife. Will and I had become friends – he the junior architect, reluctantly emptying the graveyard of St Saviour's Infirmary prior to its demolition, and me the apothecary to that now vanished hospital. These days we shared lodgings above my apothecary shop on Fishbait Lane. His friendship had saved me from an existence of lonely isolation, and I loved him more than I had ever loved anyone – anyone but Eliza.

We went from room to room, our boots loud upon the stairs. The house had been boarded up with its contents intact, and spiders and moths had been hard at work. Furnishings, once opulent, were ragged and decayed; ornaments – vases, candlesticks, picture frames – all draped with cobwebs. On the north side of the house a loose gutter had caused a great dark stain to appear on the wall. The paper hung down from it like strips of diseased flesh. The place made me shiver. More than once I looked over my shoulder, but there was never anyone there. On the first floor, as we passed the open door to the library, I thought I glimpsed a face in the over-mantel mirror – a woman's face, the eyes strange and glimmering. But when I looked again there was nothing, nothing but the dim blush of light on the dial of a stopped clock.

'What is it?' said Will.

'Nothing,' I muttered. 'Nothing but my imagination.'

But Will was hardly listening. 'Designed by Adam himself, I should imagine,' he said, peering up at the cobwebbed cornice. He slid his hand onto the smooth curl of the banister. 'Look at these stairs! The way they curve upward, as gracious as the whorl of a sea shell. The way the sunlight filters through the cupola at the top. The rooms might be decayed but their beauty is unmistakable.' He smiled. 'It is a place of air and light and beauty – three things in poor supply in this filthy city of yours.'

'It is your city too,' I said. I wondered what he would make of the structure the previous owner had erected to the rear of the house. The dissecting room and mortuary

21

– even the thought of the place made me queasy. Instead, 'It will be good to see the place lived in properly,' I said. I meant it too.

But the past was not as easy to avoid as I had hoped, for at length, we reached the upper storeys. I hesitated at the head of a dark corridor. I had been there before, and I knew what lay beyond.

Will, however, did not. 'What's in here?' he said. Without waiting for my answer, he stalked forward and threw open a door.

It had been a number of years since I had set foot inside the doctor's private anatomy museum. Then, the place had been brightly lit, full of medical students and buzzing with conversation. Now, it was dark and silent. Here and there, blades of light sliced through the shutters, skewering a six-fingered hand; a cross-sectioned brain; an unidentifiable tangle of hair and teeth, all still and silent in their glass specimen jars. Before us was a human head – pale and loose-lipped, its gaze illuminated by a shaft of silver sunlight.

'My God!' Will took a step back. 'I'd forgotten what your doctor friends got up to.'

'He was no friend of mine,' I retorted.

'What's it all doing here?'

'It's a typical arrangement for a well-known medical man, a surgeon, to set up his own anatomy school,' I said. 'If he has an anatomy museum of over five hundred pounds in value, and if the corpses can be supplied and a licence procured then the students will come. This is – was – Dr Magorian's anatomy museum. Or part of it, at least. This place was always associated with St Saviour's Infirmary – the students might examine the dead here and then examine the living there.'

'Dead bodies?' said Will. 'Here?'

'Of course dead bodies,' I scoffed. 'Usually those of the unclaimed dead. Paupers, beggars, people from the workhouse. Once upon a time their corpses would have been flung into a lime pit. Now, they are given to a grateful medical profession.'

'And yet the fellow lived here too?'

'Yes.' I could stand it no more. I longed to be back in the physic garden, the scent of turned earth and damp leaves sharp on the air, rather than in this stale and ghastly place. I crossed the floor in three strides to throw back one of the heavy wooden shutters. The sun streamed in. What had appeared ghoulish in the half-light now looked faded and banal, like bits of meat floating in aspic.

I sniffed. Spirits of alcohol, a mixture of juniper and cloves – the smell of the preserving fluid. 'I'm surprised they have not become corrupt.' I picked up one of the jars and held it high, observing its contents in the light. The diseased heart that bobbed within was pale and flabby-looking, the window cut into its left ventricle revealing greyish valves and heartstrings, for all specimens lost their colour in the end.

'Is something wrong?' said Will, seeing the look on my face.

'Someone has been here,' I said. I thought of the ghostly face I thought I had seen; the feeling I'd had that someone had been following us. 'These specimens have been cared for, even if the rest of the house has not.'

'But the place has been boarded up—'

'There's no doubt about it,' I said. I took up another jar. Inside, floating gently in the viscous liquid, was a tongue, greyish-pink and newly severed. 'This anatomy museum still has a curator.'

23

I had vowed to put the place from my mind. I had largely succeeded – not least because I had not been back to the physic garden for some weeks due to my commitments in the apothecary. But now, here we were, right at its doors. In that short space of time the property had been transformed. The windows were free of boards and shutters, the driveway occupied by wagons and cabs. The front door stood open, and within I could see shadows and movement, as if from a crowd of people. Ahead of us a pair of young men, their books under their arms, sprang from a hansom and headed for the entrance. On the air, above the rattle and din of the street, came a raucous chanting.

'A is for Arteries tied up in knots

B is for Bones boiled up thick in the pot

C is for Carotid pulsing with life

D is for Dermis we slit with our knife

E is an Embryo in a glass case

F a Foramen that pierced the skull's base . . . '

All the windows were open, blinds fluttering in the cold breeze as the voices inside rose and fell. There was a distinct smell upon the air, at once familiar and disturbing – carbolic, putrescence, preserving spirits.

'It's certainly a livelier place than it used to be,' I said, looking up at the building.

At that moment the chanting stopped, to be replaced with laughter and shouting, the sound of smashing glass and furniture toppling. An instant later a pale English mastiff rushed out of the front door. It carried something in its mouth – I could not see what. A young man with his shirt sleeves rolled up and wearing a bloodied apron plunged out after it with a roar, pursuing the creature around the untidy flower bed at the front of the house. Grinning faces appeared at an upstairs window.

'Run, Bullseye, run!' cried a voice. There was laughter and shouting as the young man in the apron caught the dog, and prised its jaws apart. A cheer rang out as he held up what looked like a shoulder blade, still ragged with meat. He aimed a kick at the dog, and headed back into the building.

A burly man dressed in black and wearing a bowler hat – evidently the porter – came out and hauled the dog inside.

'St Bride's men,' I said. 'An animated bunch.'

'So I see. And yet up until now I had always found medical students a rather serious set of fellows.'

'But the ones you've met so far have been on the wards, trailing behind famous medical men and hoping to make the right impression. You see that they leave their obsequiousness and fear of failure behind them once the Great Men are not here. I assume Dr Crowe is about his own business somewhere else.'

I had to admit that I felt somewhat out of place. Apothecary's Hall, where I had done my own training, had always had a more earnest air to it – most of us had worked as apprentices, earning our keep as we learned our trade before sitting the examinations. The young men who trained as surgeons and physicians at the Royal Colleges, the universities and private medical schools, had no such employment. They were often blessed with wealthy families who could support them until they found themselves a situation. They considered themselves a cut above us grubbing apothecaries, even those of us who ran the city's great infirmaries, for that was a job no physician or surgeon would ever take on.

'Well, well,' I said. 'We are here now, so I suppose we had better get on with it.'

We were greeted by the same porter we had seen dragging the mastiff into the building. The dog was now sitting beside its master's chair in the alcove behind the front door, wet tongue lolling. The man leaped to his feet, stuffing a half-eaten pie hastily into his coat pocket. He licked his lips. 'Got a ticket?' he said.

'No—'

'No ticket, no entry. Dr Crowe's most particular.'

'We have no ticket because we are not here for a lecture—'

'You wanting the 'natomy museum then? Still needs a ticket—'

'No,' I said. 'We are here to see Dr Strangeway.'

'Dr Strangeway don't see no one,' said the man. 'Everyone knows that.'

'Dr Crowe then?' I said. 'I have something for him.'

By now the dog was sniffing excitedly at the package projecting from my bag. The man looked at it suspiciously. 'Meat?' he said.

'In a manner of speaking—'

'Don't trouble to deny it, sir. Dead meat it is. Bullseye ain't never wrong.'

'Then yes,' I said. 'Bullseye is quite right, and I need to see Dr Crowe or Dr Strangeway as a matter of urgency.'

Beside me, Will was looking appalled. 'What have they done to the place?' he said, stepping forward. 'In only two weeks they have transformed it into . . . into . . . the antechamber to Hades!' It was true, for the hall he had so admired on our previous visit was now thick with the sulphurous reek of cheap coal, the acrid odour of preserving spirits and the sweetish stink of decay. The pink marble tiles that had glowed warm and inviting now seemed lewdly flesh-coloured, as if we were entering a giant bodily orifice. They were covered with footprints and splattered with dark, ruddy stains – perhaps iodine, perhaps blood, I could not say. The dusty pieces of furniture had been removed, but in their place was a display case of animal bones and a bank of pigeon holes for the collection and distribution of letters.

A man emerged from what had once been the morning room, a place of light and tranquillity that had entranced Will. Now it was hazy with pipe smoke and cluttered with sagging brown armchairs. I had a brief glimpse of young men slumped upon them, some reading the newspaper, some smoking and talking, others poring over books. One fellow was peering at something suspended in a specimen jar, another was holding a skull. He had it up close to his face, a magnifying glass in his hand. There was a shout from someone, and he tossed it, like a ball, across the room to another, who was warming his backside in front of the fire. The door swung closed.

'Mr Skinner,' cried the porter to the young man who had just emerged. 'If you would be so good as to take these gentlemen to Dr Crowe.'

The man Skinner seemed to be another porter, but younger and thinner than the first. We followed him through ranks of medical men gathered in the hall and waiting on the stairs.

'So, this is now an anatomy school, Skinner?' I said. 'I had no idea!'

27

'Our old place up at St Bride's was too small, sir – that and the fact that the neighbours was always complaining about the noise and the smell and the comings and goings.' He eyed me knowingly. 'I think you understand me, sir. As soon as this place came up Dr Crowe took it. Corvus Hall Anatomy School we are, sir. Been in two weeks now, but already up and running like we was always here.' He grinned. 'Still making changes, mind. Dr Crowe wants it just so, though he's much happier since we opened up the place at the back.'

The place at the back. I knew he was referring to the dissecting rooms and the dead house – a dark, icy chamber where bodies were stored prior to dissection. Built of yellow London brick, stained black by the filthy city air, its walls were damp and glistening due to its sunless position in the shadow of the main building.

Skinner ostentatiously drew out a pocket watch of battered pewter and peered at the dial. 'Better hurry,' he said. 'The doctor won't see no one after tea.'

'Tea?' muttered Will. 'Hardly an occasion to present the man with a severed hand. Unless he takes his refreshment surrounded by bones and bits of pickled organs in which case all will be well.' He watched as an orderly dressed in a brown apron started to unpack a pair of skeletons from a tea chest filled with straw. The leg bones and spines were twisted by rickets into the most grotesque of shapes. 'Poor creatures,' he said, staring at the serpentine spines, the curiously angled hips and the tangled, bandy legs.

'Don't feel sorry for them, sir,' said Skinner. 'They're the Twisted Sisters o' St Giles. Thieves and whores, the two of them. One murdered, so they say, the other hanged. Been in storage for years as we didn't have the space at St Bride's.' He snapped his watch closed. 'This way, gentlemen.'

The room we entered was quiet and comfortably furnished. 'Does Dr Crowe live in the building too?' I said. I could not keep the disbelief from my voice. To live amongst such noise and activity seemed inconceivable, and yet here we were, walking across soft carpets, past gilt-framed mirrors and mahogany sideboards as if we had entered the home of a prosperous West End gentleman.

'He lives in this wing,' replied Skinner. 'The rest is for the use of the school. We have a much better provision here than we had at our old place – for dissections I mean, as well as teaching. We have a sluice room, a mortuary, a dissecting room large enough for twenty students at a time.'

'Each with their own corpse?' asked Will.

'Oh yes!' said Skinner, with relish. 'And there's a lecture theatre, a library, a committee room, an anatomical museum that's the envy of the world, plus space for drying and preserving specimens, for clearing bones of flesh and tissue, space for storage, for students to study, the common room, rooms for lecturers. We have some of the most well-known and capable men teaching here, sir. We're still a part of St Bride's, of course.' He gave me a smug look. 'The best men north of the river are St Bride's men. It was always the case.'

I said nothing. St Bride's Infirmary had always been something of a rival to St Saviour's, though as St Saviour's had been smaller and more ramshackle, its patients more desperate and hopeless than those in St Bride's further to the west, it had not been much of a competition.

We passed through another door into a small parlour. The blinds were half drawn, the room oppressively hot, and filled with the cloying scent of lilies, for a huge funereal bunch of the things stood on the sideboard.

'Sir,' said Skinner to someone we could not yet see. 'If you would excuse me, sir, but—'

'Is it Halliday?' said an eager voice. 'We started without you, my dear fellow, you are always so *late*—'

'I've not seen Mr Halliday today, sir,' replied Skinner hastily.

'Oh,' his disappointment was clear. 'I thought—'

'It's some other gentlemen. They said it was important, sir, or I'd not have brought them through.' He stepped aside.

Dr Alexander Crowe was one of the most famous anatomists in London, a man who had trained in Paris and Edinburgh, whose books on comparative anatomy revealed the study of thousands of animals. An expert on the human spine, his essays on the liver, the lungs, and the spinal cord graced every reputable medical library in the country. I had heard he was a man of modest habits, of humility and great privacy, and I was pleased to find that, despite occupying so lofty a place in the most arrogant of professions, all of this seemed to be true.

Dr Crowe was seated in an armchair in front of a roaring fire, a cup of tea in his hands. He was of average height and stature, with a high forehead from which sprang a halo of white-grey hair. His clothes were unremarkable – the dark waistcoat and jacket, white shirt and neckerchief showed no ostentation. He regarded us through keen blue eyes behind small oval spectacles. A tray of tea things – tea pot, cups and saucers, plates of biscuits, small cakes and coloured pastries – stood on a low table before the fire. The most unusual thing about him was his companions, for sitting on hard-backed chairs beside him were three women.

The eldest was some thirty-five years old. The other two were her junior by some fifteen years. All three were clothed in plain dark dresses buttoned high at the throat. They wore their ebony hair tightly dressed and pulled close at the nape of the neck. It was a spinster's style, flat and dispirited. And yet rather than rendering them plain, it made them still more beautiful, accentuating their long slender necks, high cheek bones and pale skin. The younger two in particular were the most striking-looking women I had ever laid eyes on, all the more so because they were so similar to look at – sisters, clearly. Their lashes were raven-dark, their lips a bright scarlet against their icy pallor, as if their teacups contained blood, and they had each just taken a sip. One of them sat with her face in repose, looking down at her teacup. Her sister, and the older woman, turned their curious gazes upon us, their eyes large and dark, as Skinner stepped aside. The conversation – what there had been of it for their voices had been no more than a low murmur – fell silent.

Dr Crowe rose to his feet. 'Welcome, gentlemen. You find us at tea before the afternoon classes. Pray, take a cup, and tell us how we can help?' His voice was softly Scottish. He sounded jovial enough, though I detected a coldness in his look that made me think his natural courtesy was being sorely tested by our intrusion. But as Will and I stepped into the light his eyes lingered upon my face and, perceiving the port-wine birthmark that covered my eyes and nose like a highwayman's mask, his expression resolved into one of genuine welcome.

'Why, Mr Flockhart,' he said, grasping my hand between both of his and pumping it up and down. 'What a pleasure. We've met before, I think? But we are neighbours now. I was hoping you would call in. And Mr Quartermain, too, of course. Come, gentlemen, do sit down. These are my daughters,' he waved a languid hand, as if the gesture might somehow waft their unspoken names towards us. The three women inclined their heads. Dr Crowe's gaze shifted to take in the package still clutched in my hands. 'Do you bring us some sticks of rhubarb from the physic garden?' His eyes twinkled. 'If more of us ate the stuff there would be many a physician out of the job, what?'

'There would indeed, sir,' I said.

'Of course, the bowel is quite fascinating,' added the doctor. 'Not to mention the anus – a much underrated part of the body. What disasters befall us when it fails to work as it should! So much depends on the correct functioning of both, and yet how we take them for granted. I have a section of the bowel wall in my collection that bears a tumour the size of a grapefruit, you know. The patient died when the thing ruptured. Prior to that we had no idea what ailed him, beyond haemorrhoids and constipation of the most intractable kind. I cannot help but blame the fellow's diet – which consisted almost solely of beef and mutton. I brought the carcinoma specimen along to the Pathological Society. You might remember it, Flockhart?'

'I'm afraid I don't, sir.'

'Then I will show it to you. Strangeway made a model of

it to show to the students, though we have the real thing in the museum. We have the most extensive anatomy museum outside the Hunterian, you know, though not all our specimens are kept on the premises.' He turned to Will. 'Forgive me, sir. You are not a medical man and this can be of little interest to you.'

'We have over 10,000 specimens here,' said the eldest Miss Crowe. 'Human exhibits, rather than animal. Father's lectures draw widely upon them.'

'Ladies attend your lectures?' said Will.

'The lectures are open to all, my dear fellow. If one buys a ticket one can attend a lecture.' Dr Crowe chuckled. 'We must pay the bills somehow, and it is not as though the ladies are about to enter the profession – the sheer weight of knowledge required would be too much, not to mention the debilitating pressure of examinations. Just as well really, as we have too many doctors as it is. But a little knowledge of anatomy, of physiology, will serve to make them better wives and mothers. They come to the microscope demonstrations in their droves too. I'm not entirely sure why.' He shrugged. 'But a woman's guineas fit into my pockets as well as anyone else's. My daughters have attended every one of my lectures since they were thirteen years of age – just prior to the onset of the menses,' he said, turning to me as if the word 'menses' might leave Will, 'not a medical man', once more gaping in ignorance. 'Knowledge of the body and its changes, its functions, is desirable to anyone, wouldn't you say?'

'I would indeed, sir,' I replied.

He considered me for a moment, and then said, 'Perhaps you should consider taking your MD, Flockhart. As a surgeon-apothecary you will be something of a generalist.

Times are changing, sir, and the role your kind had in the running of our great hospitals is vanishing. All that commercial grubbing about you have to do these days too,' he wrinkled his nose, 'it can hardly be satisfying to a man of your evident talents.'

'I had no idea my talents were so apparent,' I said.

'But of course they are! I have heard of you, you know. St Saviour's – old St Saviour's – was a place of some renown. You and your father had a great deal to do with its reputation and it is a man's past that makes him who he is. But it is the future that he should look to, and I sense that you need more in your life than the chasing of costive old ladies for pennies.' He grinned suddenly. 'Or am I mistaken? I rarely am, you know.' He looked at Will. 'And what of you, Mr Quartermain? Perhaps your association with Mr Flockhart has given you some appreciation of the dark arts of medicine?' He reached down beside his chair and drew out a copy of the catalogue for the Great Exhibition. It bristled with book marks. 'I was admiring some of these just this morning. I assume you are the William Quartermain who is credited with the illustrations on pages sixty-two to sixty-eight, page one hundred and thirty, and pages two hundred to two hundred and nineteen?'

'I am, sir,' said Will. He blushed, and glanced coyly at the three Crowe women. The eldest smiled. The younger two remained unmoved.

'Excellent!' cried Dr Crowe. 'I am writing a handbook on anatomy for students and I am in need of an illustrator. I see from this catalogue that you are an excellent draughtsman. I am not looking for artistic interpretation, but an accurate and precisely executed version of what you see before you. I need clarity and detail of structure. At the same time, I want my illustrations to look appealing, in the way that this catalogue – your illustrations in particular, sir – *show* the exhibits truthfully, whilst at the same time rendering them alluring. It is a rare skill, though I am asking for no more and no less than you have already demonstrated. Pen and ink. Specimens – dissections, organs, bones, that sort of thing. Can you oblige? Four, no, five, shillings an hour. It is a good rate, and better than most medical illustrators.'

'I am not a jobbing artist, sir,' said Will. 'Nor am I a medical illustrator.'

'But that's the point. I don't *want* a medical illustrator. I want a draughtsman. A draughtsman of your calibre. Are you in employment?'

'I work for Prentice and Hall—'

'And you are currently working on – what, exactly?'

'I have just finished—'

'Well there you are! You have finished one thing, so now you may start another. Tell your masters you are hired. As of today. Your style is clean and precise. Diagrammatic but expressive. Just what I am looking for!'

'But sir, I cannot. My master—'

'Your master? Prentice, you say? Thomas Carter Prentice? I believe I removed the fellow's kidney stones some years ago. He was most obliged to me. I think I can persuade him easily enough. And as for you, Flockhart, why, we are all still awaiting the publication of your book on toxicology. You began work on it with the late Dr Bain, I recall. Perhaps you should finish it. It would be a fitting *in memoriam* to your old friend, would it not, and a worthy subject for your MD thesis. The examinations are in the spring. You have ample time to prepare. You may find some of Dr Bain's papers in the attic; I believe Halliday came across a number of them when he was settling in. He's your companion beneath the eaves, Quartermain, and a capital fellow!'

Will and I exchanged a glance. Dr Crowe had a reputation for bringing out the best in his students, for making them see more in themselves than they thought they possessed, and I could not deny that such enthusiasm was hard to resist. We had brought him a severed hand, and found ourselves being offered employment and opportunities of the most exciting kind. He was right too. I had asked myself more than once whether I really wanted to spend the rest of my life selling cough drops and purgatives. I had always prided myself on being unconcerned by titles and honours, but with a lifetime of being disdained by physicians and surgeons alike there was something in me that leaped at the chance to gain the same status. My apprentices, Gabriel and Jenny, could surely run the shop well enough; I did not have to be there all the time. And I missed the *extremis* of hospital work, no matter how I tried to pretend I did not. Will too was looking pleased. I knew that any chance to work on something that did not involve drains or filth would please him; he had enjoyed his work on the catalogue and was clearly delighted that his drawings had been singled out for praise. Dr Crowe had gone over to his desk. He scribbled a note and rang the bell for Skinner. 'By return, please, Skinner,' he said, handing it over. 'Send one of the boys.'

He went back to his chair beside the fire. 'Well then,' he said. He cleared his throat and looked meaningfully at the package I still clutched in my hands.

'Oh,' I said. 'Yes.' Through the flimsy sheath of news-paper the flesh of four dead fingers struck cold against my hands. Perhaps the doctor would feel differently about Will and me once he knew the purpose of our visit. 'Sir, I have something—'

'Jem,' whispered Will. He shook his head, and glanced at the three Crowe daughters sitting side by side, their long slim fingers cradling their half empty teacups in their laps.

'Oh my dear sirs!' cried Dr Crowe. 'Whatever you have to say you can say it in front of everyone.' He smiled as he leaned forward, his eyes upon the crumpled newspaper. 'Is it flowers? They adore flowers, don't you, my dears?'

His daughters did not speak, but inclined their heads in acknowledgement, raising their cups to their lips in unison, like a trio of automata. Two of them watched me, the third still kept her eyes downcast.

'N— no,' I stammered. 'It is not flowers.'

He clicked his tongue. 'Oh, come along, come along, sir!' and he seized the parcel from me. But the newspaper had grown damp and the stuff gave way, the hand tumbling out, crashing into the middle of the tea things to lie palm down amongst the cups and saucers. The thumb and forefinger seemed to be reaching for a macaroon. I expected uproar, but no one made a sound. I suspected it was not the first time that body parts had upstaged the pastries.

Dr Crowe blinked. He leaned forward, plucking a pair of spectacles from his pocket. He affixed them to his nose and peered down. Pulling out a pencil and using the tip as a probe, he flipped the hand over and lifted one of the flaps of skin.

'Mm,' he said. Then, still more unexpectedly, he handed the pencil to the eldest of his three daughters. 'Your observations, Lilith my dear?'

Lilith Crowe lifted the hand from amongst the crockery. She turned the thing over and dusted the sugar off its fingertips. 'Have you examined it?' she said to me.

'A little.' I glanced at the other two girls.

'Oh, don't mind them,' said Dr Crowe, noticing the dart of my eyes. He indicated the girl on the left. 'My dear Silence was born deaf. As for Sorrow—' the other girl shifted in her seat, though she kept her eyes downcast. 'Look up, my dear.' The girl raised her eyes, the first time she had done so, and I saw at once the pale gaze of ruined sight. There were all manner of childhood ailments – rubella, measles, syphilis, premature birth – that might destroy the sight, or the hearing. Having a father who was a medical man was no guarantee that life would be any less cruel.

'Yes,' said her father. 'You see it now?' His shook his head. 'They are not like other women.'

Sorrow Crowe raised her cup to her lips as the clock ticked out an awkward silence, her blind gaze fixed, I presumed, upon darkness. Her deaf sister kept her eyes trained upon my face. As for Lilith, I wondered what it was that made her 'not like other women'. I was about to find out, for without the slightest concern she lifted the skin flaps and poked at the flesh beneath. 'A neat enough incision,' she said. 'Pared away from the fascia with some skill.' She glanced up at me. 'You think a medical man did this, Mr Flockhart?'

'It is more than likely.'

She pointed to the bloody stump. 'Cleanly dismembered. Post-mortem?'

'One would hope so,' I said. 'And yet—'

'Is it possible to tell whether it was removed post-mortem, or,' Will swallowed. 'Or before?'

'It is not easy to say,' said Miss Crowe. 'The specimen is very pale, so there has clearly been blood loss, which is consistent with the removal of an extremity while the blood was still circulating.'

'Quite so,' I said. I opened my mouth to say more but she was there before me.

'And if we examine the wrist we can see that the tendons have retracted somewhat – something you see when living tendons are cut, which might suggest that it was cut from a live body.' She shrugged. 'The extent of rigor is impossible to evaluate. We cannot rule out the possibility that the subject was alive when the hand was removed. And yet we cannot say with any confidence that he was dead either.'

'Good, Lilith.' Her father smiled. 'Pray continue, my dear.'

'It is a man's hand, that much is obvious to anyone,' she said. 'But not a working man.'

'How so?' said Will.

'We are looking at the right hand. The hand almost all of us use more than the other, no matter what we are doing. The skin of this hand is too soft for the hand of a labourer. The nails are short – trimmed, and to a great extent clean, so perhaps this is the hand of a man who wishes to make the right impression. Perhaps others see his fingernails and judge his worth? A man of the middling classes, then. A dark-haired man, sallow skinned, of lean build, not above thirty years of age judging by the condition of the skin, and of average height. The length of the fingers seems fairly standard in their dimensions, so unless the fellow was unduly tall with small hands or unusually small but with the hands of a monkey, we can surmise a man of five feet and seven inches tall.'

'Excellent,' cried her father. 'Of course, you have just described many of the young men in this building. Apart from Mr Tanhauser, who has the proportions of an ape – and the mind of one, given his recent performance in class.'

'Indeed,' she said. 'Besides, I saw Mr Tanhauser not half an hour ago and he was in possession of both his hands.' She smiled at Will, though she spoke to me. 'Have I missed anything?'

'Very little, Miss Crowe,' I replied. 'Though the nails were recently cut, suggesting that his life was terminated unexpectedly – if one expects to die one does not undertake a manicure.'

'An accident, perhaps?'

'Or worse. Oh, and there is blood in the nail beds,' I added. 'Perhaps you have some ideas about that?'

'There was a card too,' said Will. 'Show them, Jem.'

I handed the card over.

It was at that moment that everything changed. '*Et mortui sua arcana narrabunt*,' read Lilith. '"And the dead shall surrender their secrets".' I saw her swallow, saw the tremor in her father's fingers as he removed his spectacles. There was silence, as if all at once there was nothing more to be said.

The clock ticked.

Dr Crowe licked his lips. 'And you found this . . . this *relic* where, exactly?' It seemed curious that he had only just thought to ask us.

I told him.

'Amongst Dr Strangeway's exhibits?'

'Yes.'

'And you say a group of students had just passed through?'

'That's right, sir.'

'Well, I think your answer lies there. In all likelihood it is nothing but a practical joke.'

'Might we see Dr Strangeway?'

'Oh, I don't think that will be necessary.' A frown creased his brow.

'Dr Strangeway doesn't like visitors,' said Lilith.

'Dr Strangeway is a very private person,' said Sorrow. Her voice was low and deep, and had a curious rough quality to it, as if it were seldom used.

Silence Crowe had not taken her eyes off me. She said nothing.

'He said he was going up to the Exhibition this morning,' added the doctor.

'Really?' said Will. 'Is it possible that this hand was meant for him to find?'

'I suppose it *is* possible—' said Dr Crowe. 'In fact, we were all meant to go to the Exhibition this morning.'

'Is it *his* hand?' cried Will recklessly. 'When did you last see him, sir?'

'This is not the hand of Silas Strangeway,' said Dr Crowe. But his face had turned pale, as if Will's words had somehow struck a chord with him. '*Et mortui sua arcana narrabunt*,' he murmured.

'Does it mean something to you, sir?' I said.

'It does not.'

I was sure he was lying. 'Very well,' I said. 'But perhaps we might ask your students what they know, as there is every reason to suspect that one of them at least is responsible.'

Dr Crowe nodded. 'Yes, of course. Would you care to come along and meet them? Dr Cruikshank is lecturing in ten minutes.' He smiled as he stood up, though it fell from his lips almost immediately. 'My daughters will look after you.' He bowed, and vanished through a door at the back of the room. Although his departure was hasty, it was courteous, and as we had taken up much of his time when he had work to do, it was easy to explain. Nevertheless, I had the distinct impression that Dr Crowe was suddenly afraid.

Chapter Three

'Vesalius told us how we should view the study of anatomy, that it is the foundation of the whole art of medicine. You've heard of *De humani corporis fabrica*, I take it?' Lilith Crowe was talking to Will as she led us out of the parlour and back towards the main body of the building. I walked behind with Sorrow and Silence. The former had her hand upon her sister's arm, and they moved in time with one another, like a single being.

'They are inseparable,' Lilith remarked in an undertone, seeing Will glance round at them. 'Between them they see and hear everything.'

'And they come to Dr Cruikshank's lectures, too?'

'They attend all the lectures they wish to attend. There will be other ladies present today. This is a class for beginners, and is popular with the public. Afterwards, I will show you where you will be working—'

'Oh, but my master, Mr Prentice—' began Will. 'I cannot—' Even as he spoke an errand boy appeared and

43

handed him a note. He glanced over it and passed it to me.

'So you have a new commission, Will,' I said. 'Congratulations. Mr Prentice says you are his very best draughtsman, an artist of the highest order whose plain style will admirably suit Dr Crowe's purposes – should you be able to stomach the job.'

'Is that something that troubles you, sir?' said Lilith. 'There is no shame in it. My father says he fainted many a time when he was first apprenticed. It can be overcome.'

'Can it?'

'Oh yes.'

We were walking down a narrow corridor. On the floor, the carpet had been replaced by a coarse grey drugget. Soon, this too disappeared and beneath our feet there were only plain quarry tiles, a rich ox-blood in colour, a practical choice that made the mopping up of fluids easier. They also camouflaged whatever stains might already be there. I could feel a slight tackiness beneath the soles of my boots. I did not look down.

The passage was dim, our way illuminated only by whatever light was admitted by the open door we had just come through. Somewhere up ahead I could hear the murmur of voices and the occasional burst of laughter. And then a banging sound started up, as if from the stamping of many feet. The students were impatient. My own medical training had taken place in the apothecary at St Saviour's Infirmary. I had learned the rest on the wards, for I had been obliged to treat everyone when our physicians and surgeons were not present. Now, as the noise grew louder, I felt a nervousness in the pit of my stomach – I always felt it when I was about to enter a room full of medical men. My existence was shot through with a constant fear of exposure, what fate would befall me if they ever discovered that they had been duped into accepting me as one of their own?

'If you could wait here while I speak to Dr Cruikshank. He is working on the anatomy manual with my father. It's his lecture you will hear this afternoon, but as you don't have tickets I must explain – perhaps you would like to meet him in person before we begin?' Lilith smiled up at Will. 'Along with my father he will be advising you on what your work requires.'

She turned to me. 'If you would excuse us, Mr Flockhart.' I opened my mouth to object, to say that I would like to come too, but they were gone.

The door closed behind them and an awkwardness descended. I became aware of Sorrow's gaze, milky and luminous in the gloom. Her eyes were wide, and would have been as beautiful as her sister's but for the pale web across the dark centre. There was a curious iridescence to them like the eyes of the drowned, washed out and sightless as if their souls had been swallowed by the deep. I saw her nostrils flare, as though she were a fox scenting me.

'Have we met before, Mr Flockhart?' she said suddenly.

'I don't believe so, Miss Sorrow.'

She uncoupled herself from her sister. 'May I?' She raised her hands, bringing them towards my face, following the direction of my voice with eerie precision. My instinct was to back away, but I fought the urge and remained still. Her fingers were cool against my skin, her face close to mine. Her eyes seemed to be looking nowhere, and yet I felt as though she could see into my very heart. I shivered, and saw her smile. I blushed then, and my skin grew warm.

'You are nervous, sir?' she said.

'No.'

'Yes,' she replied. 'Your skin is hot, your voice is light but too quick.' Her cool fingers rested on my neck. 'How your pulse races!' She smiled again, lowering her gaze so that her dead eyes were concealed behind alabaster lids and dark lashes. She looked like an angel in repose, but for the coy smile that twitched at the corners of her mouth. 'I can hear it in your voice, in the tremor of it. I can feel it in your skin.' Her fingers had travelled across my cheeks and chin, beneath my ears and against my neck. My eyelids fluttered closed as she touched them gently with those cool hard fingertips. 'Your skin is very smooth,' she observed.

'Thank you,' I said. 'I have an enviable complexion.'

I glanced at Silence, and saw with some surprise that she was smiling. 'He wears a red mask, Sorrow!' she said. 'A scarlet birthmark across his eyes.' The girl's voice was curiously flat and clumsy-sounding, the words blurring into one another.

'You can hear?' I blurted. 'And speak?'

'Of course.' She had read my lips. I had thought as much, for her gaze had been fixed hungrily upon them. The sisters smiled as they linked arms once more. They could tell I was discomfited, and I had the impression that they were glad. I had assumed the two of them to be diminished by their disabilities. Instead I found them quite extraordinary: a woman who could not see but who could detect every emotion; another who could not hear, but who saw everything, from the dilated pupil in her interlocutor's eye to the sweep of a tongue across nervous lips. They smiled, though they were not smiling at me. Had they guessed who and what I was? I was relieved when the next moment the door opened and Will reappeared.

'This way,' he said.

❧

Dr Cruikshank was a tall wiry Scotsman of some fifty years. He wore his shirt collar high against his jaw, wound about at the neck with a frothing cream kerchief. His hair had retreated to the back of his head to expose a high bulbous forehead, with features clustered above a small weak chin. What remained of his hair was gathered in a ruff about his ears and the back of his head. It was slick with oil, and had been coaxed into ringlets with a lady's curling iron. His right eye was dark and watchful, his left eye white and sightless. But what he lacked in natural attributes he more than made up for in dress. He wore a waistcoat of purple velvet, a topcoat of black wool with a lining of plum-coloured silk. A jewelled pin set with a large garnet skewered his kerchief like a blood clot, and there were two other similarly ostentatious stones glittering on his fingers. He stood behind a pulpit-shaped lectern on a raised dais, the students stacked row upon row in almost vertical standings against the surrounding walls. We'd had a similar room at St Saviour's, but not like this. I had never seen so many men crammed into so small a space, for there must have been at least three hundred of them. At the front, a row of ladies sat. Sorrow and Silence slid in alongside Lilith, who was already seated. Will squeezed onto the end of the row beside her, his gaze transfixed by her profile. There was no room for me.

'What do you have in that parcel, my good man?' cried Dr Cruikshank as I stood there foolishly. The room fell silent. He pointed at the package I was still clutching. I began to wonder whether I would ever be rid of the thing.

'A hand, sir,' I replied.

'A hand!' he cried, his voice a clear cultivated Scots. 'Pray, sir, whose hand?'

'I'm afraid I don't know, sir.' I told him how we had come across it and he laughed.

'Well well . . . Perhaps it's no bad thing for a real exhibit to find its way amongst Dr Strangeway's waxen poppets. Indeed, some might argue that the only illumination his handiwork offers a medical man is if it were turned into tapers and set alight!' His voice rose as he spoke, his hands grasping the lapels of his coat, his gaze sweeping up to his audience, so that it was clear that his disrespectful comments were meant as entertainment. There was a bellow of appreciative laughter from the assembled students. The ladies' cheeks glowed with excitement.

'Of course,' his eyes glittered. '*I*, however, am a very great admirer of Dr Strangeway's work.' The laughter stopped. Worried looks were exchanged. 'Such finely crafted simulacra are one of the wonders of art and medicine. But let me be quite plain: I cannot imagine a less useful way of training a surgeon than solely to use such things. To learn about the body and its mechanisms without even *looking* at the body and its mechanisms? What folly! Pictures, models and drawings will serve us up to a point, but they are not enough. Other schools may teach in that way, but here we do not. A medical man must *feel* the deepest recesses of the body, the movement of the organs against each other, the spiked hardness of the kidney stone, the robust texture of the veins. He must *see* for himself what lies within, *taste* the saline membrane of the urethra, *hear* the sounds the body makes, the resonance of its healthy and its morbid structures. What models might afford us this type of vital knowledge?' He shook his head. 'Here, gentlemen, you will learn with *all* your senses.

'Show me that later,' he muttered, waving me away. 'And take a seat, for God's sake, we are late enough as it is.'

As I clambered up to the topmost standing – the only place where there seemed to be a space – something outside the window caught Dr Cruikshank's eye.

'Bullseye!' he cried, springing back into the performance once more. 'Damn that creature! It stole my bread and dripping right from beneath my nose yesterday.' The dog could be seen digging excitedly in the flower bed at the end of the garden. Dr Cruikshank bounded down from the pulpit, sprang to the window and threw up the sash.

'Run, Bullseye!' cried a student. A cheer went up. Shouts of 'Run, Bullseye, run!' filled the lecture theatre, as all at once Dr Cruikshank drew a revolver from his pocket. He flourished it in the air like a pirate, and balanced it dramatically on his left forearm. Squinting along the barrel, he took aim. He fired it twice, the roar of the report ringing in our ears. The ladies screamed in horrified delight. The students cheered wildly. The dog – apparently unscathed – vanished into the undergrowth. Dr Cruikshank slammed the window closed and stuffed the pistol back out of sight.

'Old service revolver,' he said, patting the pocket in which the weapon was now concealed. 'I was at the Eastern Cape, you know. Army surgeon. Still a crack shot, as you can see. I missed the beast deliberately, of course.' He grinned at the students. 'It would never do to kill a dog in front of the ladies.'

The lecture proceeded uneventfully after that. It was about the circulation of the blood, though it seemed to be a part of Dr Cruikshank's style to share his opinions about his colleagues as he shared his knowledge about the body – much to the amusement of his students, though they were not immune either, for he did not hesitate to mock anyone he felt deserved it, saving his best Scots words for those he appeared most to disdain. The student Tanhauser was described as 'a neep heid', someone called Allardyce 'a milk sop', another absentee named Wilson was 'glaiket', and later 'an eejit'. When he had finished, the students stamped their feet and cheered. Dr Cruikshank acknowledged their enthusiasm with a languid wave of his be-ringed hand.

'Does he always dress like this?' I asked the student next to me.

'Oh yes,' he said. 'Even when he's dissecting!'

Will came up to me. 'Why did you not save me a place?' I said. 'I had to sit right up here at the top.'

He shrugged. 'There was no room. Look, Jem, I must go with Miss Crowe just now,' he said. 'She is to show me where I will work and what I have to do.'

'Good. And I shall—'

But he was already bounding back down the steps. 'Come and find me later,' he said over his shoulder. And then he was gone.

Dr Cruikshank was watching me. 'Well then,' he said as the last students filed out. 'Let us take a look at this hand of yours.'

Dr Cruikshank's room was in a state of confusion. Packing cases stood about spewing straw and shredded paper, books teetered in untidy stacks about the floor and jars of specimens stood randomly on shelves, or peeped out from beneath chairs. It was hard to tell whether the stuff was coming in or going out. Dr Cruikshank flopped into an armchair before the fire and motioned me into the one opposite.

'I see you looking at my finery,' he said, gesturing to his plush waistcoat and fine neckerchief. 'I might be obliged to labour amongst the decayed mess of humanity, but I am not without refinement or elegant manners. And I do what I must to keep my lectures lively. Anatomy can be a dull litany of facts, sir, and it is my job to make it *not* so. You have heard of Alexander Monro *tertius*, of Edinburgh? A dull slob of a man not even beloved by his own mother.' He shook his head. 'The man single-handedly managed to destroy the reputation of anatomy teaching at Edinburgh University. That is *not* the way to do it.' He screwed the rings off his fingers and tossed them into a bowl beside his chair. 'Damn, these things annoy me though,' he said. He pulled off the neckerchief. 'And this too, confound it.'

'Then why do you wear it?'

'I must look the part,' he replied. He sighed. 'In my endeavours not to teach like Monro, I seem to have taken on the manners of Knox.'

'Robert Knox?' I said. I knew he was in London somewhere, for he had long since abandoned his once thriving anatomy school in Edinburgh. Some years ago I had seen the man lecturing on comparative anatomy. His style had indeed been as flamboyant as his ideas. I grinned. 'You do look a little like him, as well as having similar voice and mannerisms.'

He shrugged. 'He was the best, though he is a far cry from what he once was. The best, of course, apart from Dr Crowe, who never needs such theatricals to hold the attention of the room.' He reached out with a sigh. 'Come along then.'

Dr Cruikshank rooted in his pocket and produced a magnifying glass. I waited while he peered through it, examining the hand from its severed wrist to its fingertips.

'Well,' he said at last. 'I'm sure you've worked out the basics, age, gender, occupation and so forth.'

'Mid-twenties, male, professional – in my view most likely a medical man, sir. You marked the blood at the base of the nail?'

'Hmm.'

'Do you recognise it?'

'No, Mr Flockhart, I do not.'

'It was left amongst Dr Strangeway's exhibits. Possibly by a group of medical students. Your medical students, I should imagine. The rest of the body may be here, may it not?'

'It is a likely place,' Dr Cruikshank shrugged. '*If* they were our students and *if* they left this hand.'

'And there was also this,' I said. I pulled out the card that I had found between the finger and thumb. '*Et mortui sua arcana narrabunt*,' he read. 'And the dead shall reveal their secrets. How curious.' His voice was quiet, his expression unreadable. And yet somehow I had the feeling he had been waiting for me to show him the small black-edged card and its childishly scrawled motto. No doubt Dr Crowe had told him what I was about.

'Does it mean anything?' I said.

'Well, I know what it *means*,' he replied tartly.

'But is it significant?'

'Significant? To me?' He shook his head. 'Why would it be? As something pertaining to an anatomy school, however, it seems more than apposite.'

All at once he sprang to his feet. 'Tell you what, Flockhart.' He thrust the severed hand back at me and produced a large silk handkerchief from his top pocket, like a conjurer. He wiped his fingers on it. 'Since you're so keen, why don't we go and see whether we can find the rest of him?'

Precognition for the murder of Mary Anderson,
18th December 1830.

Statement of CATHERINE ANDERSON, known as
Clenchie Kate, rag picker and washerwoman, residing at
Tanner's Lodgings, Cowgate, Edinburgh. Aged twenty years.

19th December 1830

My sister Mary and I used to go up to the Infirmary or to Surgeons'
Square every day for it was not far from our lodgings. The young
men liked our saucy talk and glad eye, and the way we sang, for
we had fine voices and we knew all the sad songs of the Isles, and
some from the Lowlands too for our mother had taught us them
all. But for the most part it was our spines that they loved, for our
backs were twisted about in a way that used to make the students
stare, and their teachers lick their lips. It was how we made our
living, the two of us standing at the gates, catching their coins in
the boxes we kept at our feet.

It was no secret that Dr Crowe had developed an attachment to my sister on the death of his wife, and it was not long before she was getting from him in a day what the two of us had got in a week from all the others. At first she had laughed at him, taking his money and sharing it with me, as we had always done. But after a while something changed in her. She grew secretive. She took to brushing her hair and tying it in ribbons. They were not the kind of ribbons women of our sort could afford but she would not say where she had got them. She bought a looking glass from Jamie McGregor, the pawnbroker at the foot of St Mary's Wynd, and was forever poring over her face. Sometimes, she disappeared for hours at a time. I had no idea where she went, and she would never say.

One day I saw Mary in a gown of green silk. It was too fine for the likes of her, and all trailing in the dirt on account of her twisted figure. I took it to Jamie McGregor's. She was furious when she learned where it had gone, and that the whisky she was drinking was bought with the money I had got for it. We could never afford to get it back.

Me and Mary argued like the devil – we always had. But now it was worse. One day she showed me a little silver locket. She told me Dr Crowe had given it to her. I said we must take it to Jamie McGregor, but she would have none of it. We fought, and she gave me a black eye, but the pain of it was nothing to the pain in my heart, for I knew that the worst had happened, and that she thought herself in love with Dr Crowe, and – worse still – that she thought he was in love with her.

He did not come to our house, not that I ever saw, though I was often out while Mary, saying she felt unwell, stayed in alone. When I came back she would have a glitter in her eye and a flush to her cheek. She said it was just the fever that made her so, but I knew better.

His attentions did not last long. It was only grief that had drawn him to her, anyone could see that. I cannot say what happened, or how, but one day he looked upon her as she stood at the gates to the Infirmary and I saw that he had recovered enough of himself to recognise his recent folly for what it was.

Mary never spoke of what had taken place between her and Dr Crowe. I did not ask what had occurred, but I saw it easily enough in the way her belly swelled. One day we were at our usual place at the Infirmary when Dr Crowe came by. She pulled up her skirts to show how she had grown, and cried out to him that she had his child inside her. I saw him shake his head and walk away.

Soon after that Mary stopped coming with me. She said it hurt her legs and her back. Some of the medical men came to visit her. Mr Allardyce came, with his pencils and his measuring tape. Dr Strangeway asked if he could create her likeness in wax. Mr Franklyn begged that he might make a cast of her body with plaster. She told me she would not let them near. They said they were concerned for her, but I knew they were not. She was what they liked to call a 'monster' – both of us were. Neither beast nor devil, but something twisted and crooked, a human in some ways, but put together so wrongly as to make it a wonder that we were alive at all – like a two-headed goat or a dog born without eyes. And they marvelled too at what kind of a child might be born of one such as Mary, how it might grow in so topsy-turvy a womb, the bones of her spine and hips so deformed that the baby inside must come out widdershins – if it came out at all. We had once joked with the anatomists that when we were dead they might boil us up and see how we were made. Now, I swear I could hear them sharpening their knives.

On the afternoon of the 18th I was drinking in the White Hart on the Grassmarket. I had some coins that Mr Franklyn had given me. I was there all day, and for much of the evening, with no thought to much else, and when I'd had my fill I bought some spirits for Mary and went home. When I got home the door was stuck fast. I kicked on it in case Mary was inside, for it was often swollen tight closed with the damp. There was no sound from within. I knew Mary did not like to be out in the dark, especially when the haar was getting up. I thought she might be with our neighbour, Susan Leich, but she was not. Susan and I fell to talking, and we drank the bottle I had brought home for Mary. I was there for some two hours, perhaps longer. Susan told me I slept a while, though I have no memory of it.

When I came to leave, the fog was so thick that Susan said she would come with me, as she knew I hated the dark and the haar as much as my sister did. The door to our lodgings was still shut. Susan tried it, and declared that it must be bolted from the inside for it was stuck fast. I battered upon it, and called out 'Mary! Wake up, it's me and Susan!' There was no reply. I tried to look through the windows, but the panes were too grimed with filth to see anything but shadows and a dim glowing light. I rapped on the window and called out to her to let me in. At that, the room fell into darkness. A moment later I heard the bolt draw back.

I went inside. I could see nothing, for we have no gaslights nearby. The last lamp is on the wall at the head of Robertson's Close, and after that the vennel plunges down into the darkness of the Cowgate as it runs below the South Bridge. The next lamp is under the Bridge itself. But I knew where to fumble for a candle, and where we kept the tinder box. Before I could find them I heard a noise behind me, and something moved in the darkness. I could not tell what it was, but the sound of it, and the curious, damp smell of the place made me sick with fear, and I cried out and ran from the room, back out into the street where Susan was waiting.

'Oh, Susan,' I said. 'There is something evil in there. We must have a light. I will not go in otherwise, but I will wait here if you get one.'

I stood outside while Susan ran to fetch a lantern. I could hear the sounds of drunkards further up the street. The haar was too thick to see anyone, though it comforted me to think of others so near at hand. But then I heard another sound, like the scuffle of a foot. I saw the shadows darken before me, and a shape appeared in the door to my lodgings. I could see little other than that he had lifted his arm and covered his face with his cloak, and so I stepped forward. A lantern flashed open – to blind me, no doubt, so that I might not tell who he was. I saw his nails and fingers red with blood, and I shouted out and swung my crutch. It struck home – I heard a cry, and the sound of his lantern glass smashing – and I stumbled forward to seize him. But he knew those streets as well as I, for he turned and ran straight for Robertson's Close. My fingers caught the hem of his cloak and I felt damp wool and silk rush through my fingers as he pulled away.

A moment later Susan returned. She had a light, and had brought her husband with her too. But it was my house and I would go into it myself, and so I did, though I wished I had not, for what I saw will haunt me for ever.

My sister Mary was lying on the bed in a pool of blood, her face turned towards the wall. She had on her green dress, the one I had taken to Jamie McGregor's, though it was now stained and ruined. She had ribbons in her hair. She wore a shawl too – a lace one I had not seen before – around her neck and tight about it.

After that, I hardly know what happened. I heard someone shouting 'Murder! Murder!' and from the pain in my throat I knew it was my own voice. I felt arms about me, and the rough edge of Susan's shawl against my cheek as she dragged me from the room. I heard her cry 'Murder' too, and soon there came the sound of running feet, and cries, and I saw lights bobbing in the darkness. And then all at once there were men and women everywhere, crowding to see, to help, to watch – I don't know what. The surgeons came, Dr Cruikshank and Dr Wragg, their students too – young ones with earnest faces. They went inside to look at her, closing the door behind them, and I screamed out that they must get out of my house for it was their own Dr Crowe who had killed her; it was him I had seen, his tall hat and cloak, his hand covered in blood. It was Dr Crowe who had murdered my sister, I saw him with my own eyes.

True on soul and conscience,

Catherine Anderson (Her mark)
X

Chapter Four

The dissection room was a long chamber, its arched roof punctuated by a series of northlights that looked up at the jaundiced autumn skies. Outside I could see three crows perched on the window ledge, watching the goings on inside with hungry eyes. The air was dank and chilly, the walls newly painted and adorned with posters depicting various anatomical scenes – the blood vessels of the body, a cross section of a heart, a pair of lungs, a uterus. A bucket of white wash, the brush still projecting, stood against the far wall.

'I had some of the lads spruce the place up a little,' said Dr Cruikshank, seeing my gaze. 'The useless ones – Tanhauser, Wilson, Squires. Some of them would make better tradesmen than they would surgeons, to be perfectly honest. Still, it's brightened the place up a bit and the lime wash does something to mask the smell. For a few days, at least.' He held his arms wide. 'Are we not impressive in size, sir?'

I could not disagree. Side by side, in rows leading down the room to a door at the far end, corpses were laid out on high wheeled tables. Stools were positioned around them, upon which young men were perched, busy about their tasks. The floor was strewn with portions of viscera, detached pieces of limbs, chunks of dissected muscle, fat and cellular membranes. The windows were open to try to alleviate the stink, the students working without hats and coats in a bid to prevent the smell of death and decay from permeating garments they could not wash. As a result many had colds, and the sound of coughing and hawking echoed from the walls, the floor underfoot moist with blobs of phlegm.

Fat flies droned back and forth. From the corner of my eye I saw a movement – rats gnawing on something. Dr Cruikshank saw it too and clicked his tongue.

'Gloag!' he cried. A thick-set figure in a brown leather apron emerged from the shadows. 'We seem to have rats again. Can't you keep on top of them? Fetch Bullseye, would you?' He sighed. 'Might as well get the blasted creature to do something useful – and I'm not just talking about the dog!'

Over his silken finery Dr Cruikshank had donned a brown dissecting apron, stiff with old gore and fluids. He was due to supervise the students, he said. Dr Crowe would be along soon. 'Allardyce should be here when we have so large a class,' he muttered. 'Where the devil is he? And Halliday. I can usually rely on Halliday no matter what. Mr Tanhauser,' he raised his voice. 'Have you seen Halliday?'

The student Tanhauser glanced at the package I carried. The fingers were protruding, stiff and grey, but his face registered neither surprise nor interest. 'No, Dr Cruikshank,' he said. 'Not seen Halliday since last night. We were all out at the Golden Lion on Sink Street—'

'Yes, yes, save your vile anecdotes for the common room. You were all drunk together and Halliday has not been seen since.' Dr Cruikshank muttered an exasperated expletive. 'Well, well, let us continue as we are for now, gentlemen, Dr Crowe will not be long, I am sure, and Dr Wragg might be prevailed upon to offer us the benefit of his great experience. Once I have visited the dead room with this fellow here I shall be right back. And Dr Allardyce may also deign to appear at some point, though I'm sure we can manage well enough without him on this occasion.'

I followed him between the bodies to the front of the room. The students did not look up, but continued with their work. 'Use main force, Mr Nelson!' cried Dr Cruikshank, catching sight of a nervous student hesitating over his cadaver's chest. 'Cut through the ribs with the saw and then crack them. Don't be afraid, sir, the subject is beyond screaming now.' And to another, equally hesitant, 'Come along, Mr Squires, get your hands *inside* the cavity. You will learn nothing if you just stare into his entrails! Do you hope to read your future in there? I can tell you *that*, sir. Failure, pure and simple – unless you step up and get in. That's it. Right in! *In*, sir! Good. *Good*.' He cleared his throat. 'Gentlemen,' he cried. 'Forgive the interruption, but are any of your cadavers missing a hand? To be precise, the right hand?'

The men looked up, their expressions bemused. 'No, sir,' came the reply. I saw one or two of them exchange a glance. Had they been present at the Exhibition that morning? I could not be sure. I saw one of them catch sight of something over my shoulder and his face assumed an expression of alarm. I looked back to see Sorrow and Silence standing arm in arm beside the door, the eyes of both fixed upon the young men as they worked. Dr Cruikshank saw them too and he smiled. 'Miss Sorrow,' he said, 'Miss Silence, perhaps you would care to act as demonstrators while Dr Allardyce is absent?'

'Please God, no,' muttered Squires. I saw him bend to his work, his face closed, watching the two sisters from the corner of his eyes.

'Oh, no, thank you, Dr Cruikshank,' replied Sorrow. 'We have just come on an errand for Uncle Strangeway.'

Dr Cruikshank nodded. 'Very well.' He eyed Squires and Tanhauser, for he had seen the look of relief they had exchanged. 'It pains me to say it, gentlemen, but those two girls are more skilled with the knife than you will ever be. The fingers of a lady are light and quick, which is more than can be said about *you*.'

There were a few unattended corpses here and there, and Dr Cruikshank approached them with impatient footsteps. He went from cadaver to cadaver, lifting the sheet at the right hand. 'No. No. No. They should not be left out unattended like this, though it seems all hands are accounted for, here at least. Whose body is this?' he demanded irritably of a corpse that lay shrouded in the corner. 'It stinks to high heaven.'

'Wilson was working on that one, sir,' came the reply.

'And where is Mr Wilson this fine day?'

The students shrugged. Dr Cruikshank muttered a curse. 'Perhaps the dimmest of the lot,' he said to me. 'I did his father a favour in accepting him, but I rue the day. The lad's a dolt – charming and handsome but a dolt nonetheless. He'd make an admirable physician, no doubt. I'm sure he could slap on a leech as the occasion required and dispense the necessary powders easily enough, but when it comes to anatomy and surgery he's got the finesse of a blacksmith. Gloag!' he cried to the squat attendant who had just returned with the dog. 'Take Wilson's cadaver back to the dead room. We can't have it stinking up the place like this. Why in God's name has it been left out if the fellow is not here?'

'I wonder that Dr Crowe opened this place,' I said as I watched Gloag wheel the body away. He threw Dr Cruikshank a dark look as he went. 'A private anatomy school? They are not required as much as they used to be. Everything is going to the universities.'

'Everything?'

'The bodies.'

Dr Cruikshank smiled. 'Yes, well, we don't do too badly, as you can see. We are associated with St Bride's Infirmary and Workhouse, and they provide for us well enough. Admittedly, sometimes relatives try to take the bodies for burial, but deceiving the poor about where their dead family members have gone is no great hardship. We tell them we've buried them due to the possibility of contagion, but we haven't. Sometimes they want proof, but most of them are easily frightened off with paperwork, or the threat of exhumation costs – exhumation for corpses that were never buried, ha ha!'

'So you steal their corpses,' I said. 'It went on at St Saviour's too. Not that many of our patients died,' I added hastily. 'As apothecary there I must say we had few deaths, all things considered.'

'Of course we steal them,' he said, as if I had no understanding of the situation. I wondered why he was so belligerent. He had no cause to be. I had the feeling it was a show of arrogance for my benefit, but I was not about to be put off by it. 'How else are we to manage?' he went on. 'How else are we to get the subjects we need for students to learn their trade? Would *you* like to be attended to by a medical man who had only ever looked at a wax model and an anatomy manual? I think I know the answer to *that*.' I could not disagree, though I did not share his casual attitude to the procurement of corpses by deceiving the friends and relatives of dead paupers.

'The poor are everywhere, Mr Flockhart,' he went on. 'Why not use them once they are dead, for they were of little use when they were alive. Of course, it is body snatching, the same as it always was. But now it is sanctioned by the law. Now, we snatch the bodies *before* they have gone into the ground – a great relief to our students I'm sure. The parish undertaker and the workhouse master are our new friends, just as once we relied on the sexton, and our own skills with the spade and the hooks.' He shrugged. 'I'm sure the students are glad. I never liked digging myself.'

His expression became aggrieved. 'And yet the workhouse only deals in the very worst specimens. Vagrants and beggars, mostly. The only thing they have going for them is their lack of fat. Pity they are always so old. We really want fresh young bodies. Young and slim. No fat and good musculature.' He gestured to the package I still carried, wrapped up in its damp newspaper. 'The bodies that find their way into the dissecting rooms are almost always from unclaimed corpses – the old and destitute. The owner of *this* hand was neither of those things. It is the hand of a young man, and a well-nourished one at that. And if it *were* from a young cadaver, what student would waste any part of it on a practical joke?'

'Then who does it belong to and where is the rest of it?' I asked.

'How would I know?'

'It has been cut with skill and precision. Only a medical man would know how to do that. And probably one who had undertaken more than a beginners' class in anatomy.'

He clicked his tongue. 'Pranks are common, sir. And medical students are an ebullient lot. To become a surgeon one must undertake nine hours of dissection a day, five days a week, for nine months of the year – as a minimum. It seems a lot, but it is quite essential. As a result, there is nothing but anatomy in their lives for many weeks. It is what sets them apart from quacks, from physicians – some of whom have no knowledge of the human body at all. The best dissector makes the best surgeon, there is little question about that. And there are times, sir, when the young men need a little light relief from the horror of their work.'

'So now you are telling me that you think it *is* from an anatomy school?'

His pushed his face close to mine, so that I could smell the hair oil that smothered his ringlets. I saw the sheen of sweat upon his brow, though the room was as chilly as a grave. 'What I am telling you, *sir*, is that you should let it lie. This hand might come from anywhere.'

I smiled, and answered mildly, 'I hardly think so. Hands severed neatly at the wrist do not just "come from anywhere".'

'From any anatomy school then. Did you think of that?'

'Yes, sir,' I said. I found I was enjoying his discomfiture. 'But I am not ready to give up on *this* anatomy school just yet.'

He sighed, and rubbed a hand across his eyes. We were still in the dissecting room, and although we had kept our voices low it was apparent that everyone was listening to us. 'Well then,' he gave me a grin that I did not like the look of. 'We have one last place we might try.'

He led me to the far end of the room, through a swing-door, and down a long, sloping corridor, so that I had the impression that we were heading into the bowels of the earth itself. At the end I could see another door, wide and black-painted. I had never been there before, but I knew what lay beyond.

'The dead house?' I said.

He nodded. 'In here we have the bodies that are await-ing dissection, as well as those that have been "started", as it were. We have few at present that are not currently spoken for, though there was an outbreak of the cholera at St Bride's Workhouse some three weeks ago and we benefited from that considerably. They didn't last of course. It was not *quite* the season for dissections, you see, and the weather was warm for the time of year. Winter is the season. We are entering it now and I am hoping for rich pickings – if you will pardon my anatomist's humour. The cold often sees off the weak and we are the main beneficiaries. The bodies do not go off quite so readily in the winter and we expect large classes – most lucrative.' He pulled open the large, heavy door. A cold breath of air rolled out to greet us. It stank of flesh on the turn. I had smelled it since we had first entered the building, but in that final dark passage it had grown more pungent than ever, enveloping me like a sea, forcing its way into my mouth and nose as if I were drowning in it. Dr Cruikshank buried his face in a handkerchief for a moment, and I caught the scent of eucalyptus and camphor, two powerful oils favoured by anatomists to deaden the nose.

The room beyond was illuminated by a number of small windows set high in the wall. They looked out at the damp grass at the back of the building. The bodies were laid out side by side, each of them beneath a dirty flap of waxed canvas, so that I was reminded for a moment of a flop house – dark, windowless rooms where the near destitute spend the night beneath a mound of filthy rags. The smell in such places is little better too, though there is something rich and animal about the stink of unwashed bodies in close proximity, something that proclaims life at its most desperate. Here, the smell was of death triumphant.

'Well,' said Dr Cruikshank with a sigh. 'Let us draw our search to an end.' He lifted one of the sheets. A pair of pale feet projected, the skin ingrained with dirt. The doctor tut-tutted. 'Gloag is supposed to wash them down before they are put in here, but this one is filthy. Look at those ankles! Gloag! Gloag!' He shouted into the shadows, though there was no answering movement, for which I was heartily glad. I could not imagine a worse place to spend one's time. Dr Cruikshank stepped up to the next corpse, lifting the shroud at the place where the right hand should be.

The body was a luminous white; thin, but strong, the shoulders pale and smooth. The upper arm was slender but muscular, the lower right arm freckled and covered with dark hairs. The right hand had been neatly excised at the wrist, the bones of the radius and ulna protruding from a neat cuff of receding flesh.

I drew a sharp breath of shock and surprise. 'Thank God!' I whispered. 'I was beginning to think—'

'Think what, sir?' said Dr Cruikshank. He turned to me in the gloom, his face hidden in shadow so that I could not read his expression. 'You think this is the end? Why, it is just the beginning. How dare *any* man waste *any* part of so pristine and desirable a corpse. Let us see which man has his name to it, for they are all allocated the moment they come in.'

He flung the sheet aside the way one might whisk a dust sheet from a piece of furniture. When I looked down I knew immediately that Dr Cruikshank was right. This was only the beginning.

Eyes

It is said that the last image seen in the final moment of life can be found imprinted upon the back of the eye. For those who die at the hands of another, might the face of their murderer be caught for ever, like a photograph, on the canvas of the retina?

I have made a special study of the eyes. How many have I plucked from the sockets of the dead? Over the years, hundreds. And yet I have never seen this phenomenon – the ghostly image of a face, a room, an object, stamped on that dark surface – though I have looked many times.

Man has been fascinated by eyes since medicine began. The ancient Greeks believed vision was possible because of a divine fire that burned within the eye itself, the lens directing that fire out into the world. And yet this is not so, for in fact the eye works as a 'camera obscura', with pictures of what is seen projected through the lens onto the concave surface of the retina. No wonder, then, that we who have killed should fear what final image our victim's eyes might hold.

More than any other organ of the body the eye breeds superstition and fear. Its sphere recalls the globe of the earth, as if our eyes are themselves tiny celestial orbs. The eye is the seat of clairvoyance and omniscience, those with 'second sight' seeing into the future. Would one so gifted have been able to predict my deeds? The eyes are said to be the 'windows on the soul', but what if the soul, like mine, is black?

For hundreds of years people have worn amulets to ward off 'the evil eye', a curse transmitted through the malicious glare of the envious and hate-filled. We are doctors and anatomists here, we do not invoke the protection of charms and idols. And yet what resentment seethes amongst us, and what fury was in my eyes when I came to murder?

Chapter Five

※

We stared down at the body. It was a man, that much was evident, but it was impossible to recognise who, for the skin of the head and face had been removed in its entirety, peeled away to reveal only the red, anonymous musculature beneath. I was reminded briefly of the model we had seen at the Exhibition not two hours earlier – had so little time elapsed since then? – for the face of the corpse was not unlike the left side of that flayed model – the grinning teeth, the staring eyeballs, the red, glistening cheeks. In my pocket, my hand curled around the card that I had plucked from between the dead man's fingers. *Et mortui sua arcana narrabunt.* What in God's name had Will and I stumbled upon?

'Well, well,' said Dr Cruikshank after a moment. He bent close, so that for a fleeting, macabre moment I thought he was about to plant a kiss upon its forehead. In fact he was examining the job, and, seizing a lantern from the workbench against the wall, he bent closer still. 'It is skilfully done and it is not unusual to start a dissection with the face.' He stepped back and ran his eyes along the row of shrouded bodies. 'Six,' he said. 'There were only five of them here yesterday, I remember it quite distinctly – in addition to the number we have upstairs.'

He went over to a ledger that stood on a tall angled desk beside the door. 'The bodies, and their provenance, are recorded by Gloag or by one of the students. Squires and Tanhauser take turns as it gets them out of the dissecting room and makes them look useful. We must keep a record for the Anatomy Inspector. Students must sign their bodies in and out,' he said. 'The demonstrator initials them as they enter and leave.' He ran a finger down the list, his lips moving as he counted under his breath. He shook his head. 'Definitely one extra,' he looked up at me. 'I have no idea who he is or where he has come from. An administrative error, no doubt. I shall be sure to ask Gloag about it. The bodies come up from the workhouse and from St Bride's Infirmary. The workhouse is indifferent to the fate of its corpses, and the hospital is hasty in its efforts to move them on.' He chuckled. 'Of course, we only take *un*claimed bodies from both of these places. Those from the workhouse are rarely claimed.'

'And those from the hospital?'

'I've told you already.' He had the grace to look embarrassed. 'It's no more or less than what happens at every anatomy school. It is necessary if we are to have a supply for the teaching of anatomy, but as a result of the haste required and the . . . the duplicity involved, mistakes are often made.' He flung the sheet back across the flayed corpse with a practised air. 'This fellow is one such, I have no doubt, though there is no student's name attached to him, no label affixed to his big toe – something they all must have, once dissection has started. Of course, it's not unusual for a body that has been acquired by unconventional means to be swiftly rendered unrecognisable.' All at once he seemed keen for me to be gone, pulling out his watch and raising his eyebrows as if in shock at the time. 'I will sort it out, Mr Flockhart, rest assured. And now, sir, I have an anatomy class to teach. They are awaiting me, as you saw—'

I gave him the hand, still wrapped in its damp fold of newspaper. 'Thank you, sir,' I said. 'I can't say I'm sorry to be passing this on.'

'Oh, to be sure, to be sure.' He tossed the hand onto the corpse's waxy shroud. It lay there with its fingers pointing skyward. 'And I *will* get to the bottom of the matter.' He steered me over to the door and back up the sloping corridor towards the anatomy room.

'Dr Crowe said I may attend your lectures,' I said.

'Oh.' He sounded unenthusiastic.

'Have you known Dr Crowe for a long time? You are both from Edinburgh, I think?'

'All the best men come from Edinburgh, sir, though it is not what it was, and has lost ground to the London schools in recent years. But we were trained by the best, and our anatomy museum is one of the finest in the country. The public are in thrall to it – I wish I could say the same about our students.' He led me back the way we had come, ushering me hastily out of the dissection room and into the passageway. The students watched me go, their expressions blank. 'Good day to you, Mr Flockhart.' The door swung closed and I was alone.

The afternoon was drawing on. Skinner was lighting the lamps and the students were noticeably fewer in number by the time I emerged from the dissecting room. They had probably gone out to one of the many chop houses and supper rooms on St Saviour's Street. I had told Gabriel and Jenny that I would be back before sundown. That time would soon be upon us, now that the nights were drawing in. They would be worried if I did not come back soon. And yet I had no intention of going home just yet. I had to locate Will, who was somewhere about the building. Was he still with Miss Crowe? I found myself wondering at the whereabouts of the Mr Halliday I had heard mentioned. He had clearly been expected by both Dr Crowe and Dr Cruikshank, and yet he had not appeared. Where was he? Dr Allardyce's absence also seemed to be unexpected, as did that of the student Wilson. With an anonymous corpse in the dead house and three men evidently missing, was no one concerned for them? I knew students for a boorish lot, addicted to high jinks, beer and rowdiness. But that cryptic note, that severed hand and peeled, raw face – these struck me as something beyond mere japery.

I took the stairs up to the anatomy museum. The whole top floor of the building was now given over to the display of anatomical specimens. They were all about the rest of the building too – in the library, along the hall, on either side of the stairs. They were in the dissecting room and the lecture theatre. Every time I turned a corner I seemed to stumble across an orderly unpacking another crate of specimens – whole organs, healthy and morbid, a resin cast of the veins of the foot, the skeleton of an otter or a platypus, a baby with hydrocephalus, a display of foetal bones from one month to nine months. Every surface, every shelf and niche was home to something.

I came across the porter, Skinner, carrying a large specimen jar. A lump of flesh was suspended within though I could not tell what it was.

'The anatomy museum?' he said, when I told him where I was going. 'I'll come along with you, sir. And your Mr Quartermain is that-a-way too, sir. Up at the top.'

I remarked on the rowdiness of the students, and the smell of beer and pipe smoke in the hall. 'Are they known to be playful with the corpses?' I asked. 'I saw Bullseye gnawing on a scapula when we arrived.'

'Oh, you mustn't mind them, sir,' he said. 'I admit our young men can be a bit boisterous but it's nothing more than high spirits. Take that business with the hand. My money's on Wilson, sir. Wilson's the man for a practical joke – when he's not pursuing the ladies. And I've not seen him these last two days, so my guess is he's lying low till it all blows over.'

'I see,' I said.

'They're just letting off steam. I mean, spending the day staring into the innards of a corpse, sir. Ain't surprising they wants a bit of levity sometimes. A distraction is all it is, sir. Seems a little boisterous but it ain't nothing. Mind you, there was one time they all got drunk. Last year it was, sir. Every man of them forgot to go to the examination the next day.'

'And what about Dr Strangeway?' I said. 'Does he like the rowdies?'

He shrugged. 'I can't rightly say, sir. We don't see much of him.'

'And what does he look like?'

'Hard to describe, sir.' Was it my imagination or had the orderly's stride lengthened, his urge to talk becoming strained the more questions I asked?

'And Mr Halliday? Have you seen him today?'

'Not today, sir.'

'What's he like? Dr Cruikshank seems to think him a most skilled anatomist, and yet still a student—'

'Here we are then, sir.' Skinner smiled, turning to me with evident relief as we reached the door to the anatomy museum. 'The stairs up to the preparation rooms – that's where your young friend is – they're at the back in the corner. Ask Dr Wragg. He'll show you. He's the curator of the anatomy museum. You'll find him inside.'

'What is he like?' I persisted. 'This mysterious Mr Halliday?'

Skinner's eyes flickered over my shoulder. I turned to look. Was there a movement? The swish of black skirts whisking away into the gloom? I could not be sure, but – 'You're new amongst us, sir.' His voice was louder now, smile fixed, his gaze uneasy. 'Perhaps it's best if you find out about Mr Halliday for yourself.'

Chapter Six

⁂

The museum was dark, the shades drawn down over the windows so that direct light did not fade or corrupt the specimens. At first I thought the place was deserted, but then I saw a light moving in the shadows, a wavering candle held by a shaking hand. I heard a throat being cleared, long and lavish, and the sound of sputum being hawked up from moist lungs.

'Hello? Dr Wragg?' I followed the sound, past ranks of glass jars, lead-sealed, organs and body parts floating within like curious sea creatures. The light moved away, drifting before me like the glow of an anglerfish swimming in the deep.

I was so focused upon it that I did not notice the dark shadow approaching me. I heard no footstep, no breath, and I thought later how silently they moved, how they might creep up on anyone if they so chose – without a light too, as if they knew every turn and obstacle, and could have passed through the place blindfolded.

'Mr Flockhart?' It was Sorrow who spoke, her blank eyes pearlescent in the darkness. I wondered how she knew it was me, for she could see nothing, and I had not heard her sister speak. 'I understand you have been talking to Dr Cruikshank,' she said.

'Yes,' I replied.

'About the hand.'

'Yes.'

'It is nothing,' she said. 'There is some rivalry between Dr Strangeway and Dr Cruikshank on the matter of how best to teach anatomy. Dr Cruikshank favours the cadaver, with many hours spent with the corpse. Dr Strangeway prefers models – precise and exact in every detail but wax models nonetheless. He says the excessive use of the dead encourages a lack of respect for the living, a callousness—' She stopped. 'I fear the students can be rather provoking.'

'I'm sure you are right,' I said. 'But one must be certain.'

They watched me, their faces expressionless, their white skin flawless and beautiful in the darkness. But for Sorrow's fish-scale gaze the two of them were identical. For a moment I thought the girl was about to speak again, but then all at once I heard footsteps, rapid and confident. I saw the glow of a candle reflected on the jars like a million glittering eyes, and then out of the darkness a man appeared. It was one of the students I had seen in the dissecting room. In his hand he held a bundled handkerchief. He stopped dead when he saw the sisters. He took a step back, his glance darting from one to the other, as if he feared to take his eyes off either of them. Sorrow put her head back, her blind gaze fixed upon him. I saw her nostrils flare.

'Mr Tanhauser,' she said. She smiled. 'No Mr Wilson with you today?' Tanhauser's face flushed. He glanced back the way he had come, as if he wanted more than anything to turn tail and flee.

'I've brought something for Dr Wragg,' he muttered.

Sorrow Crowe reached out, and deftly took the bundled handkerchief from him. He did not object. He seemed mesmerised by them both, terrified, like a mouse suddenly confronted by a pair of angry cats. The girl searched amongst the folds, and pulled out a kidney. It had been sliced neatly down the middle so that it opened up like the two halves of a broad bean. She ran her long, slender fingers over its surface, and held it to her face for a moment so that for an instant I thought she was about to take a bite. Tanhauser evidently thought the same for he cried out in horror and lurched back from her. But it seemed she was merely smelling the thing.

'Your corpse is old,' she said. 'But you have a good specimen here. A renal carcinoma, even one as small as this, is an excellent addition to any collection of morbid anatomy.'

'How did you know what it was?' I said.

'Oh, they *always* know,' said Tanhauser, backing away.

'I can feel it,' she replied. 'A slight firmness, a granular texture to what would otherwise be smooth. And the smell of the thing. It is quite clearly morbid.'

'I was looking for Dr Wragg,' repeated Tanhauser. 'You seen him, miss?'

She turned her dead eyes to him. 'Have *I* seen Dr Wragg?' Her voice was mocking. 'Even a dolt like *you* would know the answer to *that*.'

I glanced at Tanhauser. Like me he seemed surprised

by her change in tone, and yet he evidently found her hostility easier to deal with, for he replied, 'Well, miss, have you *smelled* him anywhere?'

She scowled at him.

'Look,' he passed a hand across his brow, 'I'm sorry. I just want to find Dr Wragg. And may I have my kidney ,please?'

'Of course,' She held the organ out, but as Tanhauser reached for it she squeezed the thing tightly in her fist. We heard it squelch horribly.

Tanhauser gasped, and stepped back. 'Keep it then,' he whispered. 'And welcome to it.' He threw me a pitying glance, and then vanished the way he had come.

'Dr Wragg is waiting for you, Mr Flockhart,' said Sorrow. She dropped the kidney onto the floor. Her sister pointed into the darkness, where I could see a light burning dimly. When I turned back the two of them were gone.

Somewhere far off a door banged. A dog barked and voices shouted. The light began to move off again.

'Confound this place,' I muttered. 'Hello?' I shouted. 'You there! Dr Wragg?'

I found a candle sitting beside a display of gunshot wounds, lumps of punctured skin and flesh, greyish now, rather than the screaming scarlet they would once have been. Beside it, wiping the glass with a slimy leather cloth, was a small man in a woollen topcoat with a high shawl collar. The elbows were worn down to the very weave of the fabric, the cuffs shaggy with frayed edges against a grubby shirt.

'Good evening, sir,' I said. 'I'm glad I caught you. You move like a will o' the wisp through these exhibits. Are you the curator here?'

'I am.' He took up a bottle containing a blob of flesh I was unable to identify in the gloom and buffed it lovingly with his handkerchief, the leather hank he had been using now tucked into his belt. 'At least, I'm one of them. The other fellow's new. I'm not new. I'm old. Very old.' He turned to me. 'Flockhart, isn't it?'

'Yes, sir.' There was a pause, a silence filled only by the squeak of cloth against glass. He stopped, and turned red-rimmed eyes upon me. 'What do you want with us, sir?'

'Why, nothing. That is, I'm looking for Mr Quartermain. Dr Crowe has employed him as an artist. A draughtsman. I believe he is nearby? If you could direct me?' I frowned. 'How long have you been here, Dr Wragg?'

'Long enough,' he said. 'I've been an anatomist, man and boy. Always.' He laughed, a hollow rattling sound like pebbles caught in a drain.

'What about this museum? How long have you been looking after this place? Here.'

'Here? Since the place was closed. I knew Dr Magorian – he owned the Hall before Dr Crowe bought it. But then you know that, don't you? He was an Edinburgh man too. And when he died, well, we couldn't just let the place rot.'

'We?' I said. 'You and who else? Dr Crowe?'

He did not reply, but replaced the jar on the shelf, turning it this way and that, until he was happy.

'Did Dr Crowe know?' I persisted. 'Did he know you were coming in here to look after the specimens even while the place was boarded up?'

He smiled at me then, revealing the most curious set of teeth I had ever seen, for they appeared to be real human teeth, but set into a plate of polished wood. They had clearly originated from a number of different mouths, for they were different sizes and colours. 'Dr Crowe doesn't stick his nose in where it's not wanted,' he said. 'Dr Crowe is a gentleman. He knows when to ask questions and when *not* to ask questions.' He picked up his candle. 'I advise you to do the same.'

'And who is the young curator?'

'Fellow called Halliday.' His face darkened. 'He's not here.' He turned away from me. 'Your friend's up there.' He pointed to a dark corner of the room. I could just about make out the serpentine coil of a spiral staircase winding up into the ceiling. A faint, flickering glow filtered down from above. I felt the old man's gaze follow me as I walked away.

Precognition for the murder of Mary Anderson,
18th December 1830.

Statement of RICHARD ALLARDYCE, apprentice
surgeon-apothecary to Dr Crowe. Currently residing at
22 East Newington Street, Edinburgh. Aged twenty-two
years.

19th December 1830

I was made aware of the death of Mary Anderson on the night
of the 18th inst. by the arrival of one Davie Knox, a young lad
of some eleven years of age who, on account of sharing his name
with the most brilliant and infamous anatomist of the day, had
decided that the two of them must surely be cousins. As a result, for
the price of a shilling he and his gang of fellow miscreants inform
the gentlemen surgeons of any deaths they know to have occurred
in the Cowgate and its surrounding streets.

Young Davie and his entourage came up to 13 Surgeons' Square at some time between nine and ten o'clock in the evening of the 18th. He told me that there was a devil of a commotion going on at the foot of the close, 'At the hoose o' Thrawn-Leggit Mary,' he said. 'She's murthered, and there's the de'il tae pay fer it.'

'Murdered?' I said. 'By whom?' He looked askance at that and said that surely I knew who it was, 'fer it's yer ain Dr Craw,' he said. 'Auld Corbie, himsel'!' I told him that this was preposterous, that Dr Crowe had gone home some hours earlier, but he would not be persuaded.

Dr Cruikshank was in the dissecting room with Franklyn. It was late for them, but the corpse they were to work on was more than a week old already and would not last much longer. Dissection by candlelight is a vile business and, for all that they had done such work a hundred times before, they were both looking very green. I told Dr Cruikshank what I had heard, and he clapped his hands, saying, 'Excellent, Mr Allardyce. This cadaver is almost beyond use, and we could do with another. Besides, a little night air and an adventure will be sure to do us good.'

There were five of us who went down to the Cowgate that night: Dr Cruikshank, Dr Strangeway, Dr Wragg, Mr Franklyn and myself. I did not send a runner for Dr Crowe, judging it best that, given his known sympathy for the girl Mary, and his recent contretemps with her in the lecture theatre, he would be better off elsewhere. The night was chill; dank and bitter with the haar, which takes on a sulphurous tang in the wintertime due to the smokiness of the air. Our lanterns were of little help, their light reflecting off the fog so that we might have been standing at the bottom of the Nor' Loch for all the difference they made. As we reached the top of Robertson's Close we could hear the murmur of voices drifting up from the dark thoroughfare below.

'Sticks at the ready, gentlemen,' said Dr Cruikshank. 'It'll be an ugly crowd that greets us.'

I had mine to hand, as I knew that feeling towards us ran high in those parts of the town, especially since the West Port murders. The mob had come boiling up from the Cowgate during those days, and our work at the dissection tables had been brought to a standstill. Dr Knox's house had been besieged, and a number of us had been attacked in the streets. Acquiring the bodies we needed to learn our craft had become harder than ever since then, and yet without them we could not be trained. We were all decided: if we had to brave the mob to get a corpse then so be it. Besides, the body of Thrawn-Leggit Mary would be a rare trophy indeed. Dr Knox himself had been after it, though as he was away in London at that time he had missed his opportunity. I gripped my stick and followed the glow of Dr Cruikshank's lantern as we headed down the close towards the waiting mob.

I could see that they were drunk. I could smell it too. The dark and the alcohol had given them courage, and we were jostled and pummelled as we passed through their ranks. I felt a wet splatter of spit against my cheek, and saw more of the same strike Dr Cruikshank's hat. But we marched forward nonetheless, the crowd reluctantly parting to allow us passage. The door to the sisters' house stood open, though it seemed no one had dared to enter.

'Be quick about it,' said Dr Wragg. 'We have no friends down here tonight.' I saw him look to the crowd, and his grip tightened about the shaft of his stick.

Dr Cruikshank, Dr Strangeway, Franklyn and I went inside. Dr Wragg, who was no stranger to the less salubrious parts of the town, awaited us in the street, guarding the door whilst we readied the corpse. The room was dark, the shadows thick and black, for the place seemed to be built into the bowels of the *city itself. The women lived at the very foot of a tall tenement, a lodging house, one of the most dilapidated, crowded and labyrinthine I have ever come across. There was hardly a stick of furniture save for a rickety table and two low chairs, the legs of which had been sawn off so that the sisters might sit in comfort on either side of the fire. The fire itself was little more than a dark hole, with a crooked iron trivet bearing a kettle, furry with soot. An equally filthy cooking pot stood on the hearth. There was a large box bed in the corner. Upon it lay the body of the woman we had known as Thrawn-Leggit Mary. She was wearing a green silk dress, and I recognised it as one that had once belonged to Mrs Crowe. Dr Cruikshank bent over her. I saw him hold his fingers to her wrist, though there was no doubt at all that she was dead.*

'Dr Strangeway,' said Dr Cruikshank. 'If you would be so good as to make a sketch of the corpse so that we might show the authorities how she was found.' There was a thump as something heavy, a clod of earth perhaps, was flung against the door, and I heard Clenchie Kate screaming out that it was Dr Crowe who had killed her sister, for she had seen him with her own eyes. We ducked as a stone smashed through the window, and Dr Cruikshank said, 'Goodness knows when the constable might arrive. We cannot wait for him here or he will have six corpses rather than one to deal with. Come along, sir,' he addressed Dr Strangeway. 'Will you draw the scene?'

But Dr Strangeway was overcome at the sight of the girl's body, his hands shaking as he handled his pencil. He had a smear of blood on his cheek, and against the white of his skin it stood out like a wound. Dr Cruikshank noticed his pallor, and his discomfiture, and he took the drawing implements from him. 'Never mind, sir,' he said, his voice gentle. 'Allardyce can do the job. He's a passable artist.'

I was glad to be given so important a task, and I speedily took the drawing materials. In a few strokes of the pencil I had captured the angle of the head and the clutching of the hands. The arms were awry, the skirts tumbled about the misshapen legs, a lace shawl knotted tightly about the throat. The dress was soaked in gore. The girl may once have flattered herself that she looked like Mrs Crowe, but there was no evidence of that similarity now. I noted the blood – the way it had pooled, the slippery mess of it against the bedding.

Outside, Dr Wragg battered on the door with the head of his stick, and cried out, 'Make haste, gentlemen, if you please!' Another window pane shattered, the stone skimming past Dr Strangeway, who was standing with his back to us, as if unable to look at the scene. 'Have you finished, Allardyce?' said Dr Cruikshank.

I said I had, though I had not been able to capture her face, for it was turned away from me and in the shadows. I asked if he would move it, so that I might make a quick sketch, but he shook his head. He stepped in front of me then, busying himself with poring over the corpse, looking, no doubt, for scraps of evidence as to who had done this and what had happened. At length he called Franklyn, who had idled away the time looking about the room, and the two of them began wrapping the dead girl in the bed sheet. But it was too bloody to act as a shroud, so Dr Cruikshank took off his coat and wrapped her in that too.

As we appeared in the street, the crowd roared their disapproval. A cudgel wielded by an unseen assailant smashed Franklyn's lantern. Hands tugged at our burden, and there was a cheer as the corpse was seized, borne aloft on a sea of shoulders and hands, the coat, and the bed sheet, unravelling as she went.

When they saw what lay beneath, however, they released their prize onto the ground with a cry, and fell back. But we had a job to do that night, and Dr Wragg and Dr Cruikshank saw to it that it was done: Dr Wragg striking out at the mob with his stick and Dr Cruikshank springing forward to snatch up the corpse. Before the crowd could gather their wits we were gone.

True in soul and conscience,

[signed] Richard Allardyce

Chapter Seven

I found Will in the attic above the anatomy museum. It was piled high with bottles and jars, hanging bladders of chemicals, waxes and resins for preserving specimens, lead for sealing jars, tanks of alcohol and other fluids. By the smell of the place I knew it was not far from the macerating room, where human specimens were soaked, and injected with preservatives, wax or alcohol. Its atmosphere was thick, gritty and unwholesome, the air motionless, despite the open window.

He was sitting at a desk, a set of pens and a pot of ink before him, a ream of thick paper to one side. Beside him was a large brass microscope.

'Yes,' he said, noticing my appraising glance. 'It is one of the very best. No, you may not look down it. It is for my private use – though I admit I am not using it now.'

Before him on the bench was a skeleton hand, a man's judging by its size. 'I am to draw what I see,' he said. 'Nothing fancy and artistic; it is about accuracy of representation. Artistic training is no use – which is just as well as I have none. It seems my eye for structure and function are just what is required, for it must be shown as it is, the various parts outlined as clearly and practically as possible.' He had drawn it already, and was sitting back admiring his handiwork. 'What do you think? Lilith – Miss Crowe – said I might start with the bones and work my way out. It seems a sensible approach.'

'Had you not better attempt an organ too? The skeleton is the easy part, in many ways. A heart, dissected to show its innards, is a different matter. Or what about a sphincter? Or some entrails? A length of duodenum, say—'

'I am unsure what those things are, Jem, though I suspect you have chosen to mention them just to appal me.'

'The sphincter is—'

'Stop!' He held up a hand. 'That's quite enough. I can't say I'm looking forward to the organs, but Dr Crowe and Dr Cruikshank say they will give me what they wish me to draw, and draw it I shall.'

'You have accepted the commission?'

'I cannot see how I could refuse. But at least I will be inside during the winter months and who knows where it might lead. Scientific illustration is not something I'd ever considered as a career, but one must take opportunities as they present themselves.' His drawing, pen and ink, was a perfect rendition of the bones set out before him. 'Dr Crowe, or Dr Cruikshank, will annotate the structure as they see fit and add text. Dr Crowe says it is to be the most comprehensive book on practical anatomy ever attempted. Testimony to their knowledge and many years of teaching.' Will sat back in his chair and stretched. 'Miss Crowe said the specimens will be fresh, thank God.' He shrugged. 'I am not so bothered by the dead meat. It will be like illustrating the contents of a butcher's window, and I must try to think of it as recording the miracle of life. It's watching you – or anyone else – do the butchering that upsets me. But I have my salts in my pocket if I need them and I dare say I will get used to it eventually.'

'Anatomists are often excellent artists,' I said. 'Though they rarely attain such professional standards as you.'

'I don't mind the job.' He looked about the room, at the boxes and bottles, the jars of fluids and coloured resins and waxes. 'But I don't like this place.' He frowned, and peered closely at the skeleton hand, and at the image he had drawn of it. 'I have a few changes I'd like to make to my work. Will you wait for me?'

I sat on a tea chest while Will turned back to his drawing. Despite the stink it was pleasingly quiet up there, away from everyone, though I could hear the faint sounds of activity far below. 'Are you alone up here?' I said, noting another desk against the far wall behind a stack of boxes.

'Apparently that chap Halliday works up here too,' said Will.

'He must be a capable young man,' I said. 'It seems he is the assistant curator of the anatomy museum as well as helping the demonstrator, and yet I believe he is still a student.' I went over to the desk, but it told me nothing, other than the fact that the man Halliday was scrupulously tidy and liked to keep his drawers locked.

'Jem.' Will shook his head. 'Stop prying. Sit still, can't you?'

But I was unable to do either of those things. Corvus

Hall unsettled me. There was something going on there, I was sure of it, though I had no idea what it might be. I tried to put it from my mind but I could not. A faceless corpse, a severed hand, both were objects of horror in any other location, but here? Here there was every likelihood they were completely innocent. And yet I was not persuaded. I thought of Sorrow and Silence Crowe, one wordless in the dark, the other squeezing a kidney to mush with her bare hand. The memory made me shiver.

I jumped up and ranged about the room. I poked about in a dark corner, pulling out this and that to see what was there. I found only the lumber of previous years; things that had been put up there when Dr Magorian owned the place, perhaps even before that. On top of it Dr Crowe had added his own belongings – books, boxes, anatomical posters rolled into tubes, crates of bones and cases containing the skeletons of animals. Layer upon layer of medical knowledge was hidden up there, laid down like sediment on a river bed. If I dug down what pasts and histories would I find? A signature on the flyleaf of a book on *materia medica* belonged to Dr Bain, my old friend from St Saviour's. A label on a bone showed it to have come from Edinburgh, though the collection it had once been a part of was long since lost. I rooted in a box. Letters, piles of them, all addressed to Dr Magorian of St Saviour's Infirmary, spilled over my hands.

And then I found something quite unexpected. It was under a box, against the dusty floor as if it had found its way there by accident. It was a letter, small and tightly folded, the wax that had sealed it like a clot of dried blood against the yellowing paper. It was addressed to Dr Bain. What caused me to snatch it up, what made my heart lurch in my chest when I saw it, was the hand it was written in. Without hesitation I stuffed the letter into my pocket. Were there more? I rooted about, suddenly feverish, anxious. But there was nothing. A box of bones that I had stacked carelessly on a chair crashed to the floor.

Will swore. 'For God's sake, Jem, can you not sit still?'

'Sorry.' I sat down, and slid my hand into my pocket. I ran my fingers over the sharp corners and edges of the paper, felt the scab of sealing wax where Dr Bain had ripped it open. It was my mother's writing, there was no doubt in my mind, for I knew the swoop of her 'S' and the generous curl of her 'B' as well as I knew my own. She had died as I was born. My father had refused to speak of her, and yet all at once here she was, a piece of her life found in a dusty corner of an old villa. I would open it later when I was on my own. Whatever it might contain, I wanted it to be for my eyes only.

❧

By the time Will had finished, the building had fallen silent. Once the day had faded the place was no use to anatomists and medical students, who needed strong clear light to do the best of their work. Lamps might serve, but they dazzled the eye, created shadows where none were wanted, and brought with them an unwelcome heat.

Will stood up from his workbench, and pulled on his jacket. 'Shall we go home, Jem? We might go via Sorley's. I am ready for a plate of mutton stew. Or pheasant! I met Sorley in the street last week and he said he had pheasant. It's sure to be in a pie by now—'

'No,' I said, though my own stomach ached for food. 'I

want to look downstairs again. I need to go to the dead house. We must wait until everyone has gone, perhaps until midnight? And then we will creep down. Something is not right here, Will. Where is Halliday? Where are Allardyce and Wilson? Where is Silas Strangeway? No one can even describe the fellow, so that I am beginning to wonder whether he even exists. Whose is that nameless corpse? Why has it been rendered faceless—?' I stopped. Will was looking at me strangely.

'A faceless corpse?' he said.

'Yes!' I told him all that had happened after he had left with Miss Crowe. To my surprise he looked less perturbed than I had expected.

He sighed. 'You know, Jem, there may be nothing untoward about this place at all,' he said. 'It's an anatomy school. There can hardly be much about it that is commonplace. Surely it is not unusual to dissect the face of a corpse? Halliday may well be sick. And Wilson too. Or perhaps he has gone to visit his mother with Allardyce!'

'There is more to Corvus Hall than the usual eccentricities of anatomists,' I said.

'And because of this baseless conviction you want to go into a place you call "the dead house" in the middle of the night? Just the two of us?'

'Yes,' I said, and then added primly, 'Though I will go alone if you would rather not accompany me.'

'Of course I would rather *not*. But if you insist, I cannot in all conscience let you go alone. One thing is for certain, however: I am not waiting here till midnight.'

'But the porters will lock the place up. We can hardly break in!'

'Well, *you* might not be a trusted employee of Dr Crowe's

anatomy school, Jem Flockhart, but *I* most certainly am.'
He reached into his pocket and pulled out a key. 'It opens
the front door,' he said. 'After all, I must do my work
whenever I can. As such I must be able to come and go
as I please. I made that perfectly clear.' He grinned, and
slipped the key back out of sight. 'And now, there is a slice
of pheasant pie and a pint or two of ale awaiting us at
Sorley's Chop House, though if you would rather spend
the next five hours sitting on that old box of bones in the
dark you are more than welcome to.'

Chapter Eight

Without the crowds of students we could see now how much the Hall had changed. Before Dr Crowe and his entourage had moved in, it had retained the air of a grand residence, forgotten, abandoned, but waiting in hope for air and light, for kind people who might turn it back into a home. What it had got was the noise and bustle of rowdy young medical men. The place had taken on a jaded institutional air; the magnificent mahogany banister with its smooth curved newel post was already scuffed by boots, bored students scraping their initials into its lustrous wood with blunt pen knives. The walls bore the marks of greasy shoulders, the floor was strewn with straw, with dirt traipsed in from the street, with scraps of paper, splatters of dried spit and the blackened plugs of spent tobacco gouged from pipes. The smell of urine hung in the air. A door opened and a porter emerged, pushing a brush before him in a desultory fashion. Behind him came a woman, fat and slatternly. She flailed a mop about the floor in a lazy figure of eight.

The last time I had seen her she had been dozing in front of the stove on the top ward of the *Blood* – the Seaman's Floating Hospital, an ex-man o' war down on the waterfront where she had found work as Matron.

'Mrs Speedicut,' I cried. 'What are you doing here—?'

The woman looked up. 'Mr Jem!' She grinned. 'I were going to come along to you after I'd finished. The *Blood's* getting a refit and there ain't no call for a matron when there ain't no patients. So here I am. Pays better too. Plus it ain't on the river – stinks something awful down there.'

'And here?' said Will, wrinkling his nose.

'Nothing I ain't smelled or seen before,' she replied. 'They took me on cause of what I know.'

'They needed a specialist in gin and idleness?' said Will. 'You surprise me.'

Mrs Speedicut assumed a wounded expression. 'House-keeper,' she said. 'Who else knows how to do *that* in a place like *this*?'

I wondered whether I should invite her to Sorley's. We had not seen her for a while and it would be interesting to discover what she thought of Corvus Hall and its residents. I looked at Will, but he shook his head. 'Don't,' he said.

'Come to the apothecary later, madam,' I said instead. 'Gabriel and Jenny will be glad to see you.'

Mrs Speedicut frowned. 'Got any pie?' she said. 'I'll only come if there's pie.'

'Bring your own pie,' said Will.

'I'll come, since you insist upon it, Mr Quartermain,' she said. 'But there better be pie. *And* ale.' She threw Will a black look, and vanished back into the burrow from which she had come.

We left then, the porter jangling his keys impatiently.

Beneath his chair in the alcove behind the door Bullseye
was gnawing on something which looked suspiciously like
a human rib.

❧

We went round to the back of the building, intending to
go through the gate in the wall that would take us into the
physic garden, and from there directly down St Saviour's
Street to Sorley's Chop House. But Corvus Hall had one last
surprise for us that evening, for at the bottom of the garden
behind the mortuary, a bonfire roared. Silhouetted against
the blaze were three figures. Gloag the mortuary attendant
stood leaning on a long rake, staring into the flames. Beside
him, the flames reflected on his spectacles in two discs of
orange flame, was Dr Crowe. Dr Cruikshank stood to one
side. He had removed his neckerchief and his plush waistcoat
and was standing in his shirtsleeves, his hands thrust into
his pockets. The fire was white hot at its core, far hotter than
was required for the burning of leaves and twigs. But they
were not burning garden refuse at the back of Corvus Hall,
not that night. The faces of the three men, crimson in the
firelight, were the faces of demons. Dr Cruikshank pointed
into the flames and Gloag reached in with his rake. A pair
of skulls burned black as coal, their eye sockets flaming with
light, rolled in the heart of the furnace.

I heard Will gasp. 'Bones!'

'Yes,' I said. 'The bones of the unclaimed dead. What
else might they do with them?'

'Bury them?'

'Possibly, but where? You remember St Saviour's
graveyard—'

'How could I ever forget it?' His voice was low. I knew the memory of that place haunted him still, though it had been some three years ago now since he had been employed to empty it.

'You recall how many hundreds of bodies you had to disinter? How many coach loads were carried away?' I said. 'It is common practice for the sextons of the city's graveyards to exhume bodies – often those that have hardly rotted away – and burn them. How else might more space be made? Those bones come from the dissecting room. Once they have been anatomised, what else might be done with them? The ground of London is thick with corpses already.'

The smell on the air was thick and choking, the smell of hot, rotten flesh and scalded bones. Behind us the Hall was dark, though I knew there must be people about the place still. A movement drew my eyes to a window on the first floor, and for a moment I thought I saw a face – a pale oval looking out at the fire as it reared and danced. And yet it was barely a face at all, for it seemed to be completely devoid of features, without eyes or nose, the mouth no more than a ragged hole. I jumped as the fire gave a great sharp *snap*, as if something deep inside it had burst. Gloag leaned forward to jab at it with the end of his rake, shuffling the coals so that the flames leaped higher. The skulls rolled, their jaws yawning wide as they vanished into the flames. When I looked back, the face – if it had been a face – was gone.

❧

Sorley's was warm and boisterous. The uneasiness I had felt as we left the anatomy school dispersed beneath its genial fug of hot fat, pipe smoke and beer fumes. We ordered our food – game pie for me, the promised pheasant pie and potatoes for Will, some of Sorley's fine beer – and found ourselves a booth near to the fire. One of Sorley's boys brought us our ale straight away, and I took a long draught of the dark, bitter liquid. My throat was dry. The way Will was glugging down his own beer told me that he felt the same. I didn't like to tell him why he was so thirsty, nor that he would feel that way every evening while he worked at the Hall on Dr Crowe's anatomy manual. I wondered whether he had noticed the dust that lay thickly upon every surface of his new workplace. It was the dust of dry bones, of desiccated hair and dead flesh, for such things filled the air there; they were a part of the bricks and mortar, and if he did not keep his window open he would be ill in no time.

I did not say any of this, however. Instead, I put down my beer and told him why I wished to return to the Hall. To the dead house. I waited until he had eaten his pheasant pie first. 'There is an extra body there, Will. Its right hand has been cut off, and its face removed – not to mention where we found the hand, and the curious message that was on the card left with it. No one seems to know who this mystery corpse belongs to, though it is evidently a young man who was in perfectly good health at the time of his death.

'It's not impossible that what Dr Crowe says is true,' I went on. 'If the body came from the hospital, or from the workhouse, and was in danger of being reclaimed by relatives, then rendering it unrecognisable would be the first priority. And yet I'm certain that Dr Cruikshank was surprised to see it. I believe he recognised it, though he pretended he did not.'

'Can you be sure?'

'I cannot be *sure*. But he works here. *He* allocates bodies to his students and he quite clearly did not expect to have an extra one. His face when he saw it—'

'So what is it you are expecting to find?'

'I don't know. At least, I am not entirely certain. I spent half the day carrying that hand around with me, and in the end I don't even know whose body it came from. There must be *some* identifying marks upon it, on the body or the hand, something that marks it out as unique, but I would need to look at it more closely.'

'It may still be a prank, Jem. Not everything is worse than it seems.'

'I know. And yet I must do this.'

I did not tell him that Dr Wragg had warned me away, that Dr Cruikshank had ushered me out of the dead room as fast as he could, and that Sorrow and Silence Crowe filled the students with a profound and unexplained dread. He had other things on his mind, I could tell.

'What about you?' I said instead. 'What happened after you disappeared with Miss Crowe?'

'Very little,' said Will. 'Lilith Crowe is a charming and intelligent woman. Before the lecture she introduced me to Dr Cruikshank.'

'What do you make of him?'

'Eccentric. Intelligent. A little in love with Miss Crowe, I suspect.'

'She would never look at a man like him,' I scoffed.

'Would she not?' he said. 'Women do not always mind a man's looks. Something you for one should be glad about.'

I grunted. 'Go on.'

'Dr Cruikshank was civil enough. I had the impression

he did not really mind who was to work on the anatomy manual, but was pleased to see Miss Crowe animated and engaged with the project.' He sipped his beer. 'It is without doubt the most unusual household I have ever been in.'

'And then?'

'Then we attended the lecture, as you saw. After that she provided me with materials – paper, pens, ink, a drawing board, and a skeleton hand. She took me to where I am to work. Her father appeared with the Exhibition catalogue and told me once again what he liked about my drawings. Then he asked me whether I would be interested in designing a new, purpose-built building at the rear of the property to hold the anatomy museum – there is more of it stored somewhere else as it is impossible to fit it all into the rooms Dr Wragg has been given.' He smiled. 'Miss Crowe was fascinated by my ideas, my suggestions for the design of a new museum.'

'I see,' I said. I took a deep draught of my beer. All at once I felt as though a shadow had fallen across me. It was new to me to feel unnecessary, as if I might be left to one side and no one, not even Will, would mind. I knew London was growing, transforming. Her old crowded streets were being cleared, her institutions – schools, hospitals, prisons – being rebuilt on far grander lines than ever before. People like Will, who could design and build, were in demand. But me? The apothecary was a generalist. Physicians disdained his jobbing quackery, and with the coming of chloroform the role of the surgeon had been transformed from a task requiring speed and strength to something with far more subtlety and finesse. Will had a future. He was in demand. But what place did I have? All at once my apothecary shop seemed quaint and medieval

– nothing but powdered leaves and barks, and bottles of coloured water. I sighed. Perhaps I *should* finish the book on poisons I had started once upon a time. I might take my MD, and at last call myself 'doctor'. I might build a reputation as an expert in poisons and ways of killing, for there were plenty of corpses and little expertise.

Usually Will was attuned to my mood, but now he seemed oblivious to it, for once more he was talking about Miss Crowe. Apparently she was to help him, was to act as amanuensis, and to liaise between Will in his draughtsman's eyrie and the two anatomists – her father and Dr Cruikshank. He was looking forward to it.

'She is like no other woman I have ever met,' he said.

'She is very beautiful,' I noted. 'And yet, unmarried.'

'Yes,' he replied. 'I cannot think why.'

'Me neither,' I said dryly. 'Which leads one to think that she either does not like men, does not want to saddle herself with one, or—'

'Or?'

'Or something else.'

'Such as?

I shrugged. 'I have no idea.'

I thought of my father. He had not married again after my mother died. It had been because of a hereditary malady, one that prevented him from sleeping and eventually drove him mad. I too lived beneath its shadow, and I feared it almost as much as he. But I could not possibly speculate as to what malady Miss Crowe might be afraid of. More likely was the realisation that any man she married would – no matter what he might say before the event – insist that she stop her work at the anatomy school, for it was evident to me that she was as involved with the place as her father.

Sorley kept two of our pipes behind the bar. The long clay stems we both favoured did not survive well in the pocket of a top coat. Sorley's boy brought them over when Will caught his eye. 'I'm surprised there aren't any students in here,' I said. I cut a lump of tobacco and began rubbing it in the palm of my hand with my thumb.

'No doubt they are used to going west,' said Will. 'Towards St Bride's and in the opposite direction to us. If we're lucky they won't come this far down St Saviour's Street at all, though I see one of them at least has found the place.' He nodded over my shoulder. In the corner, against the wall at a small table on his own, sat a tall red-headed man. He had a stack of books beside his empty coffee cup, and he was bent over a sheaf of papers, his pen moving rapidly across the page. In front of him was a jar inside of which a large pink organ bobbed in preserving fluid.

'Should we disturb him?' said Will.

'Oh, I think so,' I replied. 'Excuse me, sir!'

The man looked up, his expression alarmed.

'Would you care to join us? My name is Flockhart, I own the physic garden beside Corvus Hall, and this is my friend Mr Quartermain. As of this afternoon he's a colleague of yours, for Dr Crowe has just employed him to work on his new anatomy manual – I'm sure you know of it.'

The man hesitated, evidently unsure, but then he gathered up his accoutrements, stuffed the specimen bottle into his bag, and came over to us. 'Gentlemen,' he said. 'A pleasure to meet you both. I'm Dr Allardyce.'

'Dr Allardyce, the anatomy demonstrator?' I said.

'Yes.'

'I am relieved to meet you, sir.' I grinned. 'Dr Cruikshank was becoming worried about you.'

'Have you eaten, sir?' said Will.

'I have,' he replied.

'I mean have you eaten since lunchtime?' said Will. 'I saw you come in, and you have had nothing but a mug of coffee.' He pulled out his pocket book. 'It would be my pleasure—'

Dr Allardyce began to protest, but Will waved him aside. 'But you must! How else might we enjoy your company if we know you are hungry? Besides, one must take advantage of the return of one's appetite that the absence of the smell of cadavers brings. I had no desire for food myself earlier. Once away from Corvus Hall, however, I discovered I was starving. I have no doubt at all that you feel exactly the same, and it is only your natural diffidence that prevents you from saying so. I can recommend the pheasant, and a pot of Sorley's best ale.'

We smoked our pipes while Allardyce wolfed down a plate of meat and potatoes and a pint of beer. None of us spoke. Will and I exchanged a glance as our new friend sat back in his chair. He closed his eyes and wiped his lips with a handkerchief. I caught a whiff of the dissecting room as he did so, and I noted the stained appearance of the linen he was swabbing at his lips with. Will saw it too. His smile wavered, but he recovered himself quickly enough. 'You feel better, sir?'

'I do,' said Dr Allardyce. 'Thank you. I have had a . . . a busy few days. One sometimes forgets to eat.' He looked about as he quaffed his second pint of ale. 'Not a bad little chop house,' he said, as if he had not noticed the place earlier. He pulled off his glasses and buffed the lenses with his shirt sleeve. His eyes were red and watery from lack of sleep, and, I presumed, from staring into the bodies of the dead all day. I guessed his age to be some forty years or more – rather old to be an anatomy demonstrator. Demonstrating was something I had always associated with younger men; men with ambition.

'You enjoy your work?' I said, nodding to the bag into which he had shoved his books, his preserved specimen and his notebook. I hoped the beer he had drunk, and the food he had eaten at Will's expense, would put him in a mood of garrulous frankness.

'Yes,' he said. 'Though I would value some help in the dissecting room.'

'Do you not have this fellow Halliday?' said Will.

Dr Allardyce gave a snort. 'Halliday! I hardly think so.'

'Oh?' I said. 'I understood him to be a most capable fellow who is set to make a name in the world of surgery. A man to rival Liston in strength and skill, to outshine Syme in speed and daring – a man likely to one day take over from Crowe himself—'

Sorley's was warm, the atmosphere genial and welcoming. Will and I were lounging in our seats in a relaxed, familiar manner. As I talked, I watched Dr Allardyce's face grow darker. In my experience, one is more likely to get someone to talk if one presents them with a set of groundless assumptions on a subject with which they are both familiar and opinionated. So it proved with Dr Allardyce. I knew nothing of Halliday, only that Dr Crowe had warmly anticipated him at tea that afternoon and had been disappointed to find Will and me instead, and that Dr Cruikshank had asked for Halliday before he had looked for Dr Allardyce.

Dr Allardyce slammed his tankard down and leaned

forward. 'He is nothing of the s-sort,' he cried. 'John Halliday is the very worst kind of man. It has been my misfortune to have to work with him these last two years and on not one occasion can I say that he has shown himself to be anything like the man you describe. He is a duplicitous, self-serving, d-debauched.' Spittle flew from his lips. 'I know I should not say it,' he said. 'And yet I must. Only last week I heard that he had won the Sir David Brewster prize essay – some £200 in prize money, plus the opportunity to have his w-work published by one of the most reputable medical publishers.'

'Is it not a work of great merit?' I said. I adopted a tone of awe – and perplexity. 'The David Brewster medal! One of the highest honours in anatomy. And he is still a student?'

'Yes, sir, and that honour would have been mine if I had handed my essay in. He stole my work, gentlemen. He stole my work on the spleen and he . . . he passed it off as his own. We were both working on the subject at that time. Some of my p-papers went missing, the specimens I had prepared and upon which I was working were lost. Lost? Stolen, more like!' He sighed. 'But I did not notice the missing p-pages until I was writing up. Some of my key observations. Drawings too. Findings based on dissections I had performed, microscopic work of the most detailed and intensive kind – all of it gone. I did not notice until it was too late, until days had passed, by which time he had transferred my work into his own hand and would almost certainly have destroyed my pages.'

'And you did not speak up?' said Will.

'I did not. I *could* not. Everyone knows we have the same

interests; they would simply have said that I was speaking out of jealousy. He's a thief,' muttered Dr Allardyce. His face was dark with fury. 'He deserved what he got.'

'What did he get?' I said. My voice was mild. I took a swig of ale, glancing up at our new friend casually. My gaze, I hoped, was sympathetic.

'I must g-go,' Dr Allardyce lurched to his feet.

'Wait—'

He swayed where he stood. The alcohol had warmed his tongue, and his opinions, and the rage that had evidently been gathering within him for some time now spilled out like bile.

'I am forty-three years old, Mr Flockhart,' he said. 'I have seen men come and go, I have seen them p-pass me by, overtake me, leave me behind, laughing at me over their shoulders as they make their way in the world. I saw Halliday laughing with the others, taking part in their drunken games while I was still working. I know they wonder why I am no more than what I am. Even Dr Crowe does not trust me to give any but the most basic of lectures. He says that I lack charisma, that I stutter and mumble, and it is true. Even worse—' He held out his hands. They were shaking. 'I can cut the f-flesh when it is dead, but when it is l-living?' He shook his head. 'I do not have what it takes actually to *be* a surgeon. I do not have the courage, the speed, the delicacy of touch and p-precision, though I wish to God I did.' He closed his eyes and took a deep breath. When he opened them again I saw that he had mastered himself. He shoved his hands into his pockets. 'I am aware that resentment is a corrosive and vile emotion, Mr Flockhart. I have done my b-best to overcome it, and on the whole I have succeeded. And yet there are times—' He looked spent, as if voicing such opinions was as exhausting as keeping them secret. He turned about and lumbered towards the door.

Chapter Nine

We returned to the apothecary, having already sent Sorley's boy down with a game pie and ale enough for three. I had no wish to watch Mrs Speedicut eat, and hoped she had had her fill by the time we arrived home. Sure enough, the apothecary table bore evidence of a meal recently finished. Pie crusts, empty beer bottles, plates smeared with chutney. Mrs Speedicut was sitting in my father's armchair before the stove. I saw that she was about to doze off, but I was having none of that.

'Wakey wakey, madam,' I cried as Will and I burst in. 'Shake some life into that fire and let's hear what you have to say.'

'About what?' she said crossly. She pulled her shawl about her shoulders and shifted her great bulk, settling herself into a more comfortable position for sleeping. 'Close that door, can't you?'

'Tell us about Corvus Hall and its various residents,' I said. 'It's what I invited you for, after all.'

She watched me through half-closed eyes. 'But I've only been there a week!'

'Long enough for you to winkle out every rumour in the whole place,' said Will. 'And to discover that the alcohol used to preserve the specimens cannot be siphoned off and drunk.'

'Oh, it's vile, sir,' cried Mrs Speedicut, her eyes snapping open. 'Quite vile! Though it smells a lot like gin! I were quite surprised it didn't taste like it too.' Will and I exchanged a glance. He had been joking. Had she really tried the stuff?

'Well,' I said, unwilling to pursue the matter. 'What a pity it's *not* gin, or you would be supplied for life. Still, I have a bottle for you now if you can tell us what you know of the place.'

I'd bought some gin from Sorley, who knew Mrs Speedicut's rough tastes well enough and who had assured me that the very cheapest bottle would serve my purposes. I had added a bag of the evil-smelling shag tobacco she favoured too, to sweeten the bargain. 'Come along,' I said. 'What have you learned after a week at Corvus Hall?'

I had used Mrs Speedicut before to find out what the backstairs gossip might be. As a professional slattern with years of experience bullying others to do her work for her, she had more time for tittle-tattle than anyone I had ever met. Now, she told us that Dr Crowe kept himself to himself and had little interest in anything but his work; that Dr Cruikshank was beloved by the students and Dr Allardyce was not; that Dr Strangeway worked alone and unseen in the upper reaches of the house. It was all very well, but it was nothing we did not already know. I could not help but feel disappointed. Were the secrets of the Hall so tightly

guarded by its residents that even a gossipmonger like Mrs
Speedicut could not fathom them?

'What about Miss Crowe?' said Will. 'What can you tell
us about her?'

'Lilith Crowe?' Mrs Speedicut looked startled. Her eyes
darted towards the door, as if she feared someone might
be listening outside. 'She and her sisters strike the fear
of God into them all,' she said. 'Gloag in the mortuary
says they're witches, all three. You've seen those three
black birds that hang about outside the dissecting room
windows? Crows, they are. Nasty, beady-eyed creatures.'

'And?' said Will.

'And Gloag says that the three crows and the three
women ain't never seen at the same time.'

'So?'

'So, don't you think it's strange?'

'No,' I said. 'I think Gloag is strange if he considers such
an occurrence worth remarking on.'

Mrs Speedicut shrugged. 'I suppose it is a bit of a
stretch,' she said.

'Women who don't conform to men's expectations
have often been condemned as witches,' I added. 'But
what else can you tell us? – Apart from the absurdity and
superstition of the idiot Gloag?'

'You have to admit, Mr Flockhart, it's against nature to
have a woman grubbing about in all that dead flesh.'

'I admit nothing of the sort—'

'The way those girls wander about the Hall at all hours
too – it's not right for a lady to have such licence in a place
like that. Think about all those young medical men.' Her
face turned red and she lowered her voice. '*That's* what I've
heard about *them*.'

113

'What?' I said. 'Speak plainly, woman. What, pray, have you heard about whom?'

Mrs Speedicut's voice sank to a whisper. 'I've heard that Lilith Crowe and her sisters can seduce any man they choose. I've heard all three of 'em roams the school at night taking body parts and bones, and that they says not a word to the medical men whose corpses they've plundered. It's one o' the reasons they moved here from St Bride's, cause they were doin' it there too. Not that anything has changed, for they say Dr Cruikshank won't hear a word against any of them, no matter what.' She leaned in close. 'I've heard that Lilith Crowe's a Siren, Mr Jem. A woman what'll lure unwary men to their doom. I've heard that's what they all are, and that they've ruined many a young man who came to Dr Crowe for his education and left with something he had never bargained on.' She sat back. 'No wonder they ain't married,' she said. 'No wonder they never will be. And they've got worse since they came to Corvus. *Much* worse.'

I handed her the gin and baccy in silence.

❧

At two o'clock in the morning I went through to wake Will. I found him already up. 'I couldn't sleep,' he said. 'At least, I slept at first, but then I awoke with a foul taste in my mouth.' He was silent for a moment. 'It's the dust, isn't it? Bones and dried flesh. I could taste it in the air yesterday, feel it on my skin.' He rubbed his face. 'Corvus Hall has become a part of me already, and I a part of it.'

'I can give you some lemon cordial to drink throughout the day. It will help to cleanse the system of impurities and freshen the palate.' I shrugged. 'I don't know what else to offer.'

'Did you sleep?'

'Of course.' I grinned. 'Like the dead. I always do.'

In fact I had not slept at all. Instead, I had taken out the letter I had found in Will's attic at the anatomy school and put it on my bedside table. My mother's hand, addressed to a man who was not my father. Should I read it? It seemed a betrayal to do so. Whatever it might contain would surely be better left where it was, folded up in that small square of paper and completely forgotten about. To distract myself I had taken a look at the manuscript on poisons that I had worked on with Dr Bain. Should I continue with it? Should I use the work to gain my MD? I thought about my life as an apothecary, about the remedies I made for colds and coughs, for chilblains and sleeplessness, for menstrual cramps, boils, toothache, diarrhoea, indigestion . . . Oh, how bored I was by the mundanity of such trifling ailments.

After that I had thrown myself onto the bed, my eyes fixed upon my mother's letter. When I got up at two, still fully clothed, I had picked it up and slipped it back into my pocket.

Downstairs Mrs Speedicut was asleep in front of the stove. Its embers glowed red in the darkness. I heard a mouse scamper across the floor. Beneath the workbench Gabriel was asleep on his truckle bed. Through the door of the herb drying room I could see a faint light. Jenny. She had left her candle burning again. How many times had I told her to put it out? She would burn the place down if she were not careful for the stuff in the herb drying room was tinder-dry. I pushed open the door. She was awake, lying in her nest of blankets amongst the hop sacks, reading a book on *materia medica*. It was huge and ancient, its leather spine cracked and flaking, the recipes written in a heavy gothic script. Dated 1597 on the title page, it had been in my family for generations. Gerard's *Herball*. I had never used it, neither had my father, but Jenny was forever poring over it.

'He has a mixture to make you sleep like the dead,' she said. 'Sleeping nightshade. It says here that "it provokes a dead sleepe wherein nothynge might awaken". Can I try it?'

'No,' I said.

'There's another one in this other book I found that says the tail feathers of a raven should be burned and the ash blown into the eyes to remedy blindness. Can we try that too?'

I thought of Sorrow Crowe. I doubted she would allow Jenny to blow ashes into her eyes. I licked my fingers and pinched out Jenny's candle. 'Go to sleep,' I said. 'I'll be back in a few hours.'

❧

Will and I walked down to Corvus Hall in silence. The fog was gathering. I felt it cool and slimy against my cheek, tasted its familiar kiss of smoke and effluent on my lips. It was still little more than a veil, though I knew it would be impenetrable by the time the dawn came. I spat a gob of phlegm into the gutter and drew my scarf closer about my face and neck, pulling my hat down over my eyes and hunching my shoulders,

'You look like a house breaker,' said Will. 'Did you bring an iron bar under your coat?'

I grinned. 'I'm hoping that won't be necessary. Unless you forgot the key?'

'You think Allardyce murdered Halliday, don't you?' said Will. 'And left his body, missing a right hand and a face, in the mortuary.'

'It's not impossible.'

'But why desecrate the corpse?'

I shrugged. 'I don't know. It's not impossible that Allardyce felt such retribution was fitting – this was the hand that plagiarised the essay, the hand that stole his work.'

'But he seems such a timid fellow,' insisted Will.

'No doubt he is, for the most part,' I said. 'And yet how much might a man endure before he snaps? Dr Allardyce has been long overdue a promotion, if his own estimation of his abilities is anything to go by. And then, after years as demonstrator, he is upstaged by this arrogant young lad. He is taunted by Halliday for his diffidence, his dislike of the manly boisterousness that the others use to cope with the daily horrors of the dissecting room. Who knows what might drive a man to take matters into his own hands? Dr Crowe and Dr Cruikshank both prefer the young upstart Halliday, that much is quite evident. Perhaps Halliday styles himself after his mentor, Dr Cruikshank, cultivating a flamboyant style and a bonhomie with the students that poor earnest Allardyce, for all his abilities as a dissector, will never have.'

'But we know nothing about Halliday. This is pure conjecture.'

'It may well be conjecture, though I can tell you which of the two I would prefer to have standing over me with a knife in his hand.'

'I think I would be hard-pressed to decide. The nervous older man or the young plagiarist whose credentials may be faked or stolen.'

It was a fair point. 'It is interesting that Dr Allardyce's hands are steady as a rock when faced with a cadaver,' I said. 'He is drawn to seek the answers to the mysteries of life in the flesh and bones of the dead. He searches the body for answers, but only once it is without life, only when it is not about to rise up and mock him, criticise him, question him. A live body fills him with fear. Did you mark how his hands shook when he talked about surgery?'

I sighed. I wished I could find the same confidence and pleasure as Dr Allardyce did when poring over a corpse. For all that I was about to do it myself, it was never a job that I relished.

The Hall stood some thirty paces back from the road. The laurel hedge had grown huge and unkempt while the place was unoccupied. It had still not been trimmed, so the building itself was largely hidden from view. It had a silent brooding air, its streaky stucco ghostly in the dark. For once I would have preferred a blanket of the thickest fog so that our entry might be concealed from the night watch, should they pass down St Saviour's Street. There was no sign of life at the Hall, no light in any of the windows, no lantern glow or wavering candle flame. I presumed there was no night porter. If there was he was evidently either asleep, or deep inside the building.

We crept across the front lawn. 'Are you sure, Jem, really sure about this?' said Will when we reached the door. His eyes were wide and dark, his pupils dilated. He did not relish our night-time adventure, I knew that much, but he would come with me no matter what I asked of him. I nodded, and he slipped the key into the lock.

Inside, it was as dark as the grave. The fanlight over the door had been painted over, I had no idea why, but it meant that not even a glimmer of gaslight from the street could creep in. We waited for a moment, but there was no sign of anyone, and so I lit the lantern I had brought. Its narrow beam of light sliced through the dark like a golden knife. Will followed me across the hall and down the passage towards the dissecting room and the dead house. The stink of the place seemed to have grown in tandem with the gloom, as if the dead took over the moment the living had departed, and I saw him put his hand over his mouth as if to suppress a retch.

'Breathe through your mouth,' I cautioned. 'You'll look like a dolt, I admit, but it's a small price to pay.'

All the bodies were back in the dead house, but the sight of the tables and the stools, the microscopes and knives laid out on the benches, the stains upon the floor made my scalp prickle. The curling pictures on the walls displaying the circulation, the lymphatics, the skeleton, the nervous system, had a dry vellum-like look to them, as if they had been etched onto sheets of dead skin. The beam of my lamp reflected back at me in the eyes of a pair of rats that skirted the wall beneath the sluice. The desire to turn back was almost overpowering. I took Will's hand, glad of the warmth of his fingers.

As we crept down the passage to the dead room the smell grew thicker, the darkness deeper. I held up my lamp as Will pushed the door open. Before us, bodies were laid out side by side beneath sheets stained with blood and fluid, with alcohol, resin and wax.

'Which one did you want to look at?' said Will, aghast. He hauled a handkerchief from his pocket and plunged his face into it. 'There are so many!'

He was right, for in addition to those that had been returned at the day's end, half-butchered from the dissecting rooms, more had come in since I had been there earlier. 'Find it, then!' His voice was a hiss. 'Do whatever it is you wanted to do. But hurry. *Hurry!*'

I went from corpse to corpse, lifting one sheet after another. Some were untouched, their faces grey-white, glimmering like lard in the light of the lantern. Others were partly anatomised, chest cavities open, stomachs eviscerated, arms or legs skinned, though none, I noticed, had been started on the face.

I found it at last, against the far wall. The hand, severed, lay where Dr Cruikshank had tossed it, the face – my God! What a face it was! Without flesh to give it familiarity there was only horror. I closed my eyes. Something Dr Cruikshank had said echoed in my head: *I had some of the lads spruce the place up a little. The useless ones – Tanhauser, Wilson, Squires . . . the lime wash does something to mask the smell.* It was the hand, the hand that I wanted. I had carried it around all day, but it was the hand that would tell me who the body belonged to. Why had I not realised it sooner? I pulled a leather roll of surgical knives from my satchel, sat my lantern down beside the faceless corpse, and bent to my task.

I had not been at work for long before I heard a noise. It came from behind us, from the dissecting room. What was it? The scuffling of a rat? I listened again, my ears straining in the silence. And then I heard it. A creak – the opening of a door – and then footsteps, tiptoeing, but coming closer. I pulled the dark lantern half closed.

'Shh!' My lips were against Will's ear. 'Someone is coming. We cannot get out. Not now. Not without being seen. We must hide.'

'Hide?' hissed Will. 'Hide where? We are in a mortuary!'

The footsteps were closer now. Was it the night porter? I did not recognise the heavy tread of a man, could not hear the sigh and grunt of someone tramping through their rounds. I heard the door to the anatomy room being slowly drawn open. There was little time. A wavering light filtered beneath the mortuary door as a lantern was held high, the footsteps – measured, quiet, but assured of where they were headed – drew nearer.

I lifted a sheet, the body beneath as pale as a flounder. 'Get on.'

'I'm not—'

'You *must*, Will. We cannot be found here—' I shoved the corpse over a little. 'There's plenty of room. It's just an old man. Now get up!'

For a moment I thought Will was about to refuse, was about to say that he had had enough, that he did not care who was coming, that he would happily throw in his new commission just to be away from the place. 'We must find out what is going on here,' I whispered. 'For something *is* going on, Will. Something wicked. Murder, perhaps *worse*—'

'For you, Jem,' he hissed. 'I would do this only for you.' He stretched out beside the naked old man, and I flapped the winding sheet back down over both of them. Will's feet protruded, for he was a good four inches taller than his new bedfellow. I hoped that whoever was about to enter would not notice that two of the residents were still wearing their boots. I lifted the sheet that covered the next corpse. The skin seemed to glow greenish in the dark. I glimpsed straggling hair, eyes open and milky, lips sagging over broken teeth. It was the cadaver Wilson had been working on, 'past its best' and partly anatomised. And yet what choice did I have? I slammed the dark lantern closed and slid in beside her.

Beneath my hand I could feel the clammy skin of her withered thigh. Something damp began seeping into my sleeve. I wanted more than anything to scream, to leap up and run – instead I turned my head and peeped out from beneath the winding sheet as the door eased open.

I could not see who it was, not properly, for his back was to us, the lantern he had brought with him on the workbench against the wall. It threw his figure into silhouette, and made his shadow loom tall and crooked. There was something familiar about him, but I could not say what it was. I heard a sigh, and then the rattle of knives. They were surgeon's knives, I could tell by the shape, the glint of the steel blades in the lantern light. A gloved hand set them out side by side: the long thin boning knife, the saw, the strong, sharp Liston knife. And then all at once I saw him stiffen. Had he heard us? I was holding my breath, but perhaps he had heard my heart, for it was pounding fit to wake my dead companion. And then he turned.

His was the face I had seen at the window as we left the Hall to go to Sorley's. I had only glimpsed it then, but there was no mistaking it now, for its features – eyes, nose, mouth – were all but obliterated by what must have been one of the worst cases of confluent smallpox I had ever seen. The scarring was a whorled textured mass, the eyes almost lost to it, the nose eroded, the lips cratered and twisted. The hand that held the Liston knife was gloved, but I knew that beneath it the flesh would be as scarred as his face, the pustules melting the skin like boiling sugar. The pain of it must have almost turned his mind, and for all that I was horrified, I felt a terrible lurch of pity. Knife in hand, the man stepped towards the shrouded corpse beside which Will lay hidden. There was nothing for it but to shout out, to warn him – but it was clear that Will had seen the man too, for all at once he cried out and reared up from his place beside the workhouse corpse.

The man let out a screech of terror and reeled back, his knife clattering to the floor. I too flung back my winding sheet and leaped up. With a high-pitched scream, the man seized his lantern and vanished out of the door.

'After him!' I cried, bounding out of the mortuary. Ahead of me, the man's lantern vanished from sight. I heard the sound of footsteps running, of doors slamming, and then all was quiet. Left once more in the dark in the passage and unsure of my surroundings, I fumbled my way back.

'Why didn't you come? I could see nothing without a lantern. Did you not want to find out who he was, what he was doing here?'

'Poor fellow,' said Will. 'He must have thought the final trumpet had sounded and the dead were rising from their graves.'

I grinned. 'Lord knows what he will say about it tomorrow.'

'Well, in case there *is* actually a night porter here, we should probably leave.' He sounded cross. I saw him wrinkle his nose as he raised the lantern. 'What's that slimy stuff on your coat, Jem?'

'I don't know,' I replied. 'I'm trying not to think about it. Preservatives, I hope. But let's take these.' I picked up the Liston knife that the man had been holding, and which had clattered to the floor when he dropped it in terror. I returned it to the box of surgical knives he had left behind. Inlaid in silver in the centre of the lid two initials glittered: S. S. 'Well, well,' I said. 'I believe we have just met Silas Strangeway.'

'I thought he was about to eviscerate me.'

'Perhaps he was.' I looked at the feet of the corpse beside which Will had been lying. A label of brown card was tied with string about the big toe. It contained a single word STRANGEWAY, and the day's date. 'It seems I had inadvertently put you beside Dr Strangeway's corpse.'

'His corpse?'

'You've seen his work, Will. His models are the dead. A great many cadavers are required to make those wax sculptures.'

'Would he know how to dissect a face?' said Will. 'How to remove all outward traces of someone's countenance?'

I could see that even talking about it appalled him. The face was sacred. To violate it was to tear at the very essence of what it meant to be human, to be an individual.

'Yes,' I said. 'Though he is not the only one here to possess such skills.'

'We should tell the police.'

'Tell the police what, Will? That I believe a man to have been murdered? I have no evidence for it, apart from a body that was unaccounted for, though according to Dr Cruikshank such administrative errors happen all the time. Yes, they might come and take a look, but they would stamp about making a fuss and alerting the perpetrator to my suspicions. The police would find nothing, Will. You would lose your commission, one of the most lucrative you have had for a while.' I shook my head, and shoved the box of knives Silas Strangeway had abandoned into my satchel. 'We cannot tell them. Not yet. Not until we are sure.'

It was a decision I was to regret many times before the week was over.

Heart

The heart – is it not the most prized and revered organ in the body? A small fist of muscle, chambered, valved, taut with tendons as strong as harp strings, it gives us life with every rhythmic squeeze of its powerful walls. It is a lump of meat on my dissecting table – complex and vital, a technical anatomical masterpiece, but meat nonetheless. And yet what magical properties we give it! If we are wounded in love do we not experience a broken heart? If we follow our dreams are we not in pursuit of our heart's desire? If we are cruel and wicked are we not heartless? It is the symbol of love, romantic and divine. We idealise the 'pure at heart'. But for those whose hearts are impure? Those whose lives are marked by evil thoughts and actions are in possession of a heart of darkness.

The ancient Egyptians believed the heart could speak, could testify against its owner after death. It was taken from the corpse and bound tightly to muffle its reproachful cries. What wickedness would mine shout about me? What bindings would keep it hushed? There are none that can silence it for it does not speak to man, and no mortal can hear the cries of the heart. Instead, it calls out to God, who knows and sees all, and who judges each one of us. 'For the Lord seeth not as man seeth. For man looketh at the outward appearance, but the Lord looketh on the heart' (Samuel 16:7).

At night, alone in my bed, I listen for the beat of my heart. Sometimes it is silent. I press my fingers to my wrist, my throat, and there is nothing. I cannot hear it. I cannot feel it. At other times it is loud – a rhythmic beating in my ears, like the drumming of the hangman's leather-gloved fingers against the gallows pole.

I am not heartless, but when they cut it out, when I am anatomised, as all felons are, my heart will surely be as black as my deeds.

**Precognition for the murder of Mary Anderson,
18th December 1830.**

**Statement of JAMES FRANKLYN, apprentice surgeon-
apothecary to Dr Alexander Crowe. Currently residing at
22 East Newington Street, Edinburgh. Aged twenty-one years.**

19th December 1830

It is true that Dr Crowe developed a fascination for Mary
Anderson. Initially, it was her spine that intrigued him. How
could it not? The two women, Clenchie Kate and Thrawn-Leggit
Mary, would draw the attention of any medical man worth his salt.
Their vertebrae snake from side to side to a degree that is almost
inconceivable. Even Dr Crowe, with his many years' experience in
matters of anatomy, said that he had never come across human
spines that were so captivating in their abnormality. Dr Crowe
has taught us to see beauty and grace in the human form, in

the arrangement of the organs and the shape of the bones. Even when there is a disharmony – a morbidity, an absence of some essential part, or a deformity – there is wonder to be found in the way the human body adapts, the way its muscles, organs, nerves and sinews adjust. In this regard, Clenchie Kate and Thrawn-Leggit Mary were quite fascinating – how could such deformity exist, and yet life continue – and yet also macabre, especially in the way they moved, scuttling swiftly up the close from the Cowgate on their black crutches like a pair of grotesque spiders. They drew us in still further with the beauty of their singing, and their bewitching faces.

I have always felt an affinity with Dr Crowe. At the time of the events described here, I was hoping to be awarded the post of demonstrator of anatomy – a prestigious appointment for one as young as I. I knew Allardyce thought the post was his for the taking – he is a gentleman's son, whereas I, a mere 'lad o' pairts', must make my way in the world without the help of fortune and connections. I had thought of making Dr Crowe a gift of the crippled girl's skeleton, should I be able to gain it, for her death was inevitable, given her condition.

I was in the lecture theatre when Mary attacked Dr Crowe. Allardyce jumped up and would have dragged the girl out had we not held him back. I saw her look to him in the crowd and curl her lip, so that at first I thought it was he she had come to indict. But instead she turned to Dr Crowe. Afterwards the place was in uproar. It was apparent straight away that Dr Crowe was largely unharmed. The knife had pierced his waistcoat, but the woman had lacked the strength and stature to do any real damage. The blood we saw was from the cut to his thumb, sustained as he instinctively put up a hand to deflect the blade. Gloag finally broke the door open, and in he came with the terrier at his heels, two of the porters from Surgeons' Hall behind him. The three of them wrestled the girl out of the lecture theatre, though at the sight of three burly men manhandling a heavily pregnant crippled girl, Dr Strangeway sprang to his feet. 'Gentlemen, please,' he cried. 'Have a care!' The girl had fallen limp in their arms and they dragged her out the way a washerwoman might haul a bag of laundry towards the copper. Dr Strangeway took up her fallen crutches and followed them out. I looked to Miss Crowe. She had not moved a muscle.

'Well, well, gentlemen,' Dr Crowe said as the door banged closed and the place fell silent. 'Had she had a little more strength and a great deal more height you might have been anatomising me tomorrow morning to check the veracity of Dr Strangeway's models!' We all laughed, as we were supposed to, but I could see how discomfited he was. Miss Crowe too, who had neither laughed nor spoken, but merely sat still and silent, her cheek pale, her fingers gripping her pen tightly, so that I saw the ink had covered her fingers the way blood covered her father's.

After that he dismissed us. As we filed out, Dr Crowe called Allardyce and me to his side, for we were both his apprentices and were there to do whatever he asked of us. He told me to find Thrawn-Leggit Mary, said that he did not wish to bring her actions to the attention of the police, and bade me take her home to the Cowgate. He asked Allardyce to call a hansom, so that he and Miss Crowe might go home. He looked down at his waistcoat and put his fingers to the blood stain and the slit in the silk the knife had made. He slid his hand into his inside breast pocket and drew out a large locket, the size of a pocket watch. Inside was a painted likeness of his wife – the only image he had of her. The glass that had covered it was shattered, the gold casing punctured and dented from where Mary's blade had struck home. The miniature within was quite spoiled. Miss Crowe saw it too, and she let out a sob. Dr Crowe looked at the ruined locket for a *long while. There were tears in his eyes as he took his daughter's hand. He nodded to me, and said, 'Thank you, Mr Franklyn. I know I can rely on you to do what's right.'*

Gloag had sent for the constable, but I told him that this was against Dr Crowe's express wishes, and that he had asked me to take Mary Anderson home. After some considerable negotiation he allowed me to put the girl into a hansom and take her away. Her lodgings are not far, but due to the narrowness of the close I was obliged to take her home the long way – along the South Bridge, past the Tron Kirk and down Blair Street to the Cowgate. She sat in silence for the whole journey, her face streaked with tears. I made sure to take the girl into her lodgings – as vile and wretched a place as one might hope never to find – and was glad to leave her there, alone, though I was sure her sister would be along soon enough. I returned to Surgeons' Square to find that Allardyce and Dr Strangeway had gone back to East Newington Street with the doctor and Miss Crowe. As it was clear I was no longer required, I went, as I usually did on a Wednesday evening, to visit my mother out at Duddingston.

❧

On the evening of the 18th inst. at around nine in the evening I left my mother's house and went back up to Surgeons' Square. I had agreed to help with the preparations for the following morning's class, though the corpse we were working on was hardly fit for anything. I was to meet Allardyce and Dr Cruikshank. Neither of them was there when I arrived, though Dr Cruikshank appeared some five minutes later. I hoped to impress him, and Dr Crowe, who had asked me to show some of the first-year students how to remove the skin of a corpse so that the musculature and membranes beneath remain intact. I am proficient at this, though

I was not prepared to leave anything to chance and hoped to secure a few hours, practice on our cadaver before the night was out.

We had hardly rolled up our sleeves before Allardyce appeared. He said he had just met the boy Davie Knox, and that it appeared Thrawn-Leggit Mary was dead. I was surprised, for she had been alive when I had left her, and I could not think what might have befallen her in the meantime. We went down to the Cowgate – Dr Cruikshank, Dr Wragg, Dr Strangeway, Allardyce and I. Dr Cruikshank led the way, Allardyce close at his heels for his lantern was out and he could not see his way otherwise. I followed with Dr Strangeway, who was also without a lantern, and Dr Wragg took up the rear. A great crowd awaited us and my heart quailed within me. We had all seen the mob at the execution of William Burke. We had seen the way they had filed past his anatomised corpse in their thousands the week after; the way they had smashed every window in Dr Knox's house and carried his effigy through the streets before hanging it from a lamp-post, and I could not help but feel afraid. As soon as they saw us a great cry went up and they surged forward. I could tell at a glance that it would not take much for them to string us up from the South Bridge by our heels – or our necks – and I must admit that I was relieved when Dr Cruikshank took all of us but Dr Wragg into Tanner's Lodgings.

I have seen many corpses, those that are fresh from the earth and those that are long dead. For all that I am aware of the dealings that have taken place at Dr Knox's medical school across the square from our own I had never to my knowledge seen a body that had been murdered – until that night. Mary Anderson was lying on the bed where I had left her. Her legs were visible, plastered with gore and grotesquely twisted. Her dress, a green one I had seen Mrs Crowe wearing on many occasions, but which the girl had not been wearing when I had last seen her, was rank with blood. She looked tiny – her torso so bunched and twisted that she appeared hardly bigger than a child. Her hands were white as bone in the lamplight, curled into claws and held up stiffly, as if she sought to tear at her own throat. Something was twisted about her neck – a shawl of some kind, the red weal that it had caused as it rasped against her skin visible upon her flesh. Her face, which had once so entranced us all, was turned to the wall, hidden in shadow. From where I stood I could see that it was darkly livid.

As the others busied themselves with the corpse I contented myself with taking a look about. At the back of the room the building seemed to merge into the rock and soil at the very root of the city. To the right, set deep within the wall, was a door. As everyone else was occupied, and there seemed naught else for me to do, I went over to examine it. The door had a key, but it was not locked. I opened it and looked out. A narrow flight of steps on the left led up to the next floor, whilst to my right the passage curved around to the neighbours' house. Tanner's Lodgings is a warren of a place, its rooms divided and subdivided, with stairs climbing up to dark landings and doors leading into windowless rooms. The poor are crammed in on every floor. From upstairs I could hear weeping, from behind the neighbours' door I heard voices raised in fury, the sound of smashing crockery and a baby crying. On the stairs, just where they turned to wind out of sight, was the crumpled form of a drunken woman. The air stank of dampness and urine. Some half dozen steps down from her, just outside the doorway where I stood, sat a small boy of some seven or eight years. His face was filthy, his feet bare. He was rubbing something, a coin of some kind, on the ragged tail of his shirt. I had the impression he had been there for some time. 'Has anyone come out of this room while you have been sitting there?' I asked. He shook his head, still intent on his work. 'Are you sure?' He laid *the coin on his palm. It was a shilling, bright as a diamond in the darkness. 'Aye,' he said. He held the coin up to his eye, the way a bit faker might when examining his coins through a jeweller's loupe. I felt sorry for the lad, sitting there in so cold and vile a passage while his mother slept off her drunken stupor, a murdered girl not ten paces away. I might not be a gentleman, I thought, but I was glad I had not been born to stock as common as this. I was about to hand him a sixpence when Dr Cruikshank called me. I shut the door, and locked it.*

I helped Dr Cruikshank wrap the body, and then we were ready. We took her to Surgeons' Hall. Allardyce and I removed the girl's blood-soaked dress and under things, and laid out her corpse in readiness for our work. I looked closely at her crimson face, her raw neck from where the ligature around it had abraded the flesh, her neatly sliced open abdomen. The handiwork I judged to be particularly skilful. I said as much to Allardyce, and he agreed, remarking that the perpetrator, whoever he was, was without doubt a master with the knife. But then the constable came and we were sent away.

I did not see the body of Mary Anderson again.

True in soul and conscience,

[Signed] James Franklyn

Chapter Ten

We arrived home some time after four and woke everyone. Mrs Speedicut shook the embers back into life, and with the speed and efficiency of long practice put a pan of porridge on the stove top to simmer. How she got the stuff to look so grey and lumpy I had no idea, though with the addition of a dollop of molasses to each of our bowls I managed to make it tolerable. Will and I both stank, and something vile had dried on my coat. I bundled all our clothes up and bade Gabriel and Jenny to take them down to the washerwoman later that morning.

There was not enough time to prepare a bath, and so I filled the basin, added some drops of lavender, some bicarbonate of soda and some tea tree oil, and set it out with a wash cloth. We washed our hair under the kitchen pump. I had formulated a shampoo, based on an Indian recipe my father had bought from a sea captain. It smelled of lemon geranium, cardamom and rosemary, and by the time we were done we were as fragrant as the apothecary on a warm day. Jenny insisted that we put in a few drops of essence of yew berry, a poisonous tincture, but one which she assured me would frighten away the dead, for even bundled up our clothes made the apothecary stink as though a decayed corpse had followed us home from the mortuary.

Will seemed reluctant to talk about what had occurred. He said he had accompanied me for no other reason than because I had asked him to. 'I cannot see what has been achieved by it all,' he said peevishly. 'Other than the fact that we both stink to high heaven, you have ruined a perfectly good coat, and between us we have terrified my employer's brother-in-law almost out of his wits.' I tried to tell him what I had found, that I was sure I could now identify the owner of the severed hand, but he would not listen. He stamped up to his room to change his shirt. When he reappeared, some twenty minutes later, he was washed and brushed and smelled strongly of sandalwood and orange blossom. He seemed distracted, ignoring the coffee I offered him, and sifting anxiously through the papers on his desk. I knew that he had completed his drawing of the skeleton hand the day before, and hoped that morning to present it to Dr Crowe, to see whether it met with the man's approval. He was anxious, and preoccupied. More than that – he was excited. Breathless almost. Usually he shared all his thoughts with me, all his worries and concerns. That morning, he was silent. He wolfed down his porridge with hardly a word.

'Take this,' I said. I handed him a bottle of the cordial I had prepared to quench his thirst and act as an expectorant. 'It will help to prevent the dust from settling on your lungs.'

'Thank you,' he said, stuffing it into his satchel. 'Why don't you come up to the Hall later, Jem?' he added, though I detected no great sincerity in his voice. 'If you want to, that is. You may not be welcome after last night. I can only hope that I still am.' He brushed his hair and smoothed the nap of his hat, and then he was gone.

Soon after, Mrs Speedicut went out too. Gabriel, Jenny and I went about our tasks. I wanted the condenser set up for I had some rosemary oil to prepare. I needed Jenny to make some sulphur pills, and the herb woman was due later that morning – I owed her money, and needed some more hops, so I had to clear some space in the herb drying room and see to the accounts. After that I found I had a little time on my hands, and so I took out the fold of paper I had brought with me from the dead room, and onto which I had collected the fragments I had scraped from beneath the fingers of the severed hand. I put them onto a slide and examined them beneath the microscope. The fragments were small, but left me in little doubt as to who owned the hand.

I went up to Corvus Hall. I took some bread and cheese for Will, and Silas Strangeway's box of surgical cutlery in my satchel. I asked to see Dr Crowe.

'He's dissecting, sir,' came the reply. 'Got a ticket?'

'Then perhaps I might see Miss Crowe?' I said.

The doorman shrugged. 'Skinner!'

Skinner seemed less voluble than he had been the day before. He looked at me warily. I tried to draw the fellow into conversation, but he would not answer, apart from the 'yes, sir,' and 'I'm sure I don't know, sir,' that courtesy required.

I heard the sound of laughter and the warm buzz of

conversation as we approached the little parlour. There was something familiar about the voice that I could hear interleaved with hers, and I felt something dark uncoil inside my breast. Was it disappointment? Melancholy? Jealousy? I could not be sure, but it moved like a serpent sliding out from beneath a rock.

Will and Miss Crowe were sitting adjacent to one another. Miss Crowe was smiling, her hair glinting dark and glossy in the autumn sunshine, the few threads of grey that ran though it shining like strands of silver wire. When she smiled the crow's feet at the corners of her eyes were evident, though her cheeks glowed with pleasure as she talked, her scarlet lips parted over neat white teeth. When the door opened they fell silent, their conversation hanging on the air like an echo.

'Mr Flockhart,' she said. She rose from her chair and stepped forward to greet me, slender hand outstretched.

'Jem!' cried Will, springing to his feet. 'I said you would be along at some point, though I didn't expect you so soon. I was just showing Miss Crowe my drawings. I have another here in addition to the hand. A length of vertebrae. She thinks they will do admirably.'

His tone was cordial enough, but somehow I sensed he was put out. I was discomfited too. What had he said that had made her smile like that? His cheeks were rosy, his eyes shining. He looked happy, I realised suddenly. He never looked like that when he was with me. All at once the box of knives I was carrying seemed cold and cruel as the blades inside it, a mundane object with which I was about to interrupt their tête-à-tête. Neither of them looked annoyed to see me, and yet I detected a change in the atmosphere. The greeting that had sat so easily on my tongue as I entered the room died on my lips, and instead I simply stood there looking foolish. Will deserved his place here. He was commissioned to work on Dr Crowe's anatomy book. But I? I was superfluous.

'Tea, Mr Flockhart?' She smiled.

'No,' I said. 'Thank you.' I sat down, my satchel clutched on my lap. I saw her look at it from beneath her lashes, but she said nothing. As she moved, I caught her scent on the air. Rose and sandalwood.

'Miss Crowe,' I said. 'I fear one of your students – Wilson – has been murdered. His body, mutilated, has been left in the dead house—'

'Jem—' said Will.

'His identity was removed, though it is unclear who did so, or why.'

'Jem—'

'There can be no doubt on the matter. It *is* Wilson. I have evidence of—'

'Jem, the lad Wilson has gone to Edinburgh,' said Will. 'His friends Tanhauser and Squires confirmed it this morning. It cannot be his body in the dead house. You must be mistaken.'

'But—'

'I am grateful for your efforts, Mr Flockhart,' said Miss Crowe. 'For your desire to uncover the truth, for your . . . your concern for Mr Wilson—'

'And the flayed head?' I looked from one to the other of them. I could hear my voice getting louder, but I could not stop. 'The anonymous corpse whose hand was severed? Who is he if he is not Wilson?'

'Mr Flockhart,' she said gently, 'You know as well as I do that bodies that come to us through . . . less orthodox means are often rendered unrecognisable as soon as they arrive, if not before. It is an uncomfortable truth, but there it is.'

'And has Wilson actually been seen?' I said. 'When? By whom?'

'Jem,' said Will. 'Stop this.'

'But by whom?' I repeated. 'It is a simple enough question. Where is the proof that Wilson is alive?'

'For goodness' sake, Jem. You'll be telling us next it might be Halliday. He's not been seen either.'

'It is *not* Mr Halliday, it is Mr Wilson.'

They sat together in silence, looking at me with concern. I felt my cheeks blaze as a hot flush of embarrassment crept up my face. And yet the fragments of whitewash that I had drawn from beneath the fingernails of the severed hand left me in no doubt. And there was worse news too, for in the dead room I had examined the skinned face and neck of the corpse. I had found the windpipe to be crushed and bruised, clear evidence of strangulation. From the crimson flesh that circled the throat I had abstracted three cobalt-blue fibres. Silk – no doubt from the ligature that had been pulled tight until he was dead. I glanced at Will, at Miss Crowe, and I knew I could tell them none of this. It made me feel worse than ever to see them both in accord, united in pity for what they clearly saw as my misplaced persistence. Tears stung my eyes.

'Well then,' I said, more sharply than I intended. 'If Wilson is found, then that is that.'

Miss Crowe stirred her tea. Her face, downcast, was unreadable. On the table beside the tea tray was Will's drawing of the skeleton hand. I found myself wondering once again what they had been laughing at. What they had been talking about that had made their eyes sparkle so? She said nothing about Will and me being inside the mortuary the previous night, though she must have known. And so I said nothing too. I would find Silas Strangeway on my own, I decided. I would ask him myself what he had been doing in the mortuary. And I would discover what had really happened to Wilson.

After that there seemed little more to say. Never any good at trivial conversation – bland statements about the condition of the roads (universally terrible), or the weather (mostly abominable) – I fell into an uncomfortable silence. After a minute or two I stood up to take my leave. I thought Will would do the same, but he did not. As if by magic, for I had not seen her ring a bell, Skinner appeared. He led me back to the hall with a stony face.

⟨⟩

There were students everywhere, standing talking, lounging against the walls, passing up and down the stairs. I recognised two of them from the dissecting room, along with two of the other students we had seen at the Exhibition. Dr Allardyce was talking to a pair of young men in their shirtsleeves, their fingers still bloody from the dissecting room, their brown aprons thick with gore. Flies droned through the air above their heads. Dr Allardyce looked nervous, as if he did not enjoy speaking to anyone and would much prefer the silent company of a corpse. The two students from the Exhibition vanished into the common room. Should I follow them? I felt I had little choice if I was to make any progress with my inquiries.

I dislike having to insinuate myself into the company of strangers, and meeting young medical men always worried me. Now, I was faced with the dilemma of how to present myself. If I pretended that I was one of them, then they might expect me to share robust anecdotes about drunkenness or debauchery, and anything that caused them to dwell on my masculinity, or lack thereof, was to be avoided. Of course, people saw what they expected to see, and the port-wine birthmark across my eyes and nose distracted people from looking deeper. On the other hand, if I spoke to them as a superior, as a man more qualified and experienced than any of them, what camaraderie might I be able to foster? Probably none at all, and they would say nothing to me of any significance. Might I manage to strike a balance between the two? I pushed open the door and went inside.

The room had once been the front parlour, a place where ladies might sit to take tea in the afternoon. Its horse shoe-shaped fireplace was still grand, but was now scuffed and dirty, and dotted with calcified circles of dried phlegm, like patches of lichen. A set of tongs, a coal shovel, a brush and poker, had been flung harum-scarum on the hearth, the patterned tiles of which were now black with ashes and dirt, and cracked from the careless thumping down of the coal scuttle. Against the walls were shelves of medical books, jars containing morbid specimens, resin casts of veins and arteries and bones of all kinds. On the mantel a clock ticked, beside it a human skull and a half dozen vertebrae of different sizes. In front of the large bay window a table stood. It was littered with ink stands, pens, books and paper crawling with line after line of scribbled words. Tanhauser was hunched over an atlas of anatomy, his lips moving, his finger marking a place on the page as his eyes closed. I watched as he opened his eyes, ran his gaze down the list of names he hoped to remember, and groaned. 'I will never get this into my head.'

'What is it?' Squires was sitting on a low chair toasting a piece of bread in front of the fire, his free hand absently turning the pages of a book that rested on his knees.

'Facial nerves.'

Squires grinned. 'Even old Wilson managed those!'

Beside him, another man was lounging in an easy chair, his legs akimbo on the singed hearthrug. 'Take a break, old fellow. Fancy a bottle?' And he reached over and produced two beer bottles from a crate that was balanced on a stack of *The Medico-Chirurgical Review* beside the fireplace.

'Too early for me, Renshaw.' Tanhauser rubbed his arms. 'It's rather chilly in here. Why don't you get back from the fire, Squires, then perhaps we can all share the heat.'

'Put your coat on,' replied Squires without looking round.

'But it's you, Squires.' Renshaw shoved him with his toe. 'You and your slice of toast. It's not fair on old Tanhauser over there – unless the toast is for him, of course. He takes it with cheese, don't you, Tanhauser? Fancy one?' He held up a bottle. He must have felt the draught from the open door on his neck at that point, for he looked round at me. 'Shut the door, can't you?' he drawled. 'Can't you see we're trying to keep warm and feed ourselves?'

'Ten Zulus Buggered My Cat,' I said.

'I beg your pardon?' He stared at me for a moment as if I were completely mad.

'Facial nerves,' I said. 'Ten Zulus.'

A smile twitched at the corners of Renshaw's mouth. 'Oh, now, that *is* good!'

'What is?' said Tanhauser and Squires together.

'You have a test coming up?' I said.

'Dr Crowe's demonstrating tomorrow,' replied Tanhauser. 'With Wilson gone he's bound to ask me. He always does. "Tanhauser! List the facial nerve branches! Or – God help me – Tanhauser! List the cranial nerves! Tanhauser! Blah, blah, blah." He thinks I'm an idiot.'

'You *are* an idiot,' said Renshaw. 'Almost as much of an idiot as Squires here.'

'Good God, Renshaw, he's nowhere near as stupid as I am!'

'Well, you could both do worse than to listen to this chap,' Renshaw grinned at me. 'What did you say your name was?'

'Flockhart,' I replied. 'Ten Zulus Buggered My Cat, Mr Tanhauser – it's a mnemonic for remembering the branches of the facial nerves. Temporal, zygomatic, buccal, et cetera et cetera. Want the cranial nerves?'

'Oh, *I* do, even if Tanhauser doesn't,' said Renshaw.

'Oh, Oh, Oh, To Touch And Feel Virgin Girls' Vaginas, Ah, Heaven!' I said. 'Olfactory, optic, oculomotor, trochlear, trigeminal – need I go on?'

Tanhauser guffawed and clapped his hands. 'Virgin Girls' Vaginas, Ah, Heaven!' he said. 'Yes!'

The others grinned and sniggered. 'Wilson'll like that one,' said Renshaw, taking a swig of his beer. 'Though any virgin girl would be advised to run at the very sight of him.' He raised his bottle in a salute. 'Thanks, Flockhart. I'll remember that – though quite frankly it's unlikely

Tanhauser will. Or at least, he'll probably spout the mnemonic itself and Dr Crowe will have a fit.'

'I have more if you need them.'

'Want a bottle?'

'So where's this chap Wilson got to?' I said, taking the bottle of ale he held out to me and dropping into a vacant chair.

'God knows,' said Tanhauser. 'Said he was going back to Edinburgh so I assume that's what he did. It's what I told Cruikshank, at any rate.'

'The weird sisters made this place a bit too hot for him,' said Squires.

'Oh?' I said. 'How so?'

'Never mind that,' said Tanhauser. He frowned at Squires. 'The less said about that the better. I just need to pass my exams and get out before it's me they come for.'

'*You?*' Renshaw laughed. 'Why would the weird sisters want you?'

'It's Halliday who should watch out,' Squires shook his head. 'It's a grave mistake he's making there. Mind you, I've not seen *him* for a few days either. Perhaps he's gone to ground with Wilson.'

'What's this chap Halliday like?' I said. 'I keep hearing his name.'

Squires nodded. 'He's a good man.'

'You only think that because he forged your attendance ticket for you when you were lying abed with that whore on Craven Lane,' said Tanhauser.

'It was he who introduced me to "that whore on Craven Lane". Her name is Susie, if you must know. Dear sweet Susie.'

'A pox by any other name would smell as sweet.'

'She doesn't have the pox,' said Squires.

'I'm afraid you find us a lewd bunch, Mr Flockhart,' said Renshaw. 'Though judging by your contribution to the conversation so far you're no better.'

At that moment the door was kicked open and a man lurched in. He was in his early twenties, not much older than the rest of them, with dark blond hair and blue eyes. He looked pale, and was unsteady on his feet. His skin had an unwholesome look to it, the flesh beneath his eyes clinging to the bone in a bluish circle. He dropped into a chair and closed his eyes. Tanhauser, Squires and Renshaw stared at him in surprise. 'Dear God, Halliday,' said Renshaw at last. 'You look terrible.'

'Mild dose of the cholera,' Halliday whispered. His voice was hoarse. 'Went out drinking with Dr Allardyce. Said he wanted to talk about my prize essay. Said he wanted to congratulate me on making the connections before he did.'

'Dr Allardyce?' said Tanhauser. '*He* bought a drink?'

'Wait, though,' Squires held up his hand. 'You're not just telling us that Dr Allardyce bought a drink, but that he bought *you* a drink?'

'Bought me lots of drinks,' said Halliday. 'And food. Beer, oysters, beer, oysters – I was feeling a bit ill even before I got home, truth be told. But by midnight!' He shuddered. 'I couldn't get to the privy, or onto the chamber pot fast enough! And I was so cold. Still am, as a matter of fact. Get away from the fire, Squires, you great lump.' He pulled his jacket tighter around his shoulders. 'I got one of the landlady's boys to fetch me some sugar and salt, and I mixed it with water.' He closed his eyes and swallowed painfully. 'It's the only thing that's kept me alive, I'm sure of it. God,' he said. His bowels gurgled noisily. 'Excuse me, gentlemen.' He lurched to his feet and bounded back out into the hall.

'Cholera?' said Tanhauser. He looked alarmed. 'How come he's not dead?'

'One can recover,' I said. 'Evidently. Unless his diagnosis is incorrect, and I see no reason why it should be. His face has all the hallmarks of it.'

'But the miasma—'

I shrugged. 'The miasmic theory of contagion? It's hardly convincing. If cholera was the result of foul vapours, why is the whole of the city not perpetually afflicted by it? It stinks like a sewer everywhere. And yet, when the cholera comes it is a localised occurrence, with some streets affected badly and others not at all.'

Halliday reappeared. He took a bottle from his satchel and drank from it deeply. He wiped his lips and grimaced. 'God, it's a vile mixture.'

'Dr Crowe will be glad to see you,' I said.

'Pity he didn't send a runner,' said Halliday. 'I could have done with some help. I could hardly move a muscle this morning. I've been shitting all night.'

'There's a cure for cholera?' asked Renshaw. 'I had no idea!'

'Generally speaking, I think it unlikely,' replied Halliday, sinking back into the armchair. 'I had a light dose, though if I'd not drunk my mixture I might not be here now.'

At that moment the door flew open and Dr Allardyce himself burst in. 'Halliday!' he cried. 'I heard—'

'What?' drawled Halliday. 'You heard I'm not dead? Very disappointing for you, sir.'

Dr Allardyce blushed. 'Come now, H-Halliday—'

'Perhaps it was that place we went to,' said Halliday. 'All those oysters! You're not affected?'

Dr Allardyce shook his head. 'Not a bit. How did you . . . how did you recover?'

'It occurred to me that if I could put back in the top all that fluid that was pouring out of the bottom I might just manage to survive. And you know how Dr Cruikshank's always on at us about "using all the senses" – the number of corpses I've sniffed and licked!' He grinned. His eyes were as blue as indigo, bright against his skin's pallor. 'The moist surfaces seem to me to be mostly saline – a bit sweetish here and there, but mostly salt. Assuming it might be more than just water that was pouring out of my arse, I thought I might try to put the sweet and the saline back in. So I drank a solution of salt and sugar – every time I had to visit the privy I sank a few pints of the stuff. Seems to have done the trick. Mind you, I've got the thirst of the Devil and my head's pounding.'

'Want a beer?' drawled Tanhauser.

Halliday glugged the ale thirstily. 'Pints and pints of that nasty salty water went down my throat, pints and pints of something very similar poured out of my back end. I could hardly keep up.'

'Perhaps you should go home,' I said.

'God, no!' he replied. 'The place stinks – especially after the night I've had. I'll stay right here, thanks. Besides, lots of work to do upstairs.' He grinned at me and held out his hand. 'John Halliday,' he said. 'Anatomy student and former missing person.'

Chapter Eleven

Coming out of the common room, I ran into Will. 'Jem,' he said. 'I thought you'd gone.'

'No,' I said. 'I am still here. I have Dr Strangeway's knives.' I pulled the box from my satchel. 'I'd like to return them – with our apologies, of course.'

'You should have given them to Miss Crowe.'

'Should I?' I said. 'What good would that do?'

He pursed his lips. 'I think he is upstairs,' he said. 'His workshop is beside the anatomy museum. The public are allowed through the museum on Tuesdays and Thursdays, and later this morning, though as you are with me I'm sure it will be permissible.'

I scowled. Was I no more than a member of the public? Was I allowed into the place only as his companion? I followed him up the stairs, my face thunderous.

He led me towards what had once been the ballroom. I remembered it as two elegantly proportioned rooms that were separated by a folding wall of white-painted panelled wood. Once the wall was folded back, the room was some fifty feet long, illuminated by tall casement windows that ran east to west.

'It is another anatomy museum,' said Will. 'There is a door at the end that takes one through to the museum where Dr Wragg works.' He threw back a pair of double doors.

The room was filled with skeletons, animals of all kinds – an anteater, a wild boar, an Arabian horse, a rhinoceros, a tiger. There were apes, birds, crocodiles, fish. In front of them all, standing on a raised dais of varnished mahogany, was a woman. Her right hand was raised above her head, her legs set in a stride. She alone was more than just bone, for her skeleton had been shrouded in a glimmering layer of crimson muscle.

'What's *that*?' whispered Will, his eyes wide. 'It wasn't here yesterday.'

'It is a life sized écorché,' I said. 'A scalded woman. You see there is a man too? They are made from wax overlaying bone.' I stepped closer. The detail was extraordinary. We stood in silence, just looking. And then all at once a voice spoke: 'Come in, gentlemen.'

Behind us, the door closed. We sprang round to find Sorrow and Silence Crowe standing side by side. They led us down the room. There were one or two students bent over glass cases, their books open and papers spread out. When they saw Sorrow and Silence they gathered their books and left without a word.

Another door took us into a long narrow chamber that did office as a wax modelling studio. As the door closed behind us a man stepped forward and held out his hands; pale hands, textured and thickened with scar tissue, the characteristic whirling and pitting of smallpox. His face was expressionless, his mouth a dark hole, his eyes glittering beneath his textured lids.

'Thank you.' He reached forward and pulled the box of knives from out of my hands. 'Mine, I believe?'

'Yes, sir,' I said. 'I'm sorry.'

'You find us still unpacking,' he said, waving my apology, and my introductions, aside. 'It is the bottles and the bodies that matter most, and we are left to last.' He shook his head. 'I am always the least important. My girls the least important.' On the table top was a life-sized model of a young woman. She was lying on her back, a wax hand upon her breast. A folded pad of fine white cotton lay across her eyes, tied loosely in place with a pink silk ribbon.

'You see how carefully she has been looked after? How we wrapped her as best we could so that she would not be frightened?' He put out a hand and touched the model's hair. 'No one makes them like this anymore. It's all function and utility now. She was to be sold to a fairground, you know. A fairground! Mr Halliday was quite determined. He calls my girls "dolls". He says only a real cadaver can teach a man about the human body.' He snorted. 'He tries to be like Dr Cruikshank, but Dr Cruikshank has always admitted the value of my creations even if he prefers a corpse himself.' He turned to face me, the semblance of a frown creasing his pale, scarred forehead. 'As if every one of my girls is not the result of months and months of anatomy.'

'And yet a student of medicine must see a cadaver, must work with the real matter and substance of the body,' I said. 'Does it not behove them to meditate on the fate of all mankind as they work? What else but a corpse might encourage such reflections?'

'My models promote a scientific understanding of human anatomy based on rigorous dissection. *My* dissections. I can see the value of the cadaver, of course I can. Do we not live in a world of death, of pain and horror and suffering?' He held out his own hands. The scarred flesh pulling the fingers into curled fists. 'And yet when they use *my* models they are brought to an almost divine reflection on the glory of the human body. *Memento Mori* and anatomy lesson are one and the same. Body and soul, relic and specimen, is there a need to draw a line between the two?'

The wax girl was lying on a rumpled sheet, her head thrown back as if in ecstasy, her lips a faint smile beneath her blindfold, so that for a moment I was reminded of Annie, one of Mrs Roseplucker's girls, who had once worked from a brothel on Wicke Street. A large panel had been lifted from the girl's waxy chest and abdomen. Inside, the wax organs were visible – the heart, the lungs, the liver, all perfectly formed and neatly packed within. I noted a line in the model's hair which marked the place where the top of its head screwed off to reveal a wax brain.

Dr Strangeway was looking down at her fondly. He stroked her cheek. 'I saved her. I couldn't let her be stared at by urchins and drunkards. She's my daughter, gentlemen. One of many, but no less dear to me because of it.'

'I think I too would prefer to be taught by one of your so-called "dolls", sir,' said Will.

But Dr Strangeway seemed hardly to be listening. 'You see, for men to be instructed they must be seduced by the subject they encounter,' he said. 'And yet how might the image of death be rendered agreeable? We might show the body's constituent parts in isolation – organs, limbs, the fine tracery of the blood vessels – but it does not teach the *whole*. What might we do to overcome this? Dissection, of course, but when that fails? When men cannot bear to wallow in death, what then?'

'A manual,' cried Will. 'I am helping Dr Crowe create the perfect handbook—'

Dr Strangeway thumped his fist on the table. 'No, sir! A mere handbook will not do! Accuracy is all, Mr Quartermain! Being able to *see* the subject from every angle, the relation of one organ to another organ. *You* must know *that* much.' He turned to Will, jabbing a finger at his chest. 'I've seen what you are doing. Your illustrations are diagrams, without detail, without intimacy. You are the very worst of this new scientific method. How might *your* pictures show us anything of the beauty of the body? It is simply a catalogue of parts!'

'I merely draw what I am told to draw, sir,' replied Will. 'I make no claims about scientific method.'

Dr Strangeway sighed, and nodded. 'Forgive me, sir, I fear my outlook is at odds with everyone else's.' He ran his hand down the waxen arm of the blindfolded model. 'Some two hundred cadavers were required to craft this single figure. The speed of decay renders a cadaver useless in no time at all – what knowledge might a man acquire from stink and decay? When he is repelled, how can he learn? And you see how plump she is? How rounded? We modelled her from the best – nothing fat, nothing old or rotten. Not like those miserable cadavers from the workhouse.'

'She is beautiful, sir,' said Will. 'What medium do you use?'

He looked pleased. 'I see you are an artist, sir, though you may be apostate, and have of late sold your soul to the world of catalogues and handbooks. It is beeswax. White virgin wax from Smyrna or Venice. I mix it with turpentine, with oils and fats, until I have the consistency. Plant resin helps to sustain the structure and maintain the vivid colour. You see those flabby specimens in the anatomy museum? Grey, pale, blobs bobbing in fluid? All very well, but where is their vitality? Their lifeblood? Their visceral truth? No living being has organs that look like that! But I show what is *really* within. I use the very finest pigments, sifted through cloth and dissolved in oil. You see the blood vessels? The nerves? They are silken fibres dipped in wax. Intricate, detailed, exact. My precise mixtures and preparations are a secret, so don't ask me. No, sir!' he covered his ears as Will opened his mouth to speak. 'I will not tell!'

He took a deep breath. A sheen of sweat covered his brow. Sorrow and Silence, Will and I, stood before him without speaking. Had he finished? I saw him swallow.

'I'm sorry, gentlemen.' He pulled out a handkerchief and dabbed at his lips. 'It is a subject close to my heart, as you can imagine. Please, take a look at my work. Some of my very best pieces are in this room.'

Around the walls, standing in glass cases like crystal sentry boxes, were six more écorchés: three men and three women. They stood opposite each other at intervals down the room – wax over real human bones. Wax faces – moulages – demonstrating dermatological complaints, eczema, chancres, pustules, hung from the walls. Each face was different, but each perfectly rendered. Will was transfixed by a series of models depicting diseased genitals. Further down the room a woman gave birth by caesarean. Two pairs of disembodied male hands helped her, one holding the wound open, the other easing the waxen child into the world. The model had turned her face away, her eyes languid, her brow creased as if in no greater pain than if she were having a splinter removed.

Dr Strangeway bent over his workbench, rummaging through his pigments. Antimony white, burnt umber, cadmium yellow. He fussed about, dabbing up spillages and rearranging pots. The air was heavy with the smell of hot wax, and the inevitable stink of decay. On a bench in the middle of the room was a torso minus its head, arms and legs – no more than a ribcage and abdomen. A hole had been cut in the flesh, to reveal the organs within. I saw Will blanch at the sight. Silence saw it too and she stepped forward to cover the torso up with a sheet of thick heavy cotton.

'These days it is organs mainly,' said Dr Strangeway. 'No one wants the whole body. Of course, we need dissection for that too. I prefer to get them at night when no one is looking.' His hands were balled into fists, his eyes watery, as if even talking about it caused him pain. 'The students can be so cruel. I sometimes think their close association with the dead breeds an unkind nature. And they have certainly moved away from my models in recent years, preferring their own corpses instead. But you have seen what you wanted to see, have you not? You can go now.' He turned away from us.

'What are you making, sir?' I said. 'I am a great admirer of your work. Your recent work in particular. I saw your contribution to the Exhibition. The heart. The head and face. Extraordinary.'

'Hm?'

'At the Exhibition.'

'Oh,' he said. 'Yes. Yes. My most recent work, sir, you are quite right.'

'And you work here with Miss Crowe?'

'With Lilith, yes. But also with Sorrow and Silence.' He smiled indulgently at the two women, who had donned aprons and set about their business at the other end of the workbench. One of them attended to a pan of melted wax, the other ground up pigments in a pestle and mortar. Dr Strangeway pulled the canvas shroud off the torso. 'They will open the ribcage and reveal what lies within – heart, lungs, oesophagus. It is a complex piece. Dr Cruikshank asked for it. He sent up the torso. It is rare to have one so young to work from.'

'I thought he disliked models,' I said.

'They have their uses.'

I looked at the torso on the workbench. *Dr Cruikshank asked for it. He sent up the torso. It is rare to have one so young.* I had seen it before, I was certain, although it had been rendered even more anonymous now that it was without arms, legs, or head.

'It's Wilson,' I whispered. 'Wilson, I'm sure of it.'

I looked at Dr Strangeway, but he was rummaging earnestly amongst his paintbrushes and did not meet my gaze. '*Et mortui sua arcana narrabunt,*' I said. 'One way or another, Dr Strangeway, the dead *will* give up their secrets, whether you and your fellow anatomists like it or not.'

Chapter Twelve

ill left me after that. He seemed irritated that I persisted with 'this Wilson business,' though I knew I was right. I said I would find him later. I hoped we might sort out our differences, as I could not bear the coolness that seemed suddenly to have arisen between us. I watched him go. Usually he left me with a quip, or a remark about meeting up later, but this time he said nothing.

I went to find Dr Wragg. Might I persuade him to tell me more about the men of Corvus Hall? I had brought some of my remedies in my bag, a salve of comfrey to rub into his arthritic fingers, a tincture of cinnamon bark for the rheumatism I had noted afflicted his knees and back. Something told me that Dr Wragg would not yield information easily, but I had to try, for I knew I would get even less from Dr Cruikshank and Dr Crowe.

The public were allowed in the museum for a few hours that afternoon, and there were ladies and gentlemen sauntering about amongst the exhibits. They gasped and gawped, in much the same way that people had once looked at the mad, as something to marvel at and to exclaim over. Skinner was in attendance, and he told me that Dr Wragg hated the public, and retreated into his private room whenever it was a 'ticket day'.

'Down there,' he pointed to the far corner of the room, where a narrow flight of stairs led up into a gloom. 'Not that he likes guests much either, sir. I'd leave him be if I were you.' But I was not about to listen to Skinner telling me what I should and shouldn't do, and so I thanked him curtly and headed off through the shelves.

I found Dr Wragg in a long, low room beneath the eaves, lit by the smallest skylight I had ever seen. It must be freezing in the winter, for beyond the rough wooden planking of the sloping ceiling there was nothing but roof slates.

There was a workbench along one wall, with a tap, a sink and a drain. It was clear that it was a place of work, for there were carboys of preserving fluid, knives, bottles, books and lumps of flesh littered about the place. Flies buzzed lazily above my head, as if too fat and sated to move with any speed. It smelled of decay, the way everywhere seemed to at Corvus. I saw that Dr Wragg's room was on the same storey as Will's, and that they were separated only by the maceration room where the specimens were soaked, and by another store room filled with the stuff needed for specimen preparation. Against one wall was a brass bedstead, mounded with quilts and blankets. Dr Wragg, it seemed, preferred to sleep in his workshop. He was standing at the workbench. He had pulled his sleeve up and was worrying at his forearm with grubby fingers.

An array of dark scabs stood out against his white skin like beetles.

'Dr Wragg,' I said. 'You have eczema, sir? I might have something—'

The old man jumped, for so absorbed was he in his task that he had not heard me come in. 'No,' he snapped.

'But—'

'It's nothing. Nothing for you.'

'I have a salve—'

'I don't want a salve.' He ran a hand over his scab-studded arm. 'I've had some of these for months,' he said. He picked at the corner of a large one with a horny fingernail, and I saw that his shirt sleeve was blotched with blood. 'This one is almost ready.' He grinned at me. 'It's my scab farm.' The grin fell from his face as he turned away, pulling his sleeve back down. 'And they don't need any salve!'

He turned to his bench, plucking up a bottle and holding it up to the light. It contained what looked like a length of tapeworm. 'From a workhouse corpse,' he said without turning round. 'Wilson wanted it. Biggest I've ever seen.'

'Wilson?' I said. 'He's dead, sir. He won't be wanting it now.'

Dr Wragg turned to face me. 'Then I'll give it to Tanhauser.'

'So you know Wilson is dead?'

He nodded. There was a sluggishness to his movements, and I saw that his pupils were no bigger than pinpricks, tiny black dots in the rheumy green of his eyes. 'And the dead shall surrender their secrets,' he whispered. He held up the bottle. 'They always do.' He smiled, showing me his crooked mis-matched teeth set in their wooden gums.

'Did you know him?'

'Wilson? No more than any of them. His father is to blame for it, though he's dead now too.'

'To blame?' I said. 'For what?'

Dr Wragg's grin grew wider. 'You think I don't know your tricks, Mr Flockhart? You think I don't know you? He is to blame for sending him here – amongst other things.' He shook his head. 'This is the beginning,' he said. 'The beginning of the end. I said it would come.'

I had seen opium addiction many times, and I could tell straight away that Dr Wragg was a habitual user. Had it started for medicinal purposes? Perhaps to numb the pain from some malady or other – judging by his teeth the man had suffered badly in that quarter alone. Now, however, like so many whose use had started innocently enough, I would wager any amount of money that he was unable to live without it. He continued to work, to appear lucid, as did so many whose lives had been governed by it for years, and whose daily life was one of habit and sameness. I had no doubt that it was the opium that had rendered him less cautious than the others, though if Dr Wragg knew that the corpse was Wilson's then I was quite certain that they all did. He turned back to his workbench. There was no point in offering him the remedies I had brought, I could see that much.

'Your museum is a credit to you, sir,' I said instead.

'Indeed, sir,' he replied. 'No school can be taken seriously without one. Few students can attend enough dissections to familiarise themselves with the range of normal and diseased appearances, so they need a well-ordered representative collection.'

'And yet most anatomy museums are merely an assortment. Here, you have something far more impressive.'

'I have set nature properly in order, sir. Museum work is prized – and fought over. Being appointed curator to a pathology museum is a great honour for any man, a testament to his work and esteem, and for that reason I am proud to say that I have curated some of the best anatomy museums in the world – Paris, Edinburgh, London.' He fell silent. I saw his face cloud over, as though a wave of opium had smothered his thoughts.

'Did Wilson help you with the collection?' I said.

'Wilson? That idiot? It is Halliday who helps me. He knows how to prepare a specimen – how to preserve an organ, wet and dry. He's very good. Not that I needed him. I've been curator of this collection for twenty years, and for ten years before that. It was I who packed the collection up when we left Edinburgh, then when we left St Bride's, and I who set it all out here. I arranged everything according to the correct system by which exhibits *should* be arranged. A taxonomy favoured by Hunter, by Monro *secundus*, by Knox – some of the greatest anatomists to have lived! It was not for Halliday to decide he had developed a better way.' He shook his head. 'He came with two of his stupidest friends – Tanhauser and Wilson. One a sycophant, the other a blockhead. They had no idea what they were doing. And so I put everything back the way it had been. The way it *should* be.' He smiled faintly, his eyes narrowing. 'Edinburgh,' he murmured. '*That* was the best of them. No one questioned my methods then.' He grinned at me again, his dentures as uneven as ancient tombstones. His eyes were watery grey-green voids, like blobs of phlegm. 'Want to see my private collection? They never touched *that*! No one would dare to.'

He shambled to the back of the room and pulled a curtain aside. On a shelf were some two dozen jars, each containing an anatomical specimen. From where I was standing they looked no different to any others. 'Well?' I said.

He plucked up a jar. 'The gall bladder of William Burke.' He grinned at me, his gaze now strange and blank. It was as if he looked into the past through a haze of opium and saw it more clearly than he saw the present. 'I was there when Monro dissected the body. The crowd some two thousand strong, out in the street, out in the college quad, filing past to spit and stare. I took it for my collection.' He lifted another jar. 'The eyes of John Lawrie. Hanged in Edinburgh in 1821 for murdering three women. And this one here,' he held up a large vessel with a pale foetus curled within. 'One of the twelve babies strangled at birth by Margaret Meikle. The others she dissolved in quicklime. You see the marks on the neck?' He thrust it towards me, the lump of flesh within bobbing. He pointed to a jar containing a small, greyish coloured piece of flesh. 'You know what this is? This is the tongue of Clenchie Kate. Aye, she was a clapper-tongued besom, that one. I was glad tae see her hangit.'

His skin had grown moist, with beads of oily sweat standing out on his brow. He gazed blankly at the wall, his eyes with their pinprick pupils, though I knew that in his mind he would be seeing all manner of things. The room was stuffy, the stink from the bottles and preparations on his workbench filling the air, so that I could not help but wonder what memories such a reeking atmosphere might provoke.

All at once he blinked. He stared at me, as if wondering who I was, and then slipped the jar back onto the shelf. He wiped his hands on the rag that hung from his belt.

Bloody Wragg, the students called him, for he was rarely seen without it. He made to pull the curtain back over his grisly collection.

'And this one?' I said. I took up another jar, not unlike the one he had just put back. It contained a greyish, purple lump, about the size of a small fist. It was sliced neatly down the middle, the chambers within exposed, the tough strings that pulled the valves open and closed still fixed and taut. Dr Wragg's hand shot out and he snatched the thing off me, cradling it to his breast.

'Never you mind what this is,' he said. 'I think you've seen enough now, don't you?' He waved a hand. 'Away with ye!'

The label was old and stained, but it had been easy enough to read, the neat handwriting that Dr Wragg prided himself on still fresh and clear: *Heart. Cross Section. Mary Anderson. 19th December 1830.*

Chapter Thirteen

❧

Will was sitting at his desk, a spinal column laid out before him. It looked raw, as if it had only recently been abstracted from its owner.

'Some wear at the lumbar region,' he said. 'But apparently a good specimen, despite coming from a workhouse corpse.' He did not look up, but worked on, his hand moving steadily across the page. 'I have already done the vertebrae – each separate, showing the undulations and crenulations of the bones.' He waved a hand in the direction of some finished pages. 'Now this. It seems the spine is Dr Crowe's passion. He has written books on the matter, and down there in the museum there is a collection of some two hundred different spines.'

'Two hundred?'

Will shrugged. '"More than merely a portion of the skeleton it is essential to the whole being, the key to the entire organic world." He was telling me earlier.' He threw down his pen. 'I cannot say I share his enthusiasm, though it is certainly a miracle of strength and flexibility and could no doubt teach us much about both.' He gestured to a large earthen bowl covered with a saucer that stood to one side. 'And in there I have a set of lungs, for when I am finished with this spine. Dr Cruikshank brought them up. Apparently Halliday will cut them open for me once I am ready to draw the insides. I think he was looking for Miss Crowe, to be honest. The lungs were just an excuse.'

'Has she been up here?'

'No.' He did not look at me, and there was a pause, a sudden awkwardness.

'Look,' I said. 'That body in the dead room—'

'Jem, *please*—'

'Listen to me, Will. I *know* you want to believe Miss Crowe's story that Wilson has returned to Edinburgh – in fact it's quite likely she believes it herself. But I'm telling you that there is no question that the corpse is Wilson – at least, it *was* Wilson. Dr Cruikshank has sent his headless torso up to Dr Strangeway, so already he is no longer complete – goodness knows where his head and limbs have ended up – and I've just been talking to Dr Wragg who *admitted* that the corpse was Wilson.'

'Dr Wragg is hardly to be trusted.'

'Isn't he? He seemed very certain to me. And how often have I been wrong, Will? You never used to doubt me.'

'What do you want me to do about it?'

'I want to go to Wilson's lodgings and see what we can find out. Will you come?'

He sighed. 'Jem—'

'And . . . and there is something else.' I had to tell him. I could not bear to keep it to myself.

'Yes?'

I put my hand into my pocket, and drew out the letter. I told him I had found it in that very room. I said I had looked for others, but that I had found nothing. I laid it on the desk. 'My mother's handwriting,' I said. 'Addressed to Dr Bain.'

'Are you sure?'

'I have a book of recipes she wrote. I am in no doubt at all that it is her handwriting.'

'You have not read it?'

I shook my head. 'I have not.'

'It may be nothing, Jem. It may be no more than a laundry list, or a request for medications.' He looked at me sadly. 'And you have been worrying and thinking about this since yesterday?'

I nodded.

'Would it not be better just to open it and see? Would you like me to—?'

'No,' I said. 'I shall do it. It's just . . . seeing her writing. And the paper – it is not the stuff we used in the apothecary at St Saviour's, but is much finer. It's as if what this contains is private, is more than something that might be scribbled down on St Saviour's cheap paper. You know Dr Bain was . . . was popular. With women.'

'Yes,' said Will. 'I remember it well.'

'What if he and my mother—'

'Does it seem likely?'

'I have no idea! It *didn't*. But now . . . Now . . . '

'Anything is possible, Jem. But why not look? At least then you can be sure—'

'I will.'

'Go on then.' He handed me the letter. 'Take a look. All will be well.'

The paper was thick and creamy, the address un-faded, despite the years that had passed, so that it looked as if she had written it yesterday. I slipped the single folded sheet from the tiny envelope. It was dated some eighteen months before I was born.

'*My dear Alexander*

I am unable to see a way forward for either of us that is without pain. You have been the kindest and most patient of men, but the time has come for us to consider the path we have embarked upon and where it will lead us. Without me you will be able to continue your work. I would only hold you back, and, in time, you would resent me. I could not bear it. I am older, and, in this matter, wiser than you, and so I make this decision for both of us. For all of us.

Cathy.'

I read it over once more, then folded it up. I thought of all the hours Dr Bain and I had spent together. He had been my only friend at St Saviour's – before Will came – and I had been distraught when he died. 'He never said. Never told me that he . . . that he knew her so well.'

'Perhaps there was no need. Not while your father was alive.'

'And now they are dead,' I said. 'All of them, and I am alone.' I had not meant to sound so self-pitying, but the words tumbled out before I could stop them. Will meant more to me than any of them; was I to lose him too? For as I watched him draw closer to Miss Crowe I felt a cold draught about my heart. I could not love him more than I did, though for him, it had not been enough.

I closed my eyes. I heard Will stand up from his desk, heard him push open the skylight and felt a faint breeze

167

swirl in. He put arms around me, the arms of a true friend, and I was glad that I had told him. The rough nap of his woollen waistcoat rasped against my cheek. He smelled of ink, and pencil shavings left in the sun, as he always did. I hoped Miss Crowe liked it as much as I.

'Will you come with me?' I said. 'To Wilson's lodgings? We cannot in all conscience let him simply vanish into his own anatomy school as a collection of anonymous body parts—'

He sighed and pushed me away, holding me at arms' length. For a moment he looked into my eyes, his hands upon my shoulders. Then, 'I will always love you, Jem.' He kissed me on the forehead. 'And I will always, always come with you.'

∼

According to Mrs Speedicut, Tanhauser, Squires and Wilson had lodgings on Brush Street, a dull row of flat-fronted Georgian terraced lodging houses in varying states of dilapidation not far from the Hall. The street sweepers and night soil men seemed reluctant to visit the place, and there were mounds of excrement about the road and pavement. It had a grim darkness to it for all that the sun was shining, and I was glad the fog had lifted, for I would not like to walk its length without being able to see where I was putting my feet.

Tanhauser, Squires and Wilson lived at the end. The woman who answered the door was as thin as a lath with a baby on her hip. Another child clutched hold of her skirts with filthy fists. Both children were crying. The sound of still more of them doing the same echoed up the dark passage that led to the back of the house. She gestured up a flight of gloomy, moist-looking stairs. 'Top floor,' she said, when I explained who I was after. 'Do you know where Mr Wilson is?' she added. 'I need the rent.'

'I'm sure he will be along soon enough, madam,' I said smoothly.

'Are you?' she said. Her grumbling voice drifted after us as we began to mount the stairs.

Tanhauser and Squires were in their sitting room, the former sprawled in a sagging armchair, the latter standing before the fire staring gloomily at the small mound of greasy coals that smoked reluctantly in the grate. The hearth was littered with black plugs of spent tobacco and brown splats of dried spit. A skull sat on the mantel, alongside a row of empty beer bottles and a cracked tobacco jar. The two men were drinking ale and smoking, and the room had a thick brown atmosphere. Beneath the smoke it stank of dirty socks and stale food.

'Oh, it's you,' said Tanhauser as we entered the room. 'Well?'

I put the beer I had brought onto the table. It was littered with dirty plates, scribbled papers and scraps of food.

'You want to get your landlady to give this place a good clean,' said Will. He wrinkled his nose. 'And what's that smell?'

'It's Squires,' said Tanhauser. 'He smells like a corpse.' He drained his beer and held out his hand for another.

'I thought you two had an examination tomorrow?' I said.

'I'm giving up,' said Tanhauser. 'I'm all in. It's not for me. Can't stomach it. Can't remember anything either.'

'It hardly matters,' piped up Squires. 'Half the sawbones in England don't know their arse from their elbow.'

'Now *that* I *do* know,' said Tanhauser, pointing the mouth of his beer bottle at his companion.

'And you, Squires?' I said.

'Oh, I have to carry on,' said Squires. 'Nothing for it. Besides, I'm not quite as thick as Tanhauser.'

'Oh yes you are!' said Tanhauser. 'You're every bit as thick as I am. But now we don't have Wilson. Wilson made both of us look good.' He raised his bottle. 'To absent friends.'

'You told Dr Cruikshank that Wilson had gone back to Edinburgh?' I said.

'No. I don't know where that came from,' replied Squires. The two men exchanged a glance. 'He may well be that body you were looking at, for all we know. The one without the hand.'

'Why?'

Tanhauser shrugged. He did not answer, though the way he glanced at Squires made me think there was something he was not telling us.

'Where are his family?' I said.

'Wilson has no family,' said Squires. 'It's one of the reasons he was here. He was a Scotsman—'

'Aren't they all?' drawled Tanhauser. He sucked on his pipe and released a cloud of acrid smoke into the reeking atmosphere. 'Never met a single one I liked. They look after their own.'

'Apart from Wilson, evidently,' said Will.

'So it seems,' said Tanhauser. 'Apparently his father was keen for him to try for a surgeon – you know, the old story, wanted his son to amount to more than he had. Used to know the lot of them when they were up in Edinburgh, apparently. Thought young Wilson could do with a better profession than the one he'd had, and told him to seek out Crowe and Cruikshank.'

'That tripe about bettering yourself dogs me too,' muttered Squires. 'My father's a baker. Thinks I might one day be surgeon to the king.' He shook his head. 'If only they really knew what it was like. No jobs for anyone unless you have an uncle who can help.' He smirked. 'You tell me a man's position at any hospital in town and I'll tell you who his uncle is.'

'Yes, well, the trouble with Wilson was that he didn't take to it any more than I have,' said Tanhauser. 'He only did it for his old man's sake. The old man's dying wish, he always said. There was no reason to stay up in Edinburgh once his father was dead so he came to seek his fortune in London.'

'Where the streets are paved with gold,' said Squires. He jerked his head towards the window. 'Didn't you notice?'

'But Wilson's far too dim to make a surgeon. Mind you, if he spent as much time in the dissection room as he did chasing the ladies he might not be too bad at all.'

'What was his father's profession?' I said.

'Police constable, I believe,' said Squires.

'I think Wilson Senior had some idea that young Wilson would end up rich and famous. Crowe and Cruikshank are both doing very well. They have huge private practices, for all that they spend much of their time at the Hall.'

'It's nothing but drudgery if you ask me,' said Squires. 'Stinks too.' He sniffed his fingernails and wrinkled his nose. 'By God, Tanhauser. It *is* me!'

'Of course it's you. You never cover your clothes, *that's* why. You reek like a charnel house.' Tanhauser put his head back and closed his eyes. 'Anyway, I'm out of it. I'm going back home and I'll be glad never to see that place nor any of *them* ever again.'

'Who?' I said.

'The weird sisters, for one. All three of them. An anatomy school is no place for a woman. I mean, it's one thing sitting in a few lectures, but hanging about the place?' He shook his head. 'They tamper with the corpses, you know.'

'How so?' said Will. He looked aghast. 'But they are so—'

'What? So beautiful?' Tanhauser laughed. 'I know! I'm not sure whether that makes it better or worse.'

'I don't know which of them it is,' said Squires, frowning. 'My money's on the older one. But everyone knows it goes on. They don't come into our dissecting classes, the demonstrations, so that's a relief. But then they don't need to! They already know how to cut a body up. Dr Strangeway showed them.'

'*Uncle* Strangeway,' Tanhauser shuddered.

'They take . . . bits,' said Squires. 'We've all noticed it. Who else would do it?'

'Dr Cruikshank?' I said. 'Dr Crowe?'

'Crowe and Cruikshank don't want bits. And Strangeway never comes down. Haven't you seen the two younger ones about the place with a jar in their hands?' He lowered his voice. 'Why do you think their cuffs are always red? Surely you've noticed? Besides, Wilson said he'd seen them.'

'When?'

'Don't know. He said he saw them both. The blind one carrying it. A head, he said it was. The deaf one was leading the way.'

'And Miss Lilith?'

Tanhauser snorted. 'Not you too,' he said. He shook his head. 'Everyone's in love with Lilith Crowe.'

'Even Wilson?' I said.

'No,' Squires looked thoughtful. 'No, Wilson didn't like her at all. I don't know why. But she's even worse than the other two. Ask Halliday.'

'They can see round corners, those other two,' remarked Tanhauser. 'Wilson said that blind one knew it was him before he'd even—' He stopped.

'Before he'd even what?' I said.

Tanhauser's cheeks coloured. The two men exchanged a glance. Then, 'Oh what the hell. He shouldn't have done it and he shouldn't have told us if he didn't want anyone to know about it. And he seemed mighty pleased with himself afterwards.' He turned to Will and me. 'Wilson gave the blind one a squeeze. Thought she'd never know who it was.'

'It was more than a squeeze,' said Squires. 'She wasn't keen apparently. But Wilson is a brute, and I doubt he was interested in her opinion. The ladies usually like him. He's a handsome devil, it's true enough. Mind you, not much point having good looks when the lady can't even see you.'

'That just left his personality then.' Squires grinned. 'He doesn't have one, as I recall.'

'He forced himself on Sorrow Crowe?' said Will, his expression appalled.

'He certainly did *something*,' replied Tanhauser.

'And now the weird sisters hate us all the more,' said Squires. 'Not that they liked us before. I think the only reason they didn't tell anyone about Wilson was because they know their position here is precarious. None of the men like them around. If their father hears of anything untoward happening he'll stop them from coming. *We* might like that, but I doubt *they* would.'

'Why do you stay at Corvus Hall?' I said. 'There are other anatomy schools.'

'That's an easy enough question to answer,' said Squires. 'The fees are lower than at other schools. And Dr Crowe is the best. The very best. So is Cruikshank. But we learn our anatomy and surgery and we get out. We get out as fast as we can.'

Precognition for the murder of Mary Anderson,
18th December 1830.

Statement of JAMES WILSON, constable.

19th December 1830

On the evening of 18th inst. I was called to Tanner's Lodgings
on the Cowgate at approx. 10 o'clock, having heard reports of a
disturbance in one of the houses. I understood that there was some
to-do with the surgeons, who were close by that part of the town.
As I approached I saw that a crowd had gathered at the foot of
Robertson's Close. I could hear a wailing and lamentation above
the muttering of the crowd. The door to the ground floor house of
Tanner's Lodgings was open, the cripple woman Clenchie Kate
lay weeping on the threshold. I asked a man what had occurred.
He replied 'Thrawn-Leggit Mary is dead. The surgeons have
killed her.'

Since the trial of Burke and Hare any unexpected death in that part of the town is deemed murder and blamed upon the surgeons, so I took what he said with a pinch of salt. I knew the woman Mary Anderson by repute and by sight. I had heard that she was in the family way and could not be expected to live through it. If she were dead, therefore, I reasoned that it may well have occurred in the natural manner of things. But however she had met her end it was clear that the surgeons had wasted no time in claiming her for their own, for I was told that they had taken her body already.

I went inside Tanner's Lodgings. The building is a part of a teeming midden of rooms and dwellings, and there were a number of people inside the dead girl's house, neighbours who had come to gawk and gape. I chased them out. The other constable had not yet arrived, but I looked about the place as best I could, given how dark it was, and my lantern not the best. I saw the stain from the blood on the floor, and on the mattress. I looked beneath the mattress, and beneath the slats that covered the bed frame, and it was there that I found the knife. I took it in my handkerchief and put it into my satchel. At length, two more constables arrived, and I was able to leave them there so that I might go up to see the girl's corpse.

I arrived at Surgeons' Square to find the place in darkness. I went straight to Surgeons' Hall, for I could see a light on in one of the windows. The door was opened by Dr Wragg, a known intimate of the resurrectionists and a more dubious-looking fellow it is hard to imagine. I asked to see Dr Cruikshank, or Dr Strangeway, or indeed, any of the gentlemen who had recently been down in the house of Thrawn-Leggit Mary. I said also that I knew they had the body and that I would like to see it.

Dr Wragg led me down a narrow flight of stairs, and then out into what seemed to be the back of the building. It was dark and cold, and he carried only a candle so there was precious little light to see by. We passed all manner of cases displaying all sorts of objects, and what with the darkness and the horror of it I wished I had waited for the other constable. Dr Wragg took me through to a room. It was long and dimly lit and laid out with tables. There were bodies upon four of them, mercifully shrouded and in the shadows, though the smell of the place was enough to make any man sick, for it was the smell of the grave. Ahead of us, three men were gathered about the last of the tables, a lantern on a hook above their heads. A fourth was standing to one side, half in the shadows. I recognised him as Dr Strangeway.

'Sirs.' Dr Wragg's voice was loud in the silence, for the men were bent close over their subject, their voices low as they worked.

'What is it, Wragg?' said Dr Cruikshank. The other two were unknown to me. By their youthful looks I took them to be students.

They all put down their knives and stepped back from their work when they heard I was the constable. Their fingers were bloody. 'Forgive me, Constable, if I do not shake your hand,' said Dr Cruikshank. His manner was casual, almost indifferent.

On the table to one side was a heap of crumpled fabric, green silk, heavily blood stained, and a mass of a grey linen, also blood stained, which I took to be her under things. The girl herself lay naked on the table, her skin white in the lamplight and scarlet from where they had cut her open. I stepped closer. I saw the legs twisted most horribly, a great bloody gash across her body. I saw her hair, tangled and dark, and her skin like marble. And then I saw her face.

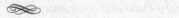

When I came to, I was lying in a dark corner on one of the dissecting tables. Dr Wragg was standing over me, a bottle of salts in his hand. The others were back at their work. He told me

that they were conducting a post-mortem and would present it to the procurator-fiscal in the morning.

I told him I must speak with Dr Cruikshank, for he was also the police surgeon, and although he might be permitted to undertake a post-mortem the other young gentlemen should absent themselves from what was the body of a murder victim, and not a corpse upon which they might practise their skills with the knife. At that, he nodded, and sent the two young men from the room. They both glared at me as they went, though they made no objection.

When Dr Cruikshank came to me I handed him the fold of canvas from inside my satchel. Wrapped within was a blade. 'I found this beneath the bed,' I said. 'Hard up against the wall, as if it had slipped down by mistake.'

He looked at it closely in the lantern light, turning it in his hands and running his fingers over the handle. He told me that it was a surgical knife. 'It makes a clean and speedy incision,' he said. 'The handle long for a firm grip, the blade short for a controlled cut. It is the very best sort for a job such as this.'

'What job?' I said.

'For slitting the belly from top to bottom,' he replied. 'The incision is neat, controlled, shallow.' He drew his finger down my body, from the middle of my chest to the buttons on my britches. But it was not her body that had so unmanned me.

'And her face?' I said to him. 'What manner of blade did that?'

He did not reply.

True on soul and conscience,

[Signed] James Wilson, police constable

178

Chapter Fourteen

⁓

The next day I went back up to the Hall. I hoped I might speak to Dr Strangeway about his years in Edinburgh, for he seemed the most likely to talk and I was becoming convinced there was something about their shared past in that city that bound them together. I was met at the door to the wax modelling studio by Sorrow Crowe. She kept her eyes downcast, their fish-scale iridescence hidden. She told me their uncle was at work in his room at the back. 'He does not let anyone in when he is working,' she said.

'Who is it, my dear?' It was Lilith's voice.

'Mr Flockhart.'

'Is he alone?'

'Yes.' I wondered how she knew.

Inside, Silence and Lilith Crowe was standing in the light from the tall north windows. Seated before them on a straight-backed chair was a fat woman in a dirty shift. She sat with her hands in her lap, a cat sleeping on the table top by her right elbow. A cape of waxed canvas had been placed over her shoulders through which her head poked. Her face was smothered in a thick layer of white plaster. There were two tubes pushed up her nose so that she might breathe, and a narrow one projecting from her mouth.

'You find us making a moulage,' said Sorrow.

'A mask,' said Silence. She looked up at me, and smiled. 'Perhaps we should do you too, Mr Flockhart.' Her voice was low. I liked it, though it was not like other voices. She could not hear how she was supposed to sound, and so the edges of her words were blurred and ill formed.

'They are usually done from the dead, are they not?' I said.

'Usually,' replied Sorrow, who of course heard everything. 'But not always. We have a technique. Sister, are we ready?'

Silence Crowe moved quickly, her hands working around the woman's head, a knife in her hand wielded with practised familiarity. There was a cracking sound and the whole mass of plaster came away. The woman beneath was covered in some sort of grease, I assumed so that the plaster did not stick to her face. She was quite hideous to look at. The scabs upon her head were crimson and painful-looking, her scalp almost completely without hair. She put up a hand to scratch at them as the plaster came away. The bridge of her nose had corroded, the bones beneath eaten away by syphilis, so that she had a melted sunken appearance. She opened her eyes, red-rimmed and cunning, and regarded me balefully.

'Mrs Roseplucker,' I said. 'I see you are not looking your best, ma'am.'

'I am not, sir,' she replied. 'But I am not dead yet so all is well. I came up to Corvus Hall to make the acquaintance of the young medical men. Ain't it a pleasure to have them back in the neighbourhood?' She grinned horribly. 'I've served the medical men all my life. I'll die doin' it too!'

'You have returned to Wicke Street?'

'I have, Mr Flock'art, me *and* my girls.'

'Ah, yes,' I said. 'The Home for Girls of an Energetic Disposition.'

'You remember us, sir! How kind! I'm sure we'll be back in Bartleby's *Book of London Pleasures* before you know it. It's not so far for the young medical men to come, and come they will, sir. They always do. You want to pay us a call. You and your virgin friend. Mr Quartermain, wasn't it? *I* can help him with that, sir—'

'I'm afraid you are a poor advertisement for your House, madam,' I said. 'Looking as you do.'

'Well I am when I'm like *this*,' she retorted. 'Where's my dress? Where's my 'at and my veil? My wig's the best in London!'

She reached behind her and seized what I had thought was a sleeping cat, and crushed it onto her head. The brindled ringlets danced about her ears. I saw her wince as the rough weave of the horsehair grazed her scabby scalp. I plunged a hand into my satchel.

'Take this salve, madam. Zinc, calendula, borage, chickweed, lavender. It will help the itch a little, soften the skin, and soothe the wounds.'

She leaned forward and snatched it from my grasp with her usual graciousness. 'Not that there's anyone in this room what's perfect, *Mr* Jem.' She sat back and sniffed at the salve, regarding me through narrowed eyes. '*They* know,' she added, pointing to the sisters. 'They know about *you*.'

'I'm sorry to see you have fallen on hard times,' I said, choosing to ignore her remark.

'Times is always hard,' she replied. 'But now this place has opened up again who knows what might happen?'

'Yes,' I said. 'Who knows?'

'I've already had some young men stop by, but it'd be nice to have some more. I came up here in my Sunday best to meet the lovely young gentlemen and these ladies saw me at the gates and asked if they might make a model of me. Of my face. Three guineas, sir!' She laughed, a grating sound, rough and hollow, like the opening of an iron coffin. 'I always said my face was my fortune.'

'It most certainly is, ma'am,' I said.

'Pity you can't say the same about yours!' She laughed again. I grinned. I was glad to see her so merry. The last time we had met she had been angry and discouraged, forced to move away from her usual haunts about St Saviour's Street and take up residence near the docks. She turned to the sisters, who had carried the mould to their workbench and were heating up a mixture on the stove top. They no longer seemed interested in either of us. The smell of hot wax filled the air. 'Perhaps I might have one for my own, miss,' she called out. 'For a present, like. Mr Jobber would be *so* pleased.'

I asked after Annie, one of Mrs Roseplucker's most long serving 'virgins' and Mr Jobber, a great dolt of a man who knew the cost of every gentleman's requirements and would fling them out into the street with their trousers about their ankles if they outstayed their welcome. 'Both still with me, sir,' she said, 'and often askin' after you and dear Mr Quartermain. Our Annie's grown up to be quite the beauty.'

'Still a virgin?' I asked.

'Oh, it makes the poor girl weep, sir. She 'as that many suitors I can't hardly keep up but not a single one will do for our Annie. Choosy, sir, that's what she is. As for poor Mr Jobber, that dear lamb, why, he almost wept with joy once he seed we was goin' back to our old place.'

Mrs Roseplucker vanished behind a screen. When she re-emerged she was battened into an ancient dress of watered silk the colour of ox blood. It was scabbed with repairs, some neat, some not, though the festoons of ragged lace that hung from her skirts did much to conceal the worst of them.

Sorrow and Silence went about their work at the far end of the room. Once they had what they wanted they appeared unconcerned with chaperoning their guest from the building. I wondered where Dr Strangeway was – they seemed not to need him for anything, and I could see Lilith bent over the workbench, her face close to a crimson mass of wax, a scalpel in her hand. She appeared hardly to have noticed that I was there. Mrs Roseplucker adjusted her wig, and crammed a large circular bonnet mounded with artificial roses on top of it. She fixed the whole teetering mass onto her head with a length of black lace, tied in a bow beneath her pudgy chin.

'Oh!' she said, suddenly catching sight of a waxen face hanging on the wall. It was another moulage showing the effects of syphilis. 'There's Maria Taylor! Used to work out of a house down on Blackcock Lane. Dead now, o' course. And there's old Mother Spendlove,' she cried, pointing to another. 'Why, I've not seen her these last ten years or more. We was girls together, she and I, back in Prior's Rents – a long time ago now. Beautiful girl she was, though not like me. I were always the favourite. She got the pox quite early on, whereas I've kept my looks.' Mrs Roseplucker nodded at the moulage. 'See? Not that it stopped her. Funny to see them here, ain't it?'

I could not reply. I hoped never to see my youthful acquaintances immortalised in a gallery of syphilitic faces. Mrs Roseplucker pocketed the money the sisters had left for her on the table. 'Will you allow me to escort you from the building, ma'am?' I said. I offered her my arm. 'Have you had many medical men coming to Wicke Street?'

Mrs Roseplucker pressed her lips together in a thin line. 'That's private, Mr Flockhart,' she said. 'I can't be telling all and sundry what gentlemen visits my girls!'

'A florin says you can.' I tossed her a coin. She snatched it from the air with grubby fingers. 'Couple o' the young ones 'ave been. I've taken to selling sheathes,' she added conversationally. 'For them what wants 'em. The young men know all about the pox,' she added. 'So they likes to look out for themselves. Can't say I blame them.'

'Names, madam,' I said. 'Can you give me any names?'

'They don't tell me who they are, Mr Jem. You knows that. Though there is one I recognise.'

'Who? Is he from Corvus Hall?'

'Course he is,' she said. 'He's the master!'

'Dr Crowe?' I said. 'Are you sure?'

'You ask our Annie.'

'I'm asking you.' I gave her another coin. 'Get on with it.'

'Not much to tell. He came some weeks ago for the first time. Wanted to see the girls – not that I've got many at the moment. Chose our Annie. She said he's transfixed by 'er back. You know she got that arse what sticks out.

Apparently there's a name for it. Can't think what. Lord something or other – trust our Annie to 'ave a deformity what 'as an aristocratic name!'

'Lumbar lordosis,' I said.

'That's it. He likes spines. So he said.'

'And?'

'And so he said he wanted a girl with an interesting spine and that's where our Annie came in. Then he made her wear a green dress he'd brought. Had it made special, he said, though Annie said it's that old fashioned she looks a complete fright in it.'

'And?'

'And so she wears it when he comes a-calling. Green dress and blue shawl. Silk! But she has to cover her face when he's doing his business. He don't actually want to see it's her. She don't mind. She's had worse and he pays well enough.' She sounded approving. 'Wish they was all as easy to manage for he ain't no bother.'

I had no idea what to make of it, and yet at the same time I felt guilty – who was I to tittle-tattle with a brothel owner about her clients' proclivities? I gave her another shilling and sent her on her way.

Chapter Fifteen

The following morning I was awakened by a persistent banging on the apothecary door. I was still groggy with sleep as I pulled it open and found Mrs Speedicut standing there. Her eyes were staring, her small mouth open in a wheezing 'o' as she tried to get her breath. She wore neither cap nor coat and had evidently run all the way. I took her by the elbow and ushered her inside. It was barely five o'clock – she would have just started her morning shift at Corvus Hall. I tried to make her sit down at the apothecary table but she would not.

'Oh, Mr Jem,' she said, wringing her hands. 'Oh, that I should see such a sight!' I poured her a cup of coffee, for the pot on the stove was still warm, and slopped a generous measure of gin into it. 'Now,' I said, shoving the cup into her hands. 'What is it?'

'It's him.' She took a noisy gulp. 'Dead!'

'Who?'

'I don't know, sir. I only saw his feet, the soles of his

boots. Oh, I can't go back there. I can't! Not this morning.' I saw her gaze slither over to look at the gin bottle and the armchair.

'You may stay here,' I said. 'For now.' Gabriel and Jenny had appeared and were looking at Mrs Speedicut in bleary surprise. 'Make sure she doesn't drink all of this,' I said, handing the gin to Jenny. 'Hide it. And find her some work to do.'

I took up my hat and coat and shouted for Will, who was already dressed and half way down the stairs. Two minutes later we were out of the door and heading towards St Saviour's Street.

'What is it?' said Will. 'Did she say it was a body?'

'Yes. More or less. But I don't know whose it is. Do you have your keys?'

In the event we did not need them, for Mrs Speedicut, the first to arrive that morning and also the first to leave, had raced out into the cold morning leaving the door ajar. There was no one else about. The hall remained unswept from the night before – the woman evidently too lazy to do it when it was supposed to be done. I was not surprised. I had been acquainted with her all my life and knew her for a lazy slattern. The place was in darkness, for it was too early for the dawn to give us any light and the only illumination came from the lantern Mrs Speedicut had brought through from the scullery. She had left it on the porter's chair, the flickering candle causing shadows to leap like demons about the walls. The two twisted skeletons so beloved by Dr Crowe grinned down at us from their glinting glass case, their bones parchment-yellow. Mrs Speedicut's broom lay abandoned in the middle of the hall, her mop and bucket flung to one side. From where we stood at the foot of the stairs we could see nothing. There was no body, nor any sign that there had ever been one.

'It's all in her imagination,' said Will. His voice was loud and echoing in the dark. 'I'm hardly surprised. This place is enough to give anyone the frights – especially at this time in the morning. Come on, Jem. There'll be a fresh pot of coffee ready by now and we can pick up a warm loaf from—'

'When I asked who it was she said she didn't know. She said she could only see his feet. "Only the soles of his boots."' All at once I caught a whiff of bowels upon the air, and my boot slipped on something wet. I looked down, and saw a pool of liquid. Beside it, a rag, stained with blood. And then I looked up.

I remembered how Will had once admired the whorl of the stairs, the way they curved elegantly upwards towards the luminous cupola at the top. Now, that graceful sweep of polished wood framed the body of a hanged man.

We took the stairs two at a time. I saw the threadbare coat, the collar high at the neck, the grubby shirt and neckerchief. The face above it was purple and swollen, the tongue a black protruding mass. The eyes bulged, scarlet with congested blood. The rope that held him was tied to the banister.

'We must cut him down,' I said.

'But what about the police? Surely this time—'

'I must examine him, preferably before anyone else does, since I seem to be the only person willing to admit that something is amiss at Corvus Hall. Besides, we cannot just leave him.'

'Who would do this?' said Will. He could not take his eyes off the dead man's face. 'Is it possible that he did it himself?'

'It *is* possible. But I think it is not probable. I didn't know Dr Wragg, but what I saw of him does not lead me to think of him as a man who would take his own life. He was an old man, he was doing what he most loved, what he had done all his life. Why would he kill himself? And in so public a way too.' And yet, I thought, the alternative was murder. Dr Wragg led a solitary life, from what I could make out. What might he have done to provoke such hatred in someone else that they were prepared to kill him – and in so brutal a way too? But I would have a clearer idea of what had happened if I were able to look at him.

The body did not weigh as much as I had expected, though it was cumbersome and we struggled to draw it up and over the banister.

'Should we call Dr Crowe?' gasped Will. 'He will be in his own wing of the building, surely. Perhaps he saw or heard something?'

'Unless Dr Crowe is the murderer,' I said. 'Though I admit that seems unlikely, given how many years the two men have worked together.'

'Besides, surely a small man like Dr Crowe would not have the strength to overpower another, wrestle him into a prepared noose and toss him into the abyss.'

'That's true enough,' I replied. 'And yet anyone might have the strength for such an undertaking if they plan it well and if they're determined.'

At that moment I heard a door open, and quiet footsteps came along the passage at the top of the house. We turned, both of us, Dr Wragg's body half draped between us across the banister. A face, white and textured, emerged out of the gloom. When he saw us he stopped dead. He put out a hand, to steady himself against the wall, as if he feared he might be about to faint.

'Dr Strangeway,' I whispered. 'Help us! Please, sir!'

We laid Dr Wragg down on the floor. He appeared to be wearing the clothes of a much stockier man, his body layered with shirts and waistcoats so that he was greatly padded, perhaps against the cold. It was as if the burly, muscular man he had once been had wasted away to nothing but skin and bone, so that he was, in death, a little old man in a suit of clothes made to fit his former self.

Dr Strangeway bent down, his fingers quick about the body. 'The hand,' he whispered. 'The hand, and the face. Are they . . . are they—?' He fumbled at Dr Wragg's sleeve. 'Thank God,' and turned the head slightly so that he could see the face. 'Oh, thank God! Thank God!'

I pulled at the noose, eventually managing to loosen the rope enough to get it over the poor man's head. 'He is long dead,' I said. 'See how the rope has cut into the neck? How the face is livid, the body stiff?'

'Who would do such a thing?' said Will.

'We must take him downstairs,' I said. 'The porter will be in soon, and then the place will start to wake up. The constable must be called—'

'The constable?' said Dr Strangeway. 'But surely—'

'He *must* be summoned, sir,' I replied. 'There is no alternative. Perhaps you could tell Dr Crowe too. Quickly now,' I said to Will as Dr Strangeway hurried away into the dark. 'We have very little time.'

We bundled up the body and carried it down the stairs, across the vestibule and along the passage to the dissecting room. Will lit another lantern and brought it over to the table.

'I can tell very little,' I said, poring over Dr Wragg's body, 'without seeing him unclothed and in full light, but we must do the best we can.' I saw that the rope had burned the skin at his neck, the wrinkled flesh rubbed red and bloody.

Will looked away. 'The face,' he said. 'I cannot bear to look. The poor fellow!'

I rummaged my hands through his clothes. A pocket book containing a few shillings, a ball of wax, a piece of lower vertebra, yellow and shining, as if he had kept it in his pocket for years, worrying at it with his thumb and finger. Other than that there was nothing. I looked at his hands. They were stained with tobacco, the fingernails grubby, but there was no sign of violence, no skinned knuckles or broken nails. Whatever had happened to Angus Wragg had taken him unawares.

'There is a bruise here,' I said. 'Against the temple. It may very well have occurred as he fell, or it may have happened before that. Perhaps he was knocked unconscious and then the rope tied about his neck. It would allow a weak man, or a woman, to hang him – I can't see how anyone would manage it otherwise.' I pulled my magnifying glass from my satchel, and peered through it at the old man's neck. 'It's hard to say,' I whispered. 'But I think there is something—' I took out my tweezers and a sheet of paper. Behind us, I could hear the building awakening. They had taken longer than I had expected – had Dr Strangeway really gone straight to Dr Crowe as I had asked? I could hear voices and footsteps. I turned my attention to the task in hand, plucking two thin blue strands from the damp raw skin of the old man's neck. I folded them up in the paper and slipped it into my pocket.

'What is it?' said Will.

'I'm not sure,' I said. 'But I think there is a chance that Dr Wragg was strangled – by something other than a rope. I found the same strands on the raw flesh at Wilson's neck.' I slipped my magnifying glass away as the doors flew open. 'But that is between you and me.'

'I heard. Is it – it can't be—' with rapid strides Dr Crowe crossed to the dissecting table. He stopped before the body, his face anguished. His eyes filled with tears. 'Oh, my poor dear friend. You should have come to me. I would have helped you.' He took the old man's hand.

'It is either self murder,' I said. 'Or—'

'Or what?' said Dr Crowe sharply. 'Dr Wragg had cancer. He had told only me and Dr Cruikshank. We tried to help him as best we could. We operated. But we could not stop it.' He shrugged. 'He was an old man, and in a great deal of pain. There was nothing more we could do for him.'

'Opiates?' I said.

'In heroic quantities and for many years. It may well have altered the balance of his mind. And Dr Wragg had long since stopped believing in God, so that would not have stopped him from taking his own life if he chose to. I have no doubt he found he was no longer able to bear the pain.' He released Dr Wragg's hand. 'He often spoke of taking his own life, though I never expected him to do so. And so there will be no talk of murder, if you please. And now,' he took a deep breath, 'if I could be alone with him for a moment.'

'The constable must be called—'

'I have sent a boy for him.'

Lilith, Sorrow and Silence entered the dissecting room. Dr Crowe motioned them closer. 'Oh, but sir,' said Will. 'Is he really a sight for . . . for ladies?'

'My daughters are strong in spirit, Mr Quartermain. They have seen enough of the dead not to fear them.'

The three women glided closer, their faces expressionless. We moved away, leaving Dr Crowe and his daughters standing for a moment over the body of their old friend.

∞

The door to the dissecting room was locked by Dr Crowe until the constable came. Will and I went upstairs to Will's room above the anatomy museum. 'Suicide?' he said.

'It's possible. No doubt Dr Crowe believes it.'

'Unless it was he who killed the fellow,' said Will. 'But what did you find?'

'I need your microscope.'

There was evidence that Halliday had been working late. His desk was busy with papers and books, a box of microscope slides, a bottle of iodine and a spleen floating in a glass jar. I was glad he was not in yet; for all that I liked the fellow I did not want him privy to our conversation. I took the fold of paper from my pocket. The fibres I had plucked from Dr Wragg's neck were almost invisible to the eye, and I was concerned in case they blew away. I held my breath, peering through my magnifying glass, my tweezers poised. At first I thought I had lost them, but there they were. One. Two. No more than mere hairs. I bade Will find a clear slide for the microscope and then we were ready. I hardly knew what they would tell me, only that looking at their colour, the shape of the fibres close-up might tell me more than I might learn with my magnifying glass. I adjusted the focus, the great brass eyepiece moving down, trained on the slide below. The fibres were smooth, a deep sky blue, though darker toward one end where they had absorbed some of the blood and fluid from Dr Wragg's neck. Silk? I was sure I had seen something of blue silk recently but I could not place it. I let Will take a look.

'You think he was throttled by something other than the rope that hanged him?'

'Yes. A scarf or a shawl, perhaps. The flimsy sort women wear sometimes.'

'You think a woman did this?'

'I think it was a woman's scarf. I don't say it was a woman who did the throttling, though it is not impossible by any means. There were no abrasions to the throat, no claw marks, which is what one might expect if he was conscious when he was attacked. So we might assume that he was *not* conscious – you saw the bruise to his temple – in which case either a man or a woman might have the strength to hang him.'

'Then why throttle him at all? Why not just hang him?'

'And if it was only throttling that was required then why hang him too?'

'To make sure he was dead?'

'Possibly. Perhaps to make it look like suicide. Perhaps the strangling was necessary to the perpetrator, but the hanging was done to conceal the murder. Certainly with suicide the police don't bother themselves to look for the culprit. As for the body of Wilson – and yes, I am sure it is him, as he is the only one missing who had been whitewashing the dissecting room – there was enough evidence about the neck to see that the muscles were bruised, the windpipe crushed even though the flesh of the head and throat had been removed. Ritual strangulation, therefore, may be common to both. I found the same blue silken threads on Wilson's neck as on Wragg's. And "ritual" is the correct word to use too, under the circumstances. Both deaths, both murders, for that is what they are – were carried out by the same hand or hands—'

'Speaking of hands,' said Will, 'if this were the same perpetrator then surely the right hand would be missing and the face sliced away.'

'And yet it is not.'

'Exactly.'

'There is time enough yet.'

'Do you have any idea who?'

I shook my head. 'Not yet. And it is a wily adversary that would dress up a murder as suicide. Besides, if Dr Wragg wished to kill himself he needed only to take an overdose of laudanum. It does not make sense for him to hang himself. What medical man would choose such a death?'

'Perhaps he ran out of laudanum and was overcome with pain,' said Will. 'Perhaps the laudanum he *had* taken put him not in his right mind?'

'It's possible,' I said.

'And besides, those fibres might have arrived there by some other means. It does not necessarily mean he was throttled by a silk scarf before he was hanged.'

'Also possible,' I said. 'And you are right, we must not jump to conclusions.'

Outside the night had grown pale and watery, a reluctant dawn leaching in from the east. I knew it would be a dark day, a day when lamps and fires smouldered continually, trying to add light and warmth but only contributing to the thickness of the dark and, by nightfall, the inevitable choking pall of fog.

'Let's take a look in Dr Wragg's accommodation,' I said. 'Before the constable comes, for he is bound to do the same.'

❧

Dr Wragg's room seemed more forlorn than ever now that he was not in it. The stove was cold, the room icy. My breath bloomed in the air before me.

'How did he bear it here?' said Will, looking about. 'And what a paltry reward this little attic is for all his years of work.'

I was wondering the same thing, though I had the feeling that Dr Wragg had wanted no more from life than what he had ended up with.

The room was no different to the last time I had seen it: untidy, with a miscellany of bottles and books lining the shelves, the bed rumpled, the workbench scattered with all the accoutrements of anatomical preservation. I spied a ledger showing which specimens he had prepared for which students. The last name in it was Wilson's, dated some three days ago, but I could see nothing that might tell us what had happened last night, or why. There was a pen and an open inkstand on the desk. Beside it, a sheet of yellowed paper bore a dozen or so scribbled words. He had started writing a note to Dr Crowe, though he had got little further than the name and date – the previous night at ten o'clock. Had something – someone – disturbed him? '*The matter is now urgent. We have in our midst—*' What was he referring to? An imposter? A murderer? Had he discovered something? Someone? Was that why he had died?

An empty bottle of laudanum rolled beneath the bed, another, half full, stood upon the wash stand. A large heavy book lay open on the floor beside the desk. There were books everywhere, but this one seemed out of place. It was a Bible. And yet Dr Crowe said that Dr Wragg had long since put aside any religious convictions. Why would Dr Wragg be looking through a Bible? I picked it up. The name inside the cover was J. H. Franklyn, beneath this were the words *Surgeons' Hall, Edinburgh, 1830*. One passage had been underlined – recently, it seemed, for the ink was quite fresh – Deuteronomy, chapter 32, verse 35. *'To me belongeth vengeance and recompense; their foot shall slide in due time, for the day of their calamity is at hand, and the things that shall come upon them make haste.'*

Something crunched beneath the heel of my boot. I bent down and picked up what looked like a broken tooth, embedded in some sort of dark wood.

'What is it?' said Will.

'It's a part of Dr Wragg's dentures,' I said after a moment. I slipped the bizarre relic into my pocket. 'I think it more than likely that he was murdered here and then dragged out onto the stairs.'

Two murders. And yet what could Dr Wragg possibly have in common with Wilson? A young uninspiring medical student and an old man at the tail end of an inauspicious career. I could not figure it out.

❧

Downstairs the constable had arrived. Dr Crowe was explaining about Dr Wragg's cancer, and the man was nodding and writing slowly and methodically in his notebook. He looked worried, staring around at the surroundings – a display cabinet of monkey skulls, the skeletons of an ostrich and a flamingo – as if he expected them to burst into life and start dancing and squawking before him. The pair of twisted skeletons stared down at him, their spines snaking, their legs tangled, their jaws wide and cackling. Sorrow and Silence were standing beneath the wall clock, their faces impassive, Sorrow with eyes fixed upon the opposite wall, her dead pupils cloudy and pale beneath half-closed lids. She seemed tense, as if alert to every sound, every whispered word, every footstep, smell or touch. Silence was watching the constable. When she saw me, she smiled, her face lighting up. The sisters were more beautiful than ever that morning, their pallor accentuated by the darkness and by the crimson inkiness of their lips, their black silken hair, the jet droplets they wore at their ears shining like beetles. Skinner appeared, along with the head porter. Bullseye whined and pulled on a leash at his side. Dr Cruikshank was there too now, though he had clearly not had time to attend to his toilet – something I assumed was a protracted and elaborate affair – for he was looking pale and haggard. His hair was wild and stringy, his rings, jewels and frothing neckerchief all absent. Instead he appeared to have flung on anything that came to hand. He was looking at Lilith, who stood beside her father with her hand upon his arm, his expression a mixture of longing and sorrow. But when he saw that I was observing him he frowned and looked away.

'And you, sir,' the constable addressed me. 'Dr Crowe says it was you who found the body.'

'Not exactly,' I said. I told him that the housekeeper at Corvus Hall was well known to me, that she had come across Dr Wragg and had run to fetch me for fear of what else to do, and in case the gentleman was still alive. 'She is a simple woman, sir,' I said. 'She only did as she thought best.'

The constable seemed quite happy to accept the fact that anyone might wish to flee from the Hall, especially on discovering a corpse dangling from the banisters. I could hardly blame him. 'Well.' He licked his lips. 'That seems to be that.' It turned out he had already viewed the body, and had accepted Dr Crowe's argument that Dr Wragg had taken his own life. He said he would present that conclusion to the magistrate, though it would be wise to have a post-mortem. It was quite clear that he too could not wait to get away from the place.

❧❧

Dr Wragg was left in the dissecting room for the next few hours, the door locked. It was a Sunday, so there were no classes and few students about. No one had any cause to go in and view the body – no one, that is, until Halliday came in sometime after 10 o'clock. I was upstairs with Will when Halliday appeared. He looked pleased to see us, but when he saw our faces his smile of welcome stalled. We told him Dr Wragg was dead and his face sagged in sorrow and surprise. 'I cannot believe it,' he said. 'I was talking to him only yesterday. He seemed quite well. A little belligerent, but that was his way. He cannot be dead! How? And when? May I see him?' His questions tumbled out in confusion. 'Killed himself, you say? Oh, the poor old fellow.' He pulled out a handkerchief and dabbed his eyes.

'His appearance . . . It is no way to remember him,' said Will. 'He does not look like the man you knew. Not now.'

'I would like to have a few moments.' Halliday's face

was crimson. 'I had no idea,' he said. 'I knew he was ill. And I confess I had . . . I had seen the laudanum bottles. And yet this? If I had known I would have let him have his own way, would have allowed him to continue with his old-fashioned arrangement of the specimens.'

We went downstairs together. Dr Crowe was in the vestibule talking to Skinner. He looked up as he heard us on the stairs. 'Halliday, my dear fellow—' he could tell by the look on Halliday's face that he had heard the news. 'Come now,' he patted the younger man's arm. 'Pay your respects, my dear boy, and then come and sit with us for a while. Lilith would be glad to see you. And there is something I would like to ask you.'

Halliday nodded, his face pink with emotion. For all that he had argued with Dr Wragg he seemed genuinely affected by the old man's death. He vanished down the passage towards the dissecting room. He was not gone more than two minutes when there was a cry. A door banged and he reappeared again, his face ashen.

'My God,' he said. His knees seemed to buckle beneath him and he steadied himself against the wall. 'My God—!'

I ran down the passage, Halliday, Will and Dr Crowe at my back as I burst into the dissecting room. Dr Wragg's body was where we had left it, and yet I could hardly believe what I saw. How had it happened? The door had been locked! With my own eyes I had seen Dr Crowe turn the key and put it in his pocket. And yet somehow, someone had been there. The winding sheet had been thrown back, the corpse exposed for all to see. The right hand had been cut from the wrist – not a clean, meticulous dismemberment but a crude, hasty butchery. The hand had gone. And the face – that was gone too.

Face

What assumptions we make about beauty, about ugliness. Those with regular, symmetrical features are assumed to be beautiful inside as well as out. Misshapen features or blighted skin are deemed ugly, as if what we see on the outside is the manifestation of some inner darkness. But what lies beneath this superficial layer of flesh by which we set so much store? Blood, sinew, tissue. Strip all that away too and there is the skull, the image of death itself – and in death are we not all equal?

Like many anatomists I am skilled at the removal of the skin of the face. How else might students see for themselves what lies beneath – what muscles might be afflicted by palsy, by what mechanisms the eyes blink, the jaw move or the lips work? It is not an easy undertaking. It requires dexterity and patience, and a gentle, some might say feminine, touch with the knife. Zygomaticus major, zygomaticus minor, corrugator supercilii, orbicularis oculi – *mouth, forehead, eye – all of us*

201

have them, layers of muscle lying in shining perfection just beneath the surface. They are essential to the expression of emotion, and is it not emotion that makes us human, emotion that lies at the very centre and soul of our being?

And yet there are those who believe that it is physiognomy, the study of the expressions and arrangement of the face, which tells the truth about who we are. It is evident in the low brow of the felon, the close-set eyes of the delinquent, the thin lips of the deceiver.

I look in the mirror and what do I see? I, who can slice off a face with such delicacy and precision, but can do nothing to cut away the signs of my own wickedness. I see high cheek bones, a proud nose and full lips. But I have read Lavater's essays on physiognomy and I know these features betoken only cruelty, jealousy and a thirst for vengeance.

Chapter Sixteen

Dr Graves came up from St Saviour's. Dr Crowe suggested him. For all that we were in an anatomy school it seemed appropriate for Dr Wragg's post-mortem to be conducted by someone who was not associated with the place. Dr Graves arrived on his corpse wagon – a boxed cart designed to carry bodies back to his lair at the new large St Saviour's which had been built on the other side of the river. At first he wished to remove Dr Wragg's body from Corvus Hall, but Dr Crowe and Dr Cruikshank refused to allow it. He offered them three guineas, 'the going rate' he said, 'for the average workhouse corpse'. He looked down at Dr Wragg's body. 'Mind you,' he said. 'It's minus a hand and a face, and being so old it's hardly worth the price. Come, sirs, three guineas is most generous. What do you say?'

'I say "no",' said Dr Crowe. 'Gloag!' He summoned the hunchback from the sluice room. 'See that Dr Graves has all he requires. And might I advise an assistant, sir?

Mr Flockhart, perhaps you could oblige us? As former apothecary to St Saviour's you know Dr Graves and his *methods*.' He eyed Dr Graves with distrust. 'I'm sure you know your way about a corpse too.'

'Yes, sir,' I said. 'I've attended many a post-mortem – almost all of them undertaken by Dr Graves.'

As the doors closed Dr Graves pulled out his box of knives. From his coat pocket he produced a handkerchief, inside of which was a hardboiled egg. He proceeded to eat it, while looking down at the corpse and considering where to begin.

'Well, well,' he said, licking his fingers. He dusted wet flecks of egg from his lapels. 'At least we are in the best place for it. The light is good and there are no interruptions.' He looked at the stump where the hand had been severed. 'Rather hastily done,' he said. 'But a reasonable job nonetheless. Where is it?'

'I've no idea, sir,' I replied.

'Students?'

'I believe that is the opinion, sir.' I hardly knew what else to tell him. 'Have you seen anything like this before?' I ventured.

'A corpse, minus its face and right hand? No.' Dr Graves bent closer, running his eye over the crimson musculature of Dr Wragg's flayed cheeks. 'We can see a lot about Dr Wragg from what has been left exposed,' he said. He pointed to the cheeks. 'Beneath the skin tells us all we might wish to know of a man's personality, his life and cares. In the young we see little. They are a blank slate. Unformed clay yet to be written on or fashioned by life into something more inflexible.' He pointed with his knife at Dr Wragg's forehead. 'Scored deep into lines by a lifetime of frowns and disappointment. Had he hoped for more from life? See the jaw clenched tight – perhaps from physical pain? And the crow's feet – the result of years spent squinting at corpses in poor light. It is a face without happiness.' Dr Graves' face hovered intimately close to Dr Wragg's. 'I met this gentleman on a number of occasions. He was a man of few words and little mirth. It is all here. I could have described him to you even if I had not met him: severe, joy-less, frowning, squinting in the darkness, troubled by pain.' He sighed. 'What will they say about me, I wonder? Well then, Mr Flockhart, shall we see what else we can find?'

We removed the old man's clothes. It was some time since I had undressed a corpse and I had forgotten how heavy and unhelpful they were. Dr Graves proceeded methodically. He noted the marks of the rope at the neck, the way the larynx was crushed and squeezed. Death by strangulation, undoubtedly. I asked whether he was sure. 'Look at the neck, Flockhart,' he said. 'The fellow dangled from a rope under his own weight for goodness knows how long – hours, is my guess. Look at his face. His neck is broken too. All in all I would say that's rather conclusive, wouldn't you?'

'You see no other . . . no other fibres?' I said.

'Fibres?' He blinked. 'No.'

'And the bruise to his temple?'

'Sustained as he fell. Now, let us get on.' He took out another of his knives, and slit Dr Wragg's body from pubis to sternum. The skin, old and wrinkled as it was, parted silkily. A layer of yellow fat beneath the dermis oozed. At the abdomen, Dr Graves's knife pressed deeper. I saw the abdominal muscles glinting darkly, parting like lips beneath the blade.

Dr Crowe was quite correct. Dr Wragg had a tumour in his lung the size of a clenched fist. There were others in his liver and spleen. It was also quite clear that Dr Wragg was a long-term user of opium. His viscera smelled strongly of the stuff – something I had often noted in those who were addicted to opiates – and his bowels were badly costive.

'Perhaps we should allow the students in,' I said once we had finished. 'Dr Crowe said Dr Wragg's organs are to go to the students – if they want them. It was his wish, apparently.'

Dr Graves was packing the organs back into the body. He was engrossed, like a child with a jigsaw puzzle. I knew he had done such a job many hundreds of times, but he still seemed to delight in it. He held up Dr Wragg's diseased spleen. 'I like the spleen,' he said. He turned it in his hands. An ugly malignancy was visible on the underside. 'Can I keep it?' He pulled out his handkerchief, the one in which he had kept his boiled egg, and began wrapping up the spleen the way a cheesemonger might swathe a half pound of Wensleydale. He stuffed it into his pocket.

'Put that back, sir!' I said. 'You cannot keep it, it belongs to Dr Wragg.'

He laughed. 'You're in an anatomy school, Mr Flockhart. The dead own nothing here. Not even themselves. What right does Dr Wragg have to his body? He has no need for any of it now.'

'And you?'

'I can show my students. I have an interest in morbid anatomy. I can put it in my collection.'

'I cannot let you take a single part of him,' I said. 'Dr Wragg's body is for the students of Corvus Hall.' I was not sure why I was defending the man. I had spent much of my life amongst bodies, both living and dead, but all at once I could not bear the dismembering, the anatomising, the pulling into its constituent parts. No wonder public feeling ran high against the anatomy schools, despite the passing of the Act that guaranteed them a supply of corpses and rendered grave robbing unnecessary. No wonder so few medical men gave their own bodies to their colleagues. I knew the students would be no more respectful than Dr Graves, and yet would it not be more fitting if Dr Wragg's body and its malignant organs were bequeathed to his own anatomy museum?

Out of the corner of my eye I saw Gloag get up from the chair he had been sitting on. He crept forward menacingly. No doubt he had been instructed to wrestle any filched organs from Dr Graves if the occasion required it. He cracked his knuckles with a sound like a child emptying a bag of marbles. Dr Graves reluctantly slid the spleen back where it belonged. I heard a moist squelch as it slipped into place. 'Very well,' he said, his voice sulky. 'But Dr Wragg owes me a spleen, even if it's his own!'

'How so?' I washed my hands at the sluice. Dr Graves rubbed his on the winding sheet and began nibbling on another boiled egg. 'Years ago,' he said. 'I knew Wragg in Edinburgh. He was the curator of the anatomy museum at Surgeons' Hall. A prestigious appointment. "Bloody Wragg", the students used to call him as he always had a filthy cloth hanging from his belt—'

'They still do.'

He grunted. 'Well, I left Edinburgh some years before Dr Wragg did. But I remember him well enough.'

'What was he like?'

'As a man? Dishonest, through and through. As a

surgeon I have no idea. He'd given that up long ago. He spent a number of years in the army before he came back to Edinburgh. After that I think he preferred the dead – he's not alone in that. But there was one occasion I had a body – one that I'd dug up myself, mark you – that had a tumour just like this one.' He eyed the spleen longingly. 'It's unusual to see one this large. I was only a student, but I knew it was quite a find. Wragg took it, and put it in Surgeons' Hall museum. I was pleased to have made a contribution, until I saw that he had put his own name on it rather than mine.' Dr Graves scowled. 'He'd do anything for a choice exhibit, especially one he could claim as his own. When I asked him about it he just laughed. Said he was sure I'd have plenty more. As it happens I have not. Apart from, with some poetic justice,' he pointed at Dr Wragg's insides, 'that one there.'

'Is that all?' I said.

'Of course that's not all, though it gives you some idea of the kind of man he was. You'll know about Robert Knox, of course. Burke and Hare, et cetera, et cetera. Well, your Dr Wragg was no better. Anything for a corpse, for an organ, for something to show the students – they were hard to come by in those days, I can assure you, and without bodies there were no students and without students,' he raised his eyebrows, 'there was no income. No reputation. Wragg had friends – in high places and low. He was close to the anatomists – he was one of them after all. But he was closer still to the resurrectionists, to the hangman, to the sick and dying. He was notorious about the Old Town, appearing like the Reaper himself at the bedside of those too poor to expect anything else before they'd even drawn their last breath. What times they were.' He grinned. 'But exciting. You can't beat the thrill of a midnight dig in a graveyard. Of course, one has to be fast. There's a technique, you know. Burrow down to the box, break through the lid at the chest, get your hooks under the arms and heave! Lord, I was fast. But not as fast as Wragg. Nor as devious.'

'What about murder?' I said.

'To get a fresh corpse?' He laughed. 'I'd not put anything past this one. You know the old rhyme, of course? *Through the close and up the stair; but and ben wi' Burke and Hare. Burke's the butcher, Hare's the thief, And Knox the boy who buys the beef.* Well, Knox might have been "the boy who bought the beef", but I'll wager Wragg was a little closer to the source of the matter, as it were. Closer than anyone cared to mention. I thought he was going to be named when the West Port murders were all anyone could talk about and it seemed likely that a surgeon would have to step up and take at least some of the blame. But he got away with it. He always did.' He licked his lips, the half-eaten egg like an eyeball in his hand. 'Bloody Wragg – the name has many connotations, Mr Flockhart.'

At the moment there was a cry from outside in the corridor. 'Help! Help! Oh! Come quickly!'

I left Dr Graves and rushed out into the passage, relieved that there were still so few students about. Instead there was only Dr Crowe and Dr Cruikshank, who emerged from the lecture theatre together. Tanhauser and Squires appeared at the door of the common room, Halliday behind them with a book in his hand. On the staircase I saw Lilith Crowe and Dr Strangeway. All of them looked alarmed, unsure of where, exactly, the cries had hailed from.

'Help,' came the voice. 'Anyone!'

'Dear God, what is it now?' said Dr Crowe stepping forward, his face white.

'Help me!'

'Upstairs,' I said.

Sorrow Crowe stood at the door to the anatomy museum, her hands bloody. 'I can smell it,' she whispered. 'Meat. And blood. I put out my hands and felt the bone, the wet flesh. The rough skin, the web between thumb and finger, the stink of the dissecting room – it is Dr Wragg.' Her blind eyes stared at me, her expression a mask of fear.

'Where?'

'Here,' she said. 'Here on this door.'

I pulled her roughly away. Behind her, nailed to the double doors of the anatomy museum, was Dr Wragg's hand. The skin of the palm had been peeled back and skewed by pins, the flesh and bone supported in between, like a butterfly against a board. Between the first and second finger was a card, no bigger than a *carte de visité*, the words *et mortui sua arcana narrabunt* scrawled upon it in black ink. The writing was clumsy, as if written by a child, the card smeared with dark clots of blood.

I saw Dr Crowe and Dr Cruikshank exchange a glance. Lilith Crowe betrayed no emotion at all, but stood with her arms around her younger sister. Beside her, Dr Strangeway wrung his scarred hands. Silence had appeared, though I had not heard her coming. She joined her sisters, and they stood side by side, Silence scrutinising the ring of faces with as much determination as I, Sorrow with her eyes downcast. I knew she was listening to everything, that she knew the sound and smell of every one of us. She raised her head, her expression sharp, her eyes a glistening mother of pearl in the light that flooded in through the cupola. She stared straight at me. What had she sensed now?

'My God!' said a voice in my ear. 'What in heaven's name is going on here?' Halliday was standing directly behind me. His face was white. 'Another prank?' Behind him, Tanhauser and Squires gaped.

'At least there can be no doubt whose hand it is,' said Will, who had come down from his room in the eaves when he heard the commotion. There was a steady *drop, drop, drop* of blood from the severed end. More of the stuff had run down the door. I wondered where Dr Wragg's face was. Perhaps we would never find it.

'Someone take it down, for God's sake,' cried a voice. It was Dr Allardyce. I had not heard him come in – and yet he was always in. Will said he was sure the fellow slept in the attic. Certainly he seemed hardly ever to leave the place. I looked at Dr Crowe, who nodded.

'Please reunite Dr Wragg's hand with Dr Wragg's body,' he said with a sigh. 'Come, my dears,' he turned to his daughters, 'come away.'

I was tempted to ask Dr Crowe whether he still thought it was a student prank, but he had already gone, chivvying the others away. He understood something of what was going on, I was certain. Dr Cruikshank too – usually so noisy and opinionated – was quiet. He seemed crushed somehow, defeated. He had donned his finery, his coloured waistcoat and his rings, 'to show he could be a gentleman as well as an anatomist'. He had a streak of blood on his shirt – as if the anatomist that day had usurped the gentleman. When he saw the severed hand and the card between its dead fingers he had glanced at Lilith Crowe, his expression as fearful as his students'. And then I saw that he had noticed Will, standing beside her, giving her hand a squeeze, and I watched his face sag.

'Yes,' he said now. 'For God's sake someone take that down and clear up the mess.' He stalked down the stairs and vanished along the passage to his office. I heard his door bang.

I took the hand and the pins. I put the card into my pocket. 'What's on it?' said Halliday. 'Is it the same? The same phrase as last time?'

'Yes,' I replied.

'What does it mean?'

'I don't know.'

'But what do *you* think? Is it a saying? Is it a motto? What about you, Allardyce? Any thoughts?'

'No.' The word blurted out of him. He took a breath. 'I have no idea. Poor Dr Wragg,' he muttered. 'You will have a lot of work to do in the museum now, Halliday. Perhaps Dr Crowe will be able to find you an assistant.'

'I don't need one,' said Halliday. 'I can manage. I'll ring for Gloag,' he added, nodding to the streaks of drying blood on the door. 'He can wipe that up.'

I took the hand back down to the dissecting room. Dr Graves had gone. I noticed that he had taken Dr Wragg's spleen after all.

'I can't stand it here,' said Will, who had followed me down. 'The stink of the place, the horrible goings on.'

As we left the building Dr Allardyce, Dr Crowe, Dr Cruikshank and Dr Strangeway were standing in a group beside the skeletons of the twisted sisters. They watched us go in silence.

Chapter Seventeen

I had never been so relieved to get to the physic garden. The day was cold – too cold even for autumn – the sky overhead a deep slate grey. We sat side by side on the bench overlooking the camomile lawn and facing away from Corvus Hall. Neither of us said a word. I rested my eyes on the lavender bushes. They needed trimming back. The whole place needed it. Perhaps I should leave Gabriel and Jenny in charge at the shop for a while and devote myself to the garden. I could start some new beds, take out some old ones, work on the poison garden. I felt a drop of rain on my hand – heavy and solid, it presaged a downpour. We ran to the hot house as the skies emptied. The rain drummed on the glass roof panes with a sound like impatient fingers. I went to the stove. The gardener kept it smouldering through the winter months though the British winters and dirty London climate were too much for all but the hardiest native species. I opened the hole at the top. It was temperamental at the best of times, the flue often choked with a bird's nest. Luck was with us that day, however, for she kindled straight away. I fed in some sticks, and some logs from the cherry tree we had felled in the early spring. I rummaged behind the door and produced two folding chairs. 'Field chairs,' I said. 'I saw ones of similar design in the Exhibition catalogue.'

'Don't talk to me about the Exhibition or the catalogue,' said Will. 'I have begun to see it as the source of all our current problems.' He shivered. I pulled out a blanket and draped it across his shoulders. It smelled of grass and lavender, and he sniffed at its coarse fibres with pleasure as he pulled it close.

We sat side by side, our legs stretched out towards the stove. The hot house grew warm – the heat, and the smell of the place comforted us both. At once earthy and familiar, it was the smell of damp twigs and leaves, of drying herbs and moist geraniums, of warm loam, and soily roots. After the Hall it was heaven itself. We had been up since before the dawn, and had eaten nothing and we were both hungry. I rooted in my bag. I had a lump of cheese in there somewhere. I sliced it into chunks and we sat toasting it, each piece skewered by a stick of cherry.

'One must be careful not to use sticks of oleander when toasting cheese,' I said conversationally. 'The oleander bush is poisonous. Bees with their hives set nearby make a poisonous honey if they drink nectar from its flowers. A piece of cheese toasted on an oleander stick would absorb the sap and kill you in an instant.'

'Oh,' said Will.

'Whole families have been wiped out by innocently toasting cheese on skewers of oleander.'

'Somehow death by poison does not seem anywhere near as awful as what is going on next door.'

'I think they are not interested in poison next door,' I said. 'They are surgeons and anatomists, they have no interest in the subtleties of physic, whether to cure or kill. You remember that procedure you watched, Will, when you first came to St Saviour's? The excision of the hip joint?' It had been his first day there. Anaesthetic had not reached St Saviour's and the job had been a grisly one. The blood, the agony of the patient, the muted screams – Will had lain in the bloody sawdust at the surgeon's feet in a dead faint.

'How could I ever forget?' he said.

'You saw how these men are. They are trained with the knife. Trained to cut fast and deep, without fear or hesitation. To hear cries of pain and suffering and to press on no matter what. There is not a single one of them who is not capable of these crimes. Not a single one.' I sighed. I had grown impatient with my work at the apothecary, had felt bored by its mundanity. But now? Now I wanted nothing but the scent of hops, comfrey, camomile and peppermint. Corvus Hall held nothing for me and the sooner I could turn my back on it the happier I would be.

Will clapped me on the shoulder. 'Let's not think of it.'

'But we must, Will,' I said. 'We have stumbled upon horror, but we cannot just go away, we cannot leave it.'

'It is between them. Something between the surgeons.'

'I know that. But nonetheless—'

'You think there is worse to come?' Will looked shocked.

'I am quite sure of it,' I said. 'But we must prevent it, if we can. Let us consider what we have seen so far. What might the connections be between people and events?'

'Between Wilson and Wragg? They were both medical men.'

'Yes.'

'They were both Scots – Edinburgh.'

'Yes. And there was something Dr Wragg said to me in the anatomy museum. That I should let sleeping dogs lie – Dr Cruikshank intimated the same thing.'

'You think there are past events at work here?'

'No doubt,' I said. 'And Dr Graves was telling me what he knew of Dr Wragg. Wragg was an old rogue. He's done Dr Crowe's bidding for years.'

'Bidding? In what sense?'

'I don't know.'

'But Wilson was young,' said Will. 'Dr Wragg is an old man. I can see no way for them to be connected.'

'And yet there *is* a connection. Wilson's father was a constable in Edinburgh. Wouldn't he be of an age with Dr Crowe and Dr Cruikshank?'

'It is certainly possible.'

'And what about Mr Halliday? And Dr Allardyce? Dr Allardyce was also in Edinburgh, years ago, with the others. He despises Halliday, but then Dr Allardyce strikes me as a weak, complaining sort of a fellow who will blame anyone but himself – especially for his lack of progress. I like Halliday, but is that enough to say he has nothing to do with all this?' I thought of Skinner's tight-lipped refusal to say anything about Halliday, *perhaps you should find that out for yourself.* Dr Wragg had been provoked by the fellow too. 'His fellow students adore him,' I said. 'He is the winner of a prize essay, and beloved by Dr Crowe. Who are we to believe? And we cannot discount the women either. Miss Crowe—'

'Miss Crowe?' Will's face turned pink. 'I hardly think she—'

'Why ever not?' I said sharply. 'She is no more above suspicion than anyone else. She is strong. Passionate too, I have no doubt.' I felt my port-wine birthmark grow warm – it always did when I felt uncomfortable. 'She certainly has the skills,' I added. 'And we know very little about her – or any of them.'

'I cannot believe it,' he said. 'She is quite the most delightful companion. Kind, amusing, interesting. She admires my work greatly. It was she who recommended me to her father even before we arrived, and she is to write much of the book my pictures will be in, though of course it's her father's name that will be on the cover. She is graceful and ladylike—'

'Despite the blood and bones she is so at home amongst?' I said.

'Yes,' he snapped. 'Even despite that! She is not like any of them.'

'How can she be any different? She must be as inured to the sight of blood and death and corpses as any anatomist. You are quite deceived if you think she is not.'

'How can you say that? *You* are not like that and *you* have spent your life surrounded by surgeons and disease. You were twenty years at St Saviour's! Why must a man lose his humility, his decency just because he works amongst the dead? Just because he treats pain for a living by cutting it out? Why might a woman be any different?'

All at once there was a knock at the door.

'Hello? Gentlemen?' It was Halliday, his shoulders beaded with rain drops. How long had he been out there? Had he been listening? 'May I come in?' He smiled. 'It looks cosy.'

'Of course.' I sprang to my feet. So did Will. We did not look at one another.

'I can't stand it in there today.' Halliday sank into the chair Will had pulled up for him. He held out his hands to the fire. A faint smell of putrescence rose off his damp clothes. No doubt Will and I smelled little better. The thought that I might stink like an anatomist perturbed me. 'Poor Dr Wragg,' he said. 'He must have been in such pain. One can only assume he was at the end of endurance and perhaps no longer in his right mind.'

'He could just as well have taken an overdose of laudanum,' I said. 'It would surely have been a more pleasant ending.'

'Indeed,' said Halliday.

'And he left no note – not that I could see, and I looked through his papers and in all the obvious places.'

'Perhaps he hardly cared,' said Halliday. 'Why should he explain himself? He had no family who would be interested. There is every chance the pain, or the laudanum he had already taken, had disturbed his mind.'

I shrugged. Perhaps he was right. But I was not prepared to accept it. I was sick of the place, sick of them all. 'Why did you come here?' I said to Halliday. 'Can we not be free of you all that you must traipse round here too?'

'Jem!' said Will. 'For God's sake—'

'Oh, it's a fair question, Quartermain.' Halliday blushed. 'The thing is, I saw . . . I saw your smoke. I knew the garden was yours. I hoped it was either empty in here, or that I might find the company of someone . . . someone who was not from Corvus. Just to get away for an hour.'

He rubbed a trembling hand across his eyes. How young he looked. He was only about twenty-four, younger than Will and me. Apart from his work he seemed to have very little else in his life. He would surely have known Dr Wragg very well. Despite their differences, the older man must have been something of a mentor. It was a lonely business forging a career in medicine without a family to lend succour, and all at once I felt a rush of pity for him. I knew what it was to have no parents, to have one's work as the sole comfort in life. I had Will now, and Gabriel and Jenny. They were my family. Might I not share a little of my good fortune?

'Look, Halliday,' I said. 'I didn't mean to sound harsh. It's been a trying day and we have been up since five. But why don't you come up to the apothecary for tea?'

'Really?' He looked so grateful I was quite ashamed of myself. He shook my hand. 'I'd like that very much,' he said. 'Thank you, Mr Flockhart, I will.'

Outside the rain had stopped. The air hung still and quiet, disturbed only by the distant sound of starlings, and water dripping from leaves and twigs. It was rare for the air to be clear, and when all was wet and shiny the world had a gleaming beauty to it that I loved. The berries of the dog rose gleamed, so that for a moment I was reminded of drops of blood, thick and crimson.

'And there will be no talk of death and corpses either!' I said. 'Just warm food and good company.' I hoped it was not too much to wish for.

***

Precognition for the murder of Mary Anderson,
18th December 1830.

Statement of HENRY CRUIKSHANK, surgeon, police
surgeon, and anatomy demonstrator at Dr Crowe's anatomy
school, 13 Surgeons' Square, residing at 4 Montague Street,
Newington, Edinburgh. Aged thirty years.

19th December 1830

Dr Crowe's wife died some twelve months ago of the smallpox.
Her death, and the manner of it, affected the doctor deeply, and
he shut himself away, ignoring his friends and his children, for
many weeks. I carried on his business – as a surgeon and as an
anatomist and teacher – as best I could with the help of Dr Wragg
and Dr Strangeway, as well as Mr Allardyce and Mr Franklyn,
Dr Crowe's two apprentices, both of whom live in, and who were
invaluable at this time. Dr Crowe did not come out to the college,

nor go up to his school, and nor would he see any patients, for some two months.

Dr Crowe is a man who has given his life to the study and teaching of anatomy, and I feared a melancholia had settled upon him, one not helped by the long dark winters we suffer here, and which had been particularly hard that year. His daughter Lilith was of the same opinion, and she and I both felt that it would be in the doctor's interests if he were able to return to his teaching duties as soon as possible. I said as much to Franklyn and Allardyce, and we agreed to coax him back to Surgeons' Square if we could.

It was Mr Franklyn who told Dr Crowe about the crippled sisters who had appeared at the gates to the Infirmary. 'The Twisted Sisters o' St Giles,' he called them. The students were most taken with them, he said. He was right, too, for the sisters were objects of fascination for us all, though I could see that Mr Allardyce disapproved of their lewd jokes and coarse humour.

Franklyn was younger than Allardyce, but a brilliant student. He knew his master's interests – and shared them – and on this occasion he succeeded where myself, Allardyce and Miss Crowe, had all failed. 'It is their spines, sir,' he said. 'The alignment of the vertebrae, the angle of the pelvis and the position of the shoulders, that is where they are especially unique. They are like nothing I have ever laid eyes on. They are like nothing you have ever laid eyes on. Sir, you must come and see them.' He added that as Dr Knox was away in London, and likely to be so for some weeks or months. Knowing that Dr Knox and Dr Crowe were competitive in their appreciation of the vertebrae in all its manifestations, it would be an opportunity of one-upmanship not to be missed.

And so Dr Crowe returned to his anatomy school at Surgeons' Square. I was glad to see that he seemed to be a little more cheerful now that he was out of the house every day. And yet, although we could initially not get him to go out, he now seemed determined to go to the other extreme, and he spent more and more time away from home.

It was Mr Allardyce who first brought up the delicate subject of Dr Crowe's fascination with Thrawn-Leggit Mary. 'Well, Dr Cruikshank,' he said to me one day. 'I hope Dr Crowe recovers himself soon, for it is a disgrace to the school and an insult to the memory of his wife if he carries on like this.' I asked him what he meant, but he would not say.

I asked Mr Franklyn what Allardyce alluded to, and he tut tutted. 'Allardyce is as purse-lipped as a dog's arse about it,' he said. 'But it seems Dr Crowe has become enamoured with the crippled beggar Thrawn-Leggit Mary, and they say it is more than her spine that he admires.' It pains me to say it, but the next day I followed Dr Crowe after he left the dissecting room. I saw him go down Robertson's Close and into the home of Mary Anderson.

A few days later I went to Dr Crowe's house on an unrelated matter. I found Miss Crowe in the morning room, her work basket out and one of her mother's dresses across her knees. I said to her that I thought all her mother's clothes had been burned, as was customary after the smallpox, and if there were any that had not been then she should not touch them, for fear of catching the disease herself. She replied that no, the blue dress remained, and the green one too. She had found them in her mother's dressing room, though she did not know how they had escaped the pyre. She asked if she might keep it. I said that she should ask her father. She replied that she would do no such thing, for he would give it away, as he had done the green one, if he knew that she had it.

'Give it away?' I said. 'To whom?'

'To the crippled girl he sits with in his study,' she replied. 'She is there now.'

I made my excuse and went in to the study. I found Dr Crowe sitting beside the fire in the company of Thrawn-Leggit Mary. She was wearing the green dress, which Mrs Crowe had looked most comely in and which she had often worn. She was sitting on a low stool for she could not manage a chair, her legs, hips, and back being all awry, and her shoulders lopsided. In the hearth lay the crutches she used to get herself about the place. She seemed somewhat cowed by her surroundings. I saw her eyes darting everywhere, as if she were calculating the cost of Dr Crowe's possessions, and wondering whether she might be able to slip a candlestick, or a snuff box, into her pocket and take them to her friends in the Grassmarket.

Mary Anderson certainly bore a likeness to Dr Crowe's wife – it was in the greenness of her eyes and her dark and glossy hair, the line of her cheek and lip, and she was an uncommonly pretty girl for all that she was a cripple. To anyone in their right mind the similarity was but superficial – evanescent, depending on the light, or the angle of her head. But I fear Dr Crowe was not in his right mind, not at that time, at least. As I left them alone to return to Miss Crowe I heard the girl singing too. She had a beautiful voice, but in my heart I likened it to the cry of a siren, for Dr Crowe was clearly lost on a sea of grief and sorrow, with no sight of land or homecoming no matter how much his friends and daughter might wish it.

I could see that Miss Crowe was sorely tried by all this. Not only had she lost her mother, but now, it seemed, her father too. He had always delighted in showing her his work, no matter that she was a woman, for he claimed that medical knowledge was never wasted. She had become adept at the dissecting table, her small fingers quick and agile, so that he often said he was as skilled with the anatomist's knives as he was himself. There is no house in the city like Dr Crowe's for specimens, and she would leave treasures out for him – a frog she had preserved, a pig's heart she had dissected, a resin cast of the veins of the hand. But now, Dr Crowe seemed hardly to notice his children at all. I knew it caused Miss Crowe distress. She was the eldest child by some twelve years, the others being mere babies, and she felt her isolation from her father keenly. I vowed to do what I could to remedy the situation.

I asked her to keep me informed of her father's behaviour, for I had my duties in my private practice, as well as at Surgeons' Square to attend to. At the end of the week she told me that Mary Anderson had been to the house every day; that her father made the girl sit in the window where his wife used to sit, with the light falling over her shoulder, and that she sang for him whenever he asked it of her – songs her mother had sung. I said that I was sure it would pass, and that for the time being we should say nothing.

For the next two weeks it continued. In the end I had no choice but to warn him of the consequences his behaviour was having – on his reputation at the anatomy school and amongst his colleagues, on his family and household, and private patients, for rumours spread quickly in Edinburgh, and already it seemed that the whole of the town knew how Dr Crowe had become enamoured of a crippled beggar. He grew furious at what he described as my 'interference'. He said he would not be monitored and reproached by me, or by anyone. It seemed an impossible situation. And so one day, with the agreement of Miss Crowe, I arranged to try to rid him of his infatuation.

I enlisted the help of Dr Wragg. He knew everything that was going on in the dark streets of the old town – he had young footpads in his pay, Davie Knox amongst them, who kept him informed of any deaths that occurred in desperate places, so that the bodies might be brought up to us without delay. At my request, he asked these miscreants to keep him acquainted with what went *on at the foot of Robertson's Close. The following night, as I was preparing for the next day's classes at Surgeons' Square, he sent word to me that we must act, and act now. I took a hansom to Dr Crowe's house. Under pretence of needing his assistance with a troublesome case, I bundled him inside.*

Dr Wragg was waiting for us when we arrived at our destination. 'Are we too late?' I asked.

He shook his head, and replied, 'No. In fact, I am glad you did not come sooner.' His cheeks were flushed, and his glance seemed half amused, half surprised.

Dr Crowe opened his mouth to speak, but I held up a hand. 'Please, sir,' I said. 'Say nothing until you have seen, and then decide if you would speak, or if you would remain silent.' I nodded to Dr Wragg, who turned and flung open the door to Mary Anderson's lodgings. The girl was wearing the green silk dress. She was on all fours. The man who mounted her had left his payment on the table top.

The matter of Dr Crowe's fascination with Mary Anderson was never alluded to again by any of us.

❧

On the evening of the 18th inst. Franklyn and I were commencing our work in the dissecting room when Mr Allardyce came in to tell us that Thrawn-Leggit Mary had been murdered. I had not witnessed her attack on Dr Crowe's person, though I had been apprised of the situation by Dr Strangeway. It seemed likely that the exertion had caused a haemorrhage of some kind, and the girl had died in childbirth before anyone could attend to her. This was my conjecture, for 'murder' seemed a rather improbable circumstance. But we were in need of a body and Mary's was considered something of a treasure amongst us anatomists. Allardyce's excitement was palpable. He already had his coat and hat on, and had picked up a lantern from the store.

'Come along then, gentlemen!' he said. 'Do you think we are the only ones young Davie has told?' It was true enough, for we are not the only anatomy school at Surgeons' Square, and I knew the agents of Dr Knox and Dr Lizars would be down there before us if we did not have a care. Franklyn went to get his hat and coat, abandoning his knives and saws where they lay. I could see in his face that he was disappointed that Allardyce had brought us the news, though he hid it as best he could. I went to find Dr Wragg, who I knew to be about the place attending to some new acquisitions for the museum that had come in from the Chirurgical Society, and Dr Strangeway. In the event I could not find Dr Strangeway, and although we were fewer in number than I would have liked, I was too impatient to look for others at that time of the night. In less than five minutes we were walking down Infirmary Street. At the top of Robertson's Close we bumped into Dr Strangeway, who agreed, though with some evident reluctance, to accompany us.

As I suspected, the mob had gathered in force outside Tanner's Lodgings. I was afraid we might not get inside, but despite their ill will towards us they let us through. I went inside the women's room with Dr Strangeway, and the apprentices Franklyn and Allardyce. Dr Wragg guarded the door. The place was dark and chill, and thick with the smell of blood. The girl was lying on the bed. Something was wound tightly about her neck, a scarf or a shawl of some kind in a sky-blue silken material. It was quite evident that she was dead, though I considered it my duty to check for her pulse nonetheless. I saw too that she had been delivered of a child by caesarean section. The babe was nowhere to be seen. Whether she had been throttled to death by the band at her neck, *or had been killed by the removal of her child I could not say. The quantity of blood that covered the bed led me to assume the second – that she had been strangled, not to the death, but very nearly so. Her death had been secured by the fact that she had been cut open soon after – the blood loss looked copious, suggesting that she had been alive, but was not as much as might be expected had her heart been beating strongly. Those, at least, were my impressions at the time.*

I knew we could not stay, that we had to act quickly, for the mob was howling outside. And yet I also wanted to capture something of the scene, and so I asked Dr Strangeway if he might draw the girl where she lay. His hands were shaking as he opened his bag and brought out his materials. He was well used to corpses, so I knew it was not that. But the dead girl had resembled his beloved sister, and he had drawn the cripple many times while she had lived. To see her dead – throttled and butchered – was, I thought, too much for him. And when I looked closer at what we had before us I saw with revulsion that my decision was the right one, for the skin of her face had been stripped away, removed in its entirety – lips, lids, cheeks, all precisely and meticulously filleted from the crimson tissue beneath. Even in the dim light I could see that the fascia, the gossamer-like membranes that lie beneath the skin, were still intact, the muscles that had given her face its beauty and expression, set out in glistening layers. It took my breath from me, and in all conscience I could not suffer Dr Strangeway to draw her as she now was. I took his pen and ink, and his notebook, and bade him await us by the door.

I gave the job to Allardyce instead, for he is a passable artist, and a man always keen to do something, especially if it meant leaving Franklyn looking idle. He asked me whether I might draw the face, if I would turn the girl towards him for she was in shadow. But I would not. I could not. The blood from the dissecting tables still glistened on the lad's fingernails so hastily had we left our work at Surgeons' Square, and at that moment I felt keenly the horror of our profession. A sorrow, and a heaviness, afflicted my heart at what wickedness we had stumbled upon.

Franklyn and Allardyce began arguing over which of them might claim the body. Franklyn said that he had arranged the matter with Clenchie Kate, who knew her sister's death was inevitable, and who had taken his shillings eagerly on the promise that the corpse should be his when the time came. Rabbie McDade the skeleton-maker had already been commissioned, he said, for the bones of the dead girl had been his even while she had walked the streets. Allardyce retorted that he had paid Thrawn-Leggit Mary herself handsomely while she was alive, with the understanding that he might take ownership of her corpse when she was dead. How else did Franklyn think the girl had got the dress back from the pawnbrokers? I told them both to shut their mouths, for the corpse would not belong to anyone if we did not get it up the close to Surgeons' Hall in the next five minutes. I wondered, not for the first time, whether we did our young medical men a disservice when we so inured them to the sight of death that they would argue over a woman's corpse as if were a side of beef won at a country fair. But there was no time for such musings, and I bade Allardyce make haste with his drawing. I called Franklyn to help me wrap the corpse, and then we were ready.

It was as well that I hurried them for the crowd was in no mood for us that night, and as we emerged from Tanner's Lodgings it was all we could do to keep a hold of our burden. Allardyce's squabbling with Franklyn had annoyed me, and as he was the last man out I was half temped to ask him to stay until the constable came to make sure no one entered the house. But there was every chance he would be torn limb from limb by the mob, and so I shouted at him to make haste. We had a brief tussle with the crowd, admirably managed by Dr Wragg, and then I heard the sound of the constable's whistle. Faces turned to look out for him, and we seized our moment and ran.

⤬

We took her to Surgeons' Hall. Dr Wragg had a key to the place; being curator of the museum he came and went as he pleased. We had not been at our work for long when we heard a battering at the door and a jangling of the bell. As I had expected, it was the constable. I had met him before – a strong, upright fellow named Wilson. He asked to see the body. I warned him it was not a sight for the faint at heart, but he would not listen. It is a common misconception that fainting is a woman's prerogative. It is not – I have seen Miss Crowe remain upright in an anatomy demonstration while the young gentlemen about her are falling like skittles. Constable Wilson took one look at the girl laid out on the slab and sank to the ground in a dead faint. It took Dr Wragg and me, along with Franklyn and Allardyce, to lift him onto one of the tables.

When he came to he told me that he had arrived at Tanner's Lodgings shortly after we had left the place. He reached for the canvas bag that he had been carrying over his shoulder, and pulled from it a folded piece of soft leather. Wrapped within was a knife. He told me he had found it beneath the bed against the wall – easy to miss, he said, making my excuses for me, for the room was dark and beneath the bed darker still. No doubt the murderer had dropped it and had not noticed. He asked me whether I recognised it.

I took the knife and turned it in my hand. The blade was sticky, the stuff that coated it drying a dark, reddish black. I rubbed at *it with my finger, scraping clean the flat surface of the steel where it met the smooth wood of the handle. The initials of its owner, engraved neatly into the head of the shaft, were etched in blood.*

True on soul and conscience,

[signed] Henry Cruikshank

Chapter Eighteen

※

Halliday appeared just as Gabriel was closing up the shop for the evening. He had brought some oranges and a pineapple. Gabriel held the pineapple reverently, in the manner of a monarch holding the Orb of State. 'I've never seen one of these before.'

'I have,' said Jenny. 'I used to live on the Seaman's Floating Hospital, and we had all kinds of fruit. Dr Aberlady, the apothecary, he used to get things all the time. Oranges, lemons, limes. We had pineapple too.'

'Then you will know how to prepare it, won't you?' I said. I handed it to her. 'We are relying on your expertise.'

'I got it from a street hawker,' said Halliday. 'Contraband, no doubt. He vanished into a side street the moment my shillings were in his hand.'

The pineapple was the centrepiece of our table, for I had nothing special for supper. I had not wanted to make a fuss, but simply wished to give Halliday a break from Corvus Hall, to let him relax for an evening somewhere that was away from his usual world of corpses and body parts – somewhere that was not his cold and lonely lodgings above the butcher's shop on Orchard Street. Gabriel had made some mutton stew, Jenny had prepared herb dumplings. It was almost ready, the smell of it warm and inviting, mixing with the scent of rosemary and mint from Jenny's chopping board.

'Thank you,' said Halliday as we sat down. He directed his remark at Jenny, who he seemed to think had made the whole meal.

'*I* made it,' said Gabriel, looking cross. 'I can do *some* things.' They started to argue – who had gone to the butcher, who had browned the meat, who had cut the herbs and made the gravy.

'I think we must thank both of you,' I said.

Jenny pressed her lips together. 'You're getting fat,' she said to Gabriel. She eyed the straining buttons on his waistcoat critically. 'You should eat less. I saw you dipping into the pot while Mr Jem was out.'

Gabriel's expression grew sorrowful. '*Am* I fat, Jenny?' He spread his hands across his stomach. 'I suppose I am a bit. Is it *too* fat?' He looked crushed.

'Oh!' she flung her arms about him. 'I'd much rather you were like this than thin.'

'Don't tease him, Jenny,' I said. 'You tell him he is fat, then you take it back. No wonder he's confused. Make yourself useful and get us some ale from the pantry.' She danced off. She still wore one of my old hats, a stovepipe with a rather old-fashioned appearance, though I made her take it off at meal times. She kept cutting her hair short, and it stood out from her head in a mess of ragged tufts. I had persuaded her to wear her dress, however, for I was determined that she should qualify as an apothecary without having to hide who she was. It was her only concession to her gender, for she still wore a pair of Gabriel's old boots beneath it. I had saved her from the Seaman's Floating Hospital, and she was proving to be the brightest and most efficient apprentice I had. Poor Gabriel, some two years her senior, and years longer as an apprentice apothecary, was already far behind. But they adored one another, and he was less annoyed about being left alone in the apothecary when I went out about the town now that he had Jenny to keep him company.

Halliday seemed rather ill at ease at first. He talked about Corvus Hall, how much work he had to do about the museum. 'Dr Allardyce is supposed to be helping but he always seems to find something better to do.' He talked about the paper he was writing, how worried he was about presenting his work to the Medico-Chirurgical Society. All at once he stopped. 'I'm sorry,' he said. 'I'm such a bore these days. I seem to have forgotten what it's like not to talk about medicine and anatomy and what-not. And yet I cannot talk about politics as I have no time to read the newspapers. I cannot talk about the theatre because I never go. I have no idea about the races, or the cricket. I have not read the latest novel and cannot comment on what might be fashionable in coats and dresses as I never buy such things and I do not have a wife or sister to inform me.' He threw up his hands. 'I am a hopeless dinner guest, gentlemen. I fear you will never have me back.'

'You're always welcome here,' I said.

'The lads tell me I'm too serious,' he said. 'I probably am. I'm probably rather dull for most people, though I manage to be less so if I have a glass of ale or two.' He took a swig from the tankard Jenny had poured, and grinned. 'You see? My demeanour is already much more cheerful!'

'But you are not dull at all when you are talking about anatomy,' I said.

He blushed. 'So Dr Crowe tells me. He had me showing the lads – the new men – their way about a corpse yesterday. He often asks me to demonstrate as it's too much for Dr Allardyce alone. He's been very kind.'

'I hear you are all charisma and humour when you are about a corpse,' said Will. 'I applaud you, sir. I am all nausea and fainting.'

'And yet the whole place seems rather serious,' I said. I thought of the way the students had looked when Sorrow and Silence had appeared in the dissecting room. The way the sisters had been with Tanhauser in the anatomy museum. 'It's unusual to have women about, in such a place, is it not?'

'I understand Dr Crowe believes they will raise the moral tone of the school, as well as affecting the way we go about our business,' replied Halliday. 'Amongst other things.'

'And is it working, would you say?'

'I have little experience of other places,' he replied. 'Though I would say that most of the men don't like it. The sisters used to be permitted in the dissecting room too, and the dead room, but there were some objections to that. Dr Cruikshank agreed. They tend to stay out of those places now – some of the time, at any rate.'

I tried to get Halliday to tell us something about himself, but he shrugged and said, 'My provenance is uninteresting, sir. My mother and father are dead. There was a little money put aside for me and I chose to spend it on a medical education. I came to London for my studies. It is probably why I am at Corvus Hall so much, as I have no family to visit and no money to spend on pleasures. And the work is fascinating.' His eyes gleamed. 'I cannot deny that.'

We talked on, about the nature of the profession (crowded, with the best posts taken by sons of the wealthy), about surgery (transformed since the appearance of chloroform 'but men dabble about in the abdomen for far too long. Is it any wonder that more of our patients die than ever before?') and about the appeal of Corvus Hall (Dr Crowe was a brilliant anatomist, Dr Cruikshank a first-rate lecturer, the anatomy museum second to none). The evening passed easily. The stew was warming and tasty, the dumplings light and fluffy, and we made sure to compliment Gabriel and Jenny equally. We finished our beer, and then Jenny told Will how best to slice up the pineapple. He did so using a long surgical blade Halliday produced from his bag. We ate the sweet golden pieces in silence.

'How did it taste?' I said to Gabriel, who had savoured every mouthful.

'Like sunshine,' he said. 'If you could slice up the sun and put it in a bowl it would taste just like this.'

We played cards for a while. Beggar My Neighbour, a game Jenny had enjoyed at the seaman's hospital. It was simple and rather childish, but it always ended in hilarity. I was pleased to see Halliday laughing as he lost the game yet again, and I was reminded of how difficult it was to be all alone in the world trying to make one's way in a competitive profession without connections or patronage. Would his ability be enough to enable him to succeed? I hoped so.

'Well, gentlemen,' he said as the apothecary clock struck eleven. 'I had better be on my way.' I fetched his hat and coat, for Gabriel and Jenny had already gone to bed – the former on his truckle bed beneath the apothecary table, the latter amongst the hop sacks in the herb drying room. At the door, as he took his leave, Halliday shook my hand. His grip was tight, and to my surprise there were tears in his eyes. 'Thank you, Jem,' he said. 'Thank you. For inviting me. For your hospitality. You have a most unusual family.'

'I have no family,' I replied.

'Neither do I,' he said. 'And yet whereas I remain alone in the world, you seem to have found yourself one. You bicker and argue, you are all separate, different, but you are together. There is a love,' he faltered, as though the words were pulled from a dark corner of himself that he hardly dared look into. 'There is a love that binds you together. You *are* a family. You will always have each other, I can see that clearly. But I? I have nothing like that.'

'You have Dr Crowe. I know he loves you—'

'He loves my speed and confidence with the knife. He loves my ability to memorise the parts of the body. He loves my ambition. But all of these are done without real care, without unconditional love; I would not look to Dr Crowe for comfort or succour—' His voice was tight, and filled with emotion. 'I fear I would not get it. Not from that quarter. No, Jem, I have no family but corpses and specimens. I stink of death, not life. But here, here in this apothecary and in your garden earlier, here it is all warmth and light, it is fragrant and filled with laughter and good cheer. I envy you, Jem, I envy what you have.'

'You will have the same,' I said. 'One day.'

'I think not.'

'Are you afraid, John?' I lowered my voice. 'Afraid you will suffer the same fate as Wilson? As Dr Wragg?'

'Wilson? Dr Crowe says there is every chance it was not his corpse at all.'

'And Wragg?'

'Suicide, surely?'

'And what if they were – if they were both murdered?'

He turned pale. 'You cannot mean it?'

I saw his alarm and I was immediately sorry. 'It is unlikely. I should never have mentioned it.' I clapped him on the shoulder. 'I have a foolish and sensational imagination. As you saw from our shelves, we have no shortage of Penny Bloods here. But if you are ever afraid, or worried, or . . . want some company then you are more than welcome in my home.'

He wrung my hand, though I could see his eyes were still troubled. 'Thank you, Jem,' he said again. 'Thank you for everything.' And then he was gone.

Chapter Nineteen

❧

Will was a fast worker – partly because he was not enjoying his job, partly because every time he finished a drawing he vanished to look for Miss Crowe, who would admire his work, his skill and sure hand, and would take the picture to her father, or Dr Cruickshank. 'Why can you not take your work to Dr Crowe yourself?' I said. 'Or to Dr Cruikshank?'

'Why would I do that? Why would I take my work to those two old curiosities when I can show it to a delightful young woman?'

'Hardly young!' I said. 'She is at least ten years your senior.'

'And what do I care about that?' He was sitting at his desk, under the eaves, the microscope in front of him. He was intent upon his task, periodically peering down at the slide, his pen moving with confidence across the page. The lemon cordial I had brought up from the apothecary to help prevent the bone dust from settling on his lungs sat untouched at his elbow. 'She is an artist in her own right! She admires my work in the most fulsome terms.' I saw his cheeks glow at the thought. I said nothing, but in my chest I felt my heart grow cold. I had no right to keep him for myself, especially when I could never offer him more than friendship. I had hoped it would be enough – for a time at least. But now, it seemed, that time had come. What chance did friendship have against romantic love? Such love was evanescent. By its very nature it was transient and subject to change. Friendship could weather all storms if it was true, as mine was. And yet how unworthy it must seem to him now that his heart had warmed to Lilith Crowe.

Halliday was busier than ever. He had recovered from his sickness and was re-ordering the anatomy museum according to a new taxonomy of pathology. He had enlisted the help of Tanhauser and Squires. He was barely older than they were, but was fast and confident, and he seemed driven by a furious energy. When he was not downstairs attending to the museum he was in the dissecting room helping Dr Allardyce or working with Dr Crowe and Dr Cruikshank. When he was not doing those things he was at his desk beside Will, peering down the microscope or scribbling in his notebooks. He would not tell us what he was working on.

'Not after that business with Allardyce,' he said when I asked him. 'I cannot risk such imputations, not again. The work I do is *my* work and *mine* alone. I cannot help it if Dr Allardyce is too slow-witted to draw the right conclusions and write up his work coherently.' Young, lively and energetic, it was impossible not to like him.

One day he put on a microscope demonstration. It had

been organised weeks earlier by Dr Cruikshank. Despite the death of Dr Wragg everyone at the Hall was keen that the event should go ahead, the work of the anatomy school continuing no matter what.

'Can you help, Flockhart?' Halliday said. 'I know you're *au fait* with the microscope. Quartermain told me, and I saw that magnificent beast of a scope you have in your shop. What was it? A Lintz and Messberger?' I could see why Dr Crowe was so fond of him. The tension that had gathered about the place on the death of Dr Wragg seemed to subside as Halliday darted about the place.

At the microscope demonstration, Dr Cruikshank was at the front. He stood with his hands behind his back, clearly enjoying the spectacle of a dozen ladies positioned behind the gleaming brass instruments, all watching him expectantly. Some of the medical students had been co-opted in to help. The ladies were encouraged to pull hairs from one another's heads to examine them. Others were given a slide upon which a dead flea had been mounted. A third slide showed them a droplet of Thames water.

At the back, Halliday and Miss Crowe stood side by side. I saw Dr Cruikshank's gaze linger on her face, calm and beautiful, and upon Halliday's face, young and smiling. Later, I came across Dr Cruikshank staring out of the window of his room. His back was to me. 'They say the study of anatomy is an immoral undertaking for a woman,' he said, without turning around. 'That it is a subject fit only for those without scruple or delicacy. I have always maintained that this is not so, that a woman may be trusted to use her knowledge of the human body and its functions with sensitivity and feeling. To use it wisely.'

'I can see no reason why women should not be as trusted with anatomical knowledge as men,' I replied.

'Then why does she behave as she does?' His voice was trembling. 'I have tried to protect her, to look after her – she is not like others. She never will be. All her life I have sought to guard her from harm – and yet how can I protect her from herself? And how . . . how can I protect *them* from *her*?' He turned to me. 'No matter what she does, or has done, I love her nonetheless.' His face was wretched, tear streaked and haggard. His curls hung limp against his collar, and his jewels seemed lustreless upon his fingers. A crimson smear of blood blotted his shirt, as if the stuff had leaked through from his broken heart. He sank into his chair and put his face in his hands. Behind him, at the bottom of the garden where the yew met the long couch grass and the tall overgrown lavender bushes waved in the sunshine, I saw Lilith Crowe and John Halliday.

Chapter Twenty

❦

We walked down St Saviour's Street, back to the apothecary as the evening drew down. Will had finished his work early and rather than starting another piece I had persuaded him to come home. Coming towards us was a burly man and a slight young woman. They wheeled a hand cart before them. The woman was pushing, for the man seemed wracked by paroxysms of sobbing, which required him to blow his nose and swab his eyes almost continually with a large grey handkerchief. He kept up a deep resonant moaning, rather like the lowing of a distressed bull, which echoed above the city's evening cacophony in a dolorous monotone. On the cart was what looked at first glance to be a great mound of laundry, but which on closer inspection turned out to be the swathed body of a mountainous corpse.

There was something about the pair that seemed familiar, and as they drew closer I saw that it was Mr Jobber and Annie from Mrs Roseplucker's Home for

Girls of an Energetic Disposition on Wicke Street. Will lifted his hat.

'My dear Miss Annie,' he said. 'What a pleasure.'

'Who's this?' I said, pointing to the cart. 'A deceased client? One of your more mature gentlemen overcome by the pleasures of Venus?'

'Or overcome by the prices,' said Will. 'It's a late hour to be dealing with the laundry.'

'Oh, sirs,' cried Annie. 'It ain't laundry. It ain't no gen'man either. It's Mrs Roseplucker.' Her face was tearful. 'She died this very afternoon. She always said she'd given her best years to looking after the medical men, and so I thought I might bring her down here now, sir.' She nodded to the gates of Corvus Hall. 'Besides, it's three pounds for a corpse as fresh as this.'

'Guineas,' I said.

'Guineas!' Her face brightened. 'There you go, Mr Jobber, Mr Flockhart says it's three guineas, so that's even more than we was expecting.' She patted Mr Jobber's arm. He was a great lumbering idiot of a man. I had no idea what relation he was to Mrs Roseplucker, but he seemed to have always been with her. He had performed an essential function at all of Mrs Roseplucker's establishments – the Home for Girls of an Energetic Disposition on Wicke Street, and more recently at the vile and wretched Number 10, Cats' Hole, near the waterfront. He kept a note of the time each gentleman spent upstairs, and jettisoned any who made trouble. Mrs Roseplucker had doted on him. I wondered whether Annie would take over where Mrs Roseplucker had left off.

'I only saw her the other day,' I said. 'Up here at the anatomy school, in fact.'

Will was staring at the mound on the hand cart. 'I can

hardly believe it,' he said. 'I always thought she would outlast us all.'

'Oh, it were a shock, sir,' said Annie. She plucked out her handkerchief, as if realising a show a grief was required. She usually wore her skirts hitched provocatively to show a skinny ankle, but today she was clothed decorously in a long sweeping dress that looked to be rather too big for her. She saw my glance. 'Now then, Mr Flockhart,' she gave me an arch look. 'Don't stare at me like that, not now. Not with me all respectable like. Not over Mrs R's dead body.'

I laughed. I could not help myself. 'I'm sure the surgeons will be delighted to receive her,' I said.

'Yes,' Annie looked down at the shrouded figure, huge beneath its wrapping of dirty sheets. 'Don't suppose I'll get that bedding back, will I?'

'Oh, I don't know. Perhaps not tonight. But you might be able to go back tomorrow to get it.'

'We bound her up nice, didn't we, Mr Jobber?'

Mr Jobber made a bovine lowing noise, and buried his face in his handkerchief.

'*I'm* Mrs Roseplucker now,' said Annie, with evident satisfaction. 'It's what she'd want.'

'I'm sure,' said Will. He grinned. 'I see you have her rings.'

Annie held her hand out. Mrs Roseplucker's rings – garnets cheaply set on thin brassy bands – hung from her fingers. 'Had the devil of a job getting the damn things off her,' she muttered. 'Mr Jobber used all the butter! But it's what she would have wanted.'

'Indeed,' I said. Although I doubted whether Mrs Roseplucker would relish the way her own corpse had been so quickly robbed and sold, such shameless profiteering was definitely what she would have recommended for anyone else.

'And do you have a wake planned?' I said. 'For all Mrs Roseplucker's girls, and . . . and clients?'

'What?' Annie pushed out her chin and put her hands on her hips in an attitude not unlike her deceased mentor. 'Spend my guineas on gin and cake for a bunch of trollops, rogues and ne'er-do-wells? I don't think so! Besides, there's only me an' Mr Jobber. The other girls wouldn't move from their beds to help us. Mrs R were looking for new girls since she come back to Wicke Street. You know,' she looked thoughtful, 'I think it were the strain of it. The strain o' coming back to Wicke Street. She said she were coming home to die, didn't she, Mr Jobber?'

Mr Jobber lowed again, his great shoulders shaking.

'She always said, "They'll carry me out of this place in my box," and so we did.'

'Well,' I gestured at the hand cart. 'Hardly a box—'

'Don't see no point in buying a box,' said Annie. 'Think she'd 'ave bought *me* a box? Mean old cow!'

'Look,' I said. 'After you've taken Mrs R up to the anatomists, why don't you and Mr Jobber come to the apothecary? Come for tea. We can have our own wake. It's the least I can do. Mr Quartermain will be there too, and my apprentices Gabriel and Jenny, and Mrs Speedicut too, no doubt, as she seems impossible to get rid of at the moment.' I smiled. 'What do you say?'

Annie pulled back the sheeting and gazed down at the woman beneath. Mrs Roseplucker's puddingy face was pale as lard. Her scabs were hidden beneath a sleeping cap of dirty cambric pulled down low over her straggling hair. A wide band of grey crepe had been passed beneath her chin, holding her lantern jaw closed and giving her a fierce, bulldog expression. She had a moist, sweaty look, as if she were fashioned from warm cheese.

'Got any gin?' said Annie.

'Of course.'

'Then Mr Jobber and I would be delighted to accept your most kind offer.' She dropped me a curtsey, and the two of them moved off towards the Hall.

❧

Mr Jobber and Annie appeared not long after Will and I had returned. Jenny and Gabriel had cleared the apothecary table and set out the food and drink I'd had sent down from Sorley's: a crate of beer, a pheasant pie, a meat pie, a roast chicken and a potato pie, some plum cake, plus – inevitably – a bag of apples from the physic garden. Mrs Speedicut had come down from the anatomy school. She looked askance at Mr Jobber and Annie, but she knew better than to make a fuss about what company I kept. Besides, I knew the prospect of a free supper would overcome all obstacles. I could see that Annie was cowed by her surroundings, as this was the first time she had been in the apothecary. I wondered how much of her life she had spent in the care of women like Mrs Roseplucker. Mr Jobber too, for although too doltish to have many thoughts at all, the food mesmerised him as much as the 'polite' company he found himself in. Will grinned at me from across the table. Already I knew he was looking forward to putting his feet up on the stove after they had all gone and going over the events of the evening.

At first, the atmosphere was strained, but Sorley's ale worked its magic soon enough. In no time at all Annie was smiling and laughing with Will and teasing Gabriel. It turned out she had once lived in the same street as Mrs Speedicut and they reminisced about old neighbours. Mr Jobber ate in silence, the occasional belch and grunt of satisfaction escaping him. Only Jenny was unusually quiet. I wondered whether it was the bawdy talk that subdued her, as Annie held forth on Mrs Roseplucker's peculiarities as a brothel owner. But Jenny had spent her early years in a similar establishment on the waterfront, so it was surely nothing new to her. Later, after we had eaten all we could, I produced a bottle of gin and we all had a glass of that too. Gabriel took out his fiddle, and – his enthusiasm outweighing his competence – began to scratch out a jig. Annie and Will, who I had never seen so animated, climbed on to the apothecary table and aped a country dance, she the blushing courtesan, he the charming lover. Mr Jobber clapped his hands like a Neanderthal smashing rocks together, and gave a bellow of approval. His chin glistened with grease, the napkin Annie had shoved between the buttons of his waistcoat splattered with spilled beer and smears of chutney. His cheeks were shining.

And then, just as the noise reached a climax of laughter and singing, the door to the apothecary crashed open. The night swirled in, dank and dark, bringing with it the smell of refuse, night soil and the river at low tide. The flames of the candles guttered and shrank, those nearest the door snuffing out altogether to trail wraiths of sticky black smoke. On the threshold was a figure, short and broad as a barrel, a pair of muddy, ill-fitting boots projecting from beneath a dirty, trailing nightshirt.

'So *that's* what you want to do to me, is it?' Her voice was thunderous as she waddled forward, kicking the door closed with the heel of her boot. I recognised them as belonging to Gloag – a pair of large overshoes that he wore in the dead room when wiping down the bodies. Annie's face had drained of blood. There was another crash as Mr Jobber slid from his chair onto the floor in a dead faint.

'Good evening, Mrs Roseplucker,' said Will. 'Would you like a glass of ale, ma'am?'

'Gin,' she barked. 'Got any?' She snatched the beer anyway and sank into one of the chairs before the apothecary stove. She pointed a stubby finger at Annie, still ashen, a piece of plum cake forgotten in her hand. 'You saucy minx!' she cried.

'I thought you was dead,' screamed Annie. 'You was just lying there with your eyes open. You weren't breathin' or nothin', ask Mr Jobber!'

But Mr Jobber was unable to answer any questions. Having lurched back to his feet he was now hunched over, weeping uncontrollably.

'I were sleeping!' Mrs Roseplucker said. 'I had a bit to drink is all. And some o' that laudanum for my tooth.' She opened her mouth and thrust a grubby finger inside. 'I'm surprised you didn't sell them too,' she said, darkly. We all looked at Mrs Roseplucker's grinning black teeth for a moment – no dentist in his right mind would want anything to do with them. 'I were just sleeping,' she growled again.

'Like the bloody dead,' cried Annie, her face sulky. She twisted the rings on her fingers. '*I'm* Mrs Roseplucker now.'

'Oh no you ain't!'

'Tell us what happened, madam,' I said. I handed her a plate. 'Pheasant pie and some of Mrs Sorley's pickle?' I fetched a bowl of hot water and, once I had eased the boots from her toes, coaxed her to put her feet in it. I gave her a shawl and bade her sit closer to the warmth. The vapours from her foot bath, laced with mint oil and rosemary, wafted about her knees in fronds of fragrant steam. She looked around covetously. 'Nice,' she said. 'Very nice. You done very well for yourself, Mr Flock'art. I said as much when I was up here before.'

'Before?' I said.

'This morning. Came for some medications. Pennyroyal and carrot seed for the girls. Laudanum for me 'ead. And me teeth. And a draught to help me sleep.' She eyed Jenny critically. 'Didn't get much of a discount, though I told 'er you and I was friends. And what was in that draught?'

I looked at Jenny. 'You didn't? That recipe from the *Herball*?'

She grinned. 'Well I had to try it on someone!'

'Get on with it, madam,' said Will. 'And as you aren't at Wicke Street you can tell us without expecting a fee.'

It turned out that Mrs Roseplucker had drunk a considerable amount of gin in addition to the laudanum she had taken and the medieval sleeping draught supplied by Jenny. She had been in her bed at the time and had fallen into a deep sleep. Annie said she had checked for breathing 'with a feather', but having perceived no response from the woman even when she had shouted in her ear and 'stabbed her foot with a pin', she had then 'made ready the corpse'. Mr Jobber, who didn't know any better, had gone along with everything.

On arriving at Corvus Hall they had been sent round

the back. It had been late in the day when they had arrived and there was only Gloag in attendance at the dead house. Of course, he had taken them at their word. A corpse was a corpse, why should he ask any questions? With the assistance of Mr Jobber, Gloag had carried Mrs Roseplucker into the mortuary, slid her onto the slab and then recorded her name in the register. He had closed the door and gone about his business elsewhere in the building. Mrs Roseplucker had lain there, still and silent, sleeping amongst the corpses for the next few hours. Eventually, the effects of the gin, the opium, and the belladonna had worn off.

'First thing I remember is feeling cold,' she said. 'Cold as the stone on which I was laid. And when I opened my eyes it were that black I hardly knew whether I were dead or alive for I could see nothing, nothing at all. Dark as the grave it was. Smelled like it too. An' quiet, quiet as the grave. But I were still not myself and I drifted off again. But then—' she looked around at us, her face aghast. 'That's when it happened.'

'What?' cried Mr Jobber. 'What 'appened?'

'The most terrible thing,' she said. 'It made my poor 'eart jump in my body like it were a live thing – which it *were*,' she glared at Annie. 'But now it were racing. Why? Because I saw that where I was laying it were suddenly less dark, that there were a light, though it weren't much of a one, just a thin glowing line, spectral-like in the gloom and it was then that I saw where I was, and that I were in a sepulchre! A house of the dead! But the horror were only just beginning, my dears, oh yes, for the next thing was the voices. Hollow, echoing voices and the sound of a door opening, slowly, slowly, like a door in a crypt. At first

I thought it were opening by itself, moved by some dire ghostly presence, but it were worse, far worse than that. Oh, my dears! What I saw next will haunt me for the rest o' my days, for it were a hand, its fingers long and thin and white as bone. I saw it creep around the edge of the door and push it open. O' course I still had no idea where I was but thought I were dead and gone to some terrible place on account of the life o' wickedness I've lived and it were the Devil himself coming to get me.' She put up a hand and spread her fingers about her flabby neck. 'I felt something about my throat, choking me, so I thought, but when I pulled at it I seed it were just a bandage. The voices came closer. Whispering I don't know what but it were like spells and incantations and all manner o' wickedness.' She lowered her voice. 'All at once I could hear them. "I thought it was behind us," one o' them said. 'And "I hoped never to think of it again." "Not think of it?" replied the other. "There is not a day goes by when I *don't* think of it." "I will do whatever it takes," said the first voice. "I did then. I will now." "It is too late for that," says the other. "Too late. For all of us. It will follow us to the grave and beyond."

'And then the door started to open. Two of them there was, two of them come to get me, dark against the light of their vile lantern. They had knives in their hands, their coats black as night, ragged as the weeds of the dead, for the dead was all around, their faces green and decayed, wrapped in blankets all bloody and foul. I thinks to jump up with a cry, but I'm that afeared I can't move a muscle. I sees the two devils looking at a huge book, like they're totting up the final reckoning for us all. They muttered together, and then they bends over a body. "No," said the one. "No, it will never be over. And yet we have work to do."

I heard a squelch, and a sigh, and it was all I could do not
to faint away with terror at the sound of it. They went away
after that, but left a lantern burning like they was coming
back at any moment. It were just about then that I found
my voice, and so I jumps up with a cry. I jumps up and I
grabs the lantern and I runs out of that terrible place as
fast as I could.'

   Gabriel and Jenny had crept forward and were now sitting cross-legged at the beldam's feet, their eyes round,
their expressions rapt. Annie too had sidled forward.
Mr Jobber, sitting in his place beside the pies, had his
gaze fixed upon his mistress. Mrs Roseplucker looked
around with satisfaction. 'I went up a dark passage and
out through a door. It were the only door I could see!
Then out again into a hall, high and bright with lamps it
were, with glass boxes on all sides filled with monsters and
creatures, with bones and bits of flesh and skin. The floor
were splotched with red, red as blood it were! There was
young men standing about and they yelled out as I passed
by, though they didn't stop me. They couldn't stop me, my
dears, for I were that fast on my feet! In a trice I were at
the front door. I felt their hands clutching at me for they
would have dragged me back in and butchered me there
and then had they got hold of me. But I were faster still.
Ask Mr Jobber, he'll tell you how fast I am. And I ran!
Lord, how I ran!

   'Well, I gets out onto the road and there's people
screaming to see me on account of my nightdress and
bandages about my face. I started for home and it took
me past the door to this here shop for I chose not to take
the back streets, not in my condition, and I heard singing.
Singing! And *music!* And the cackle of *you*, missy!' She

jabbed a finger towards Annie once more. 'Fit to wake the dead, and wake me you did, madam – not that I *were* dead. Well, I looked in and damn my eyes if it weren't *you*! And you too, Mr Jobber! How could you eat and drink and sing happy songs knowing I were dead?'

'But you weren't dead,' said Annie.

'Give me them rings back, you besom!'

'A tale fit for the pen of Prosser McLucker,' said Will, sitting back with a grin. 'That was your old pen name, I believe, madam?'

'Prosser McLucker?' cried Gabriel, sitting up straight. 'From *Tales of Violence and Blight*?'

'You wrote "The Curse of the Haunted Hand"?' said Jenny, 'and "Crimes of Captain Bloodheart"?'

'Those are mine, yes, my dears.' Mrs Roseplucker smiled, her face splitting like a rotten apple. 'You liked 'em? I took to writin' when times was hard at Wicke Street. That there pen name is just "Mrs Roseplucker" only all mixed up.'

'That were *my* idea,' muttered Annie. 'It's an annie-gram—'

Gabriel and Jenny inched closer. '"The Curse of the Haunted Hand",' said Jenny. 'I read it jus' last week!'

'Did you really see a dead man's hand move on its own?' said Gabriel.

'Course she didn't,' said Jenny. 'It's a story!' She gazed at Mrs Roseplucker with awe. 'But it's my most favourite!'

'The creeping right hand of Dick Danvers,' breathed Gabriel.

'The right hand is important, my dears,' said Mrs Roseplucker, leaning forward. 'It means strength, power and protection. It's the hand we put on the Bible when we swear an oath, the hand we sign our name with, the hand

Dick Danvers used to condemn his own brother. The right hand is the hand that reeks of guilt and shame.'

'And the left?' said Jenny

'The left is weak. It is death and decay.' She sat forward, huge in her billowing nightdress and sleeping cap. '*And if thy right hand offend thee cut it off and cast it from thee*!' she cried. 'Ain't that the truth?' She shrugged. 'That's in the Bible. Don't know where.'

Precognition for the murder of Mary Anderson,
18th December 1830.

Statement of ANGUS WRAGG, surgeon, curator of the
Anatomy Museum, Surgeons' Hall, and of Dr Crowe's
Anatomy Museum, 13 Surgeons' Square, residing at
13 Surgeons' Square, Edinburgh. Aged fifty-six years.

19th December 1830

I have known Dr Crowe for some twenty-five years. It was with
some pain that I saw him become enamoured of the crippled beggar
Thrawn-Leggit Mary of Robertson's Close. Dr Cruikshank asked
me for help in curing Dr Crowe of his unfortunate affection and I
was than happy to help – the reputation of Dr Crowe, of the
Anatomy School, and of his late wife were all dependent upon it.
I knew the woman Mary Anderson for what she was. They were
prostitutes, she and her sister, and as such the father of the child
could have been any man.

As Dr Cruikshank bade me, I watched her. One night I saw a man go in at her door. I did not know who he was at that time, but it told me that the girl would be at home and about her business that evening, and so I sent one of the corner boys to fetch Dr Cruikshank and be quick about it. When I saw who was with her I was most surprised, and glad Dr Crowe and Dr Cruikshank did not come sooner. I sent my man in directly after, the payment to be left upon the table where it might be plainly seen, and no doubt might arise about what it was for. It was just in time, for at that moment Dr Cruikshank and Dr Crowe arrived.

After that we vowed never to speak of the matter. Dr Cruikshank made it clear to all those who knew what had lately occurred that the subject of Dr Crowe's misplaced affection, and the nature of his disabusement, would on no account be alluded to again. I included Mr Allardyce in this bond, and I could see that he was mightily relieved by it.

I was not present when the girl Kate was paid by Mr Franklyn to go away from the gates of 13 Surgeons' Square, nor when her sister Mary stabbed Dr Crowe, though I was apprised of both of those events by Dr Strangeway. My next encounter with the women was when Dr Cruikshank came to get me on the evening of the 18th inst. asking me to come to the foot of Robertson's Close 'for they say Thrawn-Leggit Mary is dead,' he said. He knew me for a stout fellow – having been a surgeon some thirty years or more I have seen and done that which would make a lesser man quail in his boots. The mob did not frighten me – though when I later saw what had happened to Mary Anderson it made me glad they had not seen it too for there would have been no safety for us that night if they had.

I did not enter the hovel with them, but rather stayed outside in the street. The mob was fierce angry. They would have strung us all up if they could, for they had not forgotten the West Port murders and were sore aggrieved that not one surgeon had hanged for it. It was for this reason that I thought it prudent to remain at the door until the gentlemen inside were ready. It was not a comfortable vigil: 'I know you,' a voice shouted, once the door was closed. I could not see who for the haar was thick about. Then she stepped forward, small as a child between her two crutches. It was Clenchie Kate. 'Bloody Wragg,' she shouted. 'A man who would sell his own soul for a corpse – if he had a soul to trade.'

'They are all the same,' said another voice, a man's, though I could not see who he was.

'They took Daft Jamie for a corpse, poor lad,' said someone else.

'Aye,' cried another. 'And wee Mary Patterson.'

'And now they want our Mary too?' shouted a fourth.

'I've seen your friends coming in and out,' cried a woman I knew as Susan Leich, a shrew of a woman, and a drunkard, and a friend of both the twisted sisters. 'Those young men from Surgeons', that red-haired one with his pens and his weepin' and maitherin' about "poor Mrs Crowe". You are all of you guilty—' And so it went on, getting hotter and hotter, so that I was afeared we would indeed be set upon, and wondered what it was that kept them so long inside.

At last they were ready. Dr Cruikshank was sorely troubled by what he had seen inside that house, I could tell by his face. He was all for leaving Allardyce behind to keep the crowd from entering the room before the constable arrived, but I would not have it. They did not like Allardyce – that much was plain. They did not like any of us, truth be told, and there would be no safety for one of us left alone on the Cowgate that night. And so I said it would be better if we all returned together and Dr Cruikshank did not argue.

We took her to Surgeons' Hall, for although we did not have a licence for a post-mortem, I had the keys and if the mob followed us up the close we would be safer than if we had taken her to Dr Crowe's school. We had hardly started when the constable came up. He made us send the boys away, young Mr Franklyn and Mr Allardyce. I saw the knife he had brought up. The words upon it were well known to me. They were well known to us all, for they were the words Dr Crowe used to end all his lectures, and before starting all his dissections in front of the young gentlemen. It was a benediction, he said, one the young gentlemen would be well to respect when they picked up the knife and stood over the corpse. Et mortui sua arcana narrabunt: and the dead shall surrender their secrets. I saw the initials that were engraved on the opposite side of the blade and I knew without doubt who its owner was.

True in soul and conscience,

[Signed] Angus Wragg

Chapter Twenty-One

～

Will and I decided to go back to the Exhibition. I wanted to look again at Dr Strangeway's work – was there something about the models he had chosen to display that might help us uncover what was going on? It was a long shot, but I insisted.

There was a crowd standing before the exhibits, young men, mostly, though there were others too. To my surprise I saw that one of them was Dr Crowe. 'Wait,' I said to Will, who had been about to approach and call out a greeting. 'Let's see what happens.'

Dr Crowe was standing with his hands in his pockets. The crowd ebbed and flowed around him. I expected him to move off, but he didn't. We could not see his face, could not see what emotions he might be feeling, only that his attention was unwavering. The exhibit that held him was the head and face of the man. As in all his creations, Dr Strangeway had captured an almost divine expression: the eyelids half closed, the lips slightly parted, the cheeks smooth and flawless; the gaze, half visible beneath lowered lids fixed on some far away point. It attracted the attention of the public too, and I heard numerous voices exclaiming over the work, how skilled it was, how extraordinary in its detail, how fascinating to see what lay concealed beneath. Such order and beauty, they said, a fearful image of death and life, caught in a single frozen moment. Who was he, they wondered? What man had been immortalised in so extraordinary a way? And then they moved on, their gazes drifting to other items on display – surgical knives, leg prostheses, stethoscopes. Only Dr Crowe remained where he was. What did he see that kept him there so long?

'It's an incredible piece,' said Will. 'Who could look at it and remain unmoved? Of course, the face itself is sacred. There is beauty and order in both outer and inner views, though it is the outside that is said to be made in God's image. In this piece one side is whole and perfect, and one side is not. He made the choice concerning which side is which for a reason.'

'Really?' I said. 'There is logic to it?'

'Perhaps not logic,' said Will. 'More like superstition. You see the right side represents beauty, order, serenity. It is God and the divine. The left side, as Dr Strangeway shows us in his peeled back layers of skin, muscle and sinew, *that* side is disorder and chaos. The work of the Devil. But to the anatomist there is a beauty here too, an order and symmetry that only the initiated can appreciate.' He shrugged. 'Most of us see only death. And yet we cannot have one without the other.'

'He said as much when we were in his wax workshop. "Memento Mori *and anatomy lesson are one and the same. Body and soul, relic and specimen, is there a need to draw a*

line between the two?" D'you remember? Perhaps he sees his
work is some kind of search for grace.'

'*Forgive us our trespasses?*' said Will. 'It's present in almost
all religious art. And there is something of the divine
about many of Strangeway's pieces. The "dolls" especially
look as though they would be quite at home in a church.
These, however,' he gestured towards the exhibits. 'The
head, and the heart, these are rather different.'

'I thought you were a draughtsman, not an artist?'

'Oh, I am. But that doesn't mean I don't admire art, or
that I know nothing about it. Of course I do!' He shook his
head. 'You are so uncultured, Jem. Do you know nothing
but remedies and body parts? How prosaic your life must
be.'

'I suppose it is,' I muttered.

'Come along, let's go and speak to the man.'

But at that moment Halliday appeared. He too spotted
Dr Crowe. 'Good afternoon, sir,' he cried. Dr Crowe looked
up, and it was then that something curious happened, for
he gave a start, his face turning white with shock. It was
as if he had seen a ghost, though he recovered himself
quickly enough, and shook the younger man by the hand.
But it was quite clear that he had been momentarily taken
aback. I watched as the two of them moved off through
the crowds and I wondered who, or what, it was that he
had seen.

Brain

What manner of organ is the brain? It has no chambers, no movement, no actions visible to the eye. It is distinctively coloured and textured – grey, pearlescent, softish, opaque. We can hardly comprehend its wonders, for it tells us nothing of the workings of the mind.

Of all the organs in the body the brain is uniquely unknowable. And yet perhaps this is appropriate, for that strange matter is home to the soul and centre of our very being. It contains who we are, directs how we act, harbours our sense of right and wrong. By what means might we point out the brain of a blameless innocent, and say it is qualitatively different to the brain of a murderer? What sets apart the brain of a sane man from the brain of a mad one? And when we run mad, when we do things that defy reason or logic, when we cannot explain who we are or what we have done, what physic might there be to alleviate our suffering? What surgery might we undergo to excise the corrupt part of our mind and soul? I have no answers.

For the phrenologists, the shape of the skull corresponds to the areas of the brain beneath. The brain is divided into myriad different organs – the organ of deceit, the organ of amativeness, the organ of cruelty. A skilled phrenologist can read one's personality, one's destiny, from the contours and measurements of the cranium. Discredited as the work of quacks and charlatans, I have nonetheless read Combe, Spurzheim, Gall. And when I run my hands across my own skull I know they are right. I can feel my faculty for killing as a raised area upon my head. Beside it, my organ of compassion is small, diminished. It seems I was always destined for murder.

Chapter Twenty-Two

All at once we had a warm day. The vapours that had
beset us vanished and the sky glowed azure. I could
not remember that last time the heavens had been so
clear, and all around us people turned their faces skyward.
The anatomists would be cursing it, for they needed cold
days if their corpses were to last. Gabriel, Jenny and I went
to the physic garden. I asked Will to come with us, but he
would not. He said he had work to do, and he vanished as
soon as we had breakfasted.

Jenny glanced at me. 'Anyone would think he was off to
meet his sweetheart,' she said. 'He reeked of sandalwood
and lemon verbena.'

'It's against the stink of the corpses,' I said. 'The place
where he works is a charnel house.' I could tell she did
not believe me.

At the physic garden we made a rather subdued party.
Without Will we seemed incomplete. I plucked weeds
from the earth and trimmed back dead heads. I hoed

and dug and gathered windfalls. Jenny helped me at the poison beds. She was rather pleased with the effect her "deathly draught" had had on Mrs Roseplucker, though I had had strong words with her about experimenting on unsuspecting customers. She seemed to have no idea that anything amiss had happened. I knew it was I who was to blame. Had I been less absent she would never have dared to do such a thing. Without me there, however, she had done just as she pleased.

Gabriel gathered sticks and twigs and I made him clean out the stove in the hot house. Later, we sat in silence around a brazier, upon which I had set some apples to roast. Their skins split and oozed a sticky juice that bubbled and browned on the hot iron stove top.

'Mr Will loves your roasted apples,' said Gabriel. 'Why isn't he here?'

I told them where he was, and straight away they jumped up and stood on the old wheelbarrow to look over the wall at Corvus Hall.

'It looks horrible,' said Jenny. She sniffed. 'And it stinks.'

I went to stand beside her. She was right. Usually Corvus Hall was concealed behind a curtain of fog, the lamps burning on either side of the front door mere blobs of gritty light struggling to illuminate the gloom. Today, however, there was no fog, and the Hall could be seen clearly. How ugly it had become! The ivy had been cut back from the walls, leaving a black tracery of grasping roots. The stucco needed to be painted. The filthy London atmosphere, perpetually tainted with coal smoke, had stained it horribly, and it was streaked yellow and brown like a privy floor. In some places damp seemed to have taken hold, and lumps of plaster had fallen away showing the brickwork beneath in ugly sores. For all the bustle and activity inside, from the outside it was the image of decay.

'How long does he have to stay there?' she said.

'I don't really know,' I replied. 'Until he had finished his commission, I presume.'

'Does he like it in there?'

'I don't think so.'

'What room is he in?'

I pointed up. Will's eyrie was north facing, overlooking the garden and the dead house. His window was open wide to the breeze that blew across the city that day.

'Is that him?' said Jenny. She rooted in the satchel that she carried everywhere and produced a telescope.

'Where did you get that?' said Gabriel, clearly envious.

'I used to work on the Floating Hospital, remember? There were loads of sailors. One of them gave me this.' She pulled it its full length and put it to her eye, training it on the window at the very top of the house. 'It's him all right,' she said. 'Shall we call to him? His window is wide open. Perhaps he can come down—'

'He's working.' I took the telescope from her and peered through its brass eye. There he was, magnified and framed in a dark circle. 'We should probably leave him alone.'

'But we are only down here!' She opened her mouth to call out, but at that moment I saw someone else appear behind him. It was Miss Crowe.

'Shh, Jenny!' I said. 'Don't you dare!' Lilith Crowe stood with her back to the window for a moment. I could see the buttons on her dress, the wisps of hair at the nape of her neck. I knew I should look away, that what I was doing was spying – spying on my greatest friend – and yet I could not

266

stop. But what good do those who listen at doors or spy through keyholes ever learn? For when she turned and put her arms about his neck and kissed him, I felt a sickness to my stomach more bitter and disappointed than anything I could have imagined.

∞

Will had been in the bone room for hours and was looking ill. Before him on the bench was a pair of lungs. They had been neatly sliced and pinned open.

'Halliday did it,' he said. 'He's a marvel with the knife.' Will had drawn them as he saw them, neat, clear, almost diagrammatic. His images would make the most striking and illustrative wood engravings. I said as much, and could tell he was pleased. He showed me some of his other drawings. 'I have never worked so fast, Jem,' he said. 'Dr Crowe has set a punishing pace. He says he wants the book done as soon as possible. By Christmas! He says it is his legacy. He seems very confident.'

'I'm glad it's going well,' I said.

'Mind you, I've been in the dissecting room too – I took my drawing board down – he said I could have a desk there if I wished, but—' he grimaced. 'I refused. The place is unspeakably vile. Did you see the rats? And all the stuff about the floor? Hell could hardly be worse. He had set out a cadaver for me—'

'Let me see your drawings,' I said gently.

'I tried to give them some dignity.' He passed me a folder. 'I didn't just want a headless torso, as if who they were scarcely mattered. But at the same time I did not want to do a portrait of someone's dead mother with her cranium sliced open like a grapefruit and her brain exposed.'

'And is Dr Crowe pleased with your work?'

'He's delighted. And even if he's pushing me to work harder and longer, at least I'll be finished faster.' He turned back to his work. 'And I can get away from this infernal place.'

'Will you never be happy?' I said. 'At least you are warm and dry inside, and not digging up the dead in the freezing rain, the way you were at St Saviour's.'

'Will I never be happy,' he murmured. He glanced over at me, his gaze flickering up over my right shoulder, and he smiled. 'Maybe I shall, one day.'

I turned to see the object of his pleasure. 'Miss Crowe,' I said. 'Good afternoon.'

'Gentlemen,' she said. 'I'm glad I find both of you here. My father wonders whether you would care to join us for dinner on Sunday evening. A small gathering – Dr Cruikshank, Dr Strangeway, Mr Halliday, Dr Allardyce. A few others who knew Dr Wragg.' She had not taken her eyes off Will. It was as though I did not even exist. 'Eight o'clock? Skinner will show you through.'

We sat for a while longer, this time in silence. Was he in love with her? Did he know what she did with Halliday? I could not ask him either question. If the answer to the first was 'yes', then how would I bear it? And I could not then ask the second. I had known, always, that one day he would leave me. It is not possible for a man and a woman to remain friends for ever, not as intimately and exclusively as Will and I. Sooner or later one or other of them would be bound to look elsewhere for love. My heart was broken already, and I bore it as best I could – what remained was held together, I knew, by my feelings for Will. Now, it seemed, it was Will's turn. And yet I knew Lilith Crowe would only bring him pain. Her name alone should have told him that much, for Lilith Crowe was named for a monster of the night. A demon. Adam's first wife, banished into the wilderness for refusing to submit, her offspring had formed the evil spirits of all the world. Did she not live up to her name? I should have applauded her independence, her power, her intelligence and sensuality. Why might she not lie with any man she chose? Why should she not be as skilled with the scalpel as any of them? And yet I did not. I *could* not.

'Would you like an apple?' I said. But Will did not answer. He did not answer because he had not heard me. And he had not heard me because he was thinking of her.

I sighed. I wondered where Halliday was. His desk was covered in items he had brought up from the anatomy museum – some so ancient I had no idea what they were, their labels yellowed, the inked scrawl that had once identified them faded and brown or obliterated by leaked preserving fluid.

I heard rustling coming from Dr Wragg's room. Perhaps it was a rat – there were plenty about the place, despite the efforts of Dr Cruikshank and Bullseye. Perhaps it was Dr Allardyce. Skinner had told me that Dr Allardyce was removing Dr Wragg's belongings – which did not amount to much, when all was said and done – and had decided to move into Dr Wragg's old quarters beneath the eaves. 'He's a part of the anatomy museum himself,' Skinner had muttered. 'Just like Dr Wragg. No doubt he'll end up anatomised and bottled and sitting on the shelves too, and then he can stay here for ever.'

As if he had been conjured from my own imagination, at that very moment Dr Allardyce appeared at the door. 'Well, well,' he said. 'It seems we are to be neighbours. Where's Halliday?'

'I don't know, sir,' I said. 'Perhaps he is in the library.'

Dr Allardyce nodded. His eyes strayed over to look at Halliday's desk. 'What's he working on?'

'I'm not sure,' I said. 'Perhaps you should ask him.'

Dr Allardyce went over to Halliday's desk. He looked at the specimens that Halliday had gathered. 'Well I can't see much logic in these,' he said. 'It's all old stuff from years ago.' He laughed unpleasantly. 'You see? He's not the golden boy everyone thinks he is. If he's left to his own devices he hardly knows what to do. No wonder Dr Wragg despaired of him.'

'I think Dr Wragg respected him,' I said. 'But just disagreed with his classification of pathology.'

Dr Allardyce looked irritated. 'Damn the man,' he said. 'I try to like him, but I simply can't.'

'When we met you in Sorley's,' I said, 'you said Halliday "deserved what he got". What did you mean?'

He shrugged. 'Nothing.'

'But Halliday was ill. That was the only thing that he "got". He could have died. He *would* have died, had he not had the wit to do what he did, to drink salt and sugar to replace what his body had lost.' I smiled. I knew Dr Allardyce might be easily provoked. 'An inspired decision based on observation and experience, don't you agree? And yet perhaps it was not cholera at all. He said he had been eating oysters. Was it the oysters, sir?'

'Perhaps.' Dr Allardyce flicked through the papers on Halliday's desk.

'I think you should step away from his desk, sir,' said Will. 'Unless someone accuses *you* of plagiarism.'

'Me!' Dr Allardyce turned purple. 'How dare you! You've been listening to Halliday, haven't you?'

'No, sir,' said Will.

I smiled. 'Do you resent his success, Dr Allardyce? His skill with the knife? His easy manner with the students? You could make a friend of him, you know. It might serve you better.'

'Don't you patronise me, *apothecary*,' he snapped. 'I will not "make a friend of him". I will not watch him succeed. Why, he's not even a gentleman!'

'But you've seen many young men succeed, surely. You must have helped many of them on their way. You've been anatomy demonstrator for twenty years.'

'Yes. Twenty years and yet never a university post. Always someone *better* than me.'

'You could have gone into private practice.'

His face had become sweaty, his tongue darting across pale lips. 'I can't—'

'Why ever not? You can have no particular loyalty to this place after so long. You have practised on more corpses that anyone.'

'Yes, yes, but still.'

'It would be most lucrative. Ask Dr Crowe, Dr Cruikshank. I'm sure they would help you.'

'I cannot,' his voice was almost a scream. 'I've told you, I cannot cut a living body. I . . . I don't know why. To feel them warm, breathing; to stand over the quivering flesh, knife in hand—' He screwed his eyes closed. 'I cannot be . . . I cannot be trusted not to do harm. And so I must stay away.' He scowled again, his voice a low mutter of resentment. 'Not *quite* the man we are looking for. Not *quite* good enough. Works hard, but, not really a *London* man. And then along comes Halliday. How Dr Crowe adores him. The son he never had – both of his are dead, you know. Mere babies they were. You see how the daughters always dress in black? Even now? Halliday – blue eyed, golden haired, charming, and so, so *capable*. He has become Dr Crowe's pet, his most beloved pupil, and I? I was never beloved, not like that.' His shoulders sagged. 'A dull clod. I should expect no more, I suppose.'

'And so you took matters in your own hands. It was not cholera, was it—?'

'Of course it was! You saw him. You saw how he looked, the blue cast to the flesh, the dark circles, the wizened skin about the eyes – of course it was cholera!'

'Then how—?'

'Oh, come along, Flockhart. Surely you can see that cholera is not borne upon miasma, nor upon foul vapours and the air we breathe. I cannot be the only man who sees that theory and does not accept it. I admit the cholera is born in filth, but transmitted by the *smell* of it? What man ever died of a stink? And we all inhale the foul vapours, but we do not all get the cholera. There must be some other means of transmission. Perhaps through the skin, or the soles of the feet? The poor die more readily and they are often seen walking through the mire barefoot. Perhaps it is in the food or the water? I have mulled the matter over, and I decided that water is the most likely vector, filthy water. And so I waited until I heard that the blue death had visited the city – in the east, of course – and I went and I drew water from six different pumps in the infected streets. And then I put that water into John

Halliday's beer as we passed the evening together. It was partly an experiment – but one that I admit I hoped would not end well for him.' He shrugged. 'And yet he did have a chance. Everyone does, for there *are* those who live. And, of course, my theory might have been wrong.'

'You experimented on a colleague, a student, without his knowledge?' said Will. 'You could have killed him!'

'Exactly,' cried Dr Allardyce. 'Why on earth do you think I did it?'

'But look at what you could have achieved!' I cried. 'The city – all our great cities – are bedevilled by cholera, year after year. Theories of miasma are accepted everywhere. You could have taken your idea to the Royal Society. You could have tested it properly. You could have saved thousands by proving you were right, rather than using it to try to kill a man.' I could not believe what I was hearing. How, when, had Dr Allardyce so lost sight of the purpose of his knowledge, of his profession? When had he become so blinded by jealousy that he took the germ of a great discovery and turned it to so personal and wicked a purpose?

'You were so close, so very close to being a great man,' I whispered. 'To achieving precisely what you wanted – the admiration and respect of your peers. A place in history, even! And yet you threw it away!'

Dr Allardyce shuffled his feet. His eyes were red rimmed from lack of sleep. 'You don't understand,' he said. His face had closed to me, his eyes wary. 'You have no idea at all. But I did not kill John Halliday, for all that I tried.' He laughed. 'And you cannot prove anything.'

Chapter Twenty-Three

I knew I should stay away from the Hall. I had no real reason to be there – I did not pay to attend classes, I did not buy a ticket for the anatomy museum. Skinner let me in because he knew I came to see Will, but I felt like an interloper. I did not linger in the hallway talking to the students, but hastened through the building with my bag of bread, cheese and apples, and my bottle of cordial. Will was always pleased to see me, though there were times when he looked disappointed, as though he'd hoped my footsteps had belonged to someone else.

On one occasion I met Miss Crowe on the stairs. 'Mr Flockhart,' she said. 'I have just been to see Mr Quartermain. My father is very impressed with his work.'

'He is very skilful, Miss Crowe,' I said.

She looked at me for a moment, with a slight smile on her face, as if she were weighing up my ugly red birthmark and wondering what type of a rival she had – certainly, not one who could compete with her in terms of looks. She smiled and said, 'He is lucky to have such a chaperone. You are very vigilant about his welfare. Do you worry something will happen to him? I can assure you I am looking after him *very* well. He said you would probably come,' she added, the smile falling away. 'You always do, don't you?'

I continued up the stairs. Had the two of them been talking about me? I could not believe Will would be so disloyal.

The following day, as I approached the room where he worked I heard voices. Will's voice was no more than a murmur. And the other voice? I listened. It was Dr Crowe. At first I thought they might be talking about the anatomy textbook he was working on, but then I heard Lilith's name.

'She is not like other women,' Dr Crowe insisted. 'She has lived a sheltered life, and no matter how worldly-wise she may appear to you, Mr Quartermain, I can assure you she is not. She has received a singular education for a woman, something I have insisted upon and which I hoped would provide her with fulfilment enough to prevent her from—' He stopped, as if unable to say the last words of his sentence. What did he hope to prevent? From the way he was talking it was as if he hoped to prevent her from marrying. 'But it is not an education in the ways of the world,' he went on. 'I fear she does not understand matters of etiquette.'

'I find her outspokenness most refreshing,' said Will.

'No, sir,' said Dr Crowe. He sounded impatient, frustrated. 'She is used to young men, such as yourself, and perhaps does not always act in ways considered . . . to be the ways of a lady. I trust you will behave honourably and consider her sensibilities at all times.'

'Of course, sir,' said Will. I could tell he was mystified, and on this occasion when I appeared at the door he looked greatly relieved to see me.

'Ah, Mr Flockhart,' said Dr Crowe. 'I'm glad you are here – someone to watch over Mr Quartermain.' He laughed, and though I thought it a queer thing to say, I did not remark on it. Why would Will need to be watched over? 'Well, well,' he said, evidently unwilling to continue with the topic of his daughter, now that I had arrived. 'I must go back to my anatomists. A dull lot they are this morning. I fear Dr Allardyce has bored them half to death, which has not helped matters. Mind you, apart from Halliday they are a lacklustre group. I fear for the profession if this is the best we can get. All they do is complain – about the fees, about the teaching, about the bodies. They have no idea how lucky they are! Why, one of the first things I was expected to do when I began my medical education was to procure *myself* a corpse! It was the same for Cruikshank and Allardyce. Dr Wragg was most useful, advising where to go and how to manage it, but nevertheless we were all expected to dig up our own cadaver. A terrible business it was too – sometimes they were rotten, sometimes we were chased from the kirkyard by gangs of relatives. More than one of us was caught. One poor chap was sentenced to three years' transportation, just to make an example of him.' He shook his head. 'These young fellows have no idea!'

He smiled and turned to leave. 'Capital work, my dear Quartermain,' he said over his shoulder. 'I could not have chosen better in choosing you.'

'What was that all about?' I said.

'I'm not sure,' said Will. 'I think he was warning me away from his daughter. He said she must never marry, though I don't understand why. Why may she not, if she wishes it?' He turned back to his work. 'You're late tonight,

Jem. But I am still not finished, even so. Will you wait a while?' I nodded. I had taken to searching through the various boxes of letters that were stacked about, to see what I might find. He never asked me why and I did not say, but hours would pass with us both working in silence – he on his drawings, me searching, searching in vain for something more from my mother, another letter perhaps, a voice from the grave that told me something more of the person she had been.

The hours passed. Neither of us noticed how dark and quiet it had become until we were disturbed by a scuffling sound coming from downstairs. Somewhere deep in the building a clock chimed – nine o'clock! How late it now was! The scuffling grew louder. I heard a gasp, and then all at once there came the sound of glass shattering. I sprang to my feet and rushed out into the passage. I should have guessed that something was amiss – the silence had been too pregnant, the scuffling that had started up had had a desperate quality to it, like heels drumming and fingers scrabbling though I had been too distracted for it to register in my mind. I clattered down the stairs to the museum. The place was in darkness, and although it was clear that something was happening somewhere, I could not see where. At the sound of my feet on the stair the noise stopped – to be replaced by a gasp and a hoarse cry. I still could not see who it was or what had happened. I crept forward, through the dark ranks of glittering specimens.

Ahead of me in the gloom I saw a figure, a dark shape struggling to its feet. He sank to his knees, then tried to rise again, his hands clutched about his neck. It was Dr Strangeway. Up ahead, beyond the figure, there was nothing – and yet the darkness seemed to stir, as if someone had just that moment moved quickly through it. Dr Strangeway was now leaning against the shelves, coughing and gasping, his hand to his throat. Beside him, knocked to the floor, his candle rolled. His attacker would have been able to follow him easily through the exhibits on stealthy feet.

'Will!' I shouted, but he was already close behind me. 'Look after him,' I said. My eyes fixed on the shadowy darkness ahead, I plunged through the shelves and into the heart of the anatomy museum.

The museum was the largest room in the building. A pair of double doors half way down opened out onto the room of écorchés – the scalded men – the wax exhibits and animal bones, and from there through to Dr Strangeway's workshop. All was dark. Usually there were students, at least one or two, their candles glowing amongst the shelves, though Dr Crowe was always complaining how rarely the students used the museum. Now, there was no one at all. I wished I had a candle myself, though as my quarry did not have one either we were evenly matched. I stopped and listened. Up ahead I felt the whisper of movement, though the darkness seemed thicker than ever. Bottles and jars, usually catching the candlelight in a thousand glittering points, were dark. The blinds over the windows that protected the specimens from the glare of the sun were half raised. Halliday liked to position them that way once the day was on the wane, for he preferred to work in daylight if he could. Outside the moon was shrouded in clouds of tarnished silver. But the wind was up, and all at once the dark was swept aside. The moonlight flooded in, the museum glimmering in a ghastly monochrome. Ahead, a shadow drifted silently away.

'Stop!' My voice was as shrill as broken glass. I ran down the room, the only way out was back the way we had come or out through the doors at the end and into the écorché room and the wax workshop – Dr Strangeway's lair. Surely I could catch them before they reached it. But the moon was a capricious friend that night and all at once it vanished. The darkness it left behind was more complete than ever. Up ahead I sensed that my quarry had hesitated. Something had stalled them – now was my chance!

I plunged between the shelves. I did not see the row of glass bottles that had been set across my path until it was too late. I ran straight into them, kicking one over with the toe of my boot. It spun out across the floor, the contents spilling in a slippery pool. My feet skittered in the mess, the smell of preserving spirits rising up. I felt something soft and meaty squelch beneath my heel and I slipped, crashing down to lie amongst the wreckage. I felt a cold, yielding wet blob beneath my hand, the spike of a shard of glass, and then I was up again and moving forward. Behind me I heard a voice – Will shouting after me – but I did not answer. Part of me hoped that he thought I might be hurt, that he would worry and come after me, that he would think about me at least. The moon came out again, and then vanished once more, a strobe of silver in that gleaming world of flesh and glass and fluid. Up ahead, my quarry moved without hesitation, still no more than a dark shadow. Was it man or woman? I could not tell.

I saw a shape flit through the door up ahead and I followed it into the museum of bones. Inside, everything was suddenly, eerily, still. There was no way back other than past me, and no way forward but into the wax workshop. What would I do when I found them? I hardly knew. I heard a sound behind me – Will at last! I turned to bid him be quiet – but it was not Will at all. Instead there was only blackness, and in it, surging towards me, was a vision of hell, red muscle and white eyeballs, a grinning mouth and high bald head. I had only a moment to wonder – *were there two of them? Two working in tandem?* – before the thing was upon me – cold and hard and much heavier than I expected. Down I went, crushed to the floor beneath the female écorché. In the darkness, her face, inches from mine, seemed demonic, furious, a parody of my own crimson mask. But while my face was ugly in its lack of uniformity, she was perfect in every line and angle, possessed of a terrible fiendish beauty that made me cry out in terror, for all that I knew she was nothing but wax laid upon bone. I heard footsteps, hasty now, but light and faint. A door opened and closed and I knew they were gone. I shoved the wax model aside. Hands helped me to my feet. It was Will.

'Leave me alone,' I said, petulant that he had seen me caught out, that he had heard me scream. He stepped back while I dusted my clothes.

'Dr Strangeway was attacked in the anatomy museum,' he said. 'This was about his neck.' He held out a scarf, a thin shawl of pale blue lace stretched tight into a narrow rope. I had seen it before. I could tell by Will's face that he had too, for it belonged to Lilith Crowe.

❦

Dr Strangeway sat in his wax workshop. He was alone at his workbench with his head in his hands. Usually the place was blazing with light, but he sat now with only a candle on the table, a dim and lonely flame that made the shadows leap. The shelves that lined the walls were filled with skulls and faces, organs, limbs, malignancies, bones and torsos all perfectly rendered in wax. On the table before him lay Mrs Roseplucker's visage. Her eyes were closed, her expression set in a belligerent frown. It had been expertly painted, from her whey coloured flesh to the fine bloom of thread veins that covered her cheeks, and the moist sore at the edge of her nose. Somehow I found the image reassuring – if Mrs Roseplucker was with us then surely all was well?

'Yes,' he said, seeing where my gaze was fixed. 'It's very good, isn't it? It's from a series of moulages of syphilis we have worked on over the years. I believe Sorrow and Silence—' his voice seemed to snag on their names, as though he wished he did not have to utter them. 'I believe they found this lady at the gates. We have a series of six now.'

'You no longer make models, do you, sir?'

He shook his head and held out his hands. 'The scars,' he said. 'I had smallpox years ago. My sister – Dr Crowe's wife – and myself, we both had it. I have no idea where it came from. A nursemaid who was helping to look after the children, some said. Her cousin was afflicted,' he shrugged. 'Who can say why the disease chooses some and not others? Why some of us recovered and others did not. We had all been vaccinated.' He held out his hands. 'It did not seem too bad at first, but as time passed I lost more and more movement. I lost the desire to draw too.'

'It's Lilith, isn't it? Lilith who makes the models.'

He nodded. 'Lilith and her sisters. They do all the wax modelling. Sorrow and Silence are quite remarkable.

Especially Sorrow. She is blind, but her hands—' he shook his head. 'She does not need eyes to know what is before her.' He stood up and went to a screened-off portion of the studio. 'Come and see this.'

He pulled back a curtain. On the table behind was a bust perfectly rendered in wax.

'It's me!' I hardly knew what else to say. How had she managed to capture such a likeness with only her touch, I could not begin to imagine. There was but one crucial difference – she had omitted my scarlet birthmark. Of course she had, for she could not see it. Without it, I looked like the woman I was, my expression pensive, wary. I turned away, unsure how I felt to be confronted by my unblemished self. 'Silence helped,' said Dr Strangeway seeing my expression. 'They both did it. They find you,' he hesitated, a smile suddenly playing about his lips, 'fascinating.'

'But that night in the mortuary,' said Will. 'That was *you*. I saw *you*.'

'It was Miss Crowe,' I said. 'Was it not? I think you no longer anatomise either, do you, sir? And it is such an unladylike activity. So Lilith does it, collecting the organs she needs at night.'

'But I saw you,' said Will. 'Not her.'

'She wears a mask,' I said. 'Though what, exactly, she is hiding is not yet clear.' I looked at Dr Strangeway. 'A mask of wax, I think?'

Dr Strangeway nodded. 'The young gentlemen sometimes stay in the library all night. They work in the dissecting room until late, they appear at the oddest times, even,' he gave the faintest of smiles, 'even in the mortuary. Sometimes Gloag is there – it is so much easier, for everyone, if they all think that it is me. And I am easy to "be",' he looked at me without flinching. 'My mask is a greater disguise even than yours.' His glaze slid away. Dr Strangeway had a way of not meeting the eyes of his interlocutor. It spoke of the desire not to be seen. I had noted it also in the way that he kept to the shadows, the way he walked with his head down, the way he put a hand up to shield himself from the stares of others. They were mannerisms I had once had myself, when I was younger and more conscious of how ugly my birthmark was. People saw at a glance how he was afflicted and they looked away – in pity at his appearance, in fear at how disease might single out any one of us. It was easy for Miss Crowe to make a wax mask, the skin whorled and pitted, the eyes small and blunted by scar tissue. A cloak, some gloves, no one would notice. Silas Strangeway was known to be reclusive, eccentric, anyone might become him if they wished.

'What is going on here, Dr Strangeway?' I said. 'You know as well as I do that Wilson is dead. You know Dr Wragg was murdered. You know that those hands, severed and left to be found with that card between the fingers, are not simply a student prank. I've never seen a place less full of high spirits than Corvus Hall! Apart from in Dr Cruikshank's lecture theatre the students seem uneasy. Frightened almost. Who can blame them!' I added. 'I have no idea why they stay!'

'They love Dr Crowe and Dr Cruikshank,' he replied. 'Those gentlemen have always commanded the highest regard, the greatest respect. The men are loyal to them. They have always been so. They *must* be so, even though sacrifices sometimes have to be made—' His voice trembled with anxiety, his scarred hands twisting together.

'You mean murder?' said Will.

'The students have nothing to be frightened of.'

'I think they have every reason to be frightened,' I said. 'Look at Wilson!'

Dr Strangeway shook his head. 'You don't understand.'

Dr Allardyce had said the same thing. 'Then tell me, sir,' I said. 'What is it that I do not understand?'

He pressed his lips together, his eyes darting to the door as if in fear that someone might be out there, might be listening.

Will held out the blue silk scarf. 'Dr Strangeway, I found you with this wrapped about your neck. Someone was attempting to strangle you. Is not the time for silence long gone?'

'It's nothing.'

'It was very nearly quite definitely something.'

'I cannot say—' His glance flickered over my shoulder again. I turned, half expecting to see Sorrow and Silence. Instead, there was Lilith Crowe and Dr Cruikshank. At the sight of them, Dr Strangeway stood up. I could not tell from his expression whether he was alarmed or relieved. A muscle in his cheek quivered. 'Thank you for your help, Mr Flockhart. Mr Quartermain. But there is nothing here to worry about.' His eyes darted to Lilith.

'Is everything well with you, uncle?' she said.

'Quite well, my dear.'

'One of the écorchés has fallen,' she said. 'Did you know?'

'Oh,' he said. 'Yes. I—'

She frowned. 'It is broken,' she replied. 'Eve is broken.'

'Dr Crowe seemed to think you might still be here, Flockhart,' said Dr Cruikshank. His face was stony. 'He sent me to find you. I believe you are coming to us for dinner tomorrow. It is in honour of Dr Wragg, a dear colleague whom Dr Crowe knew for many years as a friend, as well as a mentor, and a colleague. A small gathering but enough to acknowledge the doctor's passing. He was an atheist, so there will be no funeral, no burial. He is already dissected. If there are any parts of him you would like for your own collection—'

'Thank you, no,' I said. 'But it is a most generous and tempting offer.' I wondered whether these men had spent so long amongst the dead that they no longer realised how macabre they were. I could see the expression on Will's face and all at once I struggled not to laugh. Dr Cruikshank's gaze flickered from Dr Strangeway, to the silk scarf Will still held in his hands. A look of pain seemed to cross his features. But then he assumed his act once more, seizing his lapels in his fists and jerking his head back so that his ringlets danced.

'Capital, capital!' he cried. 'The old rogue deserves a send-off. And to be pickled and lodged in his own museum for all eternity – what better way for any surgeon to end his days?' I could not share his enthusiasm. Instead, all I saw was that a second murdered body had been neatly and cleanly anatomised, its organs, limbs, appendages, like the first, now distributed far and wide beyond all hope of recovery. What justice was there for either of them in that?

Precognition for the murder of Mary Anderson,
18th December 1830.

Post-Mortem Report by Dr H. Cruikshank and
Dr A. Wragg.

19th December 1830

Post-mortem Examination of the body of Mary Anderson, 19th December 1830. Surgeons' Hall, Edinburgh. Summary of report.

By virtue of my position as police surgeon, within the mortuary at Surgeons' Hall, I, Dr Henry Cruikshank, with the assistance of Dr Angus Wragg, have conducted a post-mortem examination of a female aged approximately eighteen years and identified as one Mary Anderson by Miss Catherine Anderson and Constable James Wilson of the City of Edinburgh Police.

External Appearance

The woman was fairly well nourished, given her known lifestyle and habits, though crippled by an extreme form of rickets which accounts for her twisted lower limbs, and the softening and deformity of the bones in general. The legs are somewhat wasted, being rarely used, though the arms are well developed, and extremely muscular about the shoulders, upper arms, forearms and hands, the result of a lifetime spent propelling the subject through the streets on crutches. The body of the woman showed evidence of considerable bruising about the torso, arms and legs. The bruising was, for the most part, pre-mortem, predating the subject's death by some weeks. The marks of violence on the body that are of recent origin fall into three distinct sets:

1. *Bruising about the neck*

2. *The complete removal of the flesh of the face*

3. *The slicing open of the abdomen (from the umbilicus to the top of the pubis).*

Internal appearance

Examination of the larynx revealed that the windpipe was almost entirely crushed, the bruising of the tissue surrounding the 3rd and 4th cervical vertebrae showing clearly that violence was applied to the neck and throat.

The internal organs – the lungs were of a dark appearance, and showed evidence of the early onset of phthisis. The heart was congested, and the presence of amniotic fluid in the birth canal suggested that parturition had started at the time of death though had not taken place. The skeleton was afflicted with a spinal scoliosis that tilted the pelvis up to the right, so that it lay almost at right angles to its correct alignment.

The womb had been slit from point (A) to point (B), the cavity pulled open and the foetus removed. There was evidence that the womb had ruptured. The placenta remained in place against the uterine wall, the umbilicus neatly severed.

Opinion

From the appearance presented at dissection, and based on an interpretation of the scene of the crime and the location of the body, we the undersigned have reached the following conclusions:

1. *That the subject Mary Anderson was pregnant at the time of her death.*

2. *That the subject was strangled minutes prior to death.*

3. *That strangulation was not sufficient to cause death, but would have rendered the victim apparently lifeless.*

4. *That the subject's foetus (missing) was full term.*

5. *That the foetus was removed via caesarean section through the abdominal wall.*

6. *That the opening of the abdomen was the cause of death.*

7. *That the subject's face was mutilated post-mortem for reason or reasons unknown.*

8. *That the skinning of the face and the slicing of the abdomen were undertaken with precision and skill.*

True on soul and conscience,

[Signed] Angus Wragg, Henry Cruikshank

Chapter Twenty-Four

Gloag had kindled a huge fire at the foot of the garden. The students had taken what they wanted from Dr Wragg's corpse, slicing him up and preparing his body parts as they pleased. One of the students – Renshaw, whom I had first met in the student common room – had even taken the worn sockets of the old man's hips. I had seen him leaving the building carrying the entire pelvis, boiled and varnished, under his arm. Some bits they had added to their own collections, others had gone to the Corvus Hall anatomy museum. What remained was now shoved into the bonfire along with any other bodies that were to be got rid of that day. Dr Crowe, Dr Cruikshank, Dr Allardyce, Will and I had stood respectfully by while the flames consumed the bundled remains of Dr Wragg.

After that we made our way to the dining room along the finely carpeted hallways of Dr Crowe's wing of the building. It was a long elegantly proportioned room with two casement windows looking out onto the garden at the back of the Hall, and from which we could see the dark outline of the dead house and beyond it the dancing flames of Dr Wragg's funeral pyre. The room was comfortably furnished, with chairs beside the fire, and warm carpets upon the floor. It was easy to forget that what lay just the other side of the wall was an anatomy school.

It appeared that Dr Crowe maintained an entire household in the east wing of Corvus Hall. There was no evidence of his profession about the place, no specimens in jars, no books or drawings of body parts, no bones. Even the smell of the dead room, which pervaded the rest of the building, was mercifully absent, though I noticed bowls of herbs, citrus peel, eucalyptus and lavender stood about on side tables and on the mantel, and they did much to sweeten the air.

I hoped it would not turn into an 'evening of medical entertainment'. I had been to such things many times, when specimens were passed around for comment and discussion. Occasionally a dog would be brought forward and an experiment would take place. Sometimes drugs – medicines, poisons, new mixtures – might be tested, one or two of the company taking the stuff while the others stood by to watch, to take notes and to administer emetics and purgatives when needed. They were loud, often messy evenings, and I was not in the mood for it. I hoped the presence of ladies would prevent such activities, but knowing Dr Crowe's daughters there was every chance that it would be they who brought in the dog or produced the unusual specimen. And there they were: the sisters, Sorrow and Silence, side by side on a brocade sofa; Lilith sitting in a wing-backed chair beside the fire. Their heads turned as we entered. I saw Will's cheeks flush with

pleasure as Miss Crowe smiled at him. I dropped my gaze.
I knew Silence was watching me, I knew she could read my
feelings in my face. I wished I could talk to her, but there
was no opportunity for it here.

Beside the bookshelves Dr Crowe was talking to
Tanhauser, who was looking rather out of his depth at the
company he found himself in. His fellow student, Squires,
was speaking to Dr Allardyce – both of them occasionally
glancing towards the door, as if they wished themselves
elsewhere. I noticed that Dr Allardyce had refused a glass
of wine – perhaps he feared alcohol would cause him to
say or do something that he might later regret. He was
staring at a portrait that hung on the wall above the fire. It
showed a young woman sitting in a chair. She wore a green
dress and had a blue shawl about her shoulders. Her face
looked familiar, and I saw that her dark, expressive eyes
were the eyes of Lilith Crowe. Behind the woman was a tall
window, which looked out at the walls of another building.
It was heavily faced with great blocks of grey stone, and as
tall as a fortress – nothing like those we had in London.
Was it Edinburgh? It seemed likely. On the table before
her was a skull and, on its side, an hourglass.

'My sister,' said Dr Strangeway in my ear. I had not
heard him approach for the carpet deadened all footfall.
I noted that his neckerchief was high at his throat that
evening, and that more than once he put up his hand to
it. 'I painted it from memory. And from a . . . a model who
bore a likeness to her. It was some months after her death,
before my hands—' He held them out, both curled into
fists. 'I could not bear to do it sooner, and yet if I had not
done it at all we would have nothing to remind us—'

'She is very beautiful,' I said.

'Oh yes. You can see where she gets her looks, and her charm, of course.'

Will was looking at Miss Crowe, hoping she would look up and see him, no doubt, but she was talking to Dr Cruikshank and Mr Halliday. Dr Strangeway seized Will's arm and steered him towards Tanhauser. Both Dr Crowe and Tanhauser appeared relieved to have a third party in their midst – the former glad to escape a conversation that had run its course, the latter thankful to be no longer required to think of anything intelligent to say. At length Dr Crowe asked us if we would all take our places at the table.

'We are an informal house,' he said. 'Please, sit where you choose.'

I had instructed Will to find out what he could. 'About what?' he had replied. 'Shall I ask each in turn whether they murdered Wilson and Wragg?'

'Just listen,' I had said. 'And observe. I don't know what we will learn this evening, or whether any of it will be of any use, but to have all these people together is an unexpected opportunity. Whatever is going on here involves them all – or surely most of them. You should listen, especially to those you are not talking to.'

'You mean I should eavesdrop?'

'I think it is essential to do so.'

I had never been one for dinner parties and soirées. It seemed to me that groups of people thrown together often looked for an outsider, a scapegoat, to mock or belittle, and I had never wanted to find myself singled out in that way. What if someone had sensed my disguise or suspected that I was not what I seemed? But I saw straight away that that role tonight was most likely to fall to either Dr Allardyce or Tanhauser, the former due to his self-conscious sense of personal failure, and Tanhauser because of his stupidity. But Tanhauser was bluff and doltish and had a well-developed sense of humour – much of it directed at himself. I could not imagine that he would be the one who drew the scorn of the table that evening.

I had Dr Cruikshank on one side of me, and Silence Crowe on the other. Tanhauser waded in with a clumsy attempt at flattery by suggesting to Dr Cruikshank that Dr Crowe's daughters take the examination at the Royal Colleges, or the university, and become surgeons proper.

'An admirable idea, sir,' replied Dr Cruikshank. 'Perhaps you might ask them yourself, Mr Tanhauser, since they are sitting right beside you and – as you imply – are more than capable of thinking for themselves.'

Tanhauser blushed. 'Miss Crowe,' he said. 'I apologise.'

'No apology necessary, Mr Tanhauser,' she said. 'I would not wish to practise as a surgeon myself as my interests do not lie in surgery. Like Dr Allardyce I would rather explore the human body and understand it, than cut and sew living people.'

'I'm sure you would be more than capable of it,' said Will gallantly. 'You just choose not to.'

'And of course, she can't anyway,' said Squires loudly. 'She can't be a surgeon as she's not passed the examinations. And she can't pass the examinations because she cannot *sit* the examinations. She cannot sit the examinations because she is a woman and her mind and body would not stand it.'

I saw Miss Crowe's fingers tighten about her fork, as if she were trying to master an urge to plunge it into the back of Squires's hairy hand. I saw that Dr Cruikshank had perceived it too. He turned the subject to ask about Tanhauser's plans for the future.

Conversation remained for the most part on otherwise anodyne subjects. Occasionally conversation would flag altogether, so that all that could be heard was the crackle and snap of the fire and the scrape and chink of cutlery on china. I saw Tanhauser and Squires exchange a glance and raise their eyebrows. Dr Crowe talked about the new anatomy textbook he was writing, comparing other books that the students were often obliged to rely on. He complimented Will on his drawings.

'Thank you, sir,' said Will. 'Though I admit I am not looking forward to more work in the dissecting room.' Dr Crowe inclined his head. 'We will try to make it as pleasant as possible for you, though a corpse is a corpse and we will do our best to find you the freshest and most youthful.'

'Are you any relation to the Flockharts of Edinburgh?' said Halliday.

'My father's cousins,' I said. 'Druggists. I have never met them. You know them?'

'I know *of* them.'

'You know Edinburgh, Halliday?' said Dr Cruikshank sharply. 'I was not aware of it.'

'A little,' he shrugged. 'One can hardly study medicine without at least visiting the place. I did a year at the extra mural school. But it was not for me.'

'I think it's a dashed poor show if women become doctors,' said Squires loudly. 'The profession's crowded enough as it is without them. I'm sorry to say it, but that's how it is.'

'Why should they not?' said Sorrow. 'Why may women not enter the profession if they are good enough, if they are as good as or better than men? Why shouldn't people benefit? Women in particular might rather be treated by a female.'

'*Better?*' Tanhauser snorted. '*Better* than men?'

Dr Allardyce gave a simper. 'I have examined the female brain on many occasions and it is not fit for purpose – not when it comes to study.'

'There is little difference in brain size,' said Sorrow. 'Men are bigger overall than women, and once this is accounted for there is little enough to distinguish the brain of one from the brain of the other.'

'Strength and stamina are required for study as much as for anything else and in this the male evidently excels,' replied Squires.

'But a woman is stronger physically than the male,' replied Sorrow. 'She must gestate, must create another human being from her own body, she must give birth. What strength of mind and body, what strength of spirit is there in that?'

'Besides,' Tanhauser took a quaff of wine, his face was sweaty, and scarlet from the warmth of the room, and the quantity of wine and food he had consumed. 'The study of anatomy? Forgive me, Dr Crowe, but no wonder your daughters have never got a husband, sir. Who would have them? The things they have seen. It's all very well letting the ladies in to general lectures about hygiene and the circulation of the blood and what have you, but what about the real details? The organs of generation, the viewing of a naked body – the male body – these your daughters have seen time and again. It is hardly decent for a woman to view these things, whether it is in the name of science or no.'

'Come, sir.' Dr Crowe put his glass down. 'You forget yourself.'

Tanhauser blushed. 'I am not the only one who thinks it,' he said. 'Wilson said so too, and look what happened to him.'

The room fell silent. There was no sound other than the crackling of the fire in the grate – which served to remind us all of the fact that another body was at that very moment rather conveniently being incinerated on the back lawn of the house. And then my blood froze in my veins as Sorrow Crowe said, 'Mr Tanhauser, how do you know women are not already practising medicine? They may be amongst us even now, disguised, concealed, showing men that they are just as good, just as capable but not able to show their true selves for fear of what might befall them if they did. Would you know it if they were? Anyone might hide who they are sir, if they wish it. Anyone might deceive their friends and acquaintances, might conceal their heart, their views, their true personality. Why might not they also conceal their identity too? And how would we ever know? How many of us truly know what lies beneath the face others present to the world?'

She could not see the effect her words were having on the room. Her dead gaze swept unseeing over us all. For a moment she seemed to linger on me and I felt as if she saw into my very soul. I was overcome with the urge to leap to my feet, to cry out, 'Yes! Yes, it is I who deceives you, I who walks amongst you unseen, a woman who practises medicine as well as any man!' I felt a cold hand grasp my own beneath the table. Silence Crowe did not look at me, but held my fingers tightly in hers until the feeling passed. Only then did she let it go. I glanced over at Will, a sheen of sweat dampening my brow. But he was gazing entranced at Lilith who sat with her eyes downcast, her lashes dark against her porcelain cheeks, her hair like burnished jet in the candlelight.

'You think I don't see you all?' cried Sorrow. 'You think blindness means I have no vision? But I don't need eyes to see. I can *feel* the fear rising from you the way heat pours from a fire. You are afraid of women. You are afraid they will best you and you will have no power over us. Men are superior only in physical strength. You may overpower us and crush us, you may beat us and rape us, but you are not our masters, and you are not our betters. You are brutes, every one of you!'

'Sorrow, my dear,' said her father gently. 'Please—'

'Oh, Father,' she said. She turned her silvered eyes upon him. 'Do you not know? Do none of you know? There are more secrets around this table than there are people.'

The room fell silent, the only sound the steady ticking of the clock and the angry snap of the coals in the fireplace. I saw Tanhauser and Squires exchange a glance. Dr Allardyce's face had taken on a sickly pallor, whilst Lilith's expression was one of such horror that I thought for one moment that she was about to rise up and dash from the room. Dr Cruikshank saw it too and he sprang to his feet.

'Ladies and gentlemen, friends and colleagues, if I might say a few words about Dr Wragg,' he said. 'He was a true and loyal friend. A man I had known all my professional career, through difficult times, and many trials and troubles. I owe him a great deal. Dr Allardyce, Dr Crowe and I, we all owe him a great deal. To a dear departed friend and colleague. To Dr Wragg.' He raised his glass. We all did the same, all of us but Halliday, who looked as though he would rather hurl his glass at the doctor's head. But then, like everyone else, he raised it in a toast. 'Dr Wragg,' he said. He drained it in one gulp, as if washing down bile.

'Well, Mr Tanhauser,' said Dr Crowe, dabbing at his lips with a napkin. 'I hear you are to quit medicine. I cannot say it is a great loss to the profession.'

'Yes, sir,' he said. 'I have failed anatomy and surgery twice. Dr Allardyce has washed his hands of me.'

'Oh, that's not quite true, Tanhauser,' said Dr Allardyce. 'I n-never wash my hands of any student.'

'You're obviously not suited to medicine,' said Dr Crowe. 'But there will be a calling for you somewhere.'

Dr Cruikshank however was less tolerant. 'You are an idiot, Tanhauser,' he said. 'You have the attention span of a goldfish.'

'I can't help it. The endless lists of things – nerves and bones and organs and what not. And Dr Allardyce's demonstrations make me want to go to sleep.'

Dr Allardyce scowled. 'I cannot work with such poor material as you,' he said. 'I cannot make a silk purse from a sow's ear. Your mind is mush, Tanhauser. Unless I were asking you to remember types of beer, or the runners and riders of the Epsom Derby, in which case you would do admirably.'

'It is an art, Tanhauser, that's all,' said Halliday. He grinned. 'I've tried to help you before but you're an idle beggar and make no effort at all.'

'But it's just a list of *things*.'

'Practise!'

'I can't!'

Lilith turned to Halliday. 'Mr Halliday, if you could turn out your pockets, please?'

'But why?'

'So that I may show Mr Tanhauser how to get himself a better memory – should he consent to learn the trick from a woman.'

Halliday grinned. He seemed relieved, as we all did, that the feeling around the table had grown less prickly. 'Of course,' he said. 'Though I think it will take more than the contents of my pockets to help Tanhauser. Even the lewdest of mnemonics have failed with him. And yet his head is so huge, if we followed the logic of Mr Squires's arguments one might assume him to be a genius.'

'Alas!' said Lilith. 'I fear his brain is actually the size of a walnut and the rest is rags and straw.'

Tanhauser laughed. 'Go on then, Miss Crowe. You can surely not make me any worse.'

Halliday was wearing the coat he habitually wore when he was about his business in the anatomy museum, and although he had brushed the shoulders it was evident that it had seen better days, for the pockets were shapeless and sagging. I had seen him stuff a specimen jar into each one when he had too much to carry up the stairs to his desk. Now, he looked faintly embarrassed that his coat had attracted the attention of a lady, though he emptied its pockets without demur.

'Good Lord, Halliday,' said Dr Allardyce as Halliday spread out the contents on the dinner table. 'Do you have a magpie's nest in there?'

There was laughter at this, for Halliday's pockets did indeed contain a surprising number of things. Lilith fetched a small tea tray of polished wood and laid the items upon it, each one some two inches apart from the other. She held up her hand for silence, and then stared at the miscellany, one after the other, for a minute or more. Then she covered them with a handkerchief – also provided by Halliday. 'Now,' she said. 'I'll wager you ten shillings that I can list the things on this tray in the order in which they are placed starting from the top right. Hold up the handkerchief so that I can't see them. Mr Tanhauser, tell me if I am right.' She closed her eyes. 'A sixpence. A shilling. A length of string. A small stick of sealing wax. A candle end. A fold of blotting paper. A small key. The cog from inside a watch. A tooth. A gallstone. A pencil. A boiled sweet. The nib of a fountain pen. A small wooden whistle. The cork from a beer bottle. A ball of coloured wax. An acorn.' She spoke slowly and methodically, hesitating only once – at which point Tanhauser let out a premature roar of victory – but she resumed directly, listing them all in the order in which they were set out. She did not make a single mistake.

'Extraordinary,' said Tanhauser. Squires said nothing. Dr Allardyce too remained silent. I saw him slip his hand into his coat pocket. He watched Halliday morosely, as if he wished he could empty his own pockets onto the tray, and that his would be much better, more interesting, and far harder to memorise.

'Now you, sir,' said Lilith to Tanhauser. Her face was stony.

Of course, Tanhauser managed only four items, and two of them were not in the right order. He sat back, a sheen of sweat upon his brow as if exhausted by the effort. 'How did you do it?'

'You have heard of Aristotle, Mr Tanhauser, and the *ars memoria*?'

'Alas, no.'

She sighed. The cheer seemed to have gone out of her,

and the explanation she provided, though perhaps no more than he deserved, was dull and perfunctory. Her sisters were similarly restless. I saw her exchange a glance with Silence, and then she gathered up the miscellaneous items and handed them back to Halliday in two fistfuls.

He grinned, and stuffed them back out of sight. 'Far too disciplined for the likes of Tanhauser,' he said. But a gloom seemed to have descended as Lilith's good humour evaporated, and shortly afterwards she said she had a headache and, with her sisters in tow, left the room. Tanhauser and Squires took themselves off soon after, in the company of Dr Allardyce, and the mood lightened still further.

'Two useless boys,' murmured Dr Cruikshank. 'There are many others, just the same. Their fathers send them to be medical men but what's the use if their hearts are not in it? Fortunately not all our students are like that.' He smiled. 'Dr Crowe?'

'Ah yes! My dear boy.' Dr Crowe turned to Halliday. 'There is something Dr Cruikshank and I wanted to speak to you about. He and I – and I'm sure Dr Allardyce concurs – we believe you to be a quite exceptional young man. I realise you have had your differences with Dr Allardyce.' He sighed. 'He used to be such a bright young lad – not as bright as you, dear boy.' There were tears in Dr Crowe's eyes as he spoke. Dr Cruikshank watched him carefully, as if fearing that Crowe was about to say too much. 'You remind me of someone,' he said. 'A long time ago now. I have only daughters, you see, so who might I – who might I—'

'Dr Crowe would like you to join Dr Allardyce as one of the anatomy demonstrators,' said Dr Cruikshank. 'The students look to you for guidance. And you have a keenness, and a degree of charisma that the teaching of anatomy needs. Without such things it is dull, dull, dull. Our students do not look to Dr Allardyce. They do not . . . do not hear him, respect him.' He looked at Dr Crowe. 'I don't know why you keep him, Sandy.'

'You do know why,' replied Dr Crowe. He clapped his hands. 'But come. Halliday, my dear boy, I see in you another Hunter, another Cooper. Will you accept the position?'

Halliday's face was white, his eyes ringed by dark circles as if he had hardly slept for days. Anatomy demonstrator at only twenty-four years old – it was an honour indeed. I saw him lick his lips, his eyes darting towards the door. I frowned. Was he frightened? But of what?

Dr Crowe saw it too. A look of consternation crossed his face, as if he feared his offer was about to be rejected. 'And to mark that appointment I would like you to accept these.' Dr Crowe reached up to the mantel and took up a box. It was made from polished walnut with a clasp of gleaming silver. He buffed it with his sleeve, and then handed it over. Halliday's face had turned almost green. His lips were bloodless. His hands shook as he took the box, and saw his own initials embossed upon the lid in silvered copperplate.

'Open it,' murmured Dr Crowe. 'They are for you.'

Halliday swallowed, and eased the lid open. Inside, resting on a layer of plush velvet, was a set of surgical knives. He seemed unable to speak. I saw him swallow again, and close his eyes. Moisture beaded his upper lip. He opened his eyes and looked down at the contents of the box. All at once he cried out, the box springing from his hands as if it were burning hot, the knives cascading into the hearth like shards of ice.

*Precognition for the murder of Mary Anderson,
18th December 1830.*

From the *Edinburgh Evening Courant,* 21st December 1830

On the morning of the 20th inst. a tragic incident occurred at Surgeons' Hall. Following the murder of the woman known as Mary Anderson some two days earlier it had come to light that a knife had been found at the scene of the crime bearing the initials of one James H. Franklyn, recently appointed demonstrator at Dr Crowe's anatomy school of 13 Surgeons' Square. Mr Franklyn had been unable to account for his whereabouts between the hours of approximately half past 8 and 10 o'clock on the evening of the 18th inst., when the murder was believed to have taken place. Although he claimed to be walking to Surgeons' Hall from Duddingston at that time, no one had seen him on the road. The knife bore evidence of recent use, and was smothered with fresh blood.

On arriving at Surgeons' Square with a view to apprehending the young man, the arresting constables found that an angry mob had already gathered in anticipation of the seizure of one or other of the anatomists. Mr Franklyn was understood to have visited the deceased on many occasions, and was rumoured to have tried to purchase her corpse even before she was dead. Being aware of this, and with the dreadful events of the West Port, and the trial of Burke and Hare still fresh in the minds of the population, the mob had gathered outside Surgeons' Hall, into which building Franklyn had vanished in search of asylum. Pursued by the arresting officers, and no doubt sensing the hand of justice closing in upon him, the young man was heard to cry out that he was innocent of the crime; that Dr Crowe knew he was innocent; that they should ask Dr Crowe, and if *they* would not then *he* would. So saying he ran to a window at the rear of the building and, throwing the sash wide, attempted to jump down from the first floor.

Despite being a drop that would not ordinarily have resulted in anything more unfortunate than a broken ankle, it seems that in his haste and desperation the young man opened the wrong window, and instead of dropping onto the lawn at the back of the building fell to his death, some 40 feet into the basement area.

There are currently no other suspects in the murder of Mary Anderson. As a result, it appears that the law has, on this occasion, been served by misadventure, the young man's flight eliminating whatever doubt might have remained in anyone's mind as to his guilt.

It is to be assumed that the dead babe of the murdered woman, the body of which has never been found, was disposed of by Franklyn before he had the chance to confess its whereabouts. Franklyn's personal 'anatomy collection' has been taken by the police, and it is believed that the items contained therein will be found to include the preserved body of the missing child.

Chapter Twenty-Five

❦

Will and I walked home along St Saviour's Street in silence. The evening had been unsettling – Corvus Hall struck me as the most macabre of places, the people in it bound together by something as disturbing as it was unknown. I thought I understood medical men, that although they might seem largely driven by ambition, in their hearts they had the best of intentions. I had never allowed my experiences at St Saviour's, at Angel Meadow Asylum or on board the Seaman's Floating Hospital stop me from thinking otherwise. They were fascinated by the body and its workings, were driven to find out all they could about it, and this often led them down pathways most would baulk at – robbing graves for corpses, experimenting on animals, anatomising anything that had once drawn breath. But Corvus Hall seemed to have its own logic, its own ways of behaving. That death was its currency seemed to mean that when terrible things happened – unidentified bodies found, faces removed, hands severed – these acts were considered unremarkable. It was a world that seemed divorced from normality. I almost wished more of them were grinning, well-meaning dolts like Squires and Tanhauser.

I sensed that Will was looking at me, though I did not turn to confirm it. And, of course, there was something else that bothered me too.

'Are you in love with her?' I said. I still could not look at him. I had meant to say something quite different, something about what was going on at Corvus Hall, but Will was at the front of my mind.

'With whom?' he said mildly.

'With Miss Crowe,' I said. 'With Lilith.'

He did not speak for a moment, then 'Jem—'

'I understand,' I said. 'I cannot love you. Not the love you deserve or want. And so you must look elsewhere. You must. You cannot be happy just living with me as your friend. It's like Squires and Tanhauser—'

He grinned. 'God, Jem, I hope you never smell like either of them.' He looked away. 'But since you ask, then yes. I believe I am.' He sighed. 'She is perfect in every way. Bold, clever, unique. Did you see her this evening? The way she put that fellow Squires in his place, the way she showed Tanhauser up to be the dolt he is. I know her father has given her an unorthodox upbringing but that is all to the good. She is independent, beautiful, wise. She needs no man to make her complete, but to be her equal – who would not delight in such companionship? You saw the memory game, Jem. How she could recollect every piece. I thought she would not manage it. There was one point when she faltered – you recall?' I did recall. It was as though in her mind something had jarred, or slipped, for she had been proceeding quite smoothly up to that point. And then all at once she had hesitated. A slow smile had spread across Tanhauser's face as he thought she had failed – but she had drawn a breath and carried on. And yet she had not looked the same afterwards – at the time I had assumed it was due to the fact that she had almost failed in the task she had set herself – memorising seventeen disparate items in the correct order. And yet—

I stopped dead, the hairs on the back of my neck suddenly damp with fear. 'We must go back,' I said. 'We must go back now.'

'Why?' said Will. He sighed. In the distance the clock at St Saviour's church chimed. 'It is past midnight—'

'We must go back,' I said, 'because if we do not, then all is lost.'

We let ourselves in the front door and locked it behind us. The Hall was silent, though I knew we were not alone that night; that in the darkness there would be others waiting. Not down here, but upstairs, up on the top floors where few of the students bothered to go. For the killer those upper storeys were safe and familiar, every inch mapped out, every artefact placed just so, so that it could be negotiated blind.

A lantern had been left on the table in the hall, its light glinting off the two twisted skeletons in their glass boxes. I put my finger to my lips, and listened. At first there was nothing. Nothing but that great echoing silence. Was I mistaken? I had been so sure. I had seen what Lilith had seen, I knew what she knew. And then I heard it.

A movement, a sigh, perhaps, or a soft footfall. I could not be sure, but I knew it had begun.

'Quickly,' I cried. I bounded up the stairs. Never had the place felt so huge and empty, so dark and fearful. I led Will down the hallway towards the anatomy museum. Up ahead the door to Dr Strangeway's workshop was open, the light bright, as it always was, splashing out into the hall in a square of yellow, lurid against the pressing darkness.

Inside was in a state of terrible disorder. It was clear that there had been a struggle, the models that had stood on the table top had been knocked aside. One of the Venuses – one of Dr Strangeway's 'girls' – had been flung to the floor, her organs spilling out obscenely even as her face looked heavenwards, her expression ecstatic. The smell of wax that hung in the air was tainted with some other, richer smell, a smell at once earthy and visceral. I had smelled it before in that room the first time we had visited, the first time I had met Dr Strangeway and he had told me he had needed ten human heads to create the waxen model that had been sent to the Exhibition. It was the smell of blood.

Dr Strangeway was sitting in a high-backed chair. Around his neck was a sky-blue shawl, wound tight as a tourniquet. I realised then where I had seen it before, for there was one just like it – around the shoulders of Mrs Crowe, in the portrait that hung above the fireplace. The portrait painted by Dr Strangeway. He was dead, there seemed little doubt about it. The shawl had been wrung into a twisted rope, wrapped tight about his neck again and again, and then tied to the chair so that he might remain upright. Before him stood the sisters, Sorrow and Silence. In her hand, Silence held a long sharp Liston knife. In the bright lamplight of the wax modelling room the drop of blood that hung from its tip glittered like a ruby. There was more of the stuff dripping down the wall, for above the strangled figure of Dr Strangeway a severed hand had been nailed. A card, no bigger than a *carte de visité*, bearing the words *et mortui sua arcana narrabunt*, had been jammed between its fingers.

'Who is it?' cried Sorrow. She looked about wildly, her face anguished, tears pouring from her silver eyes. She would be able to sense death, and fear, though her world would be dark. How terrified she must be. She staggered against the chair where Dr Strangeway was positioned. Blood from the stump of his hand had pooled about the floor and sopped into the hem of her dress.

'What in God's name have you done?' cried Will. He staggered back, his hand to his head, his face grey. The sight was so horrible I was sure he would faint, but he did not.

'Help me, Will,' I said. 'Find a paintbrush.'

'A paintbrush—?'

'Just do it!' I dashed forward. 'And then get this thing from around his neck. Is he alive? Miss Crowe. Sorrow. Is he alive?'

'Yes,' she whispered. Her fingers gripped my arm like the roots of a tree. 'I was trying to . . . to—'

'To help. Yes,' I said. I seized the length of bandage that streamed from her hand. 'And this was to be a tourniquet. It is perfect.'

I slid the paintbrush beneath the tourniquet I had tied about his arm, and turned it, pulling the band tight and stopping the flow of blood. The cloth about his neck dug into his flesh but I sliced through it with the Liston knife, snatched from Silence's limp grasp. She seemed transfixed, staring at her uncle, at the blood, unable to move. Dr Strangeway slumped sideways almost onto the floor. Together, Will and I hauled him onto the workbench. He lay there, as still and silent as one of his own wax models, surrounded by his paints, pigments, varnishes, all the clutter of his life.

'Who did this?' Will said. He seized Silence by the shoulders. 'Who? Did you see them?' But she could not speak, she could not do anything but shake her head, her face paler than ever, a great splash of blood across her cheek. Her cuffs were daubed in the stuff.

'Let her go,' I said. 'She must fetch help for we do not have time to fetch it ourselves.' I took Silence Crowe by the shoulders, and looked into her eyes. 'Miss Silence,' I said. 'I need you to bring your father here. He will know what to do with Dr Strangeway. He must stop the blood. Sorrow must stay with him, the tourniquet must be pulled tight or he will die.'

I turned to leave – our night had just begun and there was no time to waste standing over a dying man – when I noticed a letter lying amongst the wreckage on the table top. The address was freshly inked, the folds recent, the sealing wax hastily done. It was addressed to me. I snatched it up and stuffed it into my pocket. 'Upstairs,' I said to Will. 'But softly.'

❧

He was sitting at his desk, the stuff of his profession, his calling, all around him in a sea of bottles, papers, bones, books. He had taken his neckerchief off and flung it aside. I thought I saw a ruby pin glittering amongst its folds, and then I realised that it was a great clot of blood, wet and sticky against the freshly laundered cambric. He was working. Somehow it did not occur to him to stop – there were jobs to be done, sections for the anatomy manual to write, specimens to be re-labelled and catalogued. He could not sit still. His work was his life, and as always he turned to it for solace. But there could be none for him that evening, for he would hang for what he had done.

'Yes? What is it?' he said, as if it was just another day and Will and I just another interruption. 'I have to get on. I have work to do before I go.'

'Go where?' I said. 'To Newgate?'

At that he stopped, and turned to look at us. 'Yes,' he said lightly. 'Yes, I suppose so.' He sighed and sat back in his chair. The candles on his desk quivered at the movement, the shadows of skulls, bones, boxes, all the lumber of generations tall and black against the wall.

'I knew you'd find me.' He sighed. 'You see, Wilson was always a problem, and he was only the beginning.'

'Wilson?' I said.

'Of course, I wanted them to know straight away what was happening, to guess that judgement had arrived – and they would guess.' Halliday leaned forward. 'I wanted them to be terrified. Terrified – of what might happen, of who would be next, terrified by their own uncertainty – how could retribution have arrived? From what quarter? How might they stop it? Should they confess? But I knew they would never do that. And so it was up to me to bring them to justice.'

'Who?' I said. 'For what?'

'Oh!' he laughed. 'Of course, you don't know, do you?'

He shook his head. Then, 'I suppose it was the game that gave me away.'

'The game?' said Will. 'What game?'

'I thought nothing of it at the time,' I said. 'But Miss Crowe knew. And then when I considered what had happened that evening, when I thought about her reaction when she had played the game, then *I* knew too—'

'Knew what?' cried Will. 'Come on, Jem, it can hardly be Halliday who's to blame for all this.'

'Oh he's certainly to blame for some of it,' I said.

'What game?'

'The memory game,' I replied. 'The tooth. The tooth that was in Halliday's pocket. It was Dr Wragg's tooth. When Miss Crowe – at that time quite innocent of whom she was talking to – asked Halliday to empty his pockets there was a tooth amongst the miscellany. Not that there is anything unusual about that for an anatomist. But this tooth was distinctive. It was a yellow front tooth, with a shard of mahogany adhering to it. It was a tooth from Dr Wragg's dentures. I found the rest of them in Dr Wragg's room. That was where you strangled him, wasn't it? He struggled – as far as an old man who is sick and addled by opium can struggle. His teeth fell out. Perhaps they broke, perhaps they were stamped on, I don't know what, but in the kerfuffle a piece lodged in your clothes, in the sagging pocket of your coat. Miss Crowe recognised it. Miss Silence too. And then they knew. Why else would it be there, if you had no involvement with his murder? And, although *I* have no idea why you have done these things, I am quite certain that *they* do.'

'An eye for an eye, a tooth for a tooth,' he muttered. 'I suppose it's fitting in a way.'

In his hand I saw he was holding another Liston knife, the blade new and gleaming and razor sharp. The box from which it had come was open upon the desk. Inside, I saw the set of surgical knives Dr Crowe had presented to him earlier that evening.

'He gave my brother a set just like these,' he said. 'And then he watched while he was wrongly accused of murder.'

'Who?' I said. 'Who accused him of murder?'

He tut tutted. Thrusting a hand into his pocket he pulled out a wad of papers, folded up long-ways and tied with a narrow pink ribbon. 'These are all you need to see,' he said. 'Copied verbatim, but you can go to Edinburgh and read the originals for yourself.'

I took them from him. *Precognition Papers for the Murder of Mary Anderson, 18th December 1830.*

'1830?' I said. 'But you must have only been—'

'Four years old,' he said. 'Yes. John Franklyn was my brother. He's in those papers. Read them and you'll see. He was accused of the most terrible of crimes, of the murder of a young woman. Of desecrating her corpse, killing her child and hiding its body. He did none of those things. I cannot believe it of him.' He stopped what he was doing, and turned to face us. 'My mother died of grief,' he said. 'Her precious boy, her clever lad who was to make her so proud – through his own brains and ambition had been chosen to be apprentice to the great Dr Crowe of Surgeons' Square. He was made demonstrator when he was twenty-one years old. So young! They gave him knives just like these as a present.' He held out one of the blades. The words engraved on it glittered darkly. '*Et mortui sua arcana narrabunt.* And the dead will give up their secrets.' His smile was bitter. 'I wondered, when they gave me

314

these, whether they knew. But they did not. *They* saw it as fitting. An appropriate reward for all my hard work and achievements. *I* saw it as a cruel taunt. They had no idea what the consequences of their gentleman's silence had been. Protecting their own, as usual.

'You see, when it really mattered, when my brother needed his medical friends, his own master, to speak up for him, they abandoned him. And when he died, trying to escape his pursuers, trying to run to the master who could have defended his honour and reputation, who could vouch for his character and integrity, they said nothing then either. His death – an accident, but the result of his flight from justice – was regarded as an admission of guilt. They say his knife was found beneath the dead woman's bed. But my brother would not kill a woman in cold blood. And if he had he would not have left his knife behind! They say he wanted the girl's corpse. But so did all of them! Would he have killed her for it? Of course not! She was doomed anyway, she could not have survived her pregnancy. All he had to do was wait.' His face was dark with fury, the knife in his hand twitching, so that it jagged against the table with a harsh scraping sound.

'And so my mother and I were left alone. My father was long gone. Jamie had taken it upon his own shoulders to look after us, and so he did, though he had little enough of a wage from Dr Crowe. But he worked hard, and we knew he was to be a great man. When he died we were left with nothing. He was a murderer, they said. The murderer of a poor crippled beggar, a defenceless girl and her innocent babe. He had lied in his statement; he had fled when his crimes had become known. In the space of an hour all we had was lost to us. Our Jamie, the reputation of our family, our old lives, all of it was gone for ever. I was now the brother of a murderer, a coward, a liar, a desecrator of corpses. Not that they cared anything for that. We were nothing to them. Even when my mother went up to Dr Crowe's house he would not see her. Why? Because if they had spoken up, if they had insisted on his innocence, then that would mean the murderer of that crippled girl was still at large.'

He coughed, his throat dry after such an impassioned speech, and he reached for the bottle of cordial that stood on his desk. He took a deep draught. 'And so I decided that I would take matters into my own hands. Why should they escape their crimes? Who really killed Mary Anderson and took her baby?' He looked about, his eyes glittering, his cheeks flushed. 'The foetus is here somewhere in the anatomy museum, I am quite certain. I have not found it yet, but I will.' He turned back to the box he was unpacking. One by one he pulled out the jars, examining the contents and the dates. 'They would keep it, just as they have kept the bones of the mother and her sister. Did you know she hanged herself? Clenchie Kate they called her. She hanged herself from the South Bridge in Edinburgh, her body swinging over the Cowgate.' He closed his eyes. 'I saw her hanging there. Her face all black. A tiny figure no bigger than a child. *I* was a child, but I can still remember it. They killed her, just as they killed her sister, and my brother. They took the girls' bodies for trophies.' His voice was a low mutter, his fingers feverish as he rooted in another box.

'Dr Wragg was meticulous,' he said. 'Despite his other failings. Every single item is labelled.' He waved a hand. 'Go on,' he said. 'Take a seat. Read those papers. They will tell you all you need to know. And I am not going anywhere tonight. Not till I find Thrawn-Leggit Mary's child.'

'You killed Wilson?' said Will. 'But why? He is younger than you. He was not in Edinburgh in 1830.'

'No, but his father was. A constable, so I discovered. The man who found the knife beneath the bed, who asked no questions about it, but assumed Dr Cruikshank had merely overlooked it.' He scowled. 'As culpable as any of them. Did he not wonder that the perpetrator of such a terrible crime was so careless as to leave his own knife behind? A knife that could belong to only one person? No. He asked no questions as it suited him to accept the simplest of explanations. He's dead, but his son, I discovered, was right here.' He lifted another bottle, peered at the label, at the pinkish globular contents, and set it aside. The room was warm, the space beneath the eaves gathering the heat of the whole building. I saw the dust hanging in the air, felt it sharp and dry against my throat. Halliday felt it too, and he swigged again from the earthen bottle of cordial.

'I was going to kill Wragg first,' he said conversationally. 'But then one evening I went out drinking with Tanhauser and the others. Wilson came along. He was as drunk as a lord. And so I took my chance – the opportunity may never have presented itself so readily again. And, I admit, I was probably not thinking as clearly as I should. I'd been drinking too – I realised that I would have the police upon me before I'd even started if I was not careful. And so I removed his face. I wanted to hide who he was, and yet it reminded them of Mary, and what had happened to her. You see I wanted Crowe, Cruikshank, Allardyce, all of them to know *exactly* what was happening – that their time had come at last. I left the hand amongst the exhibits. I wanted them to see it, in front of the students too. I had been led to believe that all of them were going up to the Exhibition – along with the students. I would not have them hide it away, and so I ensured that there could be no concealment. They would see the hand, the right hand, the hand that signed their statements, that was not raised in my brother's defence, that they had held up under oath and condemned the reputation of my family.

'Just as I was leaving the place I bumped into Allardyce. I wondered whether he'd followed me – turned out he had, but not because he had any idea about what I was doing.' Halliday gave a wild laugh. 'He said he wanted to apologise for accusing me of stealing his work! Well, of course I went along. He took me to a chop house. I don't know what happened but I ended up drunk and half dead with the cholera. By the time I got back you two were sniffing around—' he shook his head. 'Nothing was going to plan, but what could I do? Besides,' he smiled. '*They* knew what was going on. *Et mortui sua arcana narrabunt.* The words engraved on my brother's knives. The words Dr Crowe used to conclude his lectures – not that he has used them since he was in Edinburgh. But *he* knew. They all *knew*. They knew their sins had found them out, and that was enough for me. Dr Wragg was next – an old rogue with no scruples about anything, prepared to do whatever was necessary as long as there were enough bodies to ensure the students kept coming. And tonight it was the turn of Dr Strangeway – I thought you'd catch me that night in the anatomy museum, Flockhart. I'd no idea you two were still up here!' He frowned and worked faster, pushing aside the box he had just looked through and lifting another into place. 'It *must* be here.' The room had become stifling.

'But to kill them?' said Will. 'You're no better than they are. Worse, in fact. And you will hang, and they will not. And what will you have achieved?'

'I hardly care about that,' he snapped. 'Have you any idea what it is like to go to school and be taunted for your brother's crimes – crimes he did not commit? To come home every day to a mother consumed by sorrow? She never recovered. How could she? We moved away from Edinburgh, we changed our name. But still we knew, she and I, we knew that someone, and not our Jamie, had killed that girl. They would not help us. They closed ranks. Gentlemen, of course, excluding the lad o' pairts they liked to celebrate. Each one of them wrote a statement, signed it, witnessed it as being a true and honest account but at least one of them was lying.'

'Can you smell burning?' said Will. 'And it's as hot as Hades up here.'

Halliday raised his head. He staggered to his feet. He took two steps forward, and his knees buckled. I stuffed the papers he had given me into my pocket and leaped forward. 'What is it?' I said.

'I feel . . . I feel,' he blinked and put a hand to his stomach. He licked his lips and coughed. I seized the bottle of cordial and sniffed it. I poured a splash into an empty gas jar that did office as a pencil holder. It was a bright, bilious yellow.

'What's that?' said Will.

'Cadmium yellow,' I said. 'One of the most poisonous of all the tints, paints and dyes in Dr Strangeway's studio.'

'Dr Strangeway did this?'

'I doubt it. But the sisters, all of them, knew. Lilith felt the betrayal more keenly than anyone—' I stopped. Should I tell him I had seen her with Halliday? I could not.

319

But Halliday had other ideas. 'That Lilith Crowe,' he hissed. 'She's a demon.' He sank to his knees. 'A siren. Beautiful beyond compare but without scruple, without morals, without a care for anyone. I thought to seduce her, to add that to my destruction of this family, but it was she who came for me. And then once she'd had her fill she wished for nothing more. What manner of woman does *that*?'

A woman with desires and passions, I thought. Why did men assume those things to be their preserve alone? Why could they not acknowledge that whatever lusts blazed within them might also blaze inside a woman? *She can never marry,* Dr Crowe had said. *She is not like other women.* I shared a similar fate. But such enforced spinsterhood did not remove the desires that raged within us.

'You loved her?' said Will.

'I did not,' he replied. 'I had her, yes, and I was not the first either. But I did not *love* her. What man could? She is a succubus. A she-devil. I met my match in one such as her.' He clutched at his stomach and then vomited a thin stream of bright yellow liquid onto the floor. He gasped and wiped his lips. 'My God, and now she has killed me.'

I tried to look at Will's face. But he had turned away and I could not read his expression.

❧

We half dragged, half carried Halliday out into the passage. Downstairs there would be emetics of some kind that we might give him, something that might help him void the poison he had ingested. It was hot out there, and the air had a gritty smokiness to it. We reached the end, but the doors that might have led us down to the anatomy museum were locked. From beneath the door smoke wreathed. 'The museum is filled with bottles of alcohol,' said Will. 'If the place is on fire, they will explode, and it will burn like Armageddon.'

'Let's try the other way,' I said. I thought of all the times I had seen an unattended candle sitting on a shelf in the museum. It had been an accident waiting to happen, though there was, I knew, nothing accidental about the locked doors. With Halliday limp between us, we lurched along the passage to the doors at the other end. They too were locked.

From somewhere deep within the building I heard shouting – indistinct voices calling out. *Fire! Fire!* Did they know we were here? Could they save us? From beneath our feet smoke was trickling, trailing upwards to hang like a pall, gaseous and choking, in the stifling air – we would suffocate on smoke long before we were burned to death. Beneath my boots the floorboards were warm. I could hear a roaring sound, as if from a great wind, and the sound of breaking glass. The roar grew louder still, and I fought to master my rising terror at the thought of what lay beyond the locked doors – row upon row of alcohol-filled glass jars.

Halliday was unsteady on his feet, but seemed coherent enough to understand the situation. We propelled him back to the bone room he and Will had shared, and took stock of the situation. There were two skylights. If we could not go down, then our only alternative was to go up. 'Perhaps the roof?' I said. 'Or might we crawl across the rafters in the roof space, like rats?'

'I fear the roof space will already be filling with smoke,' said Will. 'And besides, the rafters are a precarious place to be at any time, never mind when we have a fire raging in the rooms below and a sick man to help. It must be the roof, Jem, for I will not leave him here and we cannot get out from this floor.'

The roof was north facing, the skylights letting in the daylight without the glare of the sun. Will stood on his desk and tried to open the window.

'The roof is sloped,' he said, peering out. 'But if we can climb up the incline it is flat on top and we will be safe – for a time at least. It will depend how quickly the fire spreads, whether we can enter the building at a point away from the blaze.'

The roaring sound had grown louder. There was an explosion that made our ears ring, and set the bones and jars dancing on their shelves. Through the skylight, I saw a fountain of orange sparks spurt towards the heavens. Will began to cough as the smoke thickened. Halliday lay unmoving, draped across his desk as though he were fashioned from melted wax. His face wore a glazed, tearful look.

'I remember when Jamie used to come home,' he said. 'He used to walk over to see us on a Wednesday night after he'd prepared for the classes the next day – it was the only time he got away. He was so proud to be working with Dr Crowe. My mother adored him. "Look at our Jamie," she used to say. "You want to be like him and go on to become a great doctor? Jamie's going to make them all sit up!" She was right about that, at least.' Tears streaked his face. He blinked them away, and suddenly reared up, his eyes staring, as if all at once everything had become clear. 'My God,' he whispered. 'What have I done?'

Will was wrestling with the window. He leaped down from the desk and seized a bone, a femur, from one of the shelves against the walls. Wielding it like a club, he smashed the window and battered the jagged pieces away.

I felt the air get sucked out into the night, and I heard the fire grow louder, the broken window acting as a flue to draw the air through the building. There was no time to lose. I flung my jacket over the shards of glass that remained and put out a hand to Halliday. 'Come on!'

I pulled Halliday onto the desk, and between us Will and I somehow managed to get him through the window. He vanished from sight, so that for a moment I thought he had either fallen, or flung himself off. But then I saw his boot scrabbling against the roof tiles and I knew he was unhurt.

'You next,' said Will.

I climbed out onto the roof, Will appearing a moment later beside me. The smoke was thick in the air, the Hall beneath us a giant tinder box, for aside from the explosive contents of the anatomy museum it was filled with old books and paper, and choking with a cloud of dust made up of skin and hair, feathers and animal flesh – it would burn to the ground, all of it, in no time at all.

Halliday lay motionless against the slope of the roof, his arms and legs spread wide like an insect clinging to a tree. 'We have to get him up,' said Will. Behind us, far below, I could see the light of the flames illuminating the lawn at the front. A dog was barking and running up and down. I could hear voices, though they were all but drowned out by the roar of the flames. Beneath us, muted by bricks and mortar, I heard the sound of glass exploding. The roof beneath us shuddered, and then right below our feet, through the skylight from which we had just emerged, a great tongue of fire spurted. The flames flailed out like a whip, before falling back to lick at the night sky. All Will's drawings, all the papers and books, the specimens collected over decades, would now be nothing but ash. The smoke stank of charred bone and flesh. We did not say a word to each other, but positioned ourselves on either side of Halliday and somehow managed to drag him up the roof slates.

All at once we were on the flat roof of the building. If we made our way along it to the other side there would surely be another way in – a skylight, a trapdoor, a window – something that would lead us back down into the building. Halliday was looking worse than ever. His steps were unsteady, but he seemed to understand that he had to move – and quickly. A dribble of yellow vomit glistened on his chin.

'Over there,' said Will, pointing to the eastern wing of the house. 'Where Dr Crowe's rooms are. There's much less smoke. Besides, the museum takes up the whole of this side of the Hall. Wherever we go it has to be as far away from here as possible.'

We moved towards the far corner of the building, though it meant that we had no choice but to cross the expanse of the roof. Behind us, there was another roar, and a great *wumph* sound, and flames and smoke poured into the sky. Beneath our feet more smoke began seeping through fissures in the roof. At first it seemed like gossamer, as if a great cobweb were drifting and billowing about our ankles. Beneath our feet dark cracks appeared, the smoke grew thick and black as ribbons, and a rending, tearing sound filled the air.

'We must move faster,' cried Will. I saw from his face that he was terrified.

Halliday dangled between us like a drowned man, an arm over each of our shoulders. We staggered forward, but something was not right. I could hardly say what it was at first, but as we moved, we seemed to glide and undulate. Beneath our feet the roof shivered, and then all at once a great chunk of it yawned open. A pillar of fire burst out before us, the sudden ingress of cold air giving the flames a new and terrible fury. It tore upwards, rearing into the night, not orange, the way fire should be, but a deep and bloody crimson, shot through with green and blue and streaked with searing yellow. The smoke that accompanied it was thick, dark and oily, the air about us alive with whirling black particles and glowing cinders. I felt my hair smoulder, the heat against my face and hands making my skin burn. I reeled back. I saw the others do the same, flinging their arms up to cover their faces. My feet skittered from under me as the roof sagged. I flung myself down and scrambled clear, hoping that by keeping low, by spreading my weight I might stop the roof from sinking further. Beside me, Halliday seemed to have realised the horror of our situation and he too dropped down, scuttling crab-like up the sagging rooftop.

Only Will was unable to follow. He had been closer to the edge, closer to the great crack that had opened up, and when the roof began to sink, he sank with it. For a moment he lay there, flat out like Halliday and me, clinging like a starfish on a rock while a sea of flame billowed and roared at his back. And then I saw him start to slide. His feet and hands clawed to find a hold, to get a purchase on something so that he might lever himself higher, might scramble to safety – but there was nothing. I crawled forward and held out my hand, craning to reach

325

his fingers as the roof bowed lower. Will stared up at me, his face anguished, his mouth and eyes round with terror. His cheeks were black with smoke smuts, and streaked with tears, the skin red and blistered from the terrible heat. I saw his hair smouldering as an ember settled.

What happened next will be imprinted upon my mind for ever. I watched Will scream as he slid towards the fire, scrabbling frantically now, his fingers bloody. And then all at once Halliday lurched to his feet beside me. He flung himself down the slope towards Will, seized him by the hand and in one heroic wrench dragged him up. It was no more than twelve inches but it was enough. I reached out and hauled him up still further, and then leaned back out to grasp Halliday.

'Give me your hand, John,' I cried. 'Quickly!'

Halliday swayed on the edge of the abyss: a tall, angular silhouette against a great wall of flame. He put out his hand to seize mine, but then seemed to change his mind. He stood for a moment looking up at me – and then all at once he smiled, opened his arms, and let himself fall back. I saw his body drop like a rag doll onto a flaming wooden beam. His back must have broken for he made no sound at all. And then the fire roared and leaped so that I had to look away. When I turned back, he was gone.

How we managed not to follow Halliday into the inferno I will never know. Somehow, we managed to skirt the hole, traversing the roof – or what remained of it – by a long circumnavigation. We entered a skylight on Dr Crowe's wing of the Hall, and from there made our way down through the building and out into the garden.

We lay side by side on the cool grass near the wall that bounded the physic garden. Neither of us spoke. I held Will's hand tight in my own. I had almost lost him again, had almost watched him slip into the flames, and I could not let him go. But his fingers were dead in mine, and I knew that something inside him was changed. I closed my eyes, as above our heads burning cinders whirled like stars into the night.

Chapter Twenty-Six

⁂

It was fortunate that the fire occurred on a Sunday night, for there had been hardly anyone inside the Hall. Dr Crowe and Dr Cruikshank had been sitting up in Dr Crowe's little parlour when Silence burst in with news about the attempted murder of Dr Strangeway, the doctor's severed right hand, still warm, tightly clutched in her own. Lilith was in her bedroom. Tanhauser, Squires, Dr Allardyce and Gloag had been in the dissecting room – Gloag helping the students bring up a body, Dr Allardyce coerced into giving them late night instruction in anatomy, as they had both drunkenly determined to demonstrate their ability to master the subject as well as any woman.

Dr Allardyce, Lilith and Dr Cruikshank had saved as much as they could from the blaze, assisted manfully by Gloag, Squires and Tanhauser, whose unexpected presence there was at last put to some useful purpose. Some stuff was neatly set aside in boxes, other things – piles of books, a group of stuffed sea birds, Dr Cruikshank's favourite armchair – lay scattered about the lawn like flotsam beached by a retreating flood. Dr Cruikshank and Gloag had carried Dr Strangeway from the building, Dr Crowe bandaging the stump of his brother-in-law's wrist as best he could. Then, from the front garden they had watched the building burn. They had seen Will, Halliday and me crawling up the slates and onto the flat roof. They had observed us as we made our way across the roof, though when we had vanished, and the flames had burst upward, they assumed we had all perished.

Appalled, horrified, they stood transfixed while Corvus Hall burned down. Then, they took themselves off to Dr Cruikshank's house – a tall town house some half a mile west of the Hall. We found them – all of them – there the next day. Dr Strangeway was upstairs in bed, though whether he would live or die was still unclear. The others sat in silence in the parlour, their expressions stunned. Dr Allardyce, Tanhauser and Squires, who had done their best to rescue some of Dr Crowe's artefacts, were sitting amongst a lumber of miscellaneous objects – one of Dr Strangeway's anatomical Venuses, slightly melted, a box of bones – legs and arms mainly – and another filled with skulls. Eve the écorché had been rescued, along with the moulage of Mrs Roseplucker's face, a singed stack of anatomy books and the coal scuttle from the students' common room. Dr Allardyce sat with his arm protectively around a packing case of assorted items culled from the museum, the library and Dr Strangeway's wax modelling studio. He exchanged a glance with Dr Cruikshank, and Dr Crowe, and then catching sight of a smoke smut on the portrait of Mrs Crowe that one of them had saved from the blaze he pulled out a filthy handkerchief, licked the corner, and began to wipe the face clean. Once more they had rallied round each other, I thought. As they always had. As they always would.

'I'm . . . I'm glad to see you looking so well, Flockhart,' said Dr Crowe. 'And you, Quartermain.' His chin trembled. 'And I'm sorry you were so nearly . . . so nearly killed.'

'Thank you, sir,' I said.

Dr Cruikshank cleared his throat. He was standing by the door, as if he hoped he might be able to leave at any moment. 'And Halliday?' he said.

'Dead,' I replied. 'But it was quick, and it was unlikely that he felt very much at all.' I glanced at the three sisters, two of them, Sorrow and Silence, standing arm in arm beside the fire, Lilith sitting still and silent in an armchair. She looked pale and drawn, the dark circles beneath her eyes making her, for once, look her age.

I told them what Halliday had said, how he had confessed to the murder of Wilson, and of Dr Wragg, that it was he who had assaulted Dr Strangeway. 'But he had ingested some yellow cadmium,' I said. 'The poison took hold of him soon enough. He would surely have died from it, and yet in the end he died saving Will. Sacrificed himself to save my friend—' I felt the tears prick my eyes. 'So perhaps we can forgive him some of the worst of his actions.'

'But why?' said Dr Crowe. 'Why did he do these things? And who poisoned him?'

'I did,' said Silence. Her voice was loud, the words gummy. 'I saw the tooth in his pocket. I knew he had killed Dr Wragg, that he would come for us all—'

Lilith reached for her sister's hand and looked into her face. 'It is no use, Silence,' she said. She turned to me. 'Mr Flockhart, it was I—'

'He died in the fire,' I said. 'It matters very little who poisoned him.'

'But why did he do these things?' said Dr Crowe. 'He was such a gifted boy. I was prepared to do all I could to help him. I knew he came from modest beginnings, but I have always sought to support those who deserve it. He was to be demonstrator, you know. So young! Why, I have no one so young since . . . since—'

'Since James Franklyn?' said Will.

'Why, yes!' His face clouded. 'We never speak of it. How did you know?'

I still had the papers Halliday had given me in my pocket. I had read them. Will too. I held them out. 'Read these, sir. They will no doubt be familiar to you anyway.' I watched his face for any flicker of emotion, and glanced around at the others. But if they knew what was contained in the bundle of ragged, sooty papers, they gave no sign of it.

'*Precognition Papers for the Murder of Mary Anderson.*' Dr Crowe looked up, his face pinched and wary. 'So?' He still did not understand.

'John Halliday was James Franklyn's younger brother,' I said. 'When Franklyn died, his family was torn apart. Halliday was the mother's maiden name – did you never notice, sir? He was James Halliday Franklyn.'

Dr Crowe shook his head. 'No. It is not an uncommon name. I have no recollection of ever seeing it.'

'John Halliday worshipped his brother, a lad o' pairts, as they say in Scotland – a young man without connections but with brains and ability who must rely on himself rather than on breeding and acquaintances to get on in the world. A lad who showed such promise that he was made demonstrator above those who were older and more experienced. To have all that snatched away, to be shamed and disgraced, his brother James branded a murderer. Halliday's mother died of grief. John Halliday stepped up to take his brother's place – and to take revenge on all those who had signed written statements which, in his mind, had led to his brother's untimely death. You see, not one of you spoke in defence of James Franklyn, but you allowed the law to hang guilt upon him, even though he was dead.'

'And Halliday harboured this for twenty years?'

'He knew no other way of viewing the world, no other way of thinking. Resentment, rage, desire for revenge, it was in every fibre of him. But he did not know who *had* killed Mary Anderson, nor who it was who had left the knife that had condemned his brother. If he had, there is every chance he would have killed only that person. *He* had no idea.' I looked about at them. '*I*, however, I *do* know who killed her.'

'No one knows who killed Mary Anderson,' said Dr Crowe sharply. 'If it was not Franklyn then who was it?'

'Franklyn had spent the evening with his mother and brother. No one saw him on the road when he returned to Surgeons' Hall, but that does not mean that he did not go there. He had been seen going into Mary Anderson's lodgings, but any man might look like Franklyn if they chose to, especially if the fog was thick, if a coat is held high at the collar, the hat pulled down low. It could be a man, it could be a woman. It is impossible to be certain, though there is someone in this room who knows. Who has always known—'

Lilith Crowe staggered to her feet, the sound of her

chair scraping across the wooden floor cutting the air like a scream. Her face was ashen. 'Please,' she whispered. 'I did not mean to . . . I tried to . . . Oh, God! After so long. Will I never be free of it?' Her hands flew to her mouth. It was the first time I had seen her appear afraid, confused, anything less than self-possessed. She looked about at us, from one face to another, as if searching for sympathy, for understanding. A teacup Tanhauser had left on the floor crunched beneath her heel, a severed toe in a jar of preserving spirits was swept to the floor by her skirts. 'Henry,' she said. 'Please.' She held out her hands to Dr Cruikshank, and then crumpled to the ground in a faint.

Womb

For many hundreds of years it was believed that the womb travelled freely around the body causing illness. Medieval doctors proposed that the womb might be possessed by demons, that it was the root cause of women's evil ways. Those who were old, or childless, whose wombs had not been put to use, were particularly susceptible. They were witches, of course, and must be put to death. Am I witch or demon? My name suggests the latter, and that I was born to be the bane of men.

The womb is the carrier of all life. As any anatomist will tell you it sits low in the abdomen, held in place by muscles and ligaments. What a precious organ it is! A place of warmth and safety, of mystery and awe. It inspires wonder – and fear. Wonder at its life-giving properties, fear at the power it exercises over us. For it is the defining organ of the female body. We are told we may not study, we may not read anything more than the catechism, as we will injure our wombs if we do. Our anatomy is our destiny, and we ignore it at our peril. Does not the presence of a womb demonstrate beyond all question that we are designed only for motherhood? And if we do not breed? What then? Hysteria. Madness. The decay of civilisation itself.

My womb is a cold and barren cavity, bloody and dark with regret. I throw aside those twin prizes, virginity and chastity, for they have no value to one such as I. I am told I may never marry, that the madness that lurks within me must not be permitted to breed. I must accept it, they say. I lie alone in my bed at night and I lay my hand across my belly and I think of all the blood I have seen and the pain I have caused.

Statement of Dr Silas Strangeway, Corvus Hall,
30th September 1851.

Corvus Hall, 30th September 1851

My dear Flockhart

It seems to me that the time has come to tell you what happened
on the night of 18th December 1830. The events have been
recorded elsewhere by others, me included, and yet there is a
version of events, a true version, that has remained a secret for
over twenty years. It has become clear in recent days, however, that
what happened in the past has not stayed in the past. Perhaps we
were naive to think that we might live our lives with impunity,
that what we hid from the world back then might be outweighed
by good deeds and hard work. We are united by it, those who were
there that night, for good or ill, and will remain so for the rest of
our lives.

After I was attacked yesterday I knew that all our striving not to think of it, all our pretence that it had not happened, had come to naught. And so here is my statement. Long overdue, perhaps, it is my account of what happened on the day we carried the body of Mary Anderson up from the Cowgate to Surgeons' Hall.

In the spring of 1830 Dr Crowe's wife died of the smallpox, leaving him the sole parent of Lilith, then some fifteen years old, and her two young siblings, both of them mere babies at the time. Dr Crowe was distraught, and for a time we believed him to have almost lost his reason. Most notable was his attitude towards a beggar woman named Mary Anderson, who went by the name of Thrawn-Leggit Mary, and who bore a strong resemblance to my late sister, Dr Crowe's wife. In time it was rumoured that Dr Crowe had had intimate relations with the girl. He denied that this was the case, though I did not believe him, especially as it was soon evident that she was pregnant. Mary Anderson always maintained that the child was Dr Crowe's. It was for that reason that on the 18th December 1830 she came up to his lecture hall to accuse him in front of all his students. The girl attacked him, attempting to stab him through the heart with a blade taken from the dissecting room.

As you are aware, Dr Crowe has always maintained that a woman has as much right to a medical education as a man. As such, it was usual for his daughter Lilith to be in the front row of his lectures. When Mary Anderson attacked her father Lilith had an uninterrupted view of it. There is no doubt that she was most distressed by what she had witnessed that day. For weeks – months – she had borne all that had been thrown at her: the death of her beloved mother; the distress this had caused her father, with whom she had always enjoyed the closest of relationships; having to care for her two young siblings – a role she had no great love for as it took her away from her studies. She had watched her father withdraw into his work, excluding her where once he had encouraged, unable to look her in the face for he saw only her mother when he did. And then came his infatuation with Mary. It was partly medical – her spine intrigued him, there was no doubt of it – and yet it was also something altogether more inappropriate and worrisome. How could this woman, this crippled beggar from the darkest of Edinburgh's streets have a face that so matched that of his beloved? Dr Crowe could talk of nothing else, and indeed the likeness between the two was most remarkable. It was only Lilith who refused to accept it. 'There is nothing of my mother in that beggar girl,' she said to me on more than one occasion. Mary Anderson had no right to such a face, she said, no right to remind anyone of her dear mother. One day I came home from Surgeons' Square to find that she had taken a scalpel to a blue dress her mother had once worn and sliced it to ribbons.

'Better this than have him give it to her,' she said.

They almost came to blows, Lilith and her father, and I was relieved when, after a few months, the whole business seemed to have blown over. But then Mary appeared at the lecture theatre. Lilith remained silent as the scene unfolded before her, stoical, no matter what. But when she saw what the girl had done – attacked her father, stabbed at his heart only to have the blow deflected by the only picture of her mother that existed – I saw a coldness in her eye, a hardness, and a determination in her face I had not seen before. With hindsight I believe that was the moment when everything changed, when Lilith determined to do all she could to rid herself and her father of Mary Anderson.

After Mary's assault, and her removal from the lecture theatre, Dr Crowe, Lilith and I returned home. As soon as we were inside, Dr Crowe, who had affected to be unconcerned by the attack, broke down, weeping uncontrollably – a shocking sight for any daughter to witness. After that he locked himself in his study, refusing to speak to anyone.

Sometime later I heard him emerge from his room. I tried to speak to him about Lilith, to tell him that he must talk to her, perhaps take her away for a few months, but he would not listen.

'I am going out, Silas,' he said. 'I must walk or I shall go mad.'

I said the haar was rising, that he would be unable to see his way, that he might be attacked and robbed or struck down by a carriage in the dark, but he cared nothing for those things. I could do and say no more, and I stood aside as he put on his walking cape and his hat, and took up his cane and his lantern. 'Tomorrow everything will be better,' he said wearily. 'But tonight – tonight I must walk.'

Some little while later I heard the sound of footsteps in the passage. At first I thought Dr Crowe had returned, that he had forgotten something and come back, or, still better, that he had decided I was right and had come to speak with Lilith. But when I looked out I saw Lilith herself, cloaked as her father had been, and carrying one of the lanterns the apprentices used when they were out in the graveyards at night. Before I had chance to say anything she had opened the door and stepped out into the fog.

Of course, I put on my own coat and set out after her. I had no idea where she might be going – my first thought was that she was following her father, but that was hardly possible as he was long gone. The only place she might go was to see Dr Cruikshank, though as it was a Wednesday he would be at work late at Surgeons' Square, and not at home. It was then that I wondered whether it was her intention to visit Mary Anderson, and that perhaps it was to Tanner's Lodgings that she was bound. And so it was to that place that I headed as fast as I could, though much hampered by the dark and the fog, for I had come out in haste and had no light.

Oh sir, I have told no one of this these twenty years or more, but that night I witnessed something I hope never to see again, *for when I opened the door to Mary Anderson's house I opened it upon a scene of carnage. On the bed lay the girl's corpse, around her neck a blue silk shawl – I recognised it immediately as one that had once belonged to Mrs Crowe. It was pulled tight. But worse still was the sight of Lilith, fingers red and slippery with gore, a knife glinting in her hands, hunched over the body of Thrawn-Leggit Mary.*

You may know, sir, that even then my niece was a skilled anatomist. At all times she carried a set of knives in her bag – Dr Cruikshank had given them to her on her fifteenth birthday. He had had them made specially, with bone handles and steel blades, the finest in Edinburgh. She held one of them in her hand now, its shaft bloody, her fingers slathered with the stuff. I saw straight away that she had cut through Mary Anderson's dress, and also through the flesh beneath. And at that moment, the moment I came in, she was pulling a child from the opening she had sliced in the wall of the dead girl's womb.

When she turned to me I hardly knew her for my niece. Her skin was white, luminous almost, but in the glow from the fire and the light from the lantern it had a Devilish crimson cast to it, smudged here and there with dark clots of blood. Her eyes were huge and wild, dark and fathomless, as if I were looking into the eyes of a demon. 'Uncle,' she said, a faint smile curling her lips. 'Look!' Her hands shook as she held out to me the red and slippery mess. I took it from her – what else could I do? The creature was the tiniest baby I had ever seen, pink, and wrinkled as a maggot and so small that I could hardly believe it would live. And then she handed me something else. I thought at first it was the placenta, but it was not. It was another baby, as small as the first but bloodier. Like two tiny sparrows they were, both girls, both living – for she had tied the cords as best she could when she cut them free from their mother.

I wrapped both babies in my waistcoat – to be sure, I could have wrapped them in my handkerchief they were so small – and said I would take them away directly. I bundled Lilith to her feet and told her she must go, go from that place and return home straight. She said she would make the girl decent, and that then she would quit the place directly. Perhaps it was wrong of me to leave her, but I took her at her word. In truth, I could not bear to remain there a moment longer. It is a failing that has haunted me ever since.

After leaving the babes at the foundlings' hospital I was returning home via Surgeons' Square when I bumped into Dr Cruikshank. He informed me that Thrawn-Leggit Mary was dead – I was surprised at how quickly the news had got out – and on his insistence I accompanied him back to Tanner's Lodgings.

It is here that I come to the most painful part of my tale, for there I found that rather than making the girl decent, as she said she would, my niece had done something quite different. The legs and abdomen she had left lewdly exposed, a pose perhaps befitting a girl who was known to be of easy virtue. Worse still, the face she had railed against so many times she had sliced clean away. I could hardly bear to look at what she had done, and my hands shook when I thought how close she must have come to being discovered. I saw too that she had left one of her knives amongst the bedding – I noted that Dr Cruikshank had also observed it, and his expression was no less appalled than mine. We exchanged a glance, but said nothing, and I saw him hide it quickly in his hand before the others could see it.

It was a long night, and hours passed before I eventually returned home. Lilith was in her room. She was asleep, and when I awoke her she had only the most fragmented memory of what had occurred that evening. She remembered her hands pulling the shawl about the girl's neck. She remembered the knife, the blood, and the two tiny infants. I believe she has retained those memories, that she knows what she did, and what she is, but, like the rest of us, she has never spoken of it.

That night she fell into a fever, no doubt brought on by the shock, and by the cold night air. She almost died. Indeed, her two young brothers caught her sickness and it took them both, adding still more to the burden of grief and sadness endured by that blighted household. Dr Cruikshank, Dr Crowe and I vowed to say nothing of what had happened, and when evidence found at the scene pointed to someone other than Lilith, we remained silent. I assumed Dr Cruikshank had seen to it, for he would do anything to protect my niece. And so it was Franklyn, Dr Crowe's apprentice and a young man of great promise, who was accused, and not one of us stood up to speak in his defence. He fell from a window trying to elude his pursuers. But he was innocent of all he was charged with.

I have carried this burden for many years. Franklyn comes to me in my dreams, even now. It is his face you see at the Exhibition, Lilith and I, working on that piece together, found we had fashioned a likeness of him before we even realised what we were doing. I cannot defend our actions. I can only say that my sole intent was to protect my niece, who was driven by passion, rage and sorrow to do what she did.

And yet, if Mary's life was taken, and the life of Franklyn was forfeit, then saving the lives of those two innocent babes was at least some recompense, for shortly before we left Edinburgh Dr Crowe adopted them both. We named them Sorrow and Silence, for that is how we have all lived since that terrible night.

I cannot undo what has been done. We have prevented Lilith from ever marrying – whatever dark force had driven her to murder must not be permitted to breed – and done all we can to keep her and her sisters safe from harm. I have no idea who it is who pursues us now, but I am quite certain that it is because *of what happened that night in Edinburgh that we are being persecuted. I accept my fate, when it comes, but I ask you to look to my nieces, Flockhart, to help Lilith and her sisters, and protect them from whoever, from whatever, awaits them in the darkness.*

Sincerely yours,

Silas Strangeway

Chapter Twenty-Seven

~~~~~

Dr Cruikshank swept forward and took Lilith in his arms.

'Dr Strangeway told me what happened,' I said. I held up the letter he had left for me in the wax workshop. 'This is his confession. His statement. The one he did not give that night in Edinburgh twenty years ago.'

'Dr Strangeway told me what had happened that night too,' said Dr Cruikshank. 'He said he had left Lilith and taken the children – we both saw what she had done. It was I who found her knife, I who took it so she would be safe. We told Dr Crowe, and then the three of us promised never to allude to it again, never to ask about it, never to speak to her, or anyone, about what she had done.'

'You put Franklyn's knife under the bed?' said Will.

'No,' said Dr Cruikshank. 'No, I did not. I assumed Dr Strangeway had done so – I never asked him. We vowed to ask nothing of one another. What we did, we did for her. We loved her, all of us.'

'But none as much as you, I think, Dr Cruikshank,' I said gently.

He sighed. 'No,' he said. He looked down at her, and stroked the hair from her face. 'None as much as I.'

'To deliver one's own sisters from their dying mother aged only fifteen, I am hardly surprised that her mind was unhinged by it,' said Will. 'And yet, to kill another human being? To desecrate the corpse? It is no wonder it could never be spoken of. No wonder she pushed it deep inside herself, so deep that she had only the most subtle memory of it.'

'Indeed,' I said. 'And what reason would those who love her have to lie about such a terrible deed?'

'But we did not lie,' said Dr Crowe quietly. 'That is what happened, though I wish to God it had not.'

'You did not lie,' I said, 'because you believe that is what happened. All of you believe it, even Miss Crowe. But it is *not* what happened. Dr Strangeway has provided us with yet another version of events, but they are still not the truth. The truth of that night has most conveniently lain hidden from all of you, and from John Halliday, for twenty years, even though it was in plain sight – had Halliday been able to step outside his vengeance for one moment, and read what he had before him slowly and objectively.'

The room was silent.

'But where?' said Dr Crowe. 'Where has it lain hidden?'

'Why, in these documents, of course.' I took up the wad of papers that Halliday had given me. '*Precognition Papers for the Murder of Mary Anderson*,' I said. Written statements collected from each of you the night that Mary was murdered. The truth has been here all along – had anyone the wit to see it.'

'Is it?' said Will. 'I could see nothing in them that pointed to anyone but Franklyn.'

'But of course it is.' I pulled open the papers. 'Look here: Clenchie Kate smashed her assailant's lantern with her crutch. Later we are told that one member of the party from Surgeons' Hall had to follow close on another as his lantern was out.'

'Who?' said Dr Crowe.

'Dr Allardyce,' said Will after a moment. 'It was Dr Allardyce.'

'So,' said Dr Allardyce. He had not moved from his chair, his arm still around the box he had saved from the fire at the Hall. 'The lanterns often went out. You cannot accuse a man of such crimes based on that!'

'Oh, but there is much more than that,' I said. 'You see, Franklyn tells us that he thought at first Mary had arrived at Dr Crowe's lecture to accuse someone else. He was referring to you, Dr Allardyce. There is also the matter of your feelings for Mrs Crowe. Dr Strangeway acknowledged the deep love you had for her. Franklyn also noted it. And we are told that you had been seen entering Tanner's Lodgings on many occasions, *weepin' and maitherin' about poor Mrs Crowe*. Can you deny that it was you who was with Mary Anderson on the night when Dr Wragg had paid a man to go with her so that Dr Crowe might have the scales fall from his eyes? Look here, when he says that no one is ever to allude to the events of the night in question – *I included Mr Allardyce in this bond, and I could see that he was mightily relieved by it*. Of course you were relieved, Dr Allardyce, for it was not only Dr Crowe who had become enamoured of Mary Anderson, was it?'

'But how on earth did I kill the woman? How was I not seen or heard?' Dr Allardyce smiled and shook his head. I had never seen him so confident. And why not, when he had kept his secret for so long?

'How? That's easy. Franklyn himself tells us how: the building at Tanner's Lodgings was like a warren, men and women were everywhere. There was a door at the back of Mary's room. It was not locked. Anyone might come in or out. Franklyn tells us that he found a boy outside with a silver shilling in his hand. Where would a boy of that age have got such a coin and not have had it snatched from his fingers by his drunken mother? I would argue that he had been in possession of it for only a short time. I suggest to you that it was Dr Allardyce who strangled Mary Anderson almost to the death, but that he was disturbed in his endeavours by Miss Crowe. Perhaps she had come to the Cowgate in search of her father. Perhaps she had come to reason with Mary Anderson. We may never know, but come she did, and it is just as well that she arrived at that moment. The memory she has of her fingers pulling the scarf about Mary's neck are a memory of her trying to loosen it, trying to save the girl. And when she could not, when she thought her dead, she did a quite extraordinary thing: drawing upon the knowledge her father had never stinted to give her, she performed a caesarean section and saved the dying girl's babies, her own half-sisters.

'And while all this was taking place, you, Dr Allardyce, were hidden in the passage at the back and had paid the lad you found there a shilling for his silence. According to Dr Strangeway, he and Lilith finished their work about the body of Mary Anderson and left, he first, she second. Dr Strangeway assumed that Lilith had murdered the woman before he arrived and then cut off her face after he left. She had no clear recollection of it. At fifteen years old to cut open a dying woman and remove her foetuses? Is it any wonder she could hardly say what she had or had not done?

'But what if those acts were committed by someone else? Someone else strangled Mary, and someone else cut off her face. That someone was hiding in the passage, waiting for Lilith and Dr Strangeway to leave before he finished off the job he had started, his last act being to take away the face that had so entranced him. It was the face of the woman he had loved, the face of Mrs Crowe, curiously possessed by the girl Thrawn-Leggit Mary, the crippled prostitute who did not deserve to have it.'

'This is complete nonsense,' cried Dr Allardyce. His hands clutched at the box on his knee, as if he were about to throw it at my head. 'How dare you accuse me—'

'And of course,' I went on, 'there is the evidence of Dr Cruikshank. *Allardyce's excitement was palpable*, he says. And yet why would you be so excited at the death of a prostitute? He also notes that *Allardyce already had his coat and hat on and had picked up a lantern from the store*. But then later he tells us—' I shuffled through the pages, searching for the bits I had marked out. 'He tells us *the blood from the dissecting tables still glistened on the lad's fingernails, so hastily had we left our work at Surgeons' Square*. But Allardyce had not been at the dissecting tables. There was no reason for him to have bloody hands, bloody cuffs. Unless he had been dissecting elsewhere that night.

'As for the knife that was left at the scene – Franklyn's Liston knife. Dr Cruikshank says that Franklyn went to get his coat *abandoning his knives and saws where they lay*.

It was the perfect opportunity for Allardyce to put one in his pocket. And he was the last man out at Tanner's Lodgings, both Dr Wragg and Dr Cruikshank remarked on it. Dr Allardyce had plenty of time to put Franklyn's knife wherever he wished.'

'Unless Cruikshank purposely wrote his statement to incriminate me,' cried Dr Allardyce. 'He was crouched over the body the whole time. He had more than enough opportunity to leave Franklyn's knife there. It is he you should be accusing. He never liked me. He still doesn't. Look how I have never been promoted beyond demonstrator. They will not even let me lecture!'

'Because you are not good enough,' said Dr Cruikshank. 'I always hoped you'd develop a private practice, more surgery less anatomy, just to get you away from the class, but you never did. I've seen you when you have the knife in your hand and the patient before you. Even now that they are etherised still you cannot make the cut.' He frowned. 'And yet you never used to be so. Back when it was speed that mattered, when they were alive and screaming under our hands, *then* you were not so bad at all.'

'And there are other matters,' I said. 'The dresses that were saved from the fire. It is customary for the possessions of a smallpox victim to be burned, and yet a couple of Mrs Crowe's dresses were saved. No one knew how. Was it you, Dr Allardyce? As Dr Crowe's apprentice you lived with him and his family, you had every opportunity to take some of Mrs Crowe's clothes. And then to see it on a crooked beggar girl? You hardly knew whether you loved it or hated it, did you? You admitted to Franklyn that it was you who had got the green dress back from the pawn shop.'

Dr Allardyce said nothing.

'And it is my belief that we might find something of great significance to the case in that box of specimens that you have so kindly saved from the inferno – an inferno started by you, I might add, for *someone* locked the doors upon us. We all saw the tooth that night, Dr Allardyce, you drew the same conclusions that Miss Crowe and I drew. You had to get rid of Halliday before he got rid of you – or before he admitted who he was and why he was here. Before he showed these precognitions to anyone and they too worked out, as I have, what happened on the night of the 18th December 1830.'

'But Dr Allardyce was with us in the anatomy room,' piped up Tanhauser. 'He was there all evening. He helped us raise the alarm. He worked all night to save Dr Crowe's possessions—'

'He was not with us the whole time,' said Squires. 'He went out to the dead house. Not for long, but long enough to go round and up to the museum.'

Will stepped forward and pulled the box from Dr Allardyce's grip. At first, I thought the man was not going to let go, for his fingers tightened about the edges, his expression darkening. And then all at once he gave it up. He sat back and closed his eyes, his face a slack mask of defeat. Will put the box on the table. One by one he lifted out jars of specimens. They were monsters and curiosities mainly – a two headed baby, a diseased pancreas, a giant liver fluke. And then, at last, there it was: a large jar, the glass thick and yellowish, the liquid within freshly changed. I lifted it gingerly and placed it on the table top. Inside, no less beautiful despite all it had been through, was the face of Thrawn-Leggit Mary.

It was a skilful job, of that there was no doubt, and Dr Allardyce had looked after it well. It swam before us, the mouth a sorrowful crescent, the eyes closed, the lips pale and waxy, the flesh with that waterlogged look all specimens take on in the end.

It should have ended there. But he had given up too easily and I might have guessed there would be more. And we were all mesmerised by the face in the jar, the face that had caused so much misfortune for so many. Allardyce was a coward, there was no question, but he was a desperate one. It took only a moment. He sprang to his feet, pulling a knife from his pocket. I recognised it as the knife Halliday had abandoned beside Strangeway's severed hand. Upon it, already darkened with blood, were the words *et mortui sua arcana narrabunt.* Holding the knife in his right hand, with his left he seized Silence by the arm, jerking her to her feet and holding her tight against his breast. She made a low moaning sound, the knife at her throat drawing a trickle of blood as the tip pierced the skin.

'Let me pass,' he said. His eyes were wild, darting here and there, his forehead beaded with oily sweat. I saw his tongue, white and anxious, flicker across dry lips. 'Let me pass and I will be gone and you will never see me again.' He dragged Silence towards the door, the knife jagging her throat so that the blood flowed faster. One slip and he would slice through her neck as if through butter. 'It is Halliday who was guilty,' he hissed. 'Not I, you saw that yourselves. And now Halliday is dead. Mary Anderson was nothing. Nothing! A crippled beggar. How *dare* she have the face of my beloved. How *dare* she! She made a mockery of my darling's memory, with her vile shuffling gait and her filthy black crutches. And so I took it. I took the face she should never have had in the first place and I kept it safe—'

He got no further. The gunshot rang out, a great roar that made our ears sing, the world turning dim and muffled as our eardrums rang. Instinctively I clapped my hands over my ears. I saw that everyone else had done the same, saw their mouths wide with horror, their lips moving as they cried out, though I could not hear what they said. Everyone, that is, but Silence Crowe, who had not heard a thing and remained where she was, standing motionless, the blood at her neck trickling into the collar of her dress. At her feet lay Allardyce, a hole between his eyes, the wall behind him an explosion of crimson mush. And behind me, her silver eyes blind and clouded, stood Sorrow Crowe, Dr Cruikshank's service revolver still smoking in her hands.

Chapter Twenty-Eight

❧

The place where Corvus Hall had stood was a place of terrible destruction. The building, so filled with dried and preserved items, with vats of wax and bottles of spirits, had burned with an incandescence that had been visible as far away as Islington Fields. What was left once the fire had burned itself out was no more than a shell. The walls loomed black and windowless. Some of the structure had been rendered unstable by the heat, and men had come and pulled it down. In its truncated form, only the ground storey and a flight of steps leading up to the non-existent front door remained. A pathetic stump of a building, it looked curiously benign, so that it was hard to imagine the activities that had taken place within its once proud walls. By spring and summer the whole area would be colonised by plants that loved scorched earth – rosebay, poppies, buddleia. Until their wild beauty softened its harsh black edges, the place would remain an ugly ruin.

What had been found inside the building's burnt out shell was even more unsettling. The boys and girls of St Saviour's Street had sifted through the wreckage in amazement, for everywhere amongst the rubble they had found what looked like tears, frozen glittering tears of melted glass. And scattered all about them were bones of all kinds, legs, arms, ribs, the bones of humans and the bones of animals – mammals and birds – and skulls, skulls everywhere. Everything was as black as charcoal, and so charred that they crumbled to ash as soon as they were touched, blowing away like ghosts upon the wind. After that the children stayed away.

But there was one last surprise from Corvus Hall. It came a week after the place had burned down. Will and I were sitting in the apothecary on either side of the fire. Above our heads were bunches of hyssop and feverfew drying in the warmth. The air was heavy with the smell of cardamom and ginger, for Gabriel was boiling up a cordial. Jenny was grinding nutmeg, and the scent of the crushed spice was warm about us. Will regarded me thoughtfully. He had been pensive, distracted, for some days, and I was becoming worried about him. He had not mentioned Lilith Crowe once, and I had not pressed him, for we had seen none of them since that night. I wondered whether he was going to mention her now, for I saw him take a breath, his gaze sorrowful, but wary.

'Look, Jem,' he said. 'You know that day in the bone room, the day you found . . . that letter from your mother.'

I blinked. 'Yes?'

'Well I found some others. A number of them. They are from . . . from some months before your birth.'

I sat up. 'How long have you had them?'

'It doesn't matter how long. The question is, do you want them?'

'Of course I do!'

'Do you? They may tell you something about your parentage that you do not wish to hear. Or they may not. Whatever they say, there is every chance it will not make comfortable reading.'

'You mean I may learn that my father was Dr Bain?' I said. 'I may learn that my mother betrayed her husband with the student who shared their lodgings?'

'If you learn that it will mean that you are free from your father's shadow,' he replied. 'Free from the threat of madness that hangs over you every day.'

'It would mean that my life so far has been an even bigger lie than I had realised,' I muttered.

'Your father did his best for you, whatever choices he made on your behalf. He believed you to be his child, that much is clear. And perhaps you are.' He held the bundle of letters on his lap. 'Or perhaps not.'

'And if I find that Dr Bain is *not* my father I should be disappointed?'

He smiled. 'I have no idea what you should feel, Jem. Only you can know that. But it is your choice to know, your choice to read these letters from your mother to Dr Bain. You may discover your true parentage, which may mean that you are truly your father's child, or it may mean that you are not. But one thing *is* clear, and that is that Jeremiah Flockhart was your father. He looked after you, he cared for you, he gave you his love of medicine, his profession, his name. Everything that you are, everything about you that we – that I – love, is because of him. And that, my dear Jem, will never change.' He held out the letters. 'Take them.'

⟡ E. S. THOMSON ⟡

They were old, faded and yellowed. They had been tied together with a narrow pink ribbon as if once upon a time they had meant something to someone, though after years at the bottom of a box it was frayed and dirty. Should I open them? Would it not be better to leave the man I had always thought of as my father with his dignity? Or should I too betray him, and read my dead mother's secret words to her lover? I ran my finger across the smooth nap of the paper, and then I slid them in my pocket.

For three days I carried them about with me. Will never asked about them, and for that I was grateful, though I knew he was watching me, knew he was ready to talk if I wished it. And then on the fourth day, I decided. I owned only a very few items that had once belonged to my mother – a Bible, a book of recipes for herbal preparations, a green cambric dress, a miniature of her that my father had loved, and the trunk in which I kept them all. I sat on my bed with the trunk open before me. Outside the sun was shining. I could hear Will whistling downstairs in the apothecary, Gabriel and Jenny singing as they worked on a tincture of black cohosh, nettle and wormwood. It had been my father's recipe, and one of his most effective against both the croup and the worms. I put the letters inside the trunk, and I closed the lid.

356

Acknowledgements

I would never have completed this book without the help of some significant people. In particular, my marvellous agent-friend Jenny Brown, and all the creative and clever people at Constable, notably, Krystyna Green, Amanda Keats, Ellie Russell, John Fairweather, Kate Truman, Brionee Fenlon, Jess Gulliver, Ellen Rockell, Andrew Davidson, and my efficient and thorough copy-editor, Una McGovern.

As ever, there are some friends and family who have made the writing journey less isolated – John Burnett, always my first reader and critic, and my super-talented writing coven Margaret Reis, Olga Wojtas and Michelle Wards. Trevor Griffiths remains the most interesting and witty man I know, and made a tough writing year much better than it might have been – thank you for everything. Thanks also to Paul Lynch, if only everyone was as complimentary about my output as you are! My mother Jean Thomson, and my lovely sons Guy and Carlo have put up with me for another long twelve months, and let me write when I needed to – love and thanks to you all.

Jacqueline Cahif, archivist at the Royal College of Surgeons of Edinburgh, gave up her time and expertise to show me the best things in her archive, as well as looking over some of my work. Jacqueline, I hope the 'Edinburgh sections' of this book do you proud. I must also acknowledge the help of Margaret Fox, who first told me about precognitions, and in so doing introduced me to my favourite historical documents of all time. Also Merlin Strangeway, brilliant wax anatomical modeller and artist who first told me about Joseph Towne, and explained wax anatomical modelling. Your emails at the start of this project were invaluable. My gratitude is demonstrated fully, I hope, by my hijacking of your marvellous surname.

Finally, my grateful thanks to Mark Mercer-Jones, consultant surgeon and former anatomy demonstrator, who was prepared to answer all manner of questions about anatomy and surgery at all times of the day or night. What a kind offer that was – how glad I am that I took you up on it. Any mistakes made in the interpretation of the information supplied are, of course, entirely mine.

Author's note/Bibliography

〜〜

The events in this book are fictitious, but are inspired by real places and people. A number of secondary sources have proved invaluable. *The Great Exhibition 1851* (Manchester University Press, 2017) edited by Jonathon Shears, and Michael Leapman's *The World for a Shilling* (Faber, 2011) provided detail about the Exhibition and the extraordinary artefacts on display. The work of Ruth Richardson was essential, notably *Death, Dissection and the Destitute* (Penguin, 1989) which explained how bodies were procured by anatomy schools after the Anatomy Act of 1832. Also invaluable was *The Making of Mr Gray's Anatomy* (Oxford, 2009) which inspired Will Quartermain's role as artist and painted a vivid picture of life for medical students in an anatomy school in the mid nineteenth century. Equally relevant on this subject was *Medical Teaching in Edinburgh in the Eighteenth and Nineteenth Centuries* (RCSEd, 2003) by Matthew Kaufman, and Druin Burch, *Digging up the Dead* (Vintage, 2008) – an earlier period but illuminating nonetheless. On the subject of wax anatomical modelling and the work of a female anatomist I drew upon *The Lady Anatomist* (University of Chicago Press, 2010) by Rebecca Messbarger, Joanna Ebenstein's *The Anatomical Venus* (Thames and Hudson, 2016), and for medical illustration consulted Richard Barnett's *The Sick Rose: Disease and the Art of Medical Illustration* (Thames and Hudson, 2014). Lisa Rosner's brilliant discussion of the Burke and Hare scandal, *The Anatomy Murders* (University of Pennsylvania, 2011), and *Anatomy of Robert Knox: Murder, Mad Science and Medical Regulation in Nineteenth Century Edinburgh* (Sussex Academic Press, 2010) by A. W. Bates were both fascinating and invaluable. Finally, the sections in the novel that deal with organs and body parts owe much to the insights of Gavin Francis's *Adventures in Human Being* (Wellcome, 2016). As always, any errors made in the interpretation of these marvellous histories are down to me.